Barbara Genier

THE STONE COTTAGE

Enjoy the read!!
Denis S Lahaie

By Denis S. Lahaie

◆ FriesenPress

Suite 300 - 990 Fort St
Victoria, BC, V8V 3K2
Canada

www.friesenpress.com

Copyright © 2021 by Denis S. Lahaie
First Edition — 2021

All rights reserved.

No part of this publication may be reproduced in any form, or by any means, electronic or mechanical, including photocopying, recording, or any information browsing, storage, or retrieval system, without permission in writing from FriesenPress.

ISBN
978-1-5255-9815-9 (Hardcover)
978-1-5255-9814-2 (Paperback)
978-1-5255-9816-6 (eBook)

1. FICTION, BIOGRAPHICAL

Distributed to the trade by The Ingram Book Company

DEDICATION

I dedicate this book to my amazing wife Helen. Your patience, support and encouragement as I worked through this, my first novel has been tremendous. I Love You and thank you from the bottom of my heart.

PROLOGUE

Cognashene
South East Shore – Georgian Bay

The stone cottage sits on a granite rock outcropping like a sentry, guarding the entrance to the treacherously narrow and rocky channel it faces. In its silent and abandoned state, it appears to be guarding the secrets of those who have lived within its walls and of those who have visited the lake just beyond the channel.

Built over a hundred years ago of stone drawn from the natural landscape surrounding it, the four corners of this small square lodging are aligned perfectly with the points of the compass. After years of neglect only the sixteen-inch-thick stone walls have remained unscathed by the often vicious weather that batters the shores of this Georgian Bay retreat.

The roof peaks in the centre of the building and splays out to the four walls in a slightly curved pagoda style. Over the years numerous storms have torn away many of the dark green shingles exposing the thick hand-hewn roofing boards beneath. Several knot holes in the aged lumber have dried out over the years and have fallen through into the cottage allowing a variety of small birds a perfect entry point in their endless search to find comfort and refuge from the elements in the inner rafters and gables. A single dormer juts out from the roof line on the west side of the cottage. Miraculously the single pane window remains intact. In years past the framework holding the panes of glass could be removed from the window casing and replaced with a screen. In the dead of summer, this feature allowed the stifling heat which so often got trapped inside, to escape from the ceiling in a form of passive air conditioning.

In the main room the four single pane glass windows are now boarded up because of their many cracks and chips. The wooden frames of the windows are split horizontally in the centre to allow the bottom half of the windows to be lifted in the summer to capture the cooling breezes that often blow off the bay on the hot sweltering nights of summer. Four rusted and tattered wire mesh window screens lie carelessly strewn in one corner of the cottage barely intact and hardly recognizable as a former barrier to the black flies and mosquitoes so common to the area.

Covering most of the south wall is a massive stone fireplace that seems disproportionate to the size of the single room cottage. The five foot square hearth is offset from the centre to the right of the fireplace giving the appearance of it being poorly designed. Its congruence is countered by a large opening on the left side which in days past provided storage space for chord wood to be stacked in. A trap door opening in the outer east wall of the cottage next to the fireplace allowed for wood to be brought in from outside without crossing the room. This reduced the tracking of dusty cord wood through the cottage and virtually eliminated any sawdust that was still on the wood from falling to the floor. The clay tile chimney flue having long ago chipped and broken has fallen into itself. The broken pieces of tile are sufficiently large enough to keep small animals like squirrels and raccoons from making this once cozy dwelling their own private lodge.

The wood plank front door once protected by a covered porch roof now leans inward at an unusual angle on its rusted hinges not providing much of a deterrent to anyone who wants to gain entrance to the cottage. The porch itself is now completely gone with only the upper ledger board remaining bolted to the mortar between the stones.

On the far south wall next to the fireplace is the back door. Years before, this door led to a lean-to style addition built on the back of the cottage. This addition was made of logs cut, then pulled by hand from the wooded area behind the cottage. Between each log a thick bead of white mortar chinking ensured that no moisture seeped through from the occasional driving rain. This room had a duel role. Primarily it functioned as a kitchen where meals were prepared. Once complete they were brought into the main part of the stone cottage to be consumed at a large homemade wooden trestle table situated under the front window overlooking the narrow channel. The kitchen also housed a set of double-bed sized bunk beds, built onto the south wall to provide the much needed extra sleeping space for the families who lived there over the years. Each spring the open pantry shelves built onto the far wall next to the stove were cleaned then covered with a decorative colourful shelf paper. This helped to add colour and a distinct coziness to the room. At a moment's glance the owners could take complete stock of the supplies that remained and make provision lists that would be brought with them on their next shopping trip into town.

A wood-burning Beech cook-stove tucked into the far corner of the room played a dual role. Not only was it a fully functioning stove (with an oven that was nearly impossible to regulate the temperature of), but it also had a water reservoir attached to the side of it. As the stove was heated for meal preparation, a full water reservoir meant there would be plenty of hot water available to pour into the wash basin for cleaning grubby hands before the meal and for washing the dishes afterwards. Additionally, on those cooler nights in the early spring and late fall the extra heat generated by the Beech was always welcome and helped make the room as comfortable as the stone walled cottage it was attached to.

After a time, the stone cottage was vacated and as the years went by, the small addition fell to ruin. Eventually its thick wood plank roofing boards and the logs from the walls were pilfered by locals. They were great for use as replacement boards on their own aging cottages or as supports for their docks which seemed to always fall victim to the ever changing heights of the water and the damage caused by the shifting ice floes in the spring.

Now all that remains of the kitchen addition is the crumbling stone and cement foundation it was built upon. The rusted out remains of the Beech cook stove are perched precariously on its side now that two of the four rusted legs have given out and can no longer support the heavy cast iron stove.

A couple of hundred feet from the stone cottage, a small protected cove near the entrance to the narrow channel holds the no longer salvageable remnants of a large dock's piers. As the water splashes against them it gives the onlooker a hint of the grandeur and the size the dock once was.

In its prime, many a splendid vessel moored to the cleats of this dock. Guests of the elegant six bedroom resort-like main cottage located a short distance from the stone cottage were always invited by the owners to "just tie up your boat and stay a while". And, "don't worry about your boat, Gilbert our caretaker who lives in the stone cottage will make sure nothing happens to it." These were common phrases the guests were likely to hear from the owners and always helped to set the tone for a pleasant and relaxing visit.

Forty years ago, a devastating fire ravaged the owner's main cottage destroying the frame structure completely and leaving only the stone and cement footings it was built upon. These footings are mostly hidden now by the sparse but hardy foliage of juniper and sumac and betray to the area the vastness and grandeur of the dwelling they once supported.

Overcome by the loss of their grand cottage retreat, the owners who lived in the nearby town of Penetanguishene at the south end of Georgian Bay never had the energy or the desire to rebuild. As their caretakers were never considered to be just "the hired help" but more like trusted lifelong friends, the owners insisted the caretakers continue to use the stone cottage as their own for as many years as they wanted or until they could no longer manage it.

As with all good things that must come to an end, so too did the point in time come for the caretakers to pack their bags for the final season and say goodbye. As their ship-lap inboard slowly pulled away from the dock pier they looked back upon the stone cottage. Tears welled in their eyes as they thought of the many good times and deep friendships they had built over the years at the stone cottage with the closely knit community of year round residents. These memories were not only of the full time residents, but of their summer-season neighbours as well who lived around the lake beyond the channel. Fondly they remembered the good times spent with the many guests that stayed, sometimes at length, at the owners' main cottage.

They thought too of all the good times they had shared on fishing expeditions with the guests. These fishing trips often culminated with shore lunches made from the day's catch. Picnics were held on the windswept outer islands reached only by cleverly dodging the many hidden shoals in the cedar strip canoes the owners so willingly allowed them to use.

Though there were many good times, their thoughts also raced back to the tragedies on the bay and the devastation those events inflicted on them as caretakers as much as it did on the owners. Their own personal stories of celebrations, good times, hardships and sorrow would never be forgotten. It left them with a certain sense of melancholy and hope that perhaps time would somehow heal the pain of those events. But, perhaps time would not be that kind.

These are their stories....

CHAPTER - 1

Maude LaJoie
Granite Bluff Inlet - North East Shore - Georgian Bay

May 1898

A solid granite bluff all but blocks the small narrow entrance to the inlet. As a natural breakwater it effectively protects and shelters the waters of the bay within in a way that no man made barrier ever could.

Rising twenty feet from the surface of the water, the casual passerby would not even know the inlet existed. Several hundred years ago, when the inlet's community was first being settled, that barrier is what had attracted the original peaceful and passive Ojibwa Nation occupants to this cove. As well as keeping the waters of the inlet calm, it also helped protect them from the aggressive tribes to the north, which were often at war.

Behind the bluff, the deep, calm waters of the inlet are a natural sanctuary for schools of small mouth bass, perch and northern pike, a staple in the diet of the community it sheltered.

The inner shores of the inlet are smooth, tan coloured granite and depending on the brilliance of the sun, change slightly to a pink hue. On a clear day the tiny particles of quartz rock embedded in the granite glitter in the sun like millions of tiny sparkling diamonds offering their faces up to the life giving sun.

The forest of white pines tower over the juniper and sumac ground cover that starts a full hundred feet back from the waters' edge. Large patches of wild blueberries and blackberries cling to the rocky shoreline straining against all odds for survival by burrowing their root bases into the tiny cracks in the rocks where small amounts of soil give life to the bushes. Thick moss covers the roots and retains just enough moisture to ensure a good crop of berries every year.

A half mile back from the shoreline, in a crater shaped granite basin, a small inland lake has formed and is fed by winter run off and the seasonal rains. The overflow from the lake trickles in small creeks as it meanders by gravity downhill to the inlet's waters' edge. After centuries of vegetative growth around the rim of the basin the lake has become somewhat overgrown with natural weeds and grasses and has become more of a marshy wetland than an actual lake. This environment became the perfect habitat for the opportunistic cranberry bushes to grow and they have flourished annually reaching a full ripened state by early October each year.

In the shelter of the inlet, set back from the shore a small community has thrived. Originally a water access only village, the Native occupants have lived a very harsh and isolated life sustained only by what nature provides with fish, deer and other wildlife. Edible berries and roots added to whatever vegetables they are able to harvest from their meagre gardens round out their subsistant diet.

When a logging road was cut into the forest, land access to the community changed it forever. The inhabitants, though still isolated, no longer had to wait for the waters of the greater Georgian Bay to calm enough for them to leave the village. Many a villager in the past had left the protected waters of the inlet to travel south for supplies at one of the larger communities along the southern end of Georgian Bay only to be either turned back by the unpredictable westerly winds or to find themselves stranded on a protected island waiting for the all to common, "three day blow" to subside.

Land access to the community through the logging road brought the predictable influx of newcomers to the village. Many visitors stayed just for a brief time, lodging with family members who had never left the area. These families had stayed behind and chose to be true to their Native heritage by continuing to live in the small but sturdy dwellings built by their ancestors. Though they were intrigued by the cultural differences from the outside communities, they possessed an overwhelming desire to ensure their own culture and language was not forgotten. They also harboured a certain fear that if they assimilated into the modern cultures that were so foreign to them, they might be drawn into that way of life and lose their identity as a nation. This sometimes gave first time visitors the impression they were standoffish and aloof or not very intelligent however it was merely their reluctance to be drawn into a different lifestyle that made them seem this way.

Other visitors, mostly of a French background, came and were so drawn to the quiet solitude and beauty of the area that it became impossible for them to leave. After negotiating a one hundred year lease with the crown for their own tracts of land they built their small homes on these rocky shores and began to carve out a new life for themselves and their families. Over the years many integrated with the Native people and their families developed a strong influence of both cultures. And thus, in this community of nearly a hundred people, as it had in many other communities along the shoreline, the Métis Nation evolved.

In time, as the logging road into the village improved, so too did the amenities that were available. A small general store was built and became the principle resource for the inhabitants. Within a short period of time it became the hub of the community warehousing not only the basic hardware, dry goods and tools but also carrying a few non-perishable food items such as fifty pound bags of flour, oatmeal, cornmeal and other staples not cultivated in the residents' small inadequate gardens which somehow managed to grow against all odds in patches between the rocks.

At the back of the general store was a small area dedicated to a post office of sorts. In truth it was more like a couple of shelves behind one of the work counters where bolts of material and lengths of rope were metered out. This is where the occasional incoming and outgoing parcels and letters could be found. The frequency of delivery depended solely upon who was going to be making the trip into one of the larger communities to the south such as Parry Sound or Penetanguishene. Often if it was known that someone was "making the trip into town," within the next few days, the number of items to be sent out on the shelves of the post office seemed to magically grow almost overnight. Conversely, the return trip from town always found the traveller loaded down with extra supplies for the villagers who had asked to have their items picked up for them since "you are making the trip into town anyway."

Over the years the number of residents in the community seemed to stabilize with very little growth in the number of new houses and the people living within. As a result, their dependence on each other grew. Although the families were self sufficient in most things, each person in the community seemed to possess some special skill or ability that was unique to them. Without hesitancy they were always willing to share this special talent at a moment's notice. As a result of their self sufficiency their reliance on the outside world was minimized. The people were very content with their lives and their lifestyle and this helped to foster camaraderie with each other. A sense of peace prevailed throughout the community and if asked, everyone who lived there would happily admit that all was well with their world.

*****

The paddle sliced into the calm clear water with clean even strokes. The sole occupant of the canoe was an expert at navigating the waters of the inlet and the trip back towards his home was done effortlessly. He was perched two thirds back from the bow and just slightly off centre. The canoe leaned into the water just enough to provide the operator perfect control of the vessel and made navigating the shallow waters near the shore so much easier.

He had been out fishing since early morning beyond the granite bluff and when he passed through the narrow channel that allowed access to the inlet, he was pleased to see as he scanned the shoreline, that the water level was higher than it had been weeks previous to this. This was a good omen as the higher water levels brought more fish into the inlet, drawn into the inlet in part by the inevitable current created as the waters of the inlet surged in and out. The catch in the inlet hadn't been very good lately and this was what had prompted him to fish out in the greater part of Georgian Bay.

Within the community the residents believed that a high water level was always thought to be a sign of good luck and in the ancient times meant prosperity, a sign that the gods were looking favourably upon them. With his wife due to give birth to their second child any day now a good omen was a very welcome sign indeed.

They had been married for nearly eight years before his wife had become pregnant. They were beginning to believe that his wife was barren or his seed was bad and that they would never have children when one day she announced she believed she was pregnant. They were thrilled with the news, however, as the months passed her belly never seemed to swell to the size that would be expected of a new mother.

Although born at full term the infant was small and frail and gave one the impression that it had been born prematurely. The infant was weak and sickly from the beginning. His wife had difficulty getting the child to latch onto the breast and although several Native women from the village tried to teach her different techniques to get the child to feed, none were successful. The child was just too weak to suckle long enough to get sufficient nourishment. Keeping the child warm was another problem the new parents were faced with. As it was the middle of winter luckily it meant the wood stove in the kitchen was always burning. Too keep the child warm enough the young couple would wrap the infant in a blanket and then open the oven door on the wood stove. They placed the child on a small table in front of the open oven door in the hope that the heat from the stove would be sufficient to keep the child's core temperature high enough.

A week after the child was born the parents noticed the newborn was having trouble being able to breathe deeply enough to keep his fingers and toes from turning a dusky grey-blue colour. When the child developed a weak cough at the slightest movement they knew that his days with them were numbered. Although they were taking turns sleeping and monitoring the child and doing everything they possibly could to sustain this wee life, the parent's worst fears were realized one stormy afternoon.

As the wind howled and whipped the snow in a furious blizzard outside the tiny domicile, the parents wept softly, comfort attained only by holding each other tightly and speaking in whispered tones to each other, sharing the grief and loss they felt, appreciating the fact that they still had each other for support.

That had been two and a half years ago. Now his wife was due to have their second child and all the signs of a healthy pregnancy were there. It seemed like from the day his wife had told him she thought she was pregnant her belly seemed to grow. Her breasts quickly became fuller and by seven months her gait had become more of a waddle than a stride. Many of the elderly women in the village thought she was going to have twins. No one could remember if twins had ever been born in the village but they were certain of one thing, it had never happened in their lifetime. If she was carrying twins, they were not sure how Mrs. King, the midwife, was going to handle this and, as old women with little else to do often do, they chatted about it endlessly.

As the fisherman paddled towards his dock he noticed the neighbours' young boy was standing on the dock waving his arms in an effort to catch his attention. The fisherman could tell, even from this distance the young boy was excited about something. Usually the young boy accompanied him on his fishing trips within the inlet but because he had planned to go out to the outer bay he did not take him. At this time of year, on the outer bay, the weather can change quickly. All too frequently it seemed the water would go from being calm to a slight ripple, to waves reaching a couple of feet within less than an hour. With the weather being that unpredictable it was not safe to bring the neighbours' young lad out that far into Georgian Bay, just in case.

On those days when he fished in the open waters of the greater bay, the young lad often sat, waiting patiently on the dock, watching for him to come back. He was always anxious to find out what luck the fisherman had had and to chat with him about what kind of fight the fish had given him as he pulled it into the canoe. He listened intently to stories about any difficulties the fisherman had in landing them, asking many questions about how he managed to get such large fish into the canoe without tipping the small vessel over.

"Mr. LaJoie! Mr. LaJoie!" the young boy shouted barely able to contain himself.

"Yes Isaac, what is it?" he asked.

"My mamma was over to visit with your wife to keep her company because you had gone out fishing and, and you hadn't come back yet and, and about an hour ago she sent me to Mrs. King's house to tell her she needed to get over to your house right away and, and she has been there for a long time now!" All this was said with near panic in Isaac's voice. He seemed to struggle to catch his breath after getting all of that out.

"Your wife told me to come down to the dock to watch for you to return. She said that as soon as I see you coming through the inlet I am to wave you down and tell you she needs you to come home right away," shouted the young lad.

Though just a lad, Isaac was fully aware that years before, the fisherman and his wife had a child that died soon after it was born and in this small close knit community, this pregnancy had gained much attention. It was being watched closely by everyone young and old.

The fisherman hastened his paddling and guided the canoe expertly to the dock. As he rose from his seat he said, "Would you tie this up for me Isaac? I better hurry."

In his frenzied state Isaac tied the canoe to the dock and raced after Mr. LaJoie, up the rocky shores to where their houses were. It wasn't until he was back sitting on the steps of his own house that he realized that he never asked the fisherman if he had caught anything. He certainly didn't remember seeing any fish in the bottom of the canoe. He'd check later he thought. Right now there were more important matters to think about. He wanted to stay close to the neighbour's house in case he was needed to run another errand or fetch additional support for Mrs. King.

*****

Although never formally trained as a midwife, Mrs. King had attended more deliveries in her day than she could count. As well as giving birth to six of her own children, she had assisted with pretty well every delivery in the village since…well…for as long as she could remember. Now in her late seventies, although her legs and hips didn't get her around as quickly as she would like, her mind was still sharp and her hands and upper arms were unusually strong, a quality she attributed to years of hard work and from the seemingly endless job of kneading dough when baking bread.

As the fisherman moved to the bedside his wife clutched his hand and said, "Oh, Oliver, I am so glad you made it back in time. I was worried you wouldn't be here when I deliver."

"Marie, when did the labour start? I knew you were due soon but I thought it would not be for another couple of weeks," he said to his wife. "I'd have never left to go fishing if I had thought you were going to deliver *this* soon!"

Mrs. King, busying herself around the tiny bedroom muttered under her breath her favourite saying. "When the apple is ripe it falls from the tree," then chuckled thinking to herself, *I wonder how many times I have said that?*

As the labour pains quickened Mrs. King put her comforting hands on Marie's belly and held them there for several minutes. "The contractions are getting stronger now Marie so you are well on your way. When you feel the contraction getting tighter push with it. From what I can tell, you're doing OK at this point." Mrs. King straightened up, stretched then rubbed her lower back with both palms. Leaning over Marie once more, she placed her hands on Marie's abdomen and said, "When it seems like it is easing off, just try to relax and rest so you don't tire yourself out to quickly. This might be a long night and you don't want to wear yourself out too soon."

Marie was comforted by the soothing way that Mrs. King spoke to her. She remembered clearly her last delivery and how Mrs. King was so confident in what she said. Just knowing she was here again brought her and Oliver the reassurance they so desperately needed at this time.

"Oliver, I think it is time to get that stove in the kitchen fired up," Mrs. King said. She looked out the tiny bedroom window at the house next door. "It looks like Isaac is sitting on the front steps next door. Get him to bring some fresh buckets of water up from the shore and start to heat it up. I am going to need some water that has been boiled hard to use while Marie is delivering and then I am going to need some water that is nice and warm for the clean up afterwards." She liked being in charge at this time and her commands although given with firmness and directness didn't come across so much as an order but as a request that made Oliver feel like he was going to be an important part of the delivery.

Oliver lit the old wood stove in the kitchen using plenty of kindling to ensure it would light. He thought, *I'll use some pine to get the fire to burn quickly. That will get the stove hot enough to boil water and then I'll use some of the oak I have in the woodshed to keep the fires burning slowly for the rest of the day.*

As he watched the small pine logs catch fire in the firebox he wondered if the men in the village were always asked by Mrs. King to boil water as the labour progressed. Was it because it was really needed or was it was because Mrs. King wanted them out of the way and this gave her a good excuse.

He went to the front door and looked out. Sure enough Isaac was sitting there on the steps but not of the house next door where he lived. It seemed that sometime between Oliver getting the order to boil the water and lighting the stove, Isaac had moved to the front steps of Oliver's house.

With the fire in the kitchen stove burning well, the kitchen started to heat up quickly. *He's a good kid,* Oliver thought as he opened the kitchen window. Even though he was only nine years old he had been good company for Oliver and Marie and was always willing to help out with chores around the house. It was for those reasons Oliver liked to take him out fishing whenever he could to show how much he appreciated the things Isaac did for them.

Isaac adored Mr. LaJoie and loved being asked to go out fishing. Sometimes they would leave from shore in the weather-beaten canoe early in the morning and would be gone for several hours. Often barely a word would be spoken between the two of them. When he did speak Mr. LaJoie always seemed to be so wise and would tell Isaac fishing stories that, like a true fisherman, he seemed to be able to stretch out into quite a yarn. He always knew what to do when Isaac latched onto a big fish and didn't mind teaching him how to play the fish on the line. He taught Isaac not to reel it in to quickly in order to tire the fish out so it would be easier to bring into the canoe. Isaac had decided long ago that when he grew up, he wanted to be a fisherman, just like Mr. LaJoie.

"Isaac, I need your help now."

"What do you want me to do?" he asked.

"Take this pail down to the end of the dock and fill it up with water. Make sure that you reach out as far as you can to get the cleanest water possible. I don't want any of the yellow pollen that is floating on the top of the water if you can help it," Oliver said.

Isaac ran down to the end of the dock. It had been windy during the night and as is so common in late spring, there was a fine yellow film of pine pollen that was floating lazily on the surface of the water. As there was just a slight breeze now, the wind had pushed most of the pollen towards the shore and around the docks. Isaac hadn't even noticed it when he had been down to the dock earlier but he wasn't surprised that Mr. LaJoie had noticed.

He moved right to the end of the dock and then lay down on his belly. He took the pail by the handle and he used the bottom of it to swish around in the water for a few seconds. This cleared the remaining pollen that had drifted towards the dock. Reaching out as far as his arms would allow he quickly scooped up a full bucket of water and brought it closer to the edge of the dock. Without losing his grip on the handle of the bucket he managed to get onto his knees and pull the bucket to the top of the dock. Quickly he stood and then started to run back towards the house. looking down at the bucket he noticed that as he ran, some of the water was spilling out so he slowed down to a quick walk so that he wouldn't spill any more.

"Thank you Isaac." said Oliver as he poured the water into the largest pots and kettle he could find in the kitchen.

"Can you get me some more?"

Without even the slightest hesitation Isaac turned around and headed back out the door thrilled to be of help at a time like this.

Just as the water was coming to a boil in the kettle Mrs. King came to the kitchen door and asked, "Is that water boiling yet?" Oliver took the wash basin from the dry sink and rinsed it with some of the freshly boiled water and then filled it again.

"Is this going to be enough?" Oliver asked.

"You need to keep that kettle full of boiling water until I tell you I don't need it any more," Mrs. King replied. Oliver was glad that Isaac had been so willing to get the extra buckets of water for him. Knowing the boy's good nature and eagerness to help he put him into service again and asked him to gather some small oak logs from the woodshed out back so that he could keep the fire in the stove going.

Even though the door was closed between the tiny bedroom and the kitchen, Oliver could hear the deep guttural moaning noises of childbirth coming from Marie. He hoped that everything was going to be all right with this delivery. He knew Mrs. King was a very competent midwife and would do everything she possibly could, but with Marie's history there was still a sense of trepidation about her having the baby at home in the village.

As the hours passed Oliver's pacing around the kitchen table increased. He began to feel an even greater apprehension about giving in to Marie's desire to stay at home for this delivery. During the pregnancy, more than once, Oliver had suggested to Marie that it might be best for her to go and stay with his relatives in Penetanguishene until she had the baby. "At least there is a doctor in that town if you have problems." Oliver's insistence however had fallen on deaf ears and he wondered if his insistence was really only to make him feel more comfortable. He knew in his heart that Marie didn't want to be away from home or from Oliver for that long. Her pregnancy had progressed uneventfully this time. She had faith in Mrs. King and she resolved that she would be all right.

Mrs. King felt inside Marie once again and felt the rim of the cervix. It was as dilated as it could possibly get and with her long and strong fingers she helped to push the rim of it up as far as she could.

"Oh, I think this is going to be a big baby Marie. I can tell by feeling the top of the head that it's a good size." Mrs. King remembered all too clearly how small the head of the last baby had felt to her. She had known from *that* moment the baby was not healthy and feared things might not be good. She had not been surprised when she heard the infant had died a week later.

"It hurts so much," Marie moaned softly. As is so typical of Native women, they are stoic when they are in labour and there was no screaming or yelling. Rather, what could be heard was a low steady moan that emanated from deep within her each time a contraction peaked. Beads of sweat formed on her forehead and across her upper lip. When she felt them starting to trickle down the side of her face she wiped them away with the sleeve of her nightgown.

"You can do it Marie. Just make sure you push as hard as you can every time I tell you to," Mrs. King said in her reassuring a voice.

"You're almost there Marie," she said encouraging her. "Keep pushing, I know you can do it."

To prevent a precipitous delivery at this point Mrs. King held a steady pressure in the opposite direction and pushed back ever so gently on the head of the baby allowing it to ease out more slowly though the birth canal with the force of the contractions. First the head crowned and soon after the right shoulder delivered. Once the shoulder was cleared the rest of the delivery was easier with the remainder of the body flowing out quickly pushed by one massive contraction. A large gush of fluid followed. With quick and deliberate movements Mrs. King gripped the infant by the ankles and held it upside down to allow any fluid that may have gathered in the mouth and lungs to drain out. Once the baby began to cry she wrapped the infant in a cloth towel and placed it on Marie's abdomen to put pressure on the uterus.

Next she tied off the umbilical cord with a strong cotton ribbon she had brought with her. Once that was completed then the placenta or afterbirth, as the Natives called it, was delivered. After a quick but thorough check of the infant she moved the baby up to Marie's open arms and congratulated her on delivering such a beautiful child.

Oliver, though still pacing in the tiny kitchen, was listening to what was going on in the bedroom behind the closed door. It bothered him to hear Marie suffering so much. Then all was quiet for what seemed like an eternity. Suddenly he heard the weak cry of a newborn and he rushed into the bedroom.

Mrs. King's practised hands felt Marie's abdomen for the top of the uterus and noted that it had started to harden somewhat already. She then started to massage Marie's abdomen with hard circular strokes feeling the top of the uterus contract fully. She placed the other hand farther down on Marie's abdomen and kept a steady downward pressure there, guarding the uterus in the lower part of the abdomen to make sure it didn't invert as she rubbed the fundus. When it was hard to the touch she stopped.

"The head is perfectly shaped. She has all her toes and fingers. I think you have a keeper here," said Mrs. King with a warm smile to the anxious fisherman. "You have a beautiful and healthy little girl Oliver," said Mrs. King. "Well, not so little I might say. I wouldn't be a bit surprised if this baby weighs eight and a half pounds. But, to me, she looks perfect."

Oliver moved to the side of the bed and stood motionless, just staring down at his wife and child. He was in awe of the miracle that had just taken place. Suddenly a feeling of complete and total love for the two of them washed over him like a wave crashing on the shore. It overwhelmed him and tears welled in his eyes. He tried to speak but found he couldn't, it was even hard for him to swallow over the lump that had formed in his throat. Even though this was their second child it did not diminish for him how special this moment was. He reached out to his wife and placed his large weathered hand on her brow wiping away some moisture that had gathered there.

"I love you so much Marie. I can't find the words to tell you how much," he said. "She looks beautiful."

He pulled up a small stool to the side of the bed and sat down. "May I hold her?" he asked.

"I don't know if I can give her up just yet. I just want to hold her and hug her and never let her go. It has taken so long for this moment to come. I don't want it to end."

"Well you are going to have to hand her over sooner or later because you and I aren't completely done just yet Marie," said Mrs. King.

Taking care not to loosen the blanket that was wrapped around the baby, Oliver lifted the new child from his wife's arms like the precious package that she was. He had never had very much experience with infants when he was growing up. The time that he had with his first child was so brief that he never did get over that typical male, stiff-armed awkwardness of handling a baby, so each time he shifted her in his arms it looked like he thought she was going to break.

"I won't be like the other fathers in the village Marie. I want to be involved. When she gets older, I am going to teach her how to fish, how to paddle a canoe, how to read the sky to predict the weather, and …." Suddenly the lump in his throat had returned and once again he found he could not speak. He just sat there and stared at his new daughter's perfect features still not really able to believe this had happened.

"Oliver, you have to give her back," Mrs. King said.

"Marie, you have to try feeding her now. This will help get things back to normal down below too. You'll probably feel some more contractions but that's normal. Do you remember what I taught you last time about getting the baby to latch on?"

"I don't think I am going to have any problems this time. She looks like she is already hungry," said Marie.

Mrs. King went around to the far side of the bed and opened the bedroom window and paused there for a moment breathing in the warm fresh air. As she turned from the window back towards Marie she said "Let me help you with getting her into a good position to feed." Then she turned to Oliver and said, "Oliver, I think you need to go outside and tell Isaac that Marie has had the baby and that everything is fine. I can see that he has gone back to his house but it looks like he is going to wear a hole in the floor of that veranda with his pacing."

Oliver stood up and turned to leave the stuffy little room. As he got to the doorway he turned and looked one more time at Marie lying on the bed, softly cooing to the baby as she held her newborn's mouth to her breast. He smiled again as a sense of completeness came over him and he thought of how proud he was of his new little family. He left the bedroom and checked the fire in the wood stove. It was still burning evenly. He decided he would be able to let the stove burn itself out now and not add any more wood. There was more than enough water already boiled if Mrs. King needed any more. As he walked down the steps at the front of his house, Isaac saw him and raced over to his side.

"Let's go for a little walk Isaac." They headed down the stone path towards the shore then walked out onto the dock. "Well, it's all over now. Thanks to your help we have a beautiful baby girl." Oliver looked down and could tell that Isaac was listening intently to every word he said. "We couldn't have done it without all your hard work fetching water and wood for the stove," he said. A large smile immediately formed across his face. Isaac knew he had only played a very small role but he appreciated Mr. LaJoie's comment and the way it made him feel like he too had had a part in this important event.

"A girl," Isaac said a bit disappointed. "I was hoping for a boy and then you and me, we could teach him how to fish, and we could go out in the canoe and, and..." he paused, "but a girl," he exclaimed, "what are we going to do with a girl?"

"You know Isaac, I have met some girls who are better at catching fish than I am," Oliver said trying to reassure Isaac. "You and I, we are going to teach her everything we know. Perhaps she will even bring us better luck than we have ever had."

Isaac thought about it for a long moment then smiled. He looked up at Mr. LaJoie and said, "OK, I'll let you, but would it be alright," he paused, "I mean, can you still let me go fishing with you until she is big enough to take with us?"

"Isaac, I wouldn't want to have it any other way."

"What's her name?" said Isaac.

"I have chosen to name her Maude," said Oliver. "Mrs. LaJoie and I had decided that if the baby was a boy, she would name him, and if it was a girl, I would name her. So, I have, and I have chosen the name Maude."

"That sounds like a fine name to me," said Isaac although he wasn't really thinking to much about what the new baby's name was. He was just relieved to hear that he would not lose his favoured place in the canoe. At least not yet anyway.

"I think you had better go home now Isaac so you can tell your mother the good news. It's starting to get dark out so you better hurry."

As Oliver stepped into the house he noticed that while he was gone, Mrs. King had tidied up the kitchen, cleaned all the basins and left them to dry on the counter near the dry sink. A bundle of towels and cloths that had been used during the delivery sat tightly wrapped in the largest of the basins ready to be washed then hung on the clothesline to dry. Though she knew Marie would not be in any shape to be doing this type of work anytime soon she was pretty sure one of the women from the village would be over tomorrow ready to help in any way that was needed. For now she had pulled the rocking chair from the kitchen close to the bedroom door and was reclined with her eyes closed, a small pillow supporting her head on the backrest. Though she appeared to be sleeping, she was merely just resting with her eyes shut, her ears tuned to any sounds that may come from the bedroom.

As Oliver moved towards the bedroom door she opened her eyes and said, "You have a beautiful wife and daughter Oliver. Both are doing just fine. And now that you are here, my work is done and I am going to take these tired old bones home and get some sleep myself." As she stood he could tell that her hips were giving her much pain. He felt badly that she had had to put in such a long day but at the same time he was eternally grateful that she had been present.

"I can't thank you enough for all that you have done for us today Mrs. King. Remember, if there is ever anything that you need please let me know and I'll be glad to help you out." He thanked her once again and helped her down the stairs at the front of the house then went back inside.

As he made his way through the kitchen he noticed that all was quiet in the darkened bedroom. Oliver bent over the small table in the bedroom and lit the single kerosene lamp that was on it. The soft yellow glow that emanated from the lamp cast shadows on the walls and provided just enough light for him to see that Marie was sleeping comfortably with Maude carefully wrapped and cuddled in her arms. He once again pulled the stool up to the bed and gently lifted the infant from Marie's arms. Marie stirred momentarily, looked up at Oliver, smiled and willingly relinquished the newborn to her husband. He cradled the baby in his arms and slowly moved the blanket that was encircling her face. As he gazed lovingly into this precious package he was holding the infant stirred, opened her eyes and for a fleeting moment stared straight into Oliver's eyes. Oliver sighed softly, took his forefinger and rubbed it ever so gently around the perimeter of her face. He thought how truly blessed he was and that the gods were looking favourably upon him. The high water level in the inlet truly was a good omen.

*****

As the years went by, Isaac and Maude became the best of friends. As an only child Isaac had never had any siblings to play with and Maude soon began to feel more like a sister to him than just a neighbour. Like a big brother he became very protective of her, always watching out for her well-being. He treated her like she was his very own little princess. Oliver, true to his word, was very involved in the care and upbringing of Maude. Although he and Marie continued to try to have another child it never did work out for them and so they devoted all of their attention and energy towards Maude and Isaac.

As Maude grew, she absorbed all of the things that her father and Isaac taught her as if she were a sponge soaking up water. She became an expert paddler and by the time she was six, Oliver was comfortable enough with their skill level to let Isaac and Maude go out in the canoe by themselves, as long as they stayed within the inlet. Isaac didn't mind giving up his prized front seat in the canoe to Maude when it meant he was able to sit at the back and guide the canoe in and out of the small coves within the inlet.

Isaac by this time was now fifteen and was very adept at teaching Maude all of the important things in life like, where to catch the fattest frogs and how to net minnows using just a wee bit of oatmeal as bait. "What you have to do is let the netting sit in the shallow water. Don't move the edges of the net or the lines that are tied to it because that will scare them away." Isaac told her. "Once the minnows swim to the surface to nibble on the oatmeal that is floating over top of the net, that's when you give a quick tug on the corners of the net to trap them." As if right on cue, a small school of minnows swam right over top of the net and with practised movements and the sudden jerking on the lines that were tied to the four corners of the minnow net, Isaac lifted it high out of the water to examine his catch. Maude squealed with delight as she watched the tiny silvery minnows flipping and flopping around in the netting. Isaac scooped his hand into the net and grabbed a handful of minnows then dropped them into the half-full pail of water he had tucked safely on the shore. "There, we'll have enough minnows now for both of us to fish off the dock this afternoon," Isaac said very pleased with his catch. "Maybe we can catch some nice bass or perch. We could have them for supper tonight." Maude agreed quickly and ran to the house to tell her mother about the minnows they had caught and that maybe they would be able to have fish for supper, just like Isaac had said.

When they would go swimming at the swimming hole with the other children from the village, Isaac never strayed to far from her side. He taught her how to swim underwater and to dive down to the bottom of the shallow pool to retrieve a shiny spoon that was kept on shore just for that purpose. When playing games with the other children in the village he always made sure that she was treated fairly by the other children.

*****

For several years now, Oliver had been taking Isaac into the outer, greater bay with him to fish for the larger northern pike and muskie that were so common in the deeper, colder waters. Those larger fish were not very often found in the inlet and one large fish could provide a couple of good feeds for the family. The first time Isaac caught and landed one of those large fish in the canoe he was both ecstatic and frightened as he was sure they would capsize. But, Oliver being the expert that he was, was able to stabilize the canoe very easily. With strong sure movements he dipped the fish net into the water well behind the fish and held it still in the water. Once the netting was soaked and no longer buoyant on the surface he came up behind the fish and quickly scooped it into the canoe. Next he slipped a rope though the edge of the fish's gill and pulled it out through the open mouth of the pike. Only then did he remove the hook and remaining bait from the fish's mouth. He tied a loop through the end of the rope and dropped the fish back into the water. Once he was happy with how far the fish was trailing behind the canoe he secured the end of the rope to the edge of his seat. He looked up at Isaac and smiled. "For a moment I thought you were going to jump out of the canoe to make room for that big fish at the front."

"Wow, that is the biggest fish I have ever caught," said Isaac. "I wasn't sure what we were going to do with it. I can't wait to go home and tell my dad about what I caught."

"Well you can do more than tell him about it, you can show him the fish when you take it home and tell your parents that tonight's supper is on you," Oliver said.

"You mean I can have this fish?" Isaac asked excitedly.

"Well you caught it; you might as well be the one who eats it. I'm pretty sure your mom and dad are going to be pleased with your big catch," Oliver said. "Once you have shown it to them you have to clean it right away so that it will be ready for supper. Do you remember how I taught you to clean a fish?"

"I have watched you fillet so many fish over the years I think I could do it with my eyes closed Mr. LaJoie," Isaac said.

"I think you'll want to keep them open, you don't want to lose any fingers with that sharp filleting knife I gave you," Oliver said. A large grin formed on Isaac's face as he thought of how proud he was of the fish that he had caught and how pleased his parents would be with him.

Maude was waiting patiently at the end of the dock when they returned from their fishing trip. She had wanted to be a part of this little expedition but her father had insisted that she stay home this time to help her mother with some of the chores around the house. Although Maude preferred to be outside and to be with Isaac and her other friends, she did enjoy it when she got the chance to spend time with her mother. She loved to help with the baking. Making bannock from a mixture of flour, water and fat was one of her favourite things to do. She was always intrigued by the way her mother was able to get the temperature of the oven just right by using a mixture of hard wood and pine to keep the temperature even. Although Maude had often tried to add wood to the fire box in the stove while they were baking, the oven always seemed to be either too cool or too hot, but, sure enough, when her mom would take over, it didn't take long and the temperature was just right.

"It's all in the way you stoke the embers at the base of the fire." Marie would say. And so as not to discourage her she added, "It took me a long time to learn how to get it just right too. Be patient, it comes with practice."

"While the stove is hot, why don't we cook something special for supper tonight? Maybe your dad would like a nice hearty stew. I know Isaac loves that too so perhaps we can invite him as well," Marie added. "Once we have the vegetables cleaned why don't you go down to the dock to wait for them to return? They should be getting back just about then and you can ask Isaac if he'd like to join us."

Maude didn't have to be told twice. As she scurried around the small kitchen gathering vegetables to be cleaned for the stew and setting the table for supper, she thought about how good it would be to see her father and Isaac pulling up to the dock. She was always full of anticipation when she waited for them because she was anxious to see if they had been able to catch any fish.

Once her work was done she quickly slipped on her moccasins and made her way outside. At the end of the dock she sat patiently and stared down the inlet towards the large granite bluff. Although she could not see the opening to the inlet from where she sat, she knew exactly where the canoe was going to appear and she kept her eyes focused on that spot.

When the canoe appeared she could tell just by the way that Isaac was sitting that they must have some fish on board. He seemed to her to be sitting straighter and taller and he was paddling with quick deep strokes. Usually when she saw them coming around the bluff, Isaac sat with a bit of a slouch to his posture and his paddle strokes were slightly more laboured, tired from the work of paddling in the waves. He usually always hated to come back to shore hoping that Mr. LaJoie would want to stay out just a little while longer. But today was different. *It's almost like he is in a hurry to get home*, she thought.

As the canoe approached the dock, she could hear Isaac chattering like a chickadee but she couldn't make out exactly what it was that he was saying. Finally when they got close enough she heard him say, "Maude, you should have been with us. It was so exciting. I caught the biggest fish I've ever seen. Your dad helped me to land it and now he says that I can take it home to show my mom and dad and then I'm going to say to them, "Well looks like supper is on me tonight."

As the canoe came alongside the dock, Maude looked down into the bottom of the boat and gasped with surprise. Isaac was right. It was the biggest northern pike she'd ever seen as well.

"Boy, he must have put up quite a fight. I wish I had been there to see that," Maude said.

"Isaac did a great job playing this fish for all it was worth. I wasn't sure who was going to get tired first, Isaac or the fish. But Isaac wins the prize today. It is a keeper like no other. My guess is it weighs a good twelve and a half pounds, that's huge for a pike you know."

Maude was thrilled. "Can I go to your house with you when you show your parents? I bet they are going to be really surprised."

Once the canoe was securely tied to the dock and the fishing lines were carefully stowed under the seats, Oliver took the bait bucket with the remaining little perch that were still swimming idly in the water and dumped it over the edge back into the water. By this time, Maude and Isaac were well on their way up the shore towards the houses and he smiled as he thought about how proud Isaac was at this moment. He remembered the time he caught his first big fish and the thrill it was for him to be able to say that he had done it himself. He knew Isaac's parents would be happy as well.

"Where are Maude and Isaac?" Marie asked as Oliver walked in the door.

"Well, I don't expect to see them any time soon," Oliver said. "Isaac caught a fair sized pike this afternoon and I told him he could keep it to give to his parents for supper tonight. When they were walking up to the house from the dock the kids were talking about how good it was going to taste and Maude was telling Isaac that when he cleans it he has to remember to do this and that and Isaac was saying "I know, I know." Then Maude started giggling about the fact that the fish was still twitching and how they might have to hold it down on the plate so it doesn't jump off the table when they are having supper."

Marie sighed and smiled. "Well, we have a big pot of stew for supper tonight with some fresh bannock that Maude and I made to have with it. We thought that Isaac would want to join us for supper but it looks like the neighbours are going to have company instead."

"Maude was so excited about that fish I don't think she even thought about asking Isaac to join us," Oliver said.

"Ah, to be a kid again," said Marie.

*****

Although as the years went by and the friendship between Maude and Isaac deepened, the difference in their ages became more apparent and the amount of time they spent together began to dwindle. They still loved to go out fishing together and to paddle around the inlet exploring the shoreline. Occasionally they would venture out beyond the bluff into the greater Georgian Bay but the chances to do this were few and far between. Isaac had taken a job with the logging company that had forged the road through the forest to the community and he was seldom home any more.

Marie, a firm believer that Maude should have more opportunities in her life than she did insisted that time would be spent daily teaching Maude how to read, write and to do simple mathematics. Maude was a quick study and soon could read and write as well as Marie. By the time she was thirteen years old, Maude was helping out in the general store and quickly learned how to keep track of the customers' purchases and how much money was due at the end of the sale. Being able to read and write meant that she soon became the person to go to in the village when someone needed to have a letter written to a relative. Occasionally when the mail would be brought into the village, some of the parcels would be wrapped in the newspapers from the larger towns. Maude would always ask if she could have the wrapping so that she could practice her reading. By the time she was seventeen her interest in what was going on in the neighbouring communities was consuming her and she started to think about moving away from the community she so dearly loved so that she could experience more of what the world had to offer.

Oliver had family members who lived in the small town of Penetanguishene a number of miles down the coast at the southern end of Georgian Bay. Though they had never been a close family, he was quite confident that if he asked, his brother and sister-in-law would be happy to provide a room for her and allow Maude to board with them.

And so it was, at the end of the summer of 1915, that Maude packed all her worldly possessions into a small cardboard satchel and planned her passage on the steamer boat that frequented the harbour in Parry Sound once a week.

She and Oliver set out in the wee hours of the morning in the canoe for the ten mile ride south to the small coastal town in order to make sure they did not miss the chance for Maude to get on board.

When it came time to leave home that morning it had been a teary goodbye. Marie held her then hugged her tightly all the while whispering in Maude's ear how much she loved her and how she would miss her. Maude promised that she would write whenever she got the chance and reassured her mother that she would be very careful. "After all, it is not like I am moving to Toronto where I could easily get lost, I am just moving to Penetanguishene. What can happen in Penetanguishene?" Maude said as much to reassure herself as her mother.

Though she loved her mother dearly it was even more painful for Maude when it came time to say goodbye to her father. She had always been his little girl. In fact even as she grew up to be a young lady she was still her dad's little princess and she knew this would be difficult for him. Suddenly Maude began to second guess herself and question whether leaving her parents home and the community she dearly loved was the right thing to do.

"This is something that you have wanted to do for a long time my little one," Oliver said trying to reassure her. "You are young and you have to go to find out if this is what you really want. That way you won't spend the rest of your life wondering, what if?"

As they waited for her to board the steamer, her father's encouraging words started to sink in and her doubts faded. She realized that soon her sense of adventure and her curiosity about what the outside world was really like got the best of her. With her father's reassurance she boarded the steamer with a renewed confidence that she was making the right decision.

As the steamer pulled away from the dock, she watched the small crowd that had gathered to see their loved ones off waving goodbye and shouting farewells. It was easy to pick out her father in that small crowd. He was the tallest one. She wasn't completely certain but it looked to her as though her father kept brushing his cheeks with the palm of his hand. At first she thought there might be a pesky black fly that was bothering him but then as she herself began to wipe a tear that had formed in the corner of her own eye she realized it wasn't a fly that was bothering her father, but tears that he was wiping from his cheeks. She knew deep in her heart that this is what her father wanted for her but just the same, it saddened her to think of how much she was going to miss her parents and how much they were going to miss her.

The captain reached up and pulled the cord attached to the ship's steam whistle and as the long steady blast resonated in the rocks of the harbour the steamer pulled out of Parry Sound harbour and headed south towards Penetanguishene. Maude wrapped the warm woollen shawl around her shoulders that her mother had made for her and thought of her parents. As the boat started to rise and fall with the swell of the waves in the open waters she left the deck and made her way to the passenger lounge. Once settled on the padded leather bench inside the cabin she rested her head on the back of the bench and let her mind wander. She wondered what adventures lay ahead of her in the days and weeks to come. What would her life be like; would she ever see her home again? She smiled as she thought of the possibilities she imagined and closed her eyes to help her relax.

CHAPTER - 2

Gilbert Valcour
Penetanguishene - South East
Shore Georgian Bay

September 1921

The log cabin shook only slightly as the early morning train rolled past on its way into town. Although the three room cabin had been built over seventy-five years ago it was well constructed and still a very sturdy dwelling, especially considering how close it was to the railway tracks.

Built on a low field-stone foundation, the cabin consisted of two bedrooms and a moderate sized great room that served as kitchen and living space. A shallow crawl space accessed by a trap door in the kitchen floor was used as a cold storage and root cellar below the house. It was the perfect place to store homemade preserves, jams, relish and the fall harvest of garden vegetables.

The property the cabin was situated on was small. At about seventy five feet square it was considerably smaller than most of the other lots at this end of town. The north border of the property was Robert Street, one of the main roads leading into town. A mere one hundred feet to the south of this lay the railroad tracks only twenty-five feet from the south border of the property. The cabin was located somewhat in the middle of the lot and although the plot of land was small, with its large maple trees providing shade in the summer and with the lawns and gardens always impeccably maintained it was an attractive, cozy spot despite how close it was to the tracks.

Hidden behind an outcropping of wild lilac bushes, an outhouse was located a short distance from the back door. Although it was pretty close to the house, to its occupants, it seemed to be more like miles away on the cold nights of winter. A decorative porcelain thunder-bowl with a hand painted ceramic lid was stored strategically under the foot of each bed and provided a welcome relief on those cold nights when you just couldn't bring yourself to go outside.

The only source of heat for the cabin was from a wood-burning cook stove in the kitchen area of the great room. This provided the much needed warmth in the winter for the entire cabin, the bedrooms staying warm as long as the heavy curtains that acted as bedroom doors were left open. If privacy was required, heat was forfeited once the curtains were closed. In the summer the great room would reach sweltering temperatures merely from meal preparation, baking breads and pies and just simply heating water for cleaning up dishes and bathing. On those days, closing the curtain on the bedroom door was a welcome relief to keep the bedrooms cooler.

Though the hydro-electric lines that ran into town were fairly close by this cabin, like most of the other houses located on this end of the street, the house did not have electricity yet, or running water for that matter. This neighbourhood, located just on the outskirts of town was known as "the west end", and considered to be the poor end of town. People here were often known as being from the other side of the tracks and though their only crime was that they were poor, they were often shunned by some of the more affluent townsfolk and considered as being "only good as hired help."

The hand dug well that serviced the cabin was not very deep at all, a mere ten feet in fact. The clay tiles that lined the walls of the well were slightly mossy and carried with them the pungent smell of closed in dampness. The water itself however was crystal clear and carried no taste. It helped that the location of the well was close to one of the many aquifers that ran haphazardly underground, fed by the multiple artesian wells in the area. For the local home owners, this ensured a constant source of water would always be available and everyone enjoyed the benefit of its pure, clean freshness. A hand pump mounted on the lid of the well, though routinely lubricated, could be temperamental at times especially on the cold days of winter when it had to be primed multiple times just to free the ice that had built up around the pipes leading into the well. On the coldest of days when the handle on the pump wouldn't move and the ice just wouldn't give, a pot of water heated on the cook stove and poured onto the pump would free things up as it dribbled onto the pipes. There were some days however when more than one pot of hot water was required and without fail, the ice build up the next day was often worse. It was a welcome relief when the warm weather of spring arrived and bringing water into the house was not a half hour job.

*****

Gilbert Valcour lay in his bunk in the small bedroom that he had shared with his brother until not so long ago. He listened for the train's steam whistle to blow as it approached the station located on the docks in the centre of the town. There was no need for the whistle to blow as it went by his house for even though it intersected with Robert Street, it was at this junction the train actually went under the Overhead Bridge as it was known to the locals.

The Overhead Bridge was the last in a series of sixteen bridges the train crossed on its way into the town of Penetanguishene. As the tracks meandered through the rolling hills of the nearby country side they passed through a series of forested then swampy areas as they made their way towards town. The other fifteen bridges were small, short structures averaging about twenty to thirty feet long. Made of heavy twelve inch square oiled timbers they spanned the numerous little creeks and small rivers that flowed towards the bay draining the watershed of that area just outside of town. The Overhead Bridge was the only bridge the train went under rather than over.

As this was the spot where Robert Street, one of the main roads into town crossed the tracks, in the interest of public safety, the railroad company decided to build a small single lane bridge for pedestrian and vehicular traffic. This was done by making use of the slopes and natural hills in the landscape at that location to become the ramps onto the bridge from either side. Since this bridge was built merely to support the weight of cars and trucks the timbers used to build this bridge were smaller in size than those needed to support the weight of the train on the other bridges and though it was a larger bridge, it had been much cheaper to build and maintain. Additionally, in the favour of the railroad company, the responsibility for maintenance and repairs to this bridge fell onto the town and thus defrayed some of the rail line's costs. By the time spring rolled around each year, the condition of the bridge was always a little questionable having fallen victim to the problems caused by the multiple freezes and thaws that occurred during the winter months. This often caused many of the timbers to sustain cracks and rot holes in them and as sure as day follows night, without fail, springtime always found labourers from the town's public works department making the necessary repairs to make sure no injuries were sustained by anyone crossing the bridge.

Even though he was only twenty four years of age, Gilbert and his mother Madelaine had already experienced their share of hardship and loss. In fact, it could be said they had experienced *more* than their fair share. In fact hardship and loss seemed to just keep coming their way. But, somehow the two of them survived it all.

Maybe it was basic survival instinct; maybe it was their profound and unwavering faith in God but there was something inherent, deep from within that drove them to find a purpose in life. Perhaps that was what kept them going. Madelaine would often say to Gilbert and her friends, "things have got to get better 'cause they can't get any worse. Someday, sometime, things will get better. I know it. They just have to."

Madelaine truly believed that time is a great healer and in time Gilbert began to realize his mother was right, for with time, he noticed that some of the pain he had felt from the loss of his father and then more recently his brother, had lessened, somewhat. Though the pain had eased he often wondered if he would ever get over missing them. Not hearing their laughter or sharing in their often spontaneous practical jokes that both his father and brother were so well known for, left a quiet emptiness in the house that both he and his mother felt was so real it was as though they could reach out and touch it.

The low and mournful whistle of the train sounded once again as it pulled into the station. Gilbert lay motionless on his bunk, reflecting as he often did, on the good times that he had shared with his father and brother.

*****

June 1906

"Gilbert, Elijah, come over here," Lucien Valcour called softly to his two young sons. "You'll want to see this! I'm pretty sure this has to be the biggest frog I've ever seen in my whole life." He looked up to see the boys splashing through the shallow water of the inland lake as they came towards him. "Don't make any noise or waves," he said, "I don't want you to scare it."

The boys stopped running then slowly made their way over to their father's side quietly and looked at the giant bullfrog that was sitting next to the shore. "I think it was trying to sit on the lily pad over there but he was too big and heavy. He kept slipping under the water. I saw it swim over here to the shore next to me and I couldn't believe how big it was," said Lucien.

With a sure and steady motion, as quick as he could, Lucien bent down and with his large calloused hand, scooped up the frog then grabbed it with the other as well to hold it more tightly so the frog couldn't wriggle free and jump back into the water. "This frog is too big to fish with but these legs would sure taste great fried in butter." The boys looked at their dad like he had rocks in his head and simultaneously cried "Yuk". At first they thought he was just kidding, another one of his practical jokes, but then they realized he was serious.

"What?" said Lucien. "Why are you looking at me like I have two heads? Haven't I ever introduced you boys to the sweet taste of a healthy set of frog's legs?" He paused as he looked at them. "You know, they are quite a delicacy for the rich folk. And," he said in a sober tone," they have to pay lots of money to eat them in their high class restaurants." He smiled. "But not us," he boasted, "we get them for free. We just have to work a little harder to get them that's all."

The boys reached out to touch the frog, rubbing the top of its head as though they were patting a family dog. The large bulging eyes of the bullfrog blinked in unison as the boys hands came close to his head but the frog didn't seem to mind being held or rubbed for that matter. Next they rubbed the underside of the frog's throat just above the belly. It was soft and slimy and it dimpled a little with the touch of their fingers but the frog seemed to like this gentle caressing and relaxed a little in Lucien's firm grip.

Eventually Lucien let the frog go back into the swampy waters at the edge of the inland lake and the boys watched with fascination as the frog slowly yet gracefully swam away, its legs bending in perfect V shapes as it brought its heels together and then with its powerful upper thighs straightened them to propel itself forward, its webbed toes fully extended for maximum thrust.

When Lucien could get time off work he would often bring his family to camp in the Cognashene area he so dearly loved. Located just half way between Penetanguishene where they lived and the Musquosh area where he worked as a logger, Lucien cherished the time that he was able to spend in Cognashene. Though Lucien was just as familiar with the areas around Go Home Bay and the entire shoreline as far north as Indian Harbour, he tended to just keep going back to the Cognashene area. This was a place he considered to be the prettiest of all the shorelines in southern Georgian Bay and what he liked to refer to as "a little slice of heaven on earth".

Lucien remembered that even as a young lad himself his father often borrowed a friend's boat whenever he could and had taken Lucien and his brother Joseph to the Cognashene area where they could spend the day catching minnows and frogs to use as bait. This was always followed by endless hours of fishing in the calm and serene back bays that were tucked slightly inland and accessed by narrow channels. They were well protected from the open waters of greater Georgian Bay and without fail there was always enough fish brought home to feed the hungry family. Sometimes his father would cook the fish over an open fire as a shore lunch and this made it even more special for the boys. They always cherished those times with their dad and never missed an opportunity to go fishing whenever they could. Now Lucien, like his father, brought his boys to the same areas to catch the bait, and to fish in the same spots. Gilbert and Elijah were never disappointed because like his father before him, Lucien without fail, always caught fish.

Over the years, it became harder and harder for Lucien to find the time to bring his family camping and fishing. Often Madelaine would have so much work ahead of her that she was not able to go with them. Sometimes there just wasn't enough money to buy gas for the boat to take them there. More often than not Lucien was away at the logging camp and could not get back home. These were the long days of summer for Gilbert and Elijah as they pined for their father to return from his logging job so they could go out fishing with him.

On a couple of occasions Lucien had taken the small row boat that he kept pulled up on shore in Penetanguishene harbour for the boys to use during the summer and rowed them across "The Gap", a large expanse of open water between Penetanguishene and Cognashene. This journey took about 4 hours and was possible only if the bay was calm and there was no wind.

One time, the day started off calm and Lucien and the boys headed out for a weekend of camping and fishing in Cognashene. Half way across the gap, the wind started to blow from the west, gently at first, then gusting stronger. They never made it to where they were headed. Instead they ended up spending the weekend plus a day longer on the exposed shore of Beausoleil Island, a huge island unsettled for the most part with only a few dwellings on the leeward side of the island where several Native families lived. With no means of communication, Lucien had no way to get a message to Madelaine to let her know they were all right. He knew she would be worried about them when the wind got up, but he also knew that with her rosary in hand, she had a direct line to God and it was probably her prayers that got them safely to shore.

They set up camp, and waited for the wind storm to blow itself out. "It will be a three day blow boys," Lucien said to Gilbert and Elijah. They could tell by the tone in their father's voice that although he was concerned, he was not too worried. If anyone had the skills to survive on an island in bad weather when they weren't planning on it, their father did. Their confidence in his ability to make the most of it was what helped them to see this as an adventure rather than a survival experience. In the end, they found a number of new fishing holes where the bass and northern pike were plentiful. Years later, Gilbert and Eli would often make their way back to that windy shoreline off Beausoleil Island to fish the hazardous shoals known as the Ginn Rocks. These shoals were so tricky to manoeuvre they often kept even the most skilled boaters away but, as local fishermen; well, they were thrilled to have this spot all to themselves.

*****

Gilbert's father Lucien had been a logger since he had been a young man working in the north cutting trees then hauling them on horse drawn wagons along the tote-roads that had been forged through the forest solely for that purpose. Once at the river the back breaking work began hauling them from the wagon to the shore then floating them as logs down the Musquosh River to the lumber mill located at its mouth. The smaller of the trees were milled into thick planks on the spot and stored on the slab docks at the entrance to the river. These were then taken by barge down to the lumber yards in the small towns of Waubaushene, Midland and Port McNicoll located on the most southerly end of Georgian Bay. These popular and highly sought after white pine planks were then loaded onto the flatbed railway cars and sold in the large city markets of Toronto, Montreal and beyond.

At the mill in Musquosh the larger trees were corralled within chained log booms and towed down to the McGibbon Sawmill in Penetanguishene where they too were milled for the fine clear lumber they provided and sold to both the local building supply stores and the markets to the south.

As a logger, Lucien was often away from home for long periods of time. In winter it was not uncommon for him and the other men on his logging team to be gone for months at a time, living out a harsh winter existence in the logging camp. Their reality was that there was no practical way to make it back home to be with family and friends. This isolated lifestyle was hard not only for the lumberjacks but for their wives as well. It wasn't easy for them to keep the family going in their absence, sustained on the meagre income they had from their husbands' work. Often the wives would have to supplement the family income by finding work in town doing things such as housekeeping and laundry and even providing nanny services for those families who had enough money to have those sorts of things done for them.

******

August 1917

It came as such a shock to Madelaine's system that she thought she would never be able to bear it. Alone in the house at the time she was always a little nervous when strangers appeared. Living in a small community provides some comfort in that you know everyone around you but when she saw the well dressed man approaching her door, Madelaine knew this could not be good news.

As she opened the door, slowly at first, she recognized him as Thomas Lampton, the owner of the lumber mill on the Musquosh River where Lucien worked. She invited him into the house and they sat at the table in the small kitchen. Though she had only met him briefly in the past, his well cut suit and confident manner spoke of the affluence he enjoyed as a result of the many businesses he owned.

"Madelaine," he said softly, "may I call you Madelaine?" Lampton asked. She nodded almost imperceptibly.

"Madelaine, I am afraid that I have some very bad news," his voice now just barely above a whisper. She could sense his uneasiness but could do nothing to comfort him. She knew what news would be coming.

"Madelaine I am afraid I have to tell you that your husband Lucien has been killed in a terrible accident up the shore." He watched as the colour drained out of her face. He reached across the table to take her hand but she pulled it away immediately and held both hands in her lap, nervously wringing a handkerchief she had pulled from her apron. She began rocking silently back and forth in her chair her shoulders trembling as though she was shivering with cold.

"How, how did this happen?" she asked barely able to get the words out around the lump that had formed in her throat.

"Lucien was a very hard worker, a good man and one of my favourite employees," he stated. "He was always very careful. He always made sure that the logs were tied down on the wagon once they were loaded even though there are support beams on the sides of the wagon to stop them from rolling off. He always put extra ropes on the load just to be sure nothing would happen."

Lampton looked at her blank expression and wondered how much of this she was actually hearing. "Lucien was always very careful; he had been doing the job a long time and knew how dangerous this work could be." He paused briefly then continued.

"Lucien was leading the team of horses that was pulling a wagon loaded with logs towards the river when one of the wheels became jammed between a couple of boulders that were to big to be moved out of the way. When the trail was cut through the forest several years ago, the men tried to move those boulders but couldn't." He paused. "The wagon slipped off the tote-road and the wheel sank into the soft soil around the boulders."

Madelaine stared blankly at him, "Go on," she said finally able to speak.

"There were three men there at the time, they used some pry bars to try to lift the wheel beyond the rocks that it was caught on and even with the horses pulling and the men lifting they weren't able to free it." He paused again.

"They decided the only way to get beyond this would be to remove the logs from the wagon and pull it forward then reload it." His voice remained calm but he was having a difficult time speaking as his mouth had dried out so badly. Madelaine could see he was very distraught by what had happened. She could tell he was a good man and that he was struggling with having to bear such bad news but she was powerless to offer him any comfort.

"As the ropes that bound the logs together on the wagon were undone the weight of the logs shifted on the wagon. Since it was already leaning, their combined weight was too much for the side supports to hold back and they broke." The one man on the top of the wagon has a very badly crushed leg. He got caught between the logs as they started to roll off the wagon. I am afraid he is going to lose that leg. The other man was at the far end of the wagon and he was able to jump back out of the way but poor Lucien." Lambert stopped barely able to speak the next words. "Poor Lucien, he was right in the middle of the wagon and when the supports broke. The logs rolled on top of him. It all happened so fast. He couldn't get out of the way."

Lampton didn't know where to look, didn't know what to say next. He sat there for a moment then once again reached out for Madelaine's hand and took it gently in his. "Madelaine, I am so sorry, so very sorry," he said as he watched the tears stream silently down her cheeks.

"Lucien was a good man and a hard worker," he repeated. "I will look after everything," he said. "You just have to tell me what you want me to do and I will look after it."

"I don't know what to do Mr. Lampton." Madelaine said her voice a mere whisper in the stillness of the cabin. "I mean, we have to get Lucien back home. Where is he now? Is he still up the shore?" Lampton nodded.

"He can't stay there. We have to get him home. How will we get him home?" As she spoke tears flowed down her cheeks, the wrinkled handkerchief she held in her hands serving a greater purpose occupying her hands rather than being used to wipe away the tears. She mumbled a few more words and she felt like she was just rambling but in her mind a thousand thoughts were flashing through. How would she survive? How will she support her boys? How would she even be able to begin to tell them about this? She couldn't think about those things right now. She just wanted to get Lucien home.

"I arranged for my boat to go to the Musquosh River. The men from another work crew I had up there have gone to where the accident happened. They are taking the man that was injured and Lucien to the river with a team of horses and then my driver will bring them both back to Penetanguishene," said Lampton.

"Is there a funeral home in town? Do you want me to arrange for him to go right to the funeral home?" he asked.

"We won't be able to afford a funeral home Mr. Lampton," said Madelaine. "We don't have any money saved. We have no life insurance either. I don't know what to do," Madelaine sobbed.

"I will look after this for you Madelaine. I will make all the arrangements for you. Lucien was a very good man, a hard worker," he repeated. "This is the least that I can do to honour him and to try and ease this pain for you and your sons."

Madelaine nodded slowly. "Lucien used to tell me that one of the reasons he kept going back to work at the logging camp was because you were a fine man to work for and you really cared about your men." With a bit of composure coming back into her voice Madelaine said, "I can see that now. I'd really appreciate it if you can look after getting Lucien back home."

"I know money will be tight for you Madelaine. I will pay the funeral costs as well as the burial expenses and I'll see to it that my office sends an extra three months salary for you," said Lampton. "Perhaps that will hold you over until you can get on your feet."

Though Madelaine was a proud woman who was more used to giving than receiving, she willingly accepted the offer of assistance from Mr. Lampton.

"Is there anything else I can do for you now?" he asked.

"No, not really. The boys will be home soon. Oh this will be so hard for them. They are so close to their father. They did so much together when he was home," her voice quivered and with that the tears flowed yet again and her sobbing came with such force her whole body heaved in the chair, her breaths coming in short gasps.

Lampton moved his chair closer to where Madelaine was sitting and sat quietly at her side. He had nothing else to say, he didn't know what else to do. He did know that just being there was important, not only for her but for him as well.

October 1917

It was called The Great War. It was to be the war to end all wars and Elijah Valcour couldn't stop thinking about signing up for it. As a child he had often thought about being a soldier. He had played war games with his older brother Gilbert and always wondered what it would be like to be a part of shaping history. In school when they studied history, Eli was always fascinated when there was discussion of the great battles for the Roman Empire. Those battles had shaped the past and he was in awe of the bravery of the soldiers and their commitment to their cause. History often repeats itself and Elijah was drawn to fighting for a cause he believed in. He truly believed that his country needed him and that he was going to make a difference in the world.

Typically Elijah was always ready with a joke or a playful tease and his usual enthusiasm for all things new and different was often infectious. He always brought a smile to Madelaine's face however this time, his mother took no comfort in his confidence and drive. She just had a feeling this would not turn out well and her feelings were more often than not right on the mark. The pain of having lost her husband several months earlier was still very fresh and the thought of possibly losing her youngest son too was more than she could think about. Though she begged him not to go, he enlisted and was soon sent off to war.

Though the conditions at "the front" were deplorable, Elijah somehow knew deep in his soul that it would only be a matter of time before things would start to turn around for the company of infantrymen he was with. They had to be. He had promised his mother he would return. He had promised her he would stay safe and he had to keep telling himself this as much for her sake as for his own sanity. He knew how she had suffered when his father had died, he knew she was struggling with making ends meet and he promised that he would send all of his money to her to make things easier at home. He could not bear to think that he too might not make it. He had to keep reassuring himself over and over again because at this moment in time, in this particular trench, things were not looking good.

The cold wet days of late fall led to even colder, wetter nights with the soldiers catching few hours of sleep in the often water soaked trenches they fought the enemy from. And then it happened. In an instant. The mortar from the enemy lines hit their trench and in a flash it was all over for them. It happened so fast, the soldiers didn't even really realize what had happened to them.

The letter from the government arrived just before New Year's and when Madelaine saw who it was from, she didn't even have to open it to know that once again, her world was about to fall apart. How much more could she possibly be expected to bear? First her husband and now her youngest son, her heart was breaking in two. How much more? She took little comfort in the words of the letter saying that Elijah had died a hero. The fact that he had been taken from her was all that she could focus on.

For Gilbert, loosing Elijah was a double blow. Not only had he lost his brother but he had also lost his best friend. From the time Elijah was born, Gilbert as the older brother had taken him under his wing, had been his protector, had watched over him. They had been inseparable and friends of the family often commented that the two of them seemed to be joined at the hip. Wherever one went the other was right there beside him like peas in a pod. While many brothers often quibble and fight as they get older, Gilbert and Eli only drew closer, their interests, their likes, even their desires to go out in the canoe, or go fishing were always in sync. When Elijah was old enough to fend for himself and the need for Gilbert to be his protector as older brother diminished, his role as confidant and companion deepened.

When Gilbert would think about his loss he knew that in time he would get over it but in his heart he knew he would never stop missing Elijah. His spirit would be with him always. He thanked God many times over for the good times they had had together and the fabulous memories he would hold dear to his heart till the day he died.

October 1921

Though Gilbert had started in the section of the West Breeze Boatworks where the hulls were made, the foreman of the shop soon began to appreciate the fine talent Gilbert possessed for "doing it right the first time." Measure twice and cut once was Gilbert's motto. Although this made him a little slower at the job than some of the other workmen, the foreman both understood and appreciated this work ethic for in the long run it saved a lot of the raw material that was used in the construction of the boats. For those reasons, not long after Gilbert had started to work at the West Breeze Boatworks, the foreman moved him to the time intensive but more responsible position of finishing the interiors of the boats being built at the factory.

This was where Gilbert's talents as a craftsman truly shone. The work he did inside the boats was more difficult than working on the hulls of the boats but he enjoyed the challenge so much more. Precision was required and his woodworking skills needed to be exact. The move to this position also provided him with slightly more money at the end of the week and this extra cash, although small, helped his mother to meet the expenses at home.

By the time Gilbert was finished with the interior of the boats he worked on, the mahogany was polished to a shiny lustre, the panel of instruments such as the gas gauge, engine temperature gauge and the alternator gauge were always precisely placed in the dash for easy viewing by the driver. On the larger boats a handsome brushed nickel compass was placed such that it could be viewed by the driver whether he was sitting at the wheel or standing up to drive. Many owners preferred to stand when they drove their boats in order to catch the fresh air blowing off Georgian Bay. As these fine boats sliced through the water under the thrust of the powerful engine the owners took pride in their purchase for, not only did the boat look great, it was also a very reliable vessel and handled well regardless of how rough the waters in The Gap became.

Gilbert had designed a slide mechanism for the driver's seat so that when sitting the driver could pull the seat forward into just the right spot to suit the driver's individual comfort yet, when the driver decided to stand, the quick flip of the latch on the slide mechanism could shift the seat backwards and out of the way when he stood. This feature added an extra comfort option to the enjoyment the owners had and soon this little invention of Gilbert's became standard fare on almost all of the boats turned out at the West Breeze Boatworks factory.

In all of the boats manufactured at the Boatworks the bench seats were covered with soft, supple leather. In order to customize the boats these fine leathers had been dyed in a variety of colours and prospective owners who placed an order for a boat were allowed to choose the colour and texture they preferred from a swatch sample provided in the showroom of the Boatworks or one of the sales offices located in either downtown Toronto or Montreal.

Designed to take the rough waters of Georgian Bay the West Breeze boats were high end boats and were at the top of the price range for boats of similar size. Not limited to just Georgian Bay these classic boats were often shipped by train to all parts of Canada as far west as British Columbia and as far east as Nova Scotia. Many a westerner boasted of the fact that they owned a West Breeze boat and their reputation as a very sea-worthy craft became legendary far and wide.

As the war raged on, the times were tough and talk of a recession coming was on everyone's lips. The orders for pleasure boats dropped off and work began to slow down at the West Breeze Boatworks. Not many of the larger boats they were building were selling even though the company sent their top local salesmen to Toronto to try to increase sales by working the larger urban market. As the orders for custom built boats dwindled there were some weeks the owner of the Boatworks were not able to meet the payroll. As the hard times of the recession hit it got to the point where several of the men who worked on building the hulls were laid off. Later that month the woman who had been working in the upholstery department was also let go.

Things did not look good all around but Gilbert stayed on in the factory as his skills were such that he could work in all areas of the boat building and finishing. Eventually the inevitable happened, the time came when even he was let go.

*****

Building canoes had always been a labour of love for Gilbert. From the time he was a young teenager he had often gone to help out old Mr. Beaudoin, a woodworker who had a small shop at the back of his house where he build cedar strip canoes. By the time Gilbert was in his late teenage years he had learned enough about building canoes from Mr. Beaudoin that he was able to make them himself from start to finish. Mr. Beaudoin didn't mind Gilbert taking over the job of making the canoes in his shop. Over the years his arthritic hands and shoulders could barely stand the rigours of shaping the wooden planks, planing, sanding then varnishing them repeatedly to get them to a shine that allowed the canoe to glide through the water with ease.

Gilbert's skills and craftsmanship in building canoes had worked in his favour when he got the job at the Boatworks. Once his talents at the Boatworks were recognized and word spread that he also built canoes in his spare time he often was hired to make a canoe, a special order of sorts by some of the labourers within the plant. Other orders came from some of the wealthy people who had purchased a West Breeze boat in the past and were interested in "adding to their fleet."

Gilbert didn't mind the extra work. He loved to make canoes and the money that he made from these special orders was being very carefully salted away in a special account at the bank. It was his intention that this money would be used as a down payment for a house when the time came.

Once he was laid off from the Boatworks he was able to devote himself full time to building canoes and although the market for powerboats had dwindled, the market for a less expensive craft that didn't need gas, or a dock to park it at, became very popular. Gilbert soon found within a very short period of time that he had enough orders to keep him busy for a year.

When he wasn't in the workshop building canoes, Gilbert, who had always been a man to tinker with things, found he was able to fix just about anything that was given to him. He was often asked by the locals for help with toasters that had stopped working, radios whose tubes had blown or those new electric kettles whose inner elements just seemed to keep blowing a fuse. He particularly liked the challenge of fixing clocks and watches that didn't keep time or had stopped working all together. With the recession in full swing, most people could only afford to get things repaired rather than purchasing a replacement. For a handyman like Gilbert, the market was ripe for his many talents

Because he often needed special supplies when building his canoes, such as the durable waterproof Spar Varnish or the tiny brass finishing nails he used to attach the cedar strips to the ribbing in the canoes, he had developed quite a relationship with the McDowell family who operated the hardware store in town. Mr. McDowell's hardware store could be counted on to always have a good supply of the parts Gilbert needed for fixing things so his work as a handyman was made easier because of this. He was in there often enough that one day Mr. McDowell said, "Gilbert, you spend so much time here, you might as well be working here. I am getting older you know and I could sure use the help."

"Oh, I have enough things to keep me busy, but thanks for the offer," said Gilbert.

"Well, if you ever change your mind, let me know," said Paddy McDowell.

Along with his canoe building business the handyman work continued and soon Gilbert's reputation as the go-to-man in town spread. Many of the townsfolk did not own a car and it was a bit challenging for most of them to bring those things they needed to have fixed all the way down to Gilbert's house at the end of Robert Street. Knowing Gilbert was often at the hardware store to purchase supplies, people started to drop off their items for Gilbert to fix at the hardware store. There seemed to be a never ending supply of things to be fixed and he soon became the town's repairman, sharpening saws, fixing radios, pumps and electric motors, replacing screens, glass cutting and replacing glass in window frames

He wasn't sure exactly when it happened but Gilbert started to fix things in the back room at the hardware store rather than cart them down to his house and then bring them back to the store to be picked up.

Then there was the issue of getting paid for his work. If he was working in the back room of the store full time then he would be there to collect what was due to him. That way he would also be there to show the customer what he had done or just how he had fixed things. Finally, because he was at the hardware store so much, Paddy McDowell started to pay Gilbert a weekly salary since he was attracting enough people into the store to make it worth his while to keep him there.

For Gilbert, it meant that he would be readily available to meet with the customers and advise them on their particular hardware needs and do-it-yourself projects. Paddy was thrilled to have him working for him because Gilbert was talented in the ways that made him a perfect fit for a hardware store. He was confident that Gilbert would be a great resource for the customers who came into the store and the customers appreciated how resourceful he was in giving advice on how to fix this or that.

Over time Gilbert became adept at fixing radios. He had the patience to work through the problems and figure out what was and wasn't working with them. It was almost like he had a sixth sense about it. He kept a supply of replacement radio tubes in the back room of the hardware store, enough of them in fact that regardless of the make or model of the radio he had replacement parts to use. When business was slow in the store, there was always an old radio that was sitting around waiting for him to trouble shoot what the problems might be. Sometimes it was something as simple as just replacing a broken dial, other times it became more complex and the only way to solve the problem was to fine tune the positioning of inner crystals to provide better reception.

Though he missed his job at the Boatworks he loved the day to day challenges he faced at the hardware store and felt a great sense of accomplishment when he knew he had solved a problem for a customer or garnered their appreciation for something he had fixed. In the evenings, he worked in the shop at Mr. Beaudoin's house building canoes. Though he had been asked once or twice for a kayak rather than a canoe, Gilbert did not rise to that particular challenge. For the amount of extra time it would take him to design, build and then make sure it was a seaworthy, he didn't think the cost would be worth it. Maybe some day he thought, when I have time, but for now he was happy turning out his much sought after cedar strip canoes.

As time went on and business stayed fairly steady, Paddy McDowell decided it was time to hire a new staff member to stock the shelves, place the supply orders and work the cash register. Paddy was convinced that if he hired another person it would free up some of his own time and allow him some much needed days off during the week so that he could attend to his second love in life, that of fishing. *I must really start looking for someone,* he though, but as often happens he would get distracted or busy and never really ever did much more about it than that.

******

The tiny sleigh bells attached above the store's front door jingled as the door opened. The bells were set just low enough that they rubbed on the top of the door when it opened, but they were hung high enough so they didn't get caught in the door when it closed.

Gilbert who had been tinkering on a particularly stubborn radio at the back of the store looked up when he heard the door open and saw a rather shy young woman step into the store. She turned slowly and let the door close softly behind her holding it all the while so that it wouldn't slam shut. For a moment she just stood there not really moving forward, not really backing up, she was just looking around the store from where she stood. She looked like she was trying to decide if she was going to stay or run away.

He walked up to the front of the store where she was standing and asked, "Is there something I can help you with?"

"Well, I...I just...I just was wondering if Mr McDowell might be in the store?" she stammered. She seemed to be very shy and kept her head down as she spoke. Though she had said very little, Gilbert could detect a slight cadence to her voice. It wasn't really an accent, it wasn't really the tone of her voice, but he could tell by the way she pronounced her words that she had a Native background. Her hair was jet black, her skin a smooth soft mocha brown. When she looked up Gilbert noticed that with her high cheekbones, black eyes that looked like obsidian glass and tanned skin she had an air of exotic radiance that caused his heart rate to quicken and he felt as if his cheeks were flushed. He had never felt anything like this before but one thing he did know, he liked feeling this way.

"Mr. McDowell isn't in right now," said Gilbert. "It's a fine summer day and he seemed to think that it was more important for him to go out and try his new fishing rod than it was to stay in the store." He smiled at her and he could see immediately that her shyness faded slightly. A wee bit of a smile crept across her face.

"It would be a great day for fishing. I don't blame Mr. McDowell one bit," she said enthusiastically.

"Do you like to fish?" Gilbert asked.

"Oh yes. It is one of my favourite things to do. I am very good at it in fact. My father is a fisherman and I know that if I was at home right now, he and I would be out in our canoe paddling around some of the back bays trying for a good feed of bass, or perhaps a nice northern pike."

"Well it looks like you and I have something in common then," said Gilbert, trying to set this lovely young woman at ease. "I love to fish as well, and on top of that, believe it or not, I make cedar strip canoes when I am not working here," he said as he waved his arm in the direction of the back of the store. He looked at her and she smiled, this time showing a full row of perfect white teeth and a beautiful full smile.

"What is it that you wanted to speak to Mr. McDowell about?" he asked.

"Well, I am not from around here. For the last couple of months I have been staying with my uncle and aunt here in town. My uncle was in the store a couple of weeks ago and Mr. McDowell mentioned to him that he was thinking of hiring someone to work in the store." She paused and looked around at the shelves, the cluttered counter and the dusty floor. She stepped forward a few paces and then said, "I worked in the general store in my village before I came to Penetanguishene and I think that I would be a good person for the job."

"Well, I know that Paddy is thinking about hiring someone. Finding someone who already has experience in a store is just what we need." He smiled at her and continued "It's not my place to hire you but what I can do is tell him when he comes in tomorrow that you were here and I think you'd be a just right for the job."

On hearing that a wide grin formed on her face, her pearly white teeth glittered in the light and Gilbert thought about how much his impression of her had changed in just a few minutes. She had gone from being a shy, Native girl to an eager and enthusiastic potential co-worker.

"Oh, if you could do that for me, I'd be really grateful." She turned to leave and as she started to reach for the door Gilbert said, "It would be my pleasure, but, there is just one thing. I don't know what your name is?"

"Maude," she said holding her head up high, "Maude LaJoie."

"Well Maude LaJoie, why don't you come back in here tomorrow just after lunch. I'll make sure old Paddy sticks around. I am sure he'll be really interested to meet you."

She glanced around the store one more time looking at all the work there was to do. "You can count on it."

*****

The next day, right after lunch, Maude was back. Paddy McDowell had indeed stayed in the store. When the door opened, he looked up from the inventory lists he was reviewing at the front counter, and was greeted by the sight of a lovely young woman. This wasn't the shy girl Gilbert had told him about. Having had her nervousness eased the day before during her friendly chat with Gilbert, Maude had more self-confidence and self-absurdness.

Gilbert had been walking towards the front of the store with a repaired toaster in his hands ready to hand it over to a waiting customer when the door opened. He was delighted to see that it was Maude who had arrived. He put the toaster on the counter and said,

"Paddy, this is Maude. She is the young lady I was telling you about this morning." Paddy put down his pencil and inventory sheets and walked around the counter to greet her.

"Nice to meet you," he said offering his hand to her to shake. "Gilbert tells me you are interested in working in the store."

"That I am," said Maude.

"Are you good in arithmetic?" he asked.

"Why yes, as a matter of fact I am."

"Gilbert told me that you used to work in the general store where you come from."

"I did, I used to do all kinds of things at the store. Usually it was me who got to sort the mail, cut fabric, sell dry goods and I looked after ordering the supplies we needed."

"Well, it sounds like you did it all." He paused and rubbed his chin as if deep in thought.

"Ordering the supplies the store needed eh?" he said with a bit of excitement in his voice. Keeping track of the inventory and making up the order lists was one of the tasks he dreaded the most about running the store. If he could delegate this job to someone else he would be a happy man.

"Yes sir. I am very good with reading and writing and I know how to make change in the cash register too," she said enthusiastically. She looked about the store. "And I noticed that some of the shelves here are kind of dusty, and the floor could be swept. I'd be happy to work at keeping the store tidy and clean as well if you'd give me the chance to."

She smiled a quick flash of a smile and then added a bit coyly, "and that would mean that you'd get more time to go out fishing."

"You are the answer to my prayers Maude. When can you start?"

"Well it's another nice day out there. Just like yesterday. I am sure that as long as Gilbert is here to show me the ropes I can start right now and you can go see if you can catch something for your supper tonight."

"It's a deal," proclaimed Paddy rubbing his hands together. "Can you work again tomorrow?"

"I can work whenever you want me to."

"Well girl, the store is open every day except Sunday. We start at eight o'clock and close at six. If those hours are good for you, they are good for me." And with that he turned on his heel and headed for the back room.

"Gilbert," he said excitedly. "I'm goin' fishin'!"

Gilbert turned to respond but only saw the back of Paddy's head as he made his way out the back door.

"Well Maude. Welcome aboard. Let me show you around and I'll tell you about how we do things around here."

CHAPTER - 3

Penetanguishene, June 1924

Gilbert had always been a quiet and pensive person, first as a child and then into his teenage and early adult life. Some who knew him, thought he seemed to be a bit distant or withdrawn but, once they got to know him better, found his kind and gentle ways always proved that he was different than that common first impression.

He had only a small network of friends his age and had spent most of his free time with his brother Elijah. Both he and his brother loved being outdoors and because they spent so much time fishing together they often kidded with each other that "no wonder we don't have a lot of friends, all we do is hang out together and go fishing."

"Yeah, and it's hard to make friends with a fish," Elijah would joke.

Gilbert had never been one to make sudden or impulsive decisions. He was never one to act quickly on anything and always took his time to think things through before he made his decision about how something should be done. As a result he always seemed to get the best outcome possible for all that he did and his success in getting things done right the first time brought him a lot of work.

For Gilbert building canoes was a labour of love. This was evident in the quality and craftsmanship found in his canoes. Every aspect of the canoes' structure was very carefully thought out, from his design for the cut of the hull to the carefully hand-planed ribbing on the inside. From the placement of the seats to allow for perfect balance in the canoe for single or multiple paddlers, to the carefully laid cedar strips on the outside, every detail was attentively thought out and painstakingly crafted. Once all the brass finishing nails had been countersunk, wood filler applied and the tiny hammer dents and small blemishes in the wood lovingly sanded out, multiple layers of Marine Spar Varnish were applied to finish the outside. This was done such that it made the grain in the wood stand out. Once the varnish had dried the texture of the cedar seemed to leap out in three dimensions. Admirers of the finished project couldn't help but run their hand over it and comment on the fine work he had done.

Gilbert found that working in the shop, by himself on tasks he loved to do was very therapeutic for him. It gave him plenty of time to think and to reflect on what was important in life. It gave him quiet-time to mourn the loss of his father and his brother but it also gave him time to think and plan for the future. This time alone provided a certain peace within him and a self-confidence in what he was able to do. The success he enjoyed in his work boosted his self-esteem and with his quiet and shy demeanour it gave him self-assurance in his ability and the "savoir faire" he possessed in all that he did. This quiet time also gave him a chance to think about Maude. He'd never had a girlfriend, had never been on a date, he was too shy for that, but for some reason he could not keep from thinking about Maude.

*****

For Maude working in the hardware store was like a dream job. She felt right at home behind the counter serving the customers and making small talk when time allowed. Her parents had instilled in her a good work ethic and to that end she was a great employee as she never sat idle. There were always shelves to dust then restock, items to be priced, inventory lists to prepare and orders to mail off to the suppliers. Though the store was a lot busier than the one at Granite Bluff Inlet the work there had prepared her well for the job she was doing now.

Old Mr. McDowell sure seemed to be fond of her. He liked the way she had cleaned up the store and she found Gilbert very easy to work with. She did notice however, from time to time, that she would find him glancing up from his work at the back of the store to watch her and it seemed to her that he was 'glancing' at her more frequently lately.

One snowy winter day, during an unusually quiet period in the store, Maude and Gilbert were taking a much deserved break sitting casually perched on stools behind the counter at the front of the store. They had been chatting about the wind whipping the snow into drifts in front of the store on the Main Street when suddenly and seemingly out of the blue Gilbert asked, "Do you have any plans for supper on Saturday night?"

Maude was so taken off guard by the question that before she even had time to think about it she said, "Well it just so happens that I have nothing planned," she said timidly, "other than eating with my aunt and uncle that is."

"I guess that would be a good thing then," Gilbert replied.

"Why Mr. Valcour, just whatever did you have in mind," she asked coyly glancing sideways at him and rapidly fluttering her eyelids in his direction the way she had seen Greta Garbo do at the movie theatre just weeks before.

"I would really like you meet my mother. She's a great cook and I have been telling her about you and, well, I was thinking if you'd come to my house for supper then it would be a chance for you to meet her."

It didn't take her long to decide. "What time is supper?"

"Well, we both have to work until six so how about if we walk to my house right after work. It's about a mile down Robert Street. Hopefully the weather won't be too bad for us to walk that far."

"Gilbert, I was raised in an isolated Native community where we either walked or canoed everywhere we went, regardless of the weather. I am pretty sure I can handle walking a mile down Robert Street to your house."

Gilbert smiled at her realizing that what he had said did sound a little lame. Of course she'd be OK with walking to his place. She was young and fit and energetic and in no way would she be daunted by a mile long walk which, as it turned out, was mostly downhill.

"I think before we go to your house though, I'll want to go to my place and get freshened up a bit. I always feel a little grubby when I get home from work after dusting shelves and stacking the shipping crates and stuff," she said. "Besides, I don't want to meet your mom for the first time in my work clothes and old overcoat."

"You look great just the way you are but if you'll feel better going to your place first, that's fine. I'll just let mom know that we will be getting in a little later than I thought so that she can plan her cooking time around that."

"Do you want me to just meet you at your house?"

"Absolutely not. It will be dark by then and you have never been there before so I'll walk with you to your place and then we can go to my home together."

"It'll give you a chance to meet my aunt and uncle that way," Maude added.

Gilbert thought for a moment then said, "I hope this will be alright with them?"

"That what will be alright with them?" she asked.

"That you are bringing me to your place to meet them and then you leaving again with me right away." He paused, "I hope they'll be OK with it."

"Oh, I don't think you have to worry about that. My uncle knows you pretty well," said Maude.

"But I haven't even met him before."

"Your reputation precedes you Gilbert." She paused as she thought about what she had just said then added. "In a good way that is. Everybody in town knows you as Mr. Fix-it, the Go-to-Guy who just happens to build the best canoes in the area," she continued.

"In fact, my uncle might just have a couple of questions for you about a few things he's been working on." She smiled. "You two can chat while I get ready."

"So it's settled then. We'll work until the store closes at six, we'll go up to your place for you to change clothes and then we'll head down to my place." Gilbert looked pensively out the window as if he was still trying to figure something out.

"What is it," she asked. "It looks like you have something on your mind."

"Well, I do actually," he said a little shyly.

"What?"

"Well," he hesitated. "This is the first time I have ever asked a girl to go somewhere with me, I've never been on a date before in my life. And well..."

"Well what?"

"Well, I don't know how long it takes for a girl to get 'freshened up,'" he stammered. "I don't know what time I should tell my mom we will get there."

"Gilbert, I am a simple girl of simple means." She smiled. "I don't really fuss too much with my hair, and I never wear make up so I am pretty sure I can be 'freshened up' in about five minutes."

A smile of relief crept across his face. "That's great. I've heard stories of it taking hours for some women to get ready."

"Oh, Gilbert," she laughed and punched him playfully on the upper arm. Smiling she turned to look out the window at the snow that continued to swirl around the storefront. Gilbert got up off his stool and said, "I guess break time is over." He headed to the back of the store. As she continued to look out the window she thought about Gilbert. She was glad that he had decided that his break was over and had returned to the workshop at the back of the store because that way he couldn't see her blushing.

Lately, in the back of her mind she had found herself thinking about Gilbert, a lot in fact. Though they had been working together for about six months now, there really had never been much of an opportunity to actually sit and chat or get to know one another. There had been hints in their conversation about the things they liked to do and it was amazing how similar they were. Being on the water, paddling back bays in canoes, fishing, swimming, all those things it seemed were high on each of their personal lists of priorities in life. The commonality of it all made for great conversation when they had the chance to chat. Maude definitely wanted to get to know Gilbert better and maybe this was going to be her chance.

As he walked home that night Gilbert realized that he had been thinking of Maude. A lot in fact. He just couldn't get her out of his mind. Usually his sense of concentration was quite strong and he could work on a project without being distracted but often, lately, he would be working on something quietly in the back of the store and suddenly realize that his concentration had faded and without even realizing it he was looking towards the front of the store to see if he could see Maude.

He was pleased that Maude had agreed to come for supper at his house and he was pretty happy with himself for getting up the nerve to actually ask her. His mother was all for it. In fact, the truth be known, it was she who suggested it. Madelaine knew how lonely Gilbert had been since Elijah had gone off to war and never returned. He had few friends and lately it seemed all he did was work, work, work. By the way Gilbert spoke about Maude to his mother she was pretty sure he had taken a fancy to her but, he was shy, and definitely could never be referred to as a ladies' man. Suggesting he ask her to the house for dinner was both an opportunity for Madelaine to meet Maude and a chance for Gilbert to ask her on a 'date' that wasn't going to cost him any money and would be in a non-threatening environment.

*****

The dinner at Gilbert's house went well. As promised the food was fantastic and Maude and Madelaine seemed to get along just fine. Maude who had been a bit shy when she first arrived had been made to feel so welcome that she didn't realize how quickly the time had flown by. Though she offered to help with the meal preparation and the clean up afterwards, Madelaine would hear nothing of it and insisted that she and Gilbert just sit and relax after their hard day at work. They chatted casually for over an hour occasionally drawing Madelaine into the conversation where ever they could.

Gilbert was so pleased that everything had gone off without a hitch it boosted his confidence to the point that as he was walking her back home to her house he asked, "would you like to do have dinner with me again sometime?"

"I can't think of anything I'd rather do Gilbert. I truly had a good time tonight. Your mom is a great lady and a wonderful cook. It sounds like she has gone through a lot in her life. I can't begin to imagine how she has been able to cope with all of it."

"It has certainly been tough on her. What with my dad dying in the logging accident and then my brother Elijah being killed in the war it hasn't been easy. I wasn't able to go to war because my father had died and as the oldest son, I had to stay home to support the family. The military have a term for that, they call it a hardship exemption. It doesn't mean that I was afraid to go to war, it just means that I had to stay home to support my mother." He paused as he thought about that then added. "Secretly I think my mom was pretty happy about that. Though she knew I wanted to enlist even if it was just to avenge my brother's death, it would have been too much for my mother to bear if something had happened to me as well."

Both Maude and Gilbert were quiet as they trudged their way through the snow back up Robert Street. Each was deep in thoughts about what Gilbert had just said but both were also thinking about how well the evening had gone.

"It's a deal," she said suddenly and seemingly out of the blue.

"What's a deal?" he asked.

"We'll do this again. We'll have supper again. Let's say next Sunday only this time it's my turn to cook."

Gilbert smiled at the prospect of spending more time with Maude then replied, "Suits me fine."

"Perfect. I'll talk to my aunt and uncle about it to make sure they are OK with it and I'm going to cook up something special. I can't see how they'll mind if I'm doing the cooking. I have a few favourite recipes up my sleeve. I'm a pretty good cook too you know."

"What are we having?"

"Why Mr. Valour," she said demurely, once again batting her long dark eyelashes in his direction. "You'll just have to come over for dinner and find out."

*****

The supper at Maude's house was nothing short of a feast. Her uncle was the local butcher in town and so there was always lots of fine meat in the house. Maude had chosen to make a scrumptious hearty beef stew with stewing beef that was so tender it easily broke into pieces with a fork. Added to that, Maude's aunt who worked at the local grocery store, had brought home the fixings for a fresh garden salad, a real delicacy at that time of year since. The snow had been covering the gardens for a long time at that point and it was almost unheard of to have a salad at that time of the year which made it all the more special. Homemade tea biscuits rounded out the meal. For dessert a three layer chocolate cake with chocolate icing was served with strong tea and when the meal was over not a single person moved away from the table hungry. In fact, all four of them had a hard time moving away from the table at all. They were stuffed. The thought of getting up and clearing the table seemed overwhelming at that moment.

Gilbert rubbed his belly and joked, "Well, I believe I am sufficiently safonsified."

"What on earth does that mean?" Maude asked.

"Oh, I think it means that I couldn't add another crumb in there" he said rubbing his belly again. "It's a phrase I heard somewhere a long time ago and I totally forgot about it until just now and for some reason it seems to fit with the way I feel right now. Filled to the brim."

The conversation between Gilbert and Maude's aunt and uncle flowed easily. It was obvious that her uncle respected Gilbert for the work that he did. He asked a lot of questions about how to do this, that and the other thing. Her uncle was amazed at how simple Gilbert made things sound when he spoke about the steps that should be taken to fix what needed fixing.

As far as Maude's aunt went, she was totally taken by Gilbert. She and her husband had never had any children and had taken Maude in under their wing as though she was their own. They were sure that Maude would be well taken care of if she were to marry Gilbert and once he left for home that night she made no bones about telling Maude she thought that he was a good catch and

Maude shouldn't let anything get in the way of them developing a long and lasting relationship.

Maude said to her aunt, "don't you think you are rushing things a little? We have only been working together for a few months and this is just the second time we get together other than at work."

"I know a good man when I meet one," her aunt replied. "I have a good sense about Gilbert and I am not usually wrong." Maude just smiled and walked upstairs to her room. It was funny that her aunt should make the comments she had just spoken because they echoed exactly what Maude had been thinking for some time now.

And so it came to be that winter that every Saturday evening Gilbert would invite Maude to his house for supper with his mother and every Sunday evening Maude would reciprocate and invite Gilbert to her aunt and uncle's house for supper. Maude and Madelaine got along famously and they worked well together in the kitchen preparing the meals they were to share. As time went by, Madelaine was comfortable enough with Maude that she would let her help with the clean up after supper. Then the three of them would sit around the table and exchange stories about what life was like for Maude growing up at Granite Bluff Inlet and what life was like for Gilbert hanging out with a fun loving brother who never really ever took anything too seriously, except for the practical jokes he loved to play.

It was on one of those Saturday evenings while Madelaine was recanting stories from her past that her philosophy on life became evident to Maude. It seemed to Maude that Madelaine was never one to hold back her hand if help was needed. She would admonish those who questioned her by saying "what were we put on this earth for if not to help one another? Doing good for others makes you feel good."

Madelaine had always been one to work hard every day. It seemed to Gilbert that she never took a day off, even on Sunday. Right after she got home from church and cooked the Sunday breakfast she would keep the wood fire burning and begin her baking for the week. Typically Saturday afternoons were set aside for making her bread dough. She would knead the dough till her hands ached and then she knew the bread would be light and fluffy enough. She would divide the dough up into loaf sized mounds then cover them with a damp dishtowel so they wouldn't dry out overnight. By noon hour on Sunday the smell of fresh baked bread could be found wafting around the neighbourhood as loaf after loaf of fresh bread was placed on the kitchen table to cool.

She had been poor her entire life and had received no formal education but she was wise in the ways of the world around her and was current with the news of the town. Once her husband died she struggled with how she was going to make ends meet. She had always been a fabulous baker and many of her friends and neighbours urged her to open a bake shop in town. She often wondered if she should however she did not have the money she needed to start up a business and was too proud to ask anyone for a loan. So, to make money to pay the bills, she started out simply by making loaves of bread on Sunday and taking them to the local grocery store in town to be sold. Soon she was getting requests for pies, tarts, cookies and sticky buns. She was amazed at how well those items were selling and in time she became a significant competition for the local bake shop. It seemed that many of the townsfolk preferred Madelaine's home-style baking to that of the bake shop and over time she gained a certain notoriety for the fine baking she did. People were always amazed that all that baking was done on an old fashioned wood burning cook stove. They knew she had had a hard life and often mysteriously a new chord of fresh chopped wood would be found stacked against the back of the log cabin. Madelaine never found out who was the kind soul who left the wood there but she certainly appreciated finding it.

To supplement the income she made from her baking Madelaine also worked as a housekeeper for a very elderly couple in town. With no pension available to them once their savings ran out they told Madelaine that she was going to have to find some other work as they could not keep her on. The kindhearted Madelaine however was not the type to walk away from someone in need so she stayed on for free, going once per week to do some light housekeeping duties and take to them some of her fresh baking to perk up their spirits.

The elderly couple asked why she was being so kind to them and she simply replied, "When my husband died and I had no money, you helped me out, you gave me work and believed in me enough to encourage me to sell my bread. One good turn deserves another. That is what we were put on this earth for, to help one another."

"There will definitely be a place in heaven for you Madelaine," the older woman replied.

Being a kind and generous person will only take you so far, it doesn't pay the bills, so Madelaine was once again looking for more work and it didn't take long. News of her kindness to the elderly couple had spread through town and as it turned out Dr. Johnson, the local physician, was in need of a housekeeper and handy man. His medical practice had become busy enough that he never seemed to get the time to get all those things he needed done around the house and he knew that since his wife, a nurse, was working with him full time in the office, she could certainly use some help with the housework.

Out for an evening stroll one day, he found himself following the railroad tracks as they led out of town. When he came to the overhead bridge at the end of Robert Street, he decided it was time to turn around but had a flash of brilliance. He walked around the fenced yard over to Madelaine's house.

A brief moment after he had gently knocked on the door Madelaine answered and appeared very surprised to see him standing there. As Gilbert was not home at the time, of course she thought the worse, the colour drained from her face and she noticeably paled.

"Oh my God," she stammered. "What has happened to Gilbert? Is he alright?"

"I have no idea where Gilbert is right now," the doctor replied. "I assume he is fine though." He paused, "That isn't the reason I've come here." He could easily see that Madelaine was visibly relieved.

"I came to ask if you would be willing to be my housekeeper. I will pay you a fair wage."

Madelaine did not need any time to think about it. "Of course, when do you want me to start?"

Surprised by Madelaine's quick response he had to think a bit about it before saying, "If you are free tomorrow, I will have you come to meet with my wife and she can show you around. We have a pretty big house you know, probably the biggest in town, and things are starting to get behind. You may have to work longer days in the beginning to get everything caught up but once that's done then you can cut your hours back a bit."

"I'll be there," she replied.

Then a second thought occurred to him. "Madelaine, it's well known throughout the town that you are a pretty amazing cook. Do you think you would be interested in preparing our meals for us as well, perhaps every other night? I don't want to over work you and I'll certainly pay you extra for that. I know that my wife will think she has died and gone to heaven if she doesn't have to start making meals when she is finished in the office."

"Dr. Johnson, I can do whatever you want. Let me sort out those details with Mrs. Johnson tomorrow when I meet with her."

"You are truly an answer to our prayers Madelaine."

He turned and started to walk away when a thought occurred to him. He turned back towards the house just as Madelaine was about to shut the door. "Oh, and by the way, do you know if Gilbert is looking for any extra work? I sure could use a handyman who is as talented as him. If he is available that is."

"Well I don't usually speak for Gilbert but since the Boatworks closed, he doesn't make as much money now at the hardware store so I am sure that if you have some work for him, he'll probably take it. He's over at Mr. Beaudoin's right now working on a new canoe if you want to stop by there on your way home and have a chat with him." She paused then added, "If you don't meet up with him, I'll ask him when he gets home and can let you know tomorrow when I go over to your house."

"Brilliant," Dr. Johnson thought as he started his walk home. "I may have just saved myself a whole lot of work."

*****

On Sunday evenings, right after the supper dishes were cleared from the dining room table, Gilbert, Maude and her aunt and uncle would take out the deck of cards and for hours on end would play the game of '58' a game invented in Penetanguishene and for the most part only played by people who were either from town or one of the small villages nearby such as Perkinsfield or Lafontaine. Though Maude had written out a 'cheat sheet' for Gilbert with the value of each card written on it, Gilbert seemed to be having a bit of a hard time catching on to the bidding for points and scoring the game.

"This doesn't seem to make any sense to me," he said. His age old habits of thinking deeply about things and trying to rationalize everything was somewhat of a burden for him as far as this game was concerned. "You say the Ace is worth one point and the King is worth 25 points but the Ace can take the King, but then the Queen is worth zero points and it can take the Jack which is also only worth one point. I don't get it at all, the nine is worth nine points, that I understand but how is it that the three is worth fifteen points. This just doesn't make logical sense to me."

He paused, thinking then added, "do you think that you could show me a set of the rules for this game? Maybe what I need to do is take them home and study them before we play again next weekend."

"There aren't any written rules for this game," admitted Maude's uncle. "This game was made up years ago in this little town by the people who settled here from France and had nothing better to do to pass the time on the cold nights of winter. You learn how to play it from someone teaching you the basic moves and how to bid for points and then it just takes practice for you to get the hang of it."

Once Gilbert learned the basics though, and mastered the concept of bidding for points, he was a force to be reckoned with as a team player. And the teams were always the same each week; it was the guys versus the girls. Sometimes the guys would win, and sometimes they would lose but whatever the score, they all enjoyed playing 58 and they all looked forward to their weekly rematch.

For the first time since his brother Elijah had died Gilbert was feeling whole again. The long stretches of melancholy that had plagued him after his brother's death seemed to be less frequent and Gilbert found that he couldn't wait to get to work in the morning so that he could see Maude again. He would often take the short cut to work by following the train tracks that passed just behind his house and made their way towards the town dock. From there it was just a quick jaunt up the hill one block to the hardware store. Though he prided himself on never being late for work, it never failed to amaze him that Maude was always there ahead of him, waiting patiently by the back door for him to unlock it. After a few months Paddy McDowell decided it was time Maude was given her own key to the store. Though he and his wife lived in the apartment just above the store, since Gilbert had started to work there, he never seemed to get his old bones down to the store before ten in the morning.

Months before, someone had brought a hotplate in to have Gilbert replace the element but they had never come back into the store to pick it up. Gilbert had tried a couple of times to get in touch with the owner but to no avail. Then one day when the customer came into the store to get something else, Gilbert rushed to the back of the store to get the Hotplate. When he got to the front of the store with it the customer said she didn't have the money to pay for the repair and told Gilbert to keep it for his trouble. So, back to the back of the store it went.

One damp and rainy morning the thought of walking to work in the inclement weather sent a chill through to Maude's bones. She got a bright idea that brought a smile to her face and it seemed to take the chill away in an instant. While she was having her breakfast and getting ready for work she bundled up some coffee grounds and an old coffee percolator from the back of the cupboard at home. Not wanting to see the Hotplate just sit there collecting dust, Maude got the bright idea to make a pot of coffee on the Hotplate right after she got into work. By the time Gilbert had made it into the store Maude had added the grounds to the dented old basket that fit onto a slender stem that rose from the bottom of the pot. She added water and the lid and set the perk on the Hotplate to brew. The smell of fresh brewed coffee permeated the whole store, a scent that was completely foreign in that building but it smelled so good Gilbert found he was salivating for a cup before it was even fully brewed.

And so a new tradition was born. Each day Maude would prepare a pot of coffee on the hotplate at the back of the store, and Gilbert would bring in a small treat for them to share, usually a couple of tea biscuits or muffins, or cookies his mom had made earlier in the week. Their morning routine was fairly simple and straight forward. While the coffee was brewing, Maude would prepare the cash register and organize her inventory sheets. Gilbert would unlock the front door and place the items such as rakes, or shovels or wheelbarrows that were on special that week out on the sidewalk in front of the store. Those items placed out on the sidewalk were always a sure fire way to attract people into the store to see what kind of a bargain was being offered that week. Once the set-up routine was complete Maude and Gilbert would sit behind the front counter perched on the old wooden stools. They would sip their piping hot coffee, munch on the treat and talk about what they had done the previous evening and how they thought their day was going to go.

CHAPTER - 4

June 1925

With spring in the air Gilbert looked forward to getting back into his canoe. He was particularly looking forward to having Maude as his passenger. It had been several years since Elijah had died and he missed having company in the boat when he was paddling in the harbour or fishing in the small coves and inlets that made up Penetanguishene Bay. The thought of going out onto the bay in one of his homemade canoes with Maude brought a smile to his face and warmth to his heart. He knew he was head over heels in love with her; they got along so well he was convinced that she was the person he wanted to spend the rest of his life with. He knew his mother liked her, and Maude's aunt and uncle thought the world of him so there was just one more thing that he had to do. He had to make his way to Granite Bluff Inlet, meet Maude's parents and ask for her hand in marriage. He wasn't sure how he was going to bring up the subject of going north to visit them but as was his nature, he took his time and thought about it in that quiet and pensive way of his.

It was a hot, sunny Sunday afternoon in early June. Gilbert and Maude were paddling up Penetanguishene harbour when Gilbert said, "The bay is lovely today, so calm and so peaceful. I bet it must be beautiful at Granite Bluff Inlet today. I would love to see it sometime."

"I was just thinking the same thing," Maude replied. "You know, it has been well over a year since I have been back there. Even though I write letters to my parents, I still miss them terribly and would love to go see them."

Ah-ha, Gilbert thought, the seed has been planted.

They were quiet for a while each lost in their own thoughts, each enjoying the tranquility of the peaceful calm water as they drifted silently in the canoe.

"You have worked for Mr. McDowell longer than I have," Maude said, "do you think he would let me have a few days off so that I could make my way home for a visit?"

"My guess is yes, but I was wondering," he paused, "perhaps you'd like some company for that visit. I would really like to meet your parents and would love to have a day to explore the Inlet. You've described it to me so many times I feel like I know the place but it isn't the same as actually being there."

"But what will Mr. McDowell do about the store if we are both gone?" she asked.

"Well before I started there, when he wanted to take some time off he used to just close up shop and put a note on the door to say when the store would be open again. 'Everyone has a right to holidays he'd say.'"

"Maybe what we could do is ask him for the time off over the Dominion Day long weekend. That way we would have Sunday as our travel day, Monday as our visiting day, and come back on Tuesday. The store would only have to be closed for one extra day."

"That's a pretty good idea Maude. I had completely forgotten about Dominion Day as a holiday, and that's coming up soon isn't it?" said Gilbert.

"How could you forget Dominion Day? Canada has been celebrating that holiday since 1879. And knowing you, it's probably the only time that you take a day off other than Christmas and New Years Day."

Gilbert sighed. Maude was right. *She's getting to know me pretty well,* he thought. He really wasn't one to take holidays preferring to work six days every week because he needed the money but usually by the time Dominion Day rolled around, he was glad to get the extra day off especially if the weather was hot and sunny.

"Well, we can certainly ask," Gilbert replied. "It never hurts to ask."

As it turned out, Mr. McDowell thought it was a splendid idea. He figured the day would come when Maude would want to bring Gilbert to her homestead and he agreed without even putting up a fuss. "I hope you kids have a wonderful time." He winked at Gilbert as if to say, *I know what you are up to.* "And don't worry about the store, everybody knows that I just live upstairs so if someone really needs something in a hurry, they'll just come knocking on my door."

Later that day Maude got busy writing a letter to her mom and dad and told them about the upcoming visit. She had spoken of Gilbert so many times in her previous letters that it shouldn't be a surprise to them that they would come for a visit, together. And it wasn't.

*****

The day they left on the SS Keewatin Steamboat heading out of Port McNicoll, it was cloudy, overcast and threatening of rain. But all of that bad weather held off and by the time they were pulling into the harbour at Parry Sound the sun had come out and the winds had died down. Their journey along the shores of Georgian Bay had only taken a few hours as the Keewatin plied through the choppy water at her average cruising speed of 14 knots. Being a vessel 350 feet long it barely responded to the three to four foot swells on Georgian Bay and the passengers rode in relative comfort totally unaware of the frothy white caps and waves pounding on the inch thick steel plated hull.

While having a light snack in the restaurant on the main deck Gilbert said to Maude, "Did you know that the Keewatin is often referred to as the sister ship to the Titanic?"

"Nope, I didn't know that," Maude said.

"Well it is. The Keewatin was built at the Fairfield Shipbuilding and Engineering Company. It's the same shipyards in Scotland that the Titanic was built in. The Keewatin was built in 1907 and the Titanic in 1909 so it is only a couple of years older. The grand staircase in the main lounge area and the triple expansion steam engines, even some of the furniture in the dining room and the deck chairs are exactly the same. Oh and by the way, this ship uses 20 tons of coal every day just to keep the engines steamed up. It would use more coal if it were to run at full throttle all day."

"Well, aren't you a fountain of knowledge," Maude said teasing Gilbert about what he had just said. "I don't think we will have to worry about any icebergs in July in Georgian Bay though." She turned slightly in her chair to gaze out at the amazing scenery of the granite shoreline.

"Where did you learn all those things about the Keewatin?" Maude asked.

"While I was waiting for our food to come I read the back of the menu card. It has a whole list of details about the ship on it."

"Here is something you may not know," said Maude. "A lot of people think that the name Keewatin is an Ojibwa word but it isn't. The Ojibwa word *'giiwedin'* and the Cree word *'kiwehtin'* are words that mean the same thing which is North

69

Wind. The word Keewatin is just a blending of the two words used by people because it is easier to say. Although I don't speak Cree some people say the word Keewatin means 'blizzard of the north' but I have no way of knowing that for sure."

"You know Maude," Gilbert said, "your English is so good, and you are so well spoken I often forget that Ojibwa is your mother tongue."

"There is no opportunity for me to speak Ojibwa in Penetanguishene so I hope that as time goes by, I don't forget it completely."

"Coming home to Granite Bluff Inlet every now and then will help you to keep it," Gilbert reassured her.

"In my mind, frequent trips back home are good for you, as long as I get to travel with you," Gilbert said hopefully.

The weather had cleared completely and it was a sunny, balmy day by the time they were pulling into the port in Parry Sound. Maude, like her father, took this to be a good sign of things to come.

Oliver was standing on the dock watching the big steamer land but he was so excited at the thought of seeing his only daughter again he couldn't contain himself. He was not by nature an impatient man however he rushed to the edge of the dock and helped to catch the heavy inch thick ropes that tied the steamer to the dock. Oliver worked quickly with the hope that if he helped with the landing that it would make things go faster. The crew on the boat tossed the mooring hawsers that were coiled on the deck of the boat and the dock crew placed them over the bollards that were securely attached to the cement dock. Once the boat was moored, the walking platform was dropped from the side of the hull and the passengers started to disembark from the steamer.

When Maude got off the boat, Oliver was there with his arms open wide. He hugged her so tightly she felt as though she was in the grips of a bear. She didn't mind at all, in fact she enjoyed the moment. It had been way too long since her father had hugged her so tightly and she could tell by the way his hand was lovingly patting her back that he was enjoying the moment as well.

"Dad," she said proudly, pulling herself out of his arms, "this is my friend Gilbert Valcour. Gilbert, this is my father, Oliver LaJoie."

The two men shook hands for what seemed like a minute. The handshake started off somewhat formally as Oliver looked Gilbert in the eyes but soon it relaxed into a friendlier shake when he saw Gilbert looking back directly into his eyes. Oliver thought Gilbert's eyes seemed to have a hypnotic quality about them, something that revealed him as a down to earth man who could be trusted.

Gilbert's warm smile and friendly greeting immediately reassured Oliver that he possessed a quiet subdued strength of character and a certain liveliness which gave the impression of unlimited energy. The face though was beginning to show the unstoppable result of aging and a hard life. Deepening lines spread from the edges of his eyes and the skin did not have the elasticity of his younger years. Gilbert it seemed was slowly achieving a weathered look. The wrinkled features around the cheeks and the forehead seemed more pronounced there but when he smiled, they all disappeared revealing pleasant and relaxed mirth lines from years of smiling.

The face of a man who has spent a lot of his time outside. A fine measure of a man, Oliver thought. *Sincere with nothing to hide.* If there was one thing that Oliver prided himself in, it was his judgment of character. First impressions meant a lot to Oliver and this one was very favourable.

"It's a pleasure to meet you Gilbert," Oliver said, "We've read so many things about you in Maude's letters. You seem to be just the way she described you." He chuckled a bit then added. "All favourable I might add."

"I hope I can live up to her praise Mr. LaJoie."

"Please, Gilbert, just call me Oliver. Mr. LaJoie makes me feel old."

"I can't wait to see mom," Maude piped in. "Is she home?"

"She sure is little one." Maude smiled at her dad's use of the pet name he had called her for years. "She's anxious to see you too and to finally get to meet Gilbert."

"I'm glad the weather cleared up," Maude said looking up to the sky and the quickly dissipating cloud formation. "It's a long canoe ride back to the inlet," Maude added.

"Oh you don't have to worry about that," Oliver said. "Isaac bought a small runabout with an outboard motor on it. He leaves it at his parent's house so that when he's home he can go out fishing whenever he wants. When he heard you were coming he insisted that I take it to Parry Sound to meet you guys. So, grab your gear and I'll get the motor started."

"Is Isaac home?" Maude asked with anticipation in her voice.

"Yup, he's on vacation this week from the logging camp. He said he hoped he'd get a chance to meet up with the two of you."

"Oh, Gilbert, I really want you to meet Isaac." Maude said excitedly. "I know the two of you will get along just great. You both have so much in common."

As Oliver tinkered with the settings on the motor, pulling the choke out and pushing it in slowly until the tiny little motor hummed. Gilbert and Maude sat patiently on the front seat of the small fourteen foot long lap-strake cedar strip boat. As a boat builder himself, Gilbert was impressed with the condition of this little boat. Though it was just a basic three seat stern driven boat, it was solidly built, the lap-strakes perfectly attached to the cedar ribbing visible on the inside. The ribbing looked like it was in very good shape and the gunwales had been formed from one solid piece of cedar. A handsome set of stainless steel oarlocks were attached to the gunwales and the oars were tucked neatly under the seats just in case there were times the motor didn't work.

As the boat headed out of the harbour it felt sturdy in the waves, the splash boards attached on the outside of the hull worked well to throw the water off to the side rather than allow it to spray into the boat. "Oliver," Gilbert shouted over the noise of the motor, "I'll bet this little boat can take a pretty good wave," Gilbert observed.

"Yes. It was a really good find." Oliver paused as he concentrated on taking a wave from a boat passing in the other direction. "Isaac was able to pick it up for a song from one of the tourists near Parry Sound who was selling his cottage." Oliver continued, "It's working out well for Isaac to have his own boat and it seems, it might come in handy for me too."

As they made their way down the harbour towards Georgian Bay, Gilbert and Maude sat silently admiring the beauty of their surroundings. A few new buildings had sprung up along the shore of the harbour since she had been there last and there were a few more out buildings nestled closely together near the railroad tracks.

A large bridge spanned over the east end of the harbour. "For the train," Oliver said when he noticed Gilbert looking at it. "They already have the plans drawn up for these huge cement reinforced piers. See that ridge on the south side of the bay," Oliver said pointing. "They are going to reinforce the bridge so that it spans right across to the far side." Maude and Oliver looked on in awe. It seemed like it would be an engineering nightmare to build a bridge that long and that high over an open expanse of water.

"But won't the bridge have to be really high to keep the tracks level?" Maude questioned.

"That's why the cement piers are going to be so big. That's the only way they will be able to support such a long and heavy metal bridge," Oliver said.

The small motor on the runabout, though noisy ran evenly and didn't seem to sputter at all. It added the perfect background to the ride as the boat made its way out of the harbour and headed towards home. The further out of the harbour they went the more Maude chatted cheerily with Gilbert. She pointed out specific details of the shoreline she thought Gilbert would like to know about. Before they knew it, they had left the harbour of Parry Sound and were well on their way home.

*****

Granite Bluff Inlet was exactly as Maude had remembered it. There had been no changes to the small Native community in the time she had been away and she was thrilled to be able to show it off to Gilbert. It was exactly as he had pictured it and he could see by the liveliness in Maude's eyes that she was as proud as can be to be able to share her homestead with him.

Marie having heard the outboard motor puttering along as it came into the inlet had already come out of the house and had made her way to the dock. Once they were tied to the dock they slowly made their way towards the house.

After a long and emotional embrace with her mother Maude said, "Mom, this is Gilbert Valcour. Gilbert this is my mom."

"It is a pleasure to finally meet you Mrs. LaJoie. Maude has cooked plenty of meals for me over the last little while and she insists that she learned how to cook from you. Every meal has been a great meal as far as I am concerned but Maude always insists that your cooking is better," Gilbert said. "If I may be so bold to say it, I'm really looking forward to having supper tonight."

"Well first off Gilbert, let's get a couple of things straight," Maude's mother said, the smile betraying the phony sternness to her voice. "First of all, I'd rather you just call me Marie, and secondly, Maude is a really good cook in her own right. I don't think I can top any of her recipes. Truth be known, before she left home to move to Penetanguishene she taught me a thing or two about cooking. She is pretty inventive when it comes to food."

"Oh mom," Maude blushed, "I'll never be as good a cook as you are."

"Speaking of eating, what time were you planning on having supper?" Maude asked.

"I didn't have any set time in mind," Marie replied. "You know how it is with the weather and living on the water. I wasn't sure the Keewatin would be in on time. And then, if your dad had trouble with the motor on Isaac's boat that could have delayed things as well so I haven't even started working on supper yet," Marie paused. "Are you hungry?"

"No, not really, we were able to grab a snack in the restaurant on the boat so we are good for now. I just wanted to know if Gilbert and I would have time to go for a canoe ride around the Inlet before supper."

"I kind of figured you'd want to do that," Oliver piped in. "The canoe and paddles are just on the shore next to the dock. Have fun you two."

*****

It was a warm and sunny afternoon and Maude was so pleased that the weather held. For Gilbert, although he had spent many hours on the waters around Cognashene and Musquosh, was still impressed with how different the shoreline looked in the Inlet. The rocks here had a pinkish hue to them with a smattering of beige, grey and white that were totally different shades from what he was used to seeing further south in the area he was so familiar with.

"There seems to be a lot of quartz in the rocks up here," Gilbert said.

"There is," said Maude. "Let me show you one of my favourite spots." They paddled on in silence for a time quietly admiring the scenery around them.

"Over there," Maude said pointing to the left with her paddle. "Steer us over to that spot where you see the streak of white quartz that goes down to the water like a white ribbon."

With little effort Gilbert expertly changed the direction the canoe was heading and guided the canoe over to the shore.

"Let's get out here," Maude said already straightening her legs out in front of her. Up until that point she had been in a kneeling position with her bum perched on the edge of the front seat. That was a position her father had always preferred when he paddled in a canoe rather than sitting on the seat. He felt it helped to lower the centre of gravity in the canoe and that made it less tipsy and easier to handle in the waves. Being closest to the shore she stepped out and held onto the gunwales of the canoe to stabilize it for Gilbert.

The water at the edge of the shore was as clear as glass. So clear in fact that it was actually deeper than it seemed. Gilbert had taken his shoes and socks off and rolled up his pant legs before getting into the canoe but he was still surprised when he stepped out of the canoe and the water went well over his rolled up cuffs.

"Whoa, that's a lot deeper than it looks. The water is so clear here," Gilbert said as he pulled the canoe up on the shore. "No wonder your dad is such a good fisherman, he can probably see the fish from a quarter mile away." Then Gilbert added. "It's almost as though he could steal the fish right out of the water with a net as it passes by. But," he shrugged his shoulders, "what is the fun in that?"

Maude laughed. "Don't tell him that. He'll be upset if he thinks you know his secret. But to be honest, my dad hardly ever uses a net when he is fishing by himself. When he catches a fish he reels it in quite close to the boat and then just plays it in the water to tire it out. Then he reaches into the water and slips his fingers under the fish's gill and pulls it out of the water that way."

"I've tried that trick," Gilbert said, "but failed at it miserably. My respect for your dad just went up another notch if he can land a fish without even using a net."

"Now, what is it that is so special about this spot my dear," Gilbert said as he walked over to her and tenderly placed his arm over her shoulder.

Maude looked at Gilbert a bit surprised. It was the first time he had ever called her by any name other than Maude. It made her feel warm inside and standing on the shore at her favourite place in the world suddenly made her feel closer to Gilbert than she had ever felt before. She took his hand and tugged slightly as they slowly made their way over the rocks. She looked into those incredible eyes of his and saw that he was serious. The blood suddenly rushed to Maude's face and she felt her knees weaken. She clutched to his arm with both hands to prevent herself from falling feeling the strong sinewy bicep beneath his shirt sleeve and wondered what was coming over her. Surprised at losing control, she stood on her toes, abruptly circled her arms around his neck and pulled him down and kissed his lips long and hungrily.

Though Gilbert had thought often that this moment would come, he was surprised that it would happen here on the rocks in Granite Bluff Inlet. He was overcome by the sudden passion of the moment and felt slightly light-headed himself. He placed both hands on her face and drew her nearer to him. He kissed her again, softly and tenderly allowing their tongues to intertwine and caress each other slowly. The stirring he felt in his loins brought a smile to his face and he slowly eased his face away from Maude's.

"What?" she asked questioning the smile on his face.

"Oh, nothing" he said knowing full well this was neither the time nor the place to take things any further. "Now," he said struggling to keep himself from taking Maude in his arms and carrying her off to a secluded spot along the shore line, "what is so special that you wanted to show me?"

"Over this way," she said sensing that there was more going on in Gilbert's mind than finding out what lay beyond the slight rise in the rocky shoreline.

As they climbed higher up the hill the steep rocks gave way to a flattened area and both stood spell bound on the crest of the rock at the sight ahead of them. The azure waters of Georgian Bay lay before them and for as far as the eyes could see, there was nothing but water and sky. The horizon was perfectly flat and you could not tell where the calm blue water stopped and the perfectly cloudless sky started.

Gilbert took Maude's hand once again and gently tugged on it as he sat down on a flattened boulder that looked like it had been planted there for the sole purpose of just sitting, gazing and admiring. He pulled her closer to him and patted the rock surface next to him. "Sit here beside me Maude," he said as he once again placed his arm around her shoulder.

They sat in silence for a long while, each lost in their own thoughts, each of them drinking in the beauty of the view that surrounded them. Occasionally a seagull would drift by aimlessly soaring on the rising thermals, eyes darting across the surface of the water constantly searching and hunting for that wee bit of food such as a minnow or small perch that would sustain him until his next meal.

As Maude snuggled in beside him he said, "I want this moment to last forever. For the first time in my life I feel perfectly at peace right here, right now. If there was some way that I could physically capture this moment in a bottle and keep it, it would become my most prized possession."

An hour went by, and they had hardly moved. Each one content to just be in the moment, enjoying the opportunity to be alone together for the first time. Finally as the sun was starting its slow and lazy fall towards the horizon Maude stood and faced Gilbert. She reached down and pulled on his hands and said,

"Well Monsieur Valcour, I think it is high time we made our way back to the house. I'm sure mom is cooking up a storm by now and we sure don't want to be late for that!"

*****

They engaged in small talk during the meal, discussing everything from the weather to fishing in the Inlet and the greater waters beyond. The meal was everything that Maude had hoped it would be. Although her mother insisted that Maude was the better cook, both Maude and Gilbert agreed that it was an incredible feast of fresh northern pike which had been cooked on an open fire in the stone pit located about half way between the house and the shore. Marie had also made a large pan of bannock into which she had added some pine nuts and blueberries that she had collected just the day before. Home fried potatoes and some root vegetables rounded out the meal. It was obvious they all had their fill as they pushed themselves away from the table stuffed. There would certainly be enough leftovers for lunch the next day.

While they sat on the front porch watching the sun sink into the far horizon Maude said jokingly to Gilbert, "Listen, you'll hear it sizzle when it hits the water."

Gilbert laughed at Maude's childish comment but understood that it was most likely a comment she had heard from Oliver a number of times in her early life.

"It will take exactly three minutes and forty-four seconds from the time the bottom of the sun touches the water until it disappears completely," said Oliver. "In the spring the sun sets much farther to the western edge of our viewpoint here in the Inlet, but by the time September rolls around the position of the sun will have shifted quite a bit to the south-west almost out of our line of sight." Oliver paused then added, "When we see that happening we know that fall has arrived and we start making our plans for the winter."

Georgian Bay had never looked so beautiful and Gilbert wondered how Maude could ever have left such a spot. When he asked her about it she simply stated, "There is more to life than beautiful sunsets and canoe rides Gilbert." After a brief pause she added, "I'll always have the memories of growing up here and will cherish them till the day I die. By the time I was a young teenager I knew I would leave here some day. As a youngster I had learned how to read really well, my mother was a great teacher. Often the elders would receive a letter from their children and grandchildren who had moved away and they would ask me to read their letters to them. I knew from reading the stories of their adventures in the big cities and far away places they had travelled to, that there was a much different life waiting for me outside of the Inlet. Occasionally a parcel would arrive wrapped in a newspaper and I would save the paper and read the news over and over again. It all sounded so grand, so exotic, it just made me realize that I wanted more out of life, more than I could find here in the Inlet. I can't say that it was easy to leave. My parents mean everything to me but I know I can come back anytime and that's what makes it OK."

After the sun set, the mosquitoes came out in full force and started to drive the neighbours off their front porches and indoors. Not wanting the evening to end Marie said, "Oliver, why don't you light a fire in the fire-pit. The smoke will keep the mosquitoes away. I'll put on a pot of tea to wash down our supper and we can sit by the fire and watch the stars come out."

She turned to Gilbert and said, "I am sure you have seen the stars shining brightly in Penetanguishene but you have never seen them from here. They are just so much more brilliant. It seems they even twinkle more. When the moon comes out you will see that it seems you can just reach out and touch it. It's no wonder our people have so many stories and beliefs of the special powers that are tied to the stars and the moon." She slowly rose from her chair and as she turned to go in the door to make the tea she turned back to Gilbert and said quietly, "You will see and you too will believe."

With a hot cup of tea in their bellies and the fire to take the chill out of the night air the four of them sat for hours getting to know each other and enjoying each others company. Marie made sure that Maude got caught up on all that had happened in the Inlet in the year since she had been gone and Maude shared best wishes and messages from her aunt and uncle with her parents. She spoke fondly of how much she enjoyed her work at the hardware store. To Marie, it all sounded very exotic and for everything that Maude mentioned she had a voracious appetite for more information and details. By the time the evening was through Marie had a really good idea of just what life was like off the reserve and in the town of Penetanguishene, a place she had never been and would probably never get to.

Gilbert and Oliver talked about the isolation of living on a reserve and the tough life the Natives of the Inlet and other reserves were facing during these hard economic times. Gilbert shared stories of his life in Penetanguishene and what it was like to live in a town where the main commerce was also threatened by the depressed economy. He explained how tough it had been on the town with the closure of the West Breeze Boatworks and how his work as a handyman/Mr. Fix-it had increased as a result. Oliver was very interested in hearing about the canoes that Gilbert made and was impressed with the details that Gilbert worked into each hull. He hoped that someday he'd get a chance to see Gilbert's handy work.

Over all, it was an amazing evening the way it turned out. The stars were so bright, the constellations so clear, Gilbert felt like he really *could* just reach out and touch them. He could easily see how difficult it would be for anyone who had known no other life, to be so enamoured with the Inlet that they would find leaving it almost impossible.

As the evening passed, Oliver came to realize that Gilbert was a good man and that his first impression of him was the right impression. He was proud that Maude had found such a hard working, kind and considerate person to have as a friend but he sensed in the way Maude and Gilbert interacted with each other that there might be more to their relationship than just friends.

The waters in the Inlet had calmed to a mirror-like quality and even though it was night time the moon was so bright you could pick out the reflection of the far shore at the water's edge. The mosquitoes had mysteriously disappeared around ten-thirty and although none of them wanted the night to end Oliver stood up, poked the fire to stir the coals and said, "Well I think it is time we call it a night."

Marie groaned a little as she stood up from the blanket she had been using as a cushion on the rocks, the arthritis in her hips giving twinges of pain with the movement. "Maude, I have made up your bed in your room for you. Gilbert, we have put together a cot for you out on the back porch. There are more than enough blankets for you so I am sure you won't be cold and I thought you might enjoy the chance to fall asleep peering at the stars under the edge of the porch roof."

"I'll be just fine there. Thanks so much for all the trouble you have gone through. When my brother Elijah and I would go for an overnight fishing trip to the Musquosh we would just sleep right out on the rocks near the rapids. The sound of the rushing water was really relaxing. Having a cot with a roof over my head is a luxury I wasn't expecting."

They all said good night and headed off to their separate beds. As Gilbert lay on his cot, listening to a loon's mournful call in the distance, he thought of the day he had just had. It had been perfect in every way. He had been completely honest with Maude when he told her he was totally at peace with himself and with the world as he knew it here at Granite Bluff Inlet. He had never felt more in love with Maude than he did today. Everything about her and her parents seemed just right. He knew he had made the right decision coming on this trip to ask Oliver and Marie for Maude's hand in marriage. *Marriage*, he thought, *Yes, marriage*. It was the right thing to do. As he thought about the tenderness and warmth he felt when he kissed Maude out at the lookout, he smiled once again as he felt that old stirring in his loins. As he drifted off to sleep he thought, *Yup, it will be the right thing to do.*

*****

Early the next morning Maude found Gilbert sitting down by the shore. The sun had not fully risen above the horizon yet and a soft fog-like mist floated about a foot off the surface of the Inlet only to be burned off as shafts of sunlight poked their way through the branches of the trees on the far shore. A loon that had been diving and fishing about one hundred feet from shore gave up its search for minnows and lazily stretched out its wings. It gave them a flutter as if preparing to take off in flight but instead it arched its back, straightened out its neck and flapped its wings furiously as if to shake off any water that had gathered during its early morning dives. Once settled back in the water, the waterline nearly at the black and white vertically striped ring around its neck, it began the never ending ritual of turning its head to the side and preening its feathers with its beak to remove any unwanted particles of algae and mossy bits it had picked up in the water. Then without warning it straightened out its neck, looked up towards the sky and let out that old familiar mournful call. The sounds of the loon's call echoed in the rocks of the granite shoreline and moments later it repeated the call, this time adding the quavering tremolo that made it sound like the loon was laughing.

"I think this loon is a female calling for her partner," said Maude. "We have a pair of loons who come to the Inlet every year and pretty much stay put for the entire summer. The male loon's call is more of a yodelling sound." Then as if on cue the female repeated her laugh-like call. Moments later a loon's call could be heard in the distance signalling that he had heard the female's call. "Do you know that loons mate for life," Maude said, "they are very faithful to each other and they are very territorial so that is why they always come back to the same spot." After a short pause she added, "I think they feel safe here."

"I can certainly understand why," Gilbert said breaking the silence. "It's amazing how long the loon can stay underwater when it dives. I like to try to predict where the loon will surface but it always fools me. Just when I think it will surface over here, up it pops over there."

Maude smiled, the same things had crossed her mind many times over the years and she realized that she and Gilbert were on the same wave length about so many things it heartened her to think about the similarities.

"Mom had the stove lit and the coffee pot on," she said. "Would you like me to bring a cup down to you so you can just relax here by the shore?"

"That would be the best way to start the day that I can think of Maude," said Gilbert reaching out and taking her hand in his.

As she left to get coffee for the two of them Gilbert thought that even though their visit to the Inlet would be a short one, it would be one of the best vacations he had ever had. He knew he would cherish it forever.

With the sun rising to shine in its full glory and with piping hot coffee in his belly he quickly became very warm sitting on the rocks down by the shore. Gilbert rolled up his pant legs, took off his shoes and socks and inched his way down to the water's edge. The cool water made his toes tingle and within minutes a small school of minnows had arrived to check out the mysterious being dangling in the water. Curious about whether they were edible or not, the minnows rushed towards his toes as if to take a nibble only to scurry away in a skittish fashion dispersing as if being frightened by a hungry fish. Both Maude and Gilbert laughed as they watched the minnows perform their little dance around his toes over and over again.

"They mustn't have much of a memory. They keep coming back for more of the same and getting nothing out of it," said Gilbert.

"I think they're hungry," said Maude. "Later we can take a bit of oatmeal and spread it on the water and they will go after that for sure. Then we can catch them and use them for bait when we go fishing." With that they stood, gathered up Gilbert's shoes and socks and headed to the house. Gilbert could feel the warmth of the rocks on his bare feet as they began to absorb the heat from the sun. Within just a few steps his feet were already dry.

Breakfast was a simple meal of bannock, and fried potatoes and more hot coffee. After the dishes had been cleared, Gilbert said to Oliver. "Do you think you and I might be able to take a ride in the canoe later today? It would be nice to spend some time together and give Maude and Marie a chance to get caught up some more on what ever it is that women need to get caught up on."

"I'd be happy to go with you," said Oliver. "Just let me know when you are ready."

"I think I'll leave that up to you Oliver. I don't know if you have any plans to do other things today so it's probably best for us to go when you have the time."

"I have nothing planned for today. Knowing that you and Maude were coming, I didn't arrange anything. We can go right now if that works for you."

"Perfect, the exercise will do me good. It will help me work off some of that big breakfast I just ate," said Gilbert.

Though Maude had taken Gilbert around the Inlet yesterday in the canoe it was still a beautiful ride, filled with scenery that Gilbert thought he would never get tired of looking at.

"Did Maude take you out beyond the Inlet yesterday?" Oliver asked.

"No, we paddled around within the Inlet and I think we went to every nook and cranny," Gilbert replied. Then a little sheepishly he added. "She took me to her favourite spot over to the west side of the Inlet. The view once you climb over the boulders is spectacular. I am really familiar with all the area around Cognashene and Musquosh but that area seems a little bit closed-in, in comparison to the wide open view you get from Maude's special spot."

"You'd be hard pressed to find a more panoramic view of the waters of Georgian Bay than you do at that spot," said Oliver. "Maude can't claim it as her spot though. It is one of my favourite spots to just go sit and ponder as well."

They paddled on in silence for a while as Oliver expertly navigated the canoe beyond the opening of the Inlet and headed north along the shoreline. The windswept white pine trees so prominent in this area seemed to be able to grow out of the tiniest of cracks in the rocks. "It is a wonder they can grow at all," said Gilbert pointing to a large pine whose biggest branches seemed to either be curling eastward from the west side of the tree or just simply growing on the east side of the tree."

"The west wind is so strong and so prevalent here the branches on the west side of the tree don't really have a chance. As they develop they bow to the winds and curl that way. I guess it's the only way they can survive in the elements," said Oliver.

"I guess that is the ultimate in adaptability isn't it," admitted Gilbert.

Soon they had paddled to the opening of another large bay and Oliver pointed out some of the sites along the way. "The fishing is best farther down in that bay. There is a small waterfall that runs from an inland lake to the east of here. The water is cooler there and quite deep and the larger pike and pickerel seem to prefer that. I guess there is a bit of a current under the water from the falls and that keeps them active." Oliver paused for a moment then added. "I don't think there has ever been a time when I didn't catch something there. I remember when Isaac was a young lad and I would take him there, he would just be in awe that there were always fish there. It's been so long since I have gone fishing with Isaac that he probably doesn't even remember this little fishing hole exists."

"Oh, I don't know," said Gilbert. "From what Maude tells me about you and Isaac and the amount of time you guys spent fishing, it isn't likely he'd forget about it."

"Let's pull up on shore for a few minutes and give our paddles a rest," joked Gilbert. Once again Oliver navigated the canoe to the shore and found just the right spot for them to get out.

Once they settled on the rocks and were comfortable, Oliver said, "What's on your mind Gilbert?"

"You're very perceptive," admitted Gilbert.

"You've been pretty quiet all morning," said Oliver. "I noticed often while we have been paddling that you seemed to have been gazing out into the open as if you are thinking of something important. I can usually tell when someone has something they want to tell me but don't know just how to go about it."

"Well," admitted Gilbert. "I do have something important on my mind that I need to talk to you about." He paused not just quite sure how to start. "I am head over heels in love with Maude and I'd like to have your permission to marry her," said Gilbert admitting for the first time to anyone that he was in love.

"Does Maude know how you feel?" asked Oliver. "Have you asked her already if she will marry you?"

"We have been seeing a lot of each other lately and I think she has a pretty good idea of how I feel but to answer your question, no, I haven't asked her to marry me. I am an old fashioned kind of guy and I thought it would be better if I had your permission before I ask her."

"Well Gilbert," said Oliver. "I have only known you for less than 24 hours, I have heard a lot about you from Maude's letters, but I am a pretty good judge of character. You are a decent man, hardworking and honest and I don't think I could hope for a better husband for my daughter or son-in-law for Marie and I." Oliver was silent for a moment then added. "You have my permission and my blessings. I know you will take good care of her."

It was like a huge weight had been lifted from Gilbert's shoulders. He realized that he had been thinking of very little else in the last few weeks and he was thrilled that Maude's parents were as warm and welcoming to him as they had been. With Oliver's permission to marry Maude the thought of spending unlimited time with her in the future was almost making him feel lightheaded. His thoughts were jumping all over the place, *will she say yes, when should I ask her, where should I ask her, when should we get married?*

Before he knew it the canoe was pulling up alongside the dock in front of the house and Oliver was saying something to him about tying the rope to the dock. He hadn't realized what a daze he had been in until he spotted Maude sitting at the shore dangling her feet in the water speaking to a man Gilbert had yet to meet. She waved excitedly at the canoe as it approached the dock but continued chattering away like a little banshee to the man beside her who seemed to be totally engaged in the conversation with Maude.

With the canoe securely tied to the dock, Gilbert walked to the shore where Maude was sitting.

"Gilbert, I am so glad you came back. This is Isaac. He was my best friend when I was growing up. I think I might have told you about him a while ago."

Gilbert winked at Isaac as he reached out his hand to shake it and with a bit of tease in his voice said, "I don't think there is anything about your childhood that I haven't heard about. Maude has told me many times about you and how she valued your friendship. I feel like I already know you. It is good to finally meet you Isaac."

"It's great to meet you as well Gilbert," said Isaac. "Maude has been filling me in on how the two of you met, and that you work together at the hardware store. I think I am a little jealous of you being able to spend so much time with my best friend," he said jokingly.

Gilbert sat on the shore next to Maude, took off his shoes and socks and let his feet dangle in the water like Maude was doing. "I wonder if the minnows will come and check out my feet again," he said.

"They've been nibbling at my toes already so I know they're around," said Maude.

As Oliver walked towards the house he smiled at the little threesome sitting on the rocks near the dock talking away like they had known each other for years. *Maude is a very lucky woman,* he thought. *She had the benefit of growing up with Isaac who, although he was older than she, adored her and was very protective of her. And now she has the love of a very good man who he was sure would be very good to her. Yes,* he thought, *she is lucky indeed.*

*****

When it was time for supper, Marie insisted that Isaac join them. Knowing that her time on this visit to the Inlet was limited Maude was happy to have him join them so they could get a respectable visit in. "It will be a good chance for you to get to know Isaac," she said to Gilbert.

"And a good chance for him to get to know me," replied Gilbert. "I must remember to ask him a few things about when you guys were growing up," he joked with Maude. "I want to see if all your stories really check out," he said with a wink and a smile.

It was to be another fabulous meal cooked on the old wood stove. Marie asked Gilbert if he could toast the homemade bread on the open fire. "What we do is use this metal hook-like lifter to take the front ring off the cook top part of the wood stove. The heat from the coals at the bottom of the firebox will toast the bread just fine." When she saw how easily Gilbert had lifted the lid, pushing it to the back of the cook top and putting the bread slices onto the wire rack that was used as a toaster she felt she had to comment.

"You seem to know your way around the kitchen stove," she said.

"It's the same way my mom and I make toast at home," said Gilbert. "In fact, we have the same wire rack toaster that you have." He smiled at Marie then said, "If your toaster ever falls apart I know a good hardware store that sells them." Marie laughed and went about with the rest of her meal preparation deep in thought and happy to be sharing the tiny kitchen space with Gilbert. Oliver had told her the news of the upcoming wedding proposal when he had returned from the canoe ride. She was happy to think that Maude was possibly going to marry Gilbert. *I couldn't have found a better man if I had picked him out myself,* she thought.

There was plenty of chatter and joking during the meal. Maude and Isaac easily got carried away in telling Gilbert stories of their childhood and what it was like to grow up together in the Inlet. The fishing, the canoeing, the swimming and diving from the high rocks at the entrance to the Inlet all seemed kind of magical as they spoke of these times in the past. The memories of sharing those good times seemed to bring it all back to them as if it was just yesterday. As the meal progressed, now and then Oliver and Marie would join in adding a few details and background information that Maude and Isaac were leaving out of the story. It helped to make the stories more realistic to Gilbert and he found himself thinking often about the good times he had had with his brother Elijah doing many of the same things. He wished, not for the first time, that Elijah could be around to meet Maude and to see how happy she made him.

When they had run out of stories to tell Isaac spoke of his work as a logger in the forests to the north and of his time spent at the saw mill. Though it was hard work he spoke proudly of it and of how much he enjoyed it. "It's a tough life and you are away from home a lot but you make really good friends with the other guys," said Isaac. "I tell you, if you ever need work Gilbert I am sure if you come to the saw mill with me I can get you a job."

Gilbert told Isaac that he appreciated the offer. "I would never say never, but I am pretty sure that being a logger is not something I would ever be interested in doing." He told Isaac about his father and how he had died. "My father loved his work too. I appreciate that it was an accident and that the work can be very dangerous. I am not worried about that part of it, but at this time I have more work than I can keep up with back home." He paused, "but, it is good to know that I would have an 'in' with someone if I do need the work."

"Maude tells me that not only do you work at the hardware store but that you build your own canoes and sell them," said Isaac. "How did you get into that?"

"As a young lad, I was looking for some work to help bring in a little extra money to our home. My dad was away logging most of the time and my mom was having a hard time making ends meet. There was a man that I knew, Mr. Beaudoin was his name, and he used to build canoes as a hobby in his shop at the back of his house. As he got older, his arthritis got to be pretty bad and he was having trouble using some of the planing tools. Since I had been hanging around his shop he asked me to give him a hand one day. Well then it became a pretty common request and I got to be very handy with the tools myself. We made fine canoes. They were almost too nice to use but there were plenty of people out there who were happy to pay for such a fine piece of craftsmanship. When it got to the point where Mr. Beaudoin couldn't do the work anymore he was quite happy to let me take over his shop and start making canoes on my own. Even now, most of the time I have several orders ahead and I could probably do that full time but there isn't enough money to be made doing that so that was why I went to work at the factory." Gilbert paused and took a sip of his tea and another bite of his toast then continued.

"I used to work at one of the factories in town a couple of years ago. It was a boat building factory and we built high end runabouts, day cruisers and mid-sized boats. They were very popular. Perhaps you have heard of the West Breeze boat line?" Gilbert asked.

"Heard of them!" Isaac exclaimed, "Everybody has heard of them. Up at the logging camp it is a common topic of conversation. Guys often say things like, 'once I make enough money working here that is one of the first things I am going to get when I get back home.' But, with those boats, I think you have to work a lot of years to be able to afford one."

"It seems his talents as a boat builder didn't go unnoticed either," said Maude. "Before the factory closed, Gilbert was one of the few men who could work on any part of the boats inside and out. Even though he was one of the last people to be hired he was one of the last people to be let go because he could do the work so well," she said proudly.

"It's too bad the factory closed. I really liked that job," said Gilbert.

"But now you work with me and that has got to be better than any other job you've ever had, right Gilbert?" Maude said poking him playfully in the ribs with her elbow.

"You are absolutely right Maude."

"He is also the town's Mr. Fix-it," said Maude. "If anything breaks down, doesn't' matter if it is a radio, a toaster, or somebody's indoor toilet that isn't working right, Gilbert can figure out what needs to be done to fix it," she paused "and," she said, "he knows what we have at the hardware store to do the job. Sometimes he has to build replacement parts with different things we have at the store but in the end, voila, it works."

Gilbert blushed a little at Maude's praise for the work that he does. There was nothing that she had said that wasn't true but by nature he was a pretty modest guy and he felt a little uncomfortable with all the things she was saying. As he thought about it though, it didn't hurt for her parents to hear about some of the work that he does. It would put him in good standing with them if Maude accepted his proposal and he became their son-in-law.

After the dishes had been cleared from the table and stacked in the washbasin the evening drew to a close. Marie said that it had been a full day and that she was tired and going to bed. Oliver agreed and started his usual routine of checking the stove and shutting the house down for the night.

"Well, I guess it is time for us to hit the sack too," Maude said to Gilbert as they stepped out onto the front porch to check out the stars.

"I'm ready. Your dad nearly wore me out with that canoe ride today. Boy, he is in good shape. You can tell how strong he is by the thrust from his paddle strokes. I always thought of myself as being in good shape but I had a hard time keeping up to his strokes today. I have no idea how far we went but I'll bet it was miles."

"My dad was raised in a canoe," said Maude, "and for years that is all he has ever had for getting around. I find the same thing when I go with him. It takes about two strokes of mine for every one of his to keep the canoe going straight."

Gilbert stood next to Maude and put his arm around her. "I've had another great day Maude, thanks again for letting me come up here with you." He turned slightly to face her and was surprised to see that she had turned towards him as well. Gently he took her in his arms and slowly gave her a long embrace. As she looked up into his eyes he bent slightly and ever so tenderly kissed her. Their lips brushed together softly at first and then more firmly with a hunger that surprised both of them. They kissed again unleashing a passion both had had bottled up inside for a long time. He could taste the sweetness of her on his lips as they stood in a long unyielding embrace. With every kiss Maude felt closer and closer to Gilbert. She loved how she felt all tingly and shaky inside when they kissed and she longed for more than just a kiss on the front porch of her parent's house.

"Gilbert," she whispered, "I think I am falling in love with you."

"That's a good thing," he said, "because I fell in love with you the day you walked into the hardware store looking for a job."

They were silent for a moment, locked in another tight embrace. Finally Maude pulled herself away from him and said, "I could stay right here in your arms forever but I have to go now. I'll see you in the morning," and with that she turned and walked into the house slowly and quietly closing the door behind her.

Gilbert stood for a long while on the front porch looking up at the sky. He had as many thoughts going through his head as there were stars in the heavens and they were all about Maude. Though he didn't really want the day to end, he made his way around to the back of the house and sat on his cot on the back porch. Without even thinking about it, he slowly undid the buttons on his shirt and removed it, folding it methodically then draping it over the railing. He bent down, removed his shoes and socks and undid the zipper to his pants. As he slid his pants off he realized he was fully aroused. He placed his folded pants over the railing next to his shirt then slipped under the thin blanket he had covered himself with the night before. He lay on his back with his hands clasped behind his head as a pillow and stared up at the night sky. *Tomorrow*, he thought. *Tomorrow I will ask her to marry me.* At peace with himself he drifted off into a deep and restful sleep.

*****

"Maude, how about you and I go out in the canoe this morning before we have to head back to Parry Sound," Gilbert said at breakfast.

"I can't think of anything I'd rather do," she said.

Once the breakfast dishes were cleared and put in the dry sink, Maude filled the pot of water on the stove and set it to boil so that she could wash the dishes.

"What do you think you are doing?" asked Marie.

"The dishes," said Maude.

"I have the rest of the day to do these. You should go with Gilbert. I think he is waiting for you down at the dock."

"I told him I would be down after I had done the dishes, he'll be surprised to see me so soon," said Maude raking her fingers through her jet black hair. She tugged tightly on her hair and pulled it back so that it fell behind her ears. "There, I think I'm ready," she said as she rushed out the door glad that her mother had kicked her out of the kitchen.

"Wow, that was fast," said Gilbert.

"Mom's taking over that job," she said, "let's get out of here before she changes her mind."

"Can you direct me back to your special place?" Gilbert said to Maude as they paddled away from the dock. Though he knew exactly where he was going he wanted to keep the conversation light so that she didn't suspect his ulterior motive for going there. "I want to have another look at the view from there so that this winter when I am fed up with the snow, I can think back on this day and that special place and it will take the winter blues away."

They paddled in silence for a while each lost in their own reverie when the silence was broken by the mournful quivering sound of the loon as it called for its mate. This is a good sign Gilbert thought. Loons mate for life and here I am about to ask Maude to marry me. It warmed his heart to know that even though it was daylight, all the stars were lining up in his favour.

Once they had reached the shore and pulled the canoe up onto the rocks Gilbert took Maude by the hand and it was his turn to lead her over the bluff and down to the flattened boulder they had sat on two days earlier. They were quiet for a while, a peaceful feeling had come over both of them. Gilbert took Maude's hands in his and he looked into her eyes.

"Maude, I have never loved anyone as much as I love you. Now that I have met you, I can't imagine what my life would be like without you in it. I want to spend the rest of my days with you. Will you marry me?"

"Yes," she replied her voice barely a whisper. She was so overcome with emotion she could barely speak. "I will marry you," she paused catching her breath. "You are the best thing that has ever happened to me and I want to spend the rest of my life with you." She swallowed hard over the lump in her throat, then continued, "I can see it in your eyes how much you love me. There is no way I'm letting you go. I just want to keep you for ever and for always."

Gilbert smiled as he leaned over to give her a quick little kiss. It seemed a bit anticlimactic after the kiss the night before. "I am so happy," he said. "I am so glad you said yes. I don't know what I would have done if you had said no."

"Don't worry," said Maude. "This has been on my mind as well. You are such a romantic to take me here to this special place to ask me to marry you. How could I have said anything else?"

They sat in silence for a while then realized that it would soon be time to leave the Inlet and head back to Penetanguishene.

"We had better hurry back," Maude said. "I don't want to just rush in to my parent's home and then have to turn around right away and head out. Besides, I want to tell my parents about your proposal. I think they'll be thrilled."

As they pulled up to the dock they were surprised to see Oliver and Marie both sitting on the dock watching them come in towards shore. "I think they must suspect something," said Maude.

"Oh I am sure they do," said Gilbert. "I had a little chat with your dad yesterday so I am sure they know already just by the smile on your face."

"Well," Marie asked coyly, "how was your ride?"

"It was the best ride ever mom," Maude said as she walked up to her mother. "Gilbert has asked me to marry him."

"And you said yes I hope."

"I did."

Marie and Oliver both gave Maude a big hug and they held that embrace for the longest time. "I am sure you will be very happy Maude, I know we are," said Oliver.

Oliver walked over to Gilbert. "Congratulations!" he said as he shook his hand. The hand shake this time was different than the one two days earlier. Before it had been a formal, reserved hand shake between two men who were strangers. Today there was a warmth and friendliness to it that spoke volumes. Both men sensed a type of energy that seemed to flow from one man to the other.

"I hate to say it but you had better get packed up little one," Oliver said to Maude. "It is well on time for you guys to get going if you are going to catch the Keewatin in Parry Sound." He laughed as he added, "It's a long paddle back to Penetanguishene if you miss the boat."

At the same time as Oliver was making his last comment they heard an outboard motor sputtering then coming to life at the dock next to the one they were standing on.

"Isaac asked if it would be OK with us if he drove you in to Parry Sound. We hope you don't mind," Marie said.

"That'll be just fine," said Gilbert.

It didn't take long for them to pack the few things they had brought with them for the weekend. After quick hugs all the way around Maude and Gilbert climbed into Isaac's boat and as it started to pull away from the dock Marie shouted, "You never told us when the wedding is."

"We didn't even talk about that yet," said Maude. "We'll sort out the details and then I will send you a letter."

The rest of that day seemed to go by in a blur. They arrived at the docks in Parry Sound with just enough time to bid farewell to Isaac and thank him for the ride. They got on board the Keewatin just as the captain blew the long melodic whistle that announced it was about to leave the dock.

Once they were settled in their seats Maude said, "Whew, that was close."

"You can say that again," agreed Gilbert.

"Now, Mr. Valcour let's talk about this wedding," said Maude as she snuggled up beside him on the bench.

CHAPTER - 5

May 1926

It was a simple wedding. Both Maude and Gilbert came from very small families and so it was no surprise to either Madelaine or Marie and Oliver when the couple decided the wedding would be small but would also be two-fold.

Maude was uneasy about forfeiting her Native status when she married Gilbert, however, her love for him ultimately exceeded the strong ties she had to her Native cultural roots. While it was important for her to acknowledge her heritage, it was also important for her to recognize that since she was stepping outside of what would be considered traditional for a woman with her background, this was a sacrifice she would have to accept.

"Gilbert, I love you more than anything else in the world but you need to understand that I am first a Native Ojibwa and that is something that I cannot change," said Maude. "There are aspects of being an Ojibwa woman, that I hold dear to my heart and for that reason I'd like to have a traditional Native wedding ceremony to reaffirm my culture before I give up my status. It is also important to me that we also have a legal civil ceremony."

"Maude, I would never expect for a moment that you should not acknowledge your heritage. I know it is very important to you and, it is important for me to understand what it means for you to be Native. Maybe you could tell me a bit about the Ojibwa as a nation so that I can understand what sacrifices you will be making."

After taking a few moments to collect her thoughts Maude started. "The Ojibwa people are a unique and complex nation. We are a nation where there is very little written word. For the most part the history of our culture exists in the minds of the people who possess the memories of years past. The spoken word, the intonation of how it is spoken is very important, and must be understood clearly as it is passed on from generation to generation verbally. Very little of my culture has been recorded. Perhaps someday it will be, but for the most part it hasn't yet."

"Tell me about your people, all that you can remember," said Gilbert.

"First of all," started Maude, "the Ojibwa people call themselves Anishinabeg or Anishinaabeg when we are referring to more than one person but we say Anishinabe when we refer to a single person. Though not many people really know our real name it translates to "first" or "original people" as we believe we were the first to inhabit this area. Our people acquired the name Ojibwa from the French fur traders. You may also see our nation referred to as Ojibwe or Ojibway. It all depends on who was spelling it at the time. If you were to go down into the United States, you would find that my people there are called the Chippewa. We all hail from the same tribe originally which happens to be one of the largest in North America but somehow we ended up with a variety of spellings and names."

"You know, I've often wondered about that," said Gilbert. "I have heard it pronounced different ways and have seen it spelled a couple of different ways. I never knew how to spell it exactly and was always wondering when writing it if I was getting it wrong. I guess what is important is to know how it is spelled and pronounced locally in our area and to stick with that."

"In our area, we are Ojibwa and it is pronounced O-jib-wa though you may hear some people on the street say it so that it ends with "way".

"Tell me about your culture, what is important to your people?" asked Gilbert.

"In our society, among our people, the things we Ojibwa value the most are generosity, strength of character, honesty, kindness, endurance and wisdom. These values are practised within the community in an almost religious fashion by setting an example to the others in the community. A man like my father who lives by these values is highly regarded and respected by all," said Maude. "As you get to spend more time at my parent's home you will see how generous the Native people are, how they are always giving to each other, how they help each other without question and share everything they have with others who are in need. They are a very peaceful somewhat passive people who seem to co-exist with each other with very little conflict. It is truly a beautiful way to live."

"Oh," said Gilbert, "there are so many people in Penetanguishene and Midland who could learn from this."

"That is why I think it is important for us to have a traditional wedding. This is not only important to me but to my parents as well. It will be symbolic to them, and symbolism is very important to my people in order to carry on tradition and reinforce our culture since so little of it is recorded," said Maude. "It will also help you Gilbert to be accepted into the community after the wedding. Just being there and following the rituals will demonstrate to the community that you recognize the diversity of our culture and embrace it."

"Tell me more about the wedding ceremony," said Gilbert. "What can I expect?"

"Well first of all both the husband and wife are called niwi'tigema'gan, or the 'one who lives with me'. Once we are wed, we are as one, so we are called by the same name. In order to get married there are few requirements we have to fulfill. The main things we will have to find are sponsors. In total we are expected to have four sponsors, generally two from the bride's family, and two from the groom. My parents can be the sponsors for me, your mother can be a sponsor for you and I'll bet if we ask Isaac, he will gladly be your other sponsor. These sponsors must commit to giving guidance and assistance to the couple throughout their married life. The sponsors are typically older, respected people from their tribe, who, during the ceremony, pledge to give spiritual and marital guidance for their entire lifetime. I know that Isaac is not yet an elder in the community but I think that that can be overlooked considering all the other rules of a traditional marriage we are breaking."

"What do you mean Maude," Gilbert asked?

"Well, I am a status Indian and will be until I marry you. And you have to realize that you are an outsider to the community even though I feel like you belong and regardless of how much the others in the community like you, you are still and always will be, an outsider."

"OK, so tell me more."

"When a couple gets married, they are forever married in the eyes of The Creator Manitou, our God. They are not allowed to divorce, so the ceremony is only performed if the couple is serious about getting married. The Pipe Carrier is the official in the ceremony, much like a priest in your religion. Before the couple say their vows they are wrapped in a ceremonial blanket, and once the vows are recited they must each smoke from the ceremonial pipe. Then while still wrapped in the blanket the couple must walk around the fire that has been lit for the ceremony and this is what binds us together as one for all eternity."

"I think it will be a beautiful ceremony. I take it the ceremony is held outside?" said Gilbert.

"Typically it is, even if it is winter. That way the ceremonial fire can be lit, and the smoke can rise to the sky to symbolize the union of our marriage rising to the heavens, to Manitou. Years ago, in our community, there used to be a huge wiigwaam that was erected, the fire was lit within the centre of it and the smoke would rise through the opening in the roof but the problem was it wasn't quite big enough for all the community to get inside. I haven't seen that wiigwaam in a long time and I don't think it is being used anymore so don't count on it."

"Wait a minute, did you say for all the community to get inside! Who all will be coming to the wedding?"

"Don't worry about that, it will just be all the people from our reserve, maybe fifty, or sixty people."

"Fifty or sixty, Maude, we can't afford to have a wedding that big!" Gilbert exclaimed.

"Oh, that is something I didn't tell you about the traditional Native wedding. It doesn't cost us anything. It is the community that provides it all. It is their gift to us. All we have to do is show up."

*****

And so, following as others had done in the past, Gilbert and Maude were married in a very small civil ceremony in Penetanguishene performed by the local Justice of the Peace and witnessed by Madelaine and a few close friends. As was common in a mixed marriage, the spiritual ceremony was planned to be held in the true Native culture and followed the customary Native traditions. For this reason, the spiritual aspect of the wedding ceremony was held at Granite Bluff Inlet. (*Author's note - As was Canadian law at that time, when a Native woman married a man who was a non-status Indian, the woman automatically forfeited her Native status. The laws did allow for a civil ceremony to take place to ensure that the marriage would be upheld legally. Bill C-31 – the pre-legislation name of the 1985 Act to Amend the Indian Act, eliminated certain discriminatory provisions of the Indian Act including the section that resulted in Indian women losing their Native status and membership when they married non-status men. Bill C-31 enabled people affected by discriminatory provisions of the old Indian Act, to apply to have their status and membership restored).*

Marie was thrilled that she was going to get a chance to meet Gilbert's mother and for weeks before the wedding was to take place made preparations for what she hoped would be a beautiful traditional Native wedding. Over the winter, as a result of the isolation of the reserve at Granite Bluff there were many times when the weather was just too bad for travel and it was not uncommon for the mail delivery to be delayed for up to three weeks at times. This made it difficult for Maude to communicate details about the wedding to her parents and she hoped beyond hope that by the time spring had rolled around, the letters with the requests that Maude had asked of her mother and the parcels she had sent had made their way to her.

On the day of the wedding Gilbert wore a pair of dress pants that he had purchased for the civil ceremony in town and was pleased to hear that Maude's mother had been able to apply the multicoloured and intricate bead work in the shape of a soaring eagle to the back of the starched white button down collared shirt that he had sent up to her months before.

Maude had asked her mother if it would be possible to be married in the traditional ribbon dress that her mother had worn at *her* wedding. Marie was honoured. Before her own wedding, it had taken Marie months to apply the intricate coloured bead-work which had been applied in a mosaic pattern and gave the appearance it had been completed by a gifted artist. To that end Marie was thrilled to have her dress used once again. The dress was long, reaching right to the ground however it flowed easily when the wearer walked, the ribbons on the bottom third of the skirt flowing and swaying like waves against the shore. As a gift from Marie to her daughter she made a fine bone and bead choker collar for her to wear around her neck. The pattern of leaves and soaring birds in the bead work matched the bead-work found on the back of the dress and the sleeve cuffs. She also made a headdress that fit like a headband and was woven into Maude's hair which had been braided back. Attached to the back of the headband was a pair of small silver rings to hold two feathers in place, the stems of the feathers once passed through the rings were woven into the braid at the back of the Maude's head. To match with the choker and headband, Marie also made earrings that had been cut from a small piece of leather and fashioned into the shape of leaves, again the bead-work matching the headband and choker.

When Gilbert saw Maude in her traditional wedding dress, her tanned mocha coloured skin contrasting perfectly with the white linen fabric of the dress and her smiling obsidian eyes he thought that he had never seen anyone so beautiful. In her hands she carried a bouquet of feathers mixed with wildflowers arranged into an elongated spray of colour. He noticed a slight trembling to her hands and that surprised him since Maude had been so confident with all aspects of the wedding preparation. He was also surprised to find that he had a lump in his throat. He wasn't typically an emotional man, but the beauty before him made him slightly weak in the knees and made it difficult to speak more than just a whisper of broken words that he was having trouble making into sentences. He felt he truly was blessed to be marrying Maude and knew that he would cherish her until the day he died.

As Maude had predicted, a fire was lit in the fire pit in front of her parent's house. The young couple were then wrapped in a vibrant red blanket that had a picture of a soaring eagle with rocks and rivulets of water painted into a multitude of colourful images. The Pipe Carrier officiated at the ceremony chanting prayers and blessings in the Ojibwa tongue. Once the chanting had ceased, Maude and Gilbert were asked to recite a few Ojibwa phrases. Next they were given the clay pipe laden with tobacco and asked to smoke from the finely whittled tip. After several puffs from the pipe, Gilbert passed it over to Maude who did the same then handed the pipe back to the elderly Pipe Carrier. Oliver approached them with a reverence that Maude had never seen her father exhibit before and led them around the fire to symbolize the sealing of the marriage vows. When they returned to their place in front of the Pipe Carrier, he took one final puff of the tobacco, then raised the pipe into the air, as high as his arms could reach and everyone present clapped and cheered.

"I guess this means we are really married now," said Gilbert.

"I guess we are, and I couldn't be happier," replied Maude. "I guess you must really love me Gilbert. You have married me twice in just a few weeks," Maude laughed and Gilbert smiled at the thought.

Soon the area around the fire had been cleared of people and thick brown blankets were spread upon the rocks. Food items for the feast were spread out upon the blankets in a buffet style and included fry-bread, venison, fish, squash, beans, corn, corn soup, potato soup and many desserts. Fresh fruits such as blueberries, raspberries, and the 'heart' berry, (strawberries), were served in tiny bowls. Once the food was blessed the Elders of the community and the officiant ate first, then the bride, groom, sponsors and other guests. None of the food was wasted. At the end of the day the food that had not been eaten was given away to the Elders who brought it back to their home to share with their families.

It was a perfect day, the weather cooperated and when all was said and done everyone agreed Maude and Gilbert looked like a couple who were perfectly matched and suited to be together forever.

*****

Madelaine stayed on with Gilbert and Maude in Marie and Oliver's house at the Inlet for a few days. Madelaine, not ever having been very adventurous didn't want to make the trip back to Penetanguishene on her own after the wedding and the LaJoie's were thrilled to be able to keep her and the newlyweds with them as long as they wanted. Though it had only been a little over a year since Maude had left home, it seemed like an eternity for Marie to have her daughter living so far away. If Maude had said that she and Gilbert were going to move back to the Inlet from Penetanguishene it would have been more than alright with her.

For Madelaine it was the first time she had been away from home since her husband had died and getting the opportunity to stay at the Inlet for a few extra days was like having the holiday she never thought she'd ever have again. A chance for once to be able to sit on a veranda and gaze out at the water and not feel guilty about all the work that needed to be done inside, or the bread that needed to be baked or the clothes that needed to be washed and ironed. She enjoyed helping Marie with the day to day tasks around her house, but with the two of them working at it, they were done in no time which left plenty of time for the two of them to sit on the veranda, sip on strong tea and get to know each other.

For Gilbert and Maude, taking a few extra days at the Inlet was their honeymoon. Though it seemed a bit odd for them not to go away together by themselves, getting the opportunity to sleep in a bit, be care free, swim and canoe when ever they liked was the best kind of honeymoon they could have hoped for.

There were plenty of tears when it was time to leave. Everyone had had such a good time no one wanted it to end. Marie hugged Maude so hard and for so long as she said her goodbye's that Maude was starting to have trouble breathing.

"I am so sad to see you and Gilbert leaving," said Marie.

"Mom, I'm going to come back," she said. "Before you know it you'll be getting a letter saying we are on our way. I promise, it won't be a year and a half before our next visit." Soothed by those comments, Marie turned to Gilbert and hugged him as well in a tight embrace.

"Take care of my little girl Gilbert," she said then paused, "I know that you will, but as a mother," she paused again as she wiped a tear that had formed in the corner of her eye, "I just have to say it."

Gilbert smiled and hugged her tightly to him. "Don't you worry about a thing. Maude and I were meant for each other. Everything will work out just fine. We'll be back before you know it. I love being here at the inlet too much to stay away."

Since Isaac's boat was not quite big enough to take everyone in one trip back to Parry Sound to catch the Keewatin for the return trip home, Oliver first brought Maude and Gilbert to the harbour and then came back for Madelaine.

"Promise me that you will come back and stay with us again Madelaine," Marie said tearfully. "I truly enjoyed our time together. Having you here with us was like a breath of fresh air. It can get lonely up here and thinking about you coming back to stay with us will help the time go by."

"I will, I promise," said Madelaine. "You and Oliver have been so good to me, I feel like a new person now that I have had a couple of days to relax and actually enjoy myself for the first time in years." She looked around at the Inlet. "I will hold you to your offer and trust me, I will come back, you can count on it." She turned and started to leave then turned again to face Marie and said, "Don't forget, you are always welcome to come to stay with me in Penetanguishene if you ever come my way."

CHAPTER - 6

July 1926

"I think the house looks beautiful Gilbert," Maude said. "I know you say it needs some work but the price is right and I don't know anyone handier than you in town." Maude strolled a short distance down the sidewalk to get a better view of the house. "We can take our time and fix it up bit by bit." She returned to where Gilbert was standing looking at the house. "We can save the money we need for each project and then fix it up the way we want it," Maude said excitedly as she and Gilbert stood staring at it. Arm in arm they slowly and casually strolled on the sidewalk back and forth in front of the house dreaming of living there.

The house, a two story red brick dwelling had a large wrap around covered veranda across the north and west side of the house. It looked charming from the road. Though the house had been built almost seventy years earlier it appeared to be still structurally sound. The foundation to the house was made of field stone and was high enough that it had a four foot crawl space before the wooden framework of the first floor began. Gilbert had been passing this house on his way to and from work for years but he had never paid much attention to it until just recently when he heard the owners were thinking of putting it up for sale. Though the house was old he noticed it had good bones, the windows looked like they were still in pretty good shape, and the roof line was straight with no sagging in the centre or any of the corners. This indicated to him that the supporting structures under it were still solid. There were a few places where the cedar shakes used for the roofing were coming lose and there were a few places where they were missing all together. *Those would have to be fixed right away,* thought Gilbert, *before the rain drives in and causes damage on the inside.* The fascia across the entire house was sorely in need of paint and the once decorative

Victorian style gingerbread trim that rimmed the top of the entire veranda was desperately in need of some tender loving care. In a few spots the trim needed to be replaced altogether, as did a few balusters on the railing.

Though Water Street, where the house was located, was at least a quarter mile from the harbour, there was enough of a grade to the hill that from the front veranda, and from the windows in the kitchen, dining and living room, it was easy to see the entire length of Penetanguishene Bay. In fact they could see all the way up to Magazine Island, a small low sandbar type island that had acquired its name during the war of 1812 when the British military used it to store their kegs of gun powder for their muskets at a safe distance away from their fort.

The house was located on Water Street and only a half block from Main Street and the hardware store as it turned out. It had running water and indoor plumbing something that both Maude and Gilbert were going to be quite happy to have.

"Well if we have any problems with the plumbing, I know just the man to call to fix it," said Maude. "Oh, and there is electrical power too. Does this mean there is a hot water tank?" Maude asked.

"Yes it does. In fact we just sold the owners a new hot water tank about three years ago so it should still be working pretty well," said Gilbert.

"I can't wait to have a nice long hot bath in my own bath tub," said Maude.

"Wait till you see the bathtub in here," Gilbert said. "The other day on my way home from work, the owners were outside and I was asking them some questions about the house. They offered to take me in to see it and as soon as I saw the big cast iron six foot long bath tub I thought of you right away."

"If you need my vote I say, let's buy it," said Maude. "Now we just have to figure out how we are going to get enough money to put a down payment on it."

"I've got that covered," said Gilbert. "You know those canoes I've been building all this time? Well, I knew some day I'd want to buy my own house and so I have never spent a cent of the money that I made from selling my canoes. I put all that money in a special account at the bank and have never taken any money out of it. There isn't a lot of money there, but we should be able to pay at least half of the price of the house with the money I have saved in that account."

"And I have been saving some money too since I got the job at the store. Maybe we can use your money to make the down payment and the money I have saved can be used to start fixing the things that need it the most," said Maude.

"Like the roof." Gilbert said, then added, "Well, since you like it too, I guess I'll talk to the owners and see if they still want to sell."

"When do you want to do that?" asked Maude.

"Since we are here, I can do it right now. Why don't you go home and help my mother get supper started and I'll talk to the owners right now," he said. "I know them pretty well from the hardware store so let me see what kind of deal we can work out."

"Perhaps tonight will be a night to celebrate," Maude said animatedly waving her arms in the air then hugging herself tightly. "I'm so excited!" She stood up on her tip toes, and planted a kiss on Gilbert's cheek then sped off in the direction of Madelaine's house where they had been living since their wedding.

This is going to make her so happy, thought Gilbert as he walked up the cement steps towards the front veranda. *I hope we can afford it.*

And afford it they could. The elderly couple who owned the house were at the point where they couldn't manage the house and large property any more. It was built on a double lot so there was about a half acre of grass to cut and flower beds to look after. A beautiful hedge of lilac bushes ran for at least thirty feet on the property line between the vacant portion of the lot and the neighbours to the west and although they looked nice during the spring and summer, come autumn the number of leaves that fell from this hedge really added to the workload of looking after the place. The owners were planning on moving out to the country to live with their son and his family and maybe give them a hand with managing the farm while their health was still good enough to be of some help. The couple were happy to sell to Gilbert and Maude and accepted Gilbert's first offer right off the bat.

*****

"I think they were just happy to have someone interested in the house," Gilbert told Maude and his mom as they sat at the table for supper. "They didn't seem to be interested in making money on the place, they are just anxious to move out and reduce their day to day workload. Can you believe it? There was no dickering on the price, I offered them a thousand dollars less then they were asking and they took it just like that," he said happily. He had been recounting to them everything that had happened from the time Maude and he parted on the sidewalk. Gilbert was pretty happy that Maude and he were going to have a house of their own. Though they were comfortable living with Madelaine and she enjoyed having Maude and Gilbert around the house, it was time for them to have their own place.

"Now, I just have to go to the bank to arrange the mortgage on what is left owing and then to the lawyer's office and have him draw up the paperwork. It won't be long now and I think we will be able to say we are homeowners Maude."

"I can't wait to see the inside. I probably won't sleep very well tonight, I'm too excited," she said.

"On my way in to work tomorrow I'll stop and speak to the owners and ask them if it is OK for me to bring you to see the house after work," said Gilbert. And that is exactly what happened. The newlyweds were thrilled when they walked into the house together for the first time. Though the house was move in ready, the handyman-carpenter in Gilbert saw a few things right off the bat that he thought he'd like to change. *Somethings I'll need to talk to Maude about*, he thought.

Overall though, it was just what Gilbert and Maude were looking for. Though it did not seem to be very big from the outside the inside was much larger than it seemed. There was a good sized kitchen, dining room and bathroom on the first level. Then there were two steps up into a large living room that went across the front of the house. Even though there was a covered veranda across the front and side of the house all the rooms seemed to be bright and airy because of the number of windows in each room. Behind the living room wall was a staircase that led to three large bedrooms on the second level. The floors in all the rooms seemed to be quite solid. Gilbert noticed that the floors on the upper lever were well worn tongue-in-groove pine planking and the creaks in the flooring followed him with each step that he took but, when he bounced up and down in the centre of every room, there was no give to the floor and nothing shook.

"A good sign of a house well built," he said to Maude.

One of the redeeming features of the house was the oversized workshop attached to the back of the house. It was poorly insulated but it did have a Franklin wood stove in the corner near the barn-style entrance door. The door big enough to get canoes in and out of with no problem and was certainly an additional bonus to the workshop. Gilbert was thrilled that he wouldn't have to go to Mr. Beaudoin's house any more to build canoes. He could work on them right here at his own house. He figured he could probably build several more

The Stone Cottage

canoes per year with the time he would save walking to and from his mother's house at the far end of town down to Mr. Beaudoin's house.

"Also," he told Maude, "if the workshop is right at the house, when I have a half hour or an hour that I could spend on the canoes I can just pop into the shop and tinker a bit at what needs to be done. That's an option I've never had before when I had such a distance to go to get to the workshop. Sometimes it isn't worth it to go all that way when I only have a short bit of time to work on them, but now…" his voice trailed off as he thought of having all his tools and canoe moulds right at home.

"This is going to be a great house for us for so many reasons," Maude added.

It wasn't long before the deal was closed and the couple were making plans to move into their home. With the money that Maude had saved Gilbert was able to replace all the cedar shakes on the roof that were in disrepair and he was able to put some putty around a few windows in the bedrooms that had seen a lot of weather but not a lot of paint over the years. Once he moved all his tools from Mr. Beaudoin's house to his own shop he used the remaining money to purchase some finishing lumber to fix what was in disrepair. A coat of shiny white paint to cover all of the trim around the roof, the framing around the windows as well as the gingerbread trim at the top of the covered veranda was all that it took. The exterior of the house was really coming together and looked great.

Gilbert's plan was to continue to make canoes in the evenings and any money he made from selling them would be put into that special account at the bank. Once there was enough in the bank to do extra work to the house he and Maude would decide on which project was their next priority.

When Gilbert and Maude moved into their home later that summer there was much to do, many plans to make and changes to think about in the days and weeks that followed. In a way, though they did not realize it, they were weaving the first strands of the tapestry that would become their lives together.

*****

It had been several months now since Gilbert had been doing handy man work around Dr. Johnson's house. The home was, just what most of the town-folk referred to it as, a mansion. It was the biggest house in town. Built on a large plot of land on a hill overlooking Penetanguishene Bay the house was constructed in a Georgia southern plantation style with a huge two story sweeping veranda across the front with large white Corinthian style pillars supporting the upper level. When you entered the house through the front door you were welcomed by a forty foot long, fifteen foot wide foyer brightly lit by light coloured plaster walls and a massive chandelier. The grand staircase that led to the upper level was along the right hand side of the foyer. On the main floor, to the right of the foyer was a large living room, the focal point being a large wood-burning stone fireplace. A solid oak mantel ornately carved with images of hunting scenes on the face of it was a constant source of conversation for anyone seeing it for the first time.

The dining room located next to the living room held a finely crafted honey coloured oak dining table large enough to sit sixteen people comfortably. Matching china cabinets, credenza's and sideboards completed the dining set. To the left of the entrance had been a library and parlour when they moved in. To make the home more functional for Dr. Johnson to run his medical practice from, these rooms were converted to the doctor's home office waiting room and examination room. The kitchen located at the far end of the foyer spanned the entire back of the house. A small but efficient wood burning stove added to the coziness of the kitchen when it was lit on those cold winter mornings. Large windows in this room provided a beautiful view of the sloping back lawns. A large all season sun room provided excellent views of the flower gardens in the back and side yards and added to the appeal of this majestic home. On the second level were five bedrooms and one three piece bath which possessed a six foot long, iron claw-foot bathtub big enough for even the largest person to stretch out in. Originally built by one of the lumber tycoon's in the area, it had been sold and purchased a couple of times in the last twenty five years before the doctor and his wife bought it.

One day, late in the month of September when Gilbert was installing some lattice work around the bottom of the elegant Georgia style veranda on the front of the house, Dr. Johnson appeared on the veranda with two cups of steaming freshly brewed coffee on a handmade wooden serving tray.

"Your mom just put a fresh pot on. She knows how you take it so I thought I'd take a break from some paperwork in the office and come check out what you've been doing here," he said as he handed a steaming hot cup of coffee to Gilbert.

"Thank you very much, I was just thinking about having a little break," said Gilbert. There was a comfortable silence between the two men as they looked out at the view from the veranda. Gilbert walked over to the far end of the veranda and said, "See how you have all these nice white Corinthian pillars across the front of the veranda? They don't just look nice they support the second story veranda and I think this pillar on the far left will need to be replaced in the next couple of years."

"Is it weak, should we be replacing it now?" asked Dr. Johnson.

"No, I think it will be OK for the next little while but on the bottom, outside edge there seems to be a bit of dry rot that is starting."

"Yes I see that," said the doctor examining the corner of the post Gilbert had pointed to. "Is it sturdy enough to still be able to use the upper veranda until it is replaced?" He bent down to take a closer look at the pillar. "I sure hope we can we still use the upper veranda."

Gilbert nodded in affirmation as he took a long slow sip of the coffee. "Don't worry. It's fine to use the upper veranda. I'll keep my eye on it"

"Great because I love getting up in the morning and having my first cup of coffee up there. The view is so beautiful and it is a peaceful way to start the day. Lord knows, as the only physician in town right now most of my days are far from peaceful."

"I'm sure it will be alright," Gilbert repeated as he walked over to the pillar and gave it a firm shake. "It's still really solid. I'll keep my eye on it and when it needs to be replaced I'll let you know." He rubbed his chin as if deep in thought then added. "that is one project I will need to have some help with when the time comes 'cause that's a really big pillar and we'll need to put some sturdy support posts in place while we are taking this one out and putting the new one in."

"Let me know when you think it needs to be done and I will hire a carpenter to come and help you."

As they sipped their coffee the two men went down the stairs and onto the front lawn to look at the spot Gilbert had been working on.

"I went to the library the other day and was looking up some pictures of houses that have been built in the same style as your house," said Gilbert.

"I found a picture in a book that is almost the same as your house. I think it is from a plantation down in South Carolina but what they did on that house was put some decorative lattice work between the floor of the veranda and the ground. Then they painted it a contrasting colour and it made the whole veranda look so much more complete, so much more elegant."

Dr. Johnson nodded as he looked at the work that Gilbert was doing.

"I hope you don't mind," Gilbert said a bit sheepishly, "but I went ahead and had the lumber yard deliver enough lattice work to do all around the veranda." Gilbert paused then added, "I wanted to talk to you about it but every time I came here either you had an office full of patients or your wife said you were at the hospital." Then he added quickly, "She said that if I thought it was a good idea she was pretty sure you'd think so too so I just went ahead with it."

"Gilbert, I don't mind at all. In fact, I really like the idea and I don't know why I didn't think of this before. There are some old cottages up the lakes that have the space under their verandas closed in with latticework and it looks great so please, go ahead."

Gilbert was relieved to have the doctor's approval and was glad he wasn't angry with him for starting with the project before the doctor knew about it.

"There is just one thing about this though Gilbert," Dr Johnson added with a bit of an edge to his tone.

"What's that?"

"Well it looks nice and once it is painted will look even better but that stuff isn't easy to paint and in a few years when it starts to peel, it will need to be done again. I can't do it, I just don't have the time."

"Well I'll be more than happy to keep it looking nice. Perhaps I can think of it as job security Dr. Johnson," Gilbert added, and the two men started to laugh.

"You know Gilbert. Speaking of up the lakes are you familiar with the Cognashene area?"

"I know it like the back of my hand," Gilbert replied.

"Well, last summer, my wife and I were invited to spend a week at a small resort not far from the outer islands of Cognashene. It is down the Freddie Channel about a mile and the place is called Franceville. It's owned and operated by Wilf and Winifred France and they have several hotel-like buildings on their property."

"Oh yeah, I know it well," said Gilbert. "They are really busy running that place. It is actually getting to be pretty famous in fact. Did you know the Wright Brothers have actually stayed there?"

"That's what I heard," said Dr. Johnson. "Mr. France had become a 'friend of a friend' of Orville Wright and this friend suggested Mr. Wright needed a holiday. Orville needed to get away from the grind and pressures of being in the lime light and media for being the world's first pilot. He had also been very busy developing and running several other businesses that relate to airplanes so he suggested Mr. Wright should take a holiday and go to Franceville. Orville liked it so much that he ended up buying a property on Lambert Island near the Musquosh river entrance. Seems he likes the anonymity that comes with being in Canada and this wilderness escape.

"But, what I was getting at was, while we were up there at Franceville old Wilf France took us for a ride down the Freddie Channel and out to the outer islands. We had a little tour of some of the places where the Group of Seven have been painting. A.Y. Jackson is one of his friends too as it turns out. But, I digress; there is one island that is right out in the open part of Georgian Bay. It has a really nice cottage on it. Seems the artists like to hang out there since it has such scenic views of the water, granite rocks, windswept pines all that stuff artists like to paint. I think the locals call it the Artist Colony Island. It's right near the Hangdog Channel."

"This all sounds pretty familiar to me so far," said Gilbert.

"Just south of there, is a narrow channel that leads into Cognashene Lake and just before you go through the channel, there is a beautiful piece of property on the right that is for sale." Dr. Johnson paused, "Well, I guess I should clarify that. It was for sale. I just bought it last week," the doctor said proudly.

"Isn't there a big, white clapboard cottage there with a huge veranda? I think there is also a small stone cottage on that property too," Gilbert said.

"Yup that's it. Obviously you know the area very well don't you?"

"Yes I do. My father used to take my brother and I fishing in the Narrows all the time. I think we fished every spot there is between the open shores of Georgian Bay right through to the channels around Musquosh."

"Well I have a proposal for you Gilbert." He smiled then continued, "This is something that I want you to think about before you give me an answer. And," he added," make sure you talk to Maude about it. My wife and I have been discussing this for a week now and this is what we would like." The doctor paused, took a long sip of his coffee then continued.

"I'd like to hire you to be my permanent caretaker. I have this large home and property here and as you know the place in Cognashene is awfully big as well. It's going to need a lot, and I mean a lot of work. It hasn't been lived in by anything but mice and bats for the last 5 years but I know with some TLC and your talents, the place can become a beautiful get away for my wife and I and our friends from the city. When it's done, I think we will name it 'My Shangri-la.'"

"Sounds like a great name for that place." Gilbert was quiet for a moment while he finished the dregs of the coffee that was left in his cup. "That's a pretty generous offer Dr. Johnson, but I don't have a boat to get back and forth with every day and even if I did have a boat I'd never be able to afford the gas for it either. I suppose I could get a tent and pitch it on the rocks and stay up there during the week while I work on the place."

"Nonsense. The stone cottage is a bit rough but it is certainly more habitable than the main cottage is right now and a lot more comfortable than staying in a tent would be. My wife and I have talked this through and here is what we propose. How about if you fix up the stone cottage first so that it is OK for you and Maude to live in during the summer, rent free of course, and then while you are staying there, you can work on what needs to be done to the main cottage? When summer is over you can come back to town and be my caretaker for this property."

"I don't know what to say!" said Gilbert excitedly. "It's like a dream job that you are offering me."

"Well you don't have to say anything right now, talk to Maude about it and we can chat again some other time. Winter is coming so we will have lots of time to work out the details before you would get started up there."

Though nearly speechless at the thought of this offer Gilbert added, "As you know, Maude was raised at Granite Bluff Inlet. She loves being on the water and everything you are offering would be right up her alley too. It would feel like a homecoming for her."

"I know," said the doctor. "That is what makes it perfect for us as well. I get the benefit of having the best handyman-carpenter in the area doing my work for me and you get to bring your wife who was raised in a similar environment with you. Knowing that you both have a background of being on the water means I won't have a thing to worry about either of you being up there."

"I'll talk to Maude about it. I can't speak for her but, if I were a betting man I'd say the odds are pretty good she is going to jump at the chance to live on the water again even if it is only a couple of months at a time."

*****

It didn't take long for Gilbert to finish putting the lattice work on the front veranda of the doctor's house on Water Street. Though his hands were busy with the labour of the task before him, his mind was reeling with the thoughts of having the opportunity to spend the summer "up the shore" as the locals liked to refer to the Cognashene and surrounding area.

As soon as Gilbert walked in the door at home, Maude could tell he was excited about something. The usual calm, quiet guy she had married had suddenly been transformed into a happy, smiling man with a spring in his step. He looked like he was just about to burst with some good news story.

"Maude, you'll never guess what. You aren't going to believe it," Gilbert said excitedly as soon as the screen door to the kitchen closed behind him.

"Just tell me Gilbert, it looks like you are on cloud nine and I don't want to waste any time playing guessing games, just tell me," replied Maude.

"Well I was working on the front veranda at Dr. Johnson's house this afternoon and he came out to talk to me. I thought he might be mad about me installing decorative lattice work under that huge veranda they have without talking to him about it first but he wasn't mad at all. In fact, he is thrilled about it, he likes the way it looks and says as far as he's concerned he thinks it really adds to the look of the place. It seems he is really happy with my work."

"Well that *is* really good news Gilbert, I'm happy for you but I never thought you'd get this excited about it," said Maude.

"No, no. That's not it at all. He says he has just bought the big white cottage with the dark green trim at the entrance to the Narrows in Cognashene. You know the one with the small stone cottage off to the right hand side of the small cove. I have been admiring that place for years and last summer when I showed it to you we talked about what it would be like to own it." Gilbert paused to catch his breath. "I think you said something like, 'in your dreams Valcour' or something like that."

"Oh yeah, I remember the place well. You said if you owned it you'd enlarge the front veranda and wrap it around to face the channel and screen it in; you'd replace the side wall of the kitchen that has some boards on it with dry rot and add a larger window so you can see the cove better." Gilbert's eyes widened in surprise. He was impressed with her memory. Maude smiled, "We did spend some time dreaming about that place but thought we'd never in a million years be able to afford it. I'd kind of forgotten about the place after that," she said.

"Dr. Johnson says that he knows the place needs a lot of work, but he also sees the potential in it too. Do you know what else he told me this afternoon?"

"I haven't a clue but by the way you are so excited about this I think it involves you," said Maude.

"Well you guessed it but not just me," Gilbert said excitedly. "He wants you and I to go up there for the summers." Gilbert paused. "He said that he wants us to talk about it and think it through before we make a decision but, he'd like us to become his permanent caretakers for the cottage as well as the big house here on Water Street. He said that both places are too big for him to look after and he wants to hire us to be up there all summer long. He said we can stay in the stone cottage and live right up there while I do the work that needs to be done on the main cottage. In the spring and fall, I can work on the projects that need to done to his house here in town and then once the weather is nice, we can move to the stone cottage and continue work on the place up there. Oh and here is the best part, we get to stay at the stone cottage rent free. It will be like being paid to be on vacation."

Gilbert paused to catch his breath then said, "and once the work on the main cottage is done Doc wants to let his friends from the city come to stay there even if he and his wife aren't there. He said we can be like the caretakers who help the guests with whatever they need and we can take them fishing and out in the canoes if they'd like us to guide them." He smiled then said, "can you imagine Maude, we would be getting paid to go fishing. Your dad is never going to believe this!"

"But what will we do for money in the winter," Maude asked.

"Well I have been thinking about that," Gilbert replied. "I can talk to Mr. McDowell and see if he'd be OK with me working there during the winter months. He always has young guys coming into the store looking for work so maybe he could hire one of them for the summer and then when they have to go back to school in the fall he could take me back for the winter."

Always the pragmatist Maude said, "But would that be enough for us to live on?"

"I think that with my handy-man work that I do for other people, all the Mr. Fix-it jobs that people get me to do, and the canoe's that I build, I am pretty sure it will be enough. Dr. Johnson didn't say how much he'd pay me but he'd have to know that if he wants me to take the job he'd have to pay me at least what I make at the store or I wouldn't be able to afford to do it."

Gilbert stopped talking for a minute and let this entire concept sink in not just with Maude but with himself as well. Just telling Maude about it and sorting out the details of it out loud made him all excited again. It truly was like a dream job.

"It sounds like a really great opportunity for us," said Maude. "Do you think he'd let us go up for a week this fall to stay at the stone cottage so we can figure out just what needs to be done? That way we'll get an idea about how long it will take us to do the work and then we can decide?"

"Maude, did you say take 'us' to do the work?"

"I know I am not as handy as you are with building and fixing things but I do know how to swing a hammer and work a hand saw. It would be a way for the two of us to keep working together. Otherwise, I don't think there would be enough for me to do up there in the beginning."

"That's a great idea. My memory of the stone cottage is that it does need a bit of work to be done to the kitchen at the back of it but for the most part; the main stone section is in pretty good shape. I'll ask Dr. Johnson if he'd let us do a little trial run at living up there this fall. Like you say, it will give us a good chance to see if we think we can make a go of it for next summer."

*****

"Marvellous, marvellous. What a great idea. Of course you and Maude can spend a week at the stone cottage," said Dr. Johnson. "When were you thinking you'd like to go Gilbert?"

"Well, the sooner the better. I know we are getting into the fall season and it has been a bit cool at night, but we still haven't had Indian Summer yet and I am hoping we can hit it just right and get a couple of days of really good weather before it gets to be too cold."

Gilbert paused and shifted from one foot to the other as he spoke to the doctor who was sitting in his leather chair behind his office desk.

"I had a long talk with Mr. McDowell at the hardware store yesterday about what you have offered Maude and I."

"Oh yeah? How did that go?" asked the doctor.

"I have to say that he wasn't too thrilled about the idea of losing Maude and I at the store but things have been slowing down a bit now that summer is over and that seemed to take some of the edge off of what I was asking. I think if it had been a really busy day in the middle of summer he might have thought differently about it."

Gilbert paused as if he was a bit reluctant to say any more. "I told him that Maude and I would like to take a week of vacation and go up the shore and give this proposal of yours a try. I told him both Maude and I would continue to work at the store for the winter and we will stay on long enough to train any new people he hires in the spring. He was pretty happy about that."

"It seems all of this is falling nicely into place. My wife will be pleased to know that you and Maude are seriously considering it. Wilf France comes to town about twice a week to pick up supplies. I'll leave a message for him with the wharf-master at the town dock to come and see me. I'll arrange for you and Maude to ride up with him on his next trip up. I'll leave it with you to make the arrangements with him for you to come back to town."

*****

Everything really is falling right into place, thought Gilbert as he walked home. It seemed to him that ever since he had met Maude his life had taken a complete one hundred and eighty degree turn. *A turn for the better,* he thought. A couple of years ago, when he reflected on his life as it was and what he hoped for the future, he had no idea it would turn out to be this way. Life as he knew it after Eli and his father had died had been pretty bleak with not much hope for something to stimulate him in the future. He was thrilled with the many twists and turns that had occurred along the way and he thought, *It looks like things are just going to keep on getting better.*

At suppertime that evening Gilbert said to Maude, "I talked to Dr. Johnson today and told him what happened when I spoke with Mr. McDowell," he paused, "He seemed to be OK with it all and is going to make arrangements for Mr. France to take us up in the next week. Oh yeah, and he is going to pay me the same amount I'd make if I was still at the store. He said it is worth it to just to have someone he trusts doing the work." He looked at Maude who seemed to be a bit quieter than normal.

The Stone Cottage

"Are you still OK with this? You seem to be a bit quiet today. Are you having second thoughts about you and I going up to spend the summer at Cognashene?"

"No, I'm not. I really am looking forward to it but… I don't think it will be just you and I going up to the cottage for the summer."

"What do you mean, have you asked someone else to come along?"

"No Gilbert. I didn't ask anyone else but I am pretty sure we will be having company up there." Maude smiled at Gilbert, those dark obsidian eyes reflecting the light that came in from the dining room window. "I am pretty sure I'm pregnant Gilbert. I still need to make an appointment with the doctor to be sure but I have a strong feeling we will be bringing a baby to the stone cottage with us."

Gilbert was stunned. He knew that having children some day was in their plans for the future. They had spoken of having children often, first when they were engaged and again after they had bought their house and were deciding which bedroom upstairs they were going to take for themselves and which one they would save as a room for the baby.

Maude had been raised as an only child but she cherished the stories that Gilbert told of his brother Elijah and was convinced that she wanted to have several children so that they too could experience the joy, love and friendship that would come with having a sibling or two. Gilbert too believed in the benefit of having several children. He had never thought to much about how many children that he and Maude would have, but he did know one thing for certain; it would be more than one.

CHAPTER - 7

March 1927

The birth notice in the newspaper simply stated;

> "Gilbert and Maude Valcour
> of Water St., Penetanguishene
> are pleased to announce the
> birth of their twins
> Benjamin Oliver and Emma Marie
> on March 18th, 1927. Mother and
> babies are doing well, father is still
> in shock at the news that he is the
> father of twins."

The hospital in Penetanguishene was a small facility. A large old two story Victorian style home located centrally in town, it had been donated by an elderly couple who could no longer maintain it. It was converted by the town to be used as the town's medical facility. Because of the limited amount of space in the hospital, typically children were born at home. In most cases the doctor and his nurse would go the house to deliver the child and barring any issues, mom and babe never had to be admitted. Maude was delivering twins however and so the decision was made late in the pregnancy that Maude would be admitted to the hospital at the end of her term so that she could be closely supervised as her labour progressed. It was a difficult delivery to say the least. Maude's labour lasted over 36 hours and it took a long time for Dr. Johnson to manipulate the infants into position for delivery but once the first baby was born the second was delivered without incident.

"I love the names that we have chosen for the twins," Maude said to Gilbert several weeks after Maude and the twins were discharged home from the hospital. I completed the birth registration paperwork and had your mother mail it off to Toronto and as I think back to the names we chose I am really happy with our choice." Maude paused with what she was saying to Gilbert as she adjusted one of the babies into a little more comfortable position to make it easier for the baby to suckle at her breast.

"I'm glad your mom was able to pick up "The Book of Names" from the library for me, it helped a lot in the decision making. I would have loved to have given our children Native names but because they are going to be going to school here in town, I didn't want any name that the other children in their class would struggle with or tease them about."

"I really like the name Benjamin Oliver," said Gilbert. "It is such a strong name."

"I like it too. In that book I was telling you about, it says that the name Benjamin, comes from the old Hebrew name Benj which means "associated with the right hand side which traditionally is a reference to 'strength' and in a name it refers to 'strength of virtue,'" said Maude.

"It's nice that it flows so well with your father's name, and what an honour it is for him to have his first grandson named after him," said Gilbert.

Maude continued, "I really liked the name Mallory. I think that it is a cute name for a little girl but when I looked it up in the book it is a variation of the French word 'mal' and in a name it refers to 'unfortunate or unlucky' and that is definitely not what our daughter is. The name we chose, Emma, is from the Germanic name Erma which means 'strong, and refers to strength of character'. It is good that the names are so different but have the same meaning especially since they are twins. I can't wait to get a letter back from my mom to see what she and dad think of us adding their names into the names of our children. "

"I'm sure they'll be pleased," said Gilbert smiling as he looked down at his wife who was cuddling the twins in their post, breast fed milk-drunk slumber.

The stress of the birth of their children was behind them now and with that worry out of the way they had settled into somewhat of a routine at home. The winter months had seemed to drag on this year and now that spring was just around the corner it was time for Maude and Gilbert to move forward with their plans for spending the summer up in Cognashene.

The Stone Cottage

*****

May 1927

Gilbert had been a hard worker his entire life and this self-discipline served him well when it came to figuring out his first set of tasks that had to be completed at the cottage and then getting to them. His priority was to get the stone cottage habitable and safe for his family. To that end he had come to the stone cottage by himself for nearly three weeks so he could work and clean uninterrupted. It was a good thing that Gilbert wasn't afraid to 'rough-it' for a little while because his first week at the stone cottage was just one step up from wilderness camping, something he had done as a young lad in the past with his father and brother but not something he was a big fan of these days. He was glad to get the chance to make the stone cottage habitable before Maude and the babies came up. It wasn't a great place to be bringing newborn twins while it was in this condition.

For the most part the main room of the stone cottage needed very little. There was a trap door built into the side of the east wall of the cottage next to the large stone fireplace. This trap door was really handy for bringing wood for the fireplace into the cottage without having to go too far from the outside wood pile next to the cottage. Simply open the trap door and the firewood could be placed right next to the hearth. A simple idea really and it sure cut down on the traffic through the cottage front door and across the floor. Gilbert's first task was to replace the trap door and the frame it was attached to. Over the years the mortar used to hold the door frame to the stone walls crumbled and the wood frame developed dry rot. In time the door itself had begun to deteriorate and this made a perfect entrance for a family of raccoons that seemed to think they liked the idea of living in such a nice sheltered spot.

Once the door was fixed, cleaning up the nest and mess the raccoons had made in the cottage was the next priority. Everything had to be scrubbed and scrubbed again. The stench of the feces and urine on the cement and flat rock floor was enough to make Gilbert's eyes water and even a good scrubbing with strong bleach and a stiff bristled brush hardly seemed to make a difference. So, day after day, that first week, Gilbert's first task of the day was to scrub the floor and then spread a fine layer of baking soda onto it to see if that would help. Then he would leave the door and windows open for the day to air it out and help dry things up.

His only set back with it was one day while the front door was left open to air out the cottage a fair sized fox snake decided that it was an open invitation to spend time sunning himself on the warm granite rock just inside the entrance. To encourage the snake to go out the door rather than slither further indoors, Gilbert made his way through the kitchen window and into the main part of the cottage. Then with a long pike pole he pushed the snake out of the cottage and into the shrubs leading to the water. Luckily the snake never returned but from that moment on, Gilbert kept a wary eye in the cottage to make sure his sibilant friend hadn't come back. In the end it didn't, and Gilbert was happy. *First crisis averted*, he said to himself, *I'll have to tell Maude about it though. Not to frighten her, but to make her aware that if it happened once it could happen again.*

He was glad the door from the main part of the cottage into the kitchen had remained closed over the years. He didn't even want to think about what kind of mess he would have encountered if the raccoons had made their way into the kitchen and taken to destroying the mattresses piled on the bunks against the far wall of the kitchen.

Each day while the floor was drying in the main part of the cottage Gilbert was busy with other tasks. Just as it was with the trap door on the side wall, at the front of the cottage the caulking around the windows and front door where they met the stone walls also needed to be replaced. Though he had initially hoped he could salvage them, the screens in the windows had to be completely rebuilt. Without any electricity running to the cottage everything had to be cut by hand. Not an easy task when it came to building something as delicate as window screens. His years of experience doing the finish work on the boats at the Boatworks came in handy and Gilbert was glad he had purchased the right size of trim to use for the frames. This meant that the hardest part of the task was to make his 45 degree corner cuts using a mitre saw and old fashioned mitre board he had build at home years before. He fastened the frame together with long finishing nails to make a perfect corner and was pleased with how tight the seam was. Stiff fine-wire mesh was cut to size over the frame and then held onto the frame with half inch square strips of wood and smaller finishing nails. Once those were complete, it meant that the mosquitoes would be held at bay in the evening when it was almost impossible to sit outside after the sun went down.

The kitchen addition at the back of the cottage was another story all together. The outside walls were made completely out of six inch half logs and over the years as the wood dried out the chinking between the logs had fallen out in many places. Various tenants of the stone cottage had used a variety of things to fill the cracks, from old rags, to bits of mortar to a pasty sawdust that had been mixed with putty. The effect was dismal to look at and not very effective at keeping the driving rain and mosquitoes out. There were freestanding cupboards, a sideboard and two shelving units lining the walls and these hid most of the mess. Additionally, there were also spaces on the walls where open shelves had been built and secured with long brackets right onto the wall. In many places you could easily see right through to the outside and the effect of years of rain driving in through these cracks had left indelible water stains on the flat surfaces of the half logs. Gilbert wasn't going to take a chance that just filling the spots where he could see outside through the cracks in the walls was going to be enough to keep the bugs and the cold winds out of the kitchen. He decided the only way to fix it properly was to remove all of the "crack-fillers" in the entire room and replace it with a properly mixed mortar. Not an easy task but he was up to it. If he expected his wife and children to be comfortable at the stone cottage he had to do what was needed to make it habitable and a place they wanted to be.

Using a heavy duty putty knife and a chisel as his main tools Gilbert attacked the project with enthusiasm. Removing the rags, and putty-like sawdust was the easy part and this encouraged him to continue. Chiselling out the old mortar between the logs however took a long time and a lot of elbow grease as the mortar that had actually remained was as hard as a rock and nearly impossible to pry out of the cracks between the logs. In the middle of the afternoon of the third day he noticed that the wind had gotten up and it surprised him when he realized that the reason he had noticed this was that he could feel the breeze blowing through the cracks in the walls. Mixing the mortar by hand was another difficult task. Isolated as he was, he didn't have a cement mixer or even a large old tub or barrel to mix it in so as a result he was only able to mix small amounts at a time in an old rusty hand basin he had found lying with several other discarded items in a small dump site about one hundred feet from the back of the cottage. It was hard to get the consistency of the mortar to be exactly the same every time but, *on a positive note* he thought, *at least I don't have to worry about the mortar drying out before I get to apply it to the walls.*

In the end, once he got started it took three days to complete but it was well worth it, in fact it nearly transformed the look of the room. Gone were the old droopy rags, the grey putty mixture, the odd bits of twigs and strips of wood that had been nailed over some of the larger cracks. Now the water stains had been sanded down, the mortar was a solid white colour and although the lines were not exactly straight, which was impossible to accomplish given the variations in the rough hewn logs, the effect was that of a well built and cozy log room. *I'm sure Maude will be pleased with this,* Gilbert thought to himself. *Now all I need to remember is to get her to pick out whatever fancy shelf paper she'd like to use in the cabinets and on the shelving units and side board. I am sure she'll find something bright and colourful and that will be all it will take to brighten this place up.*

The two small windows in this room were in pretty good shape. Their only problem was that some of the glass panes in the four pane windows were a bit loose. Gilbert had replaced the glass in many broken windows that were brought into the hardware store and he was a master at sealing the windows with just the right amount of putty to hold the glass in the window frame without affecting the view out of even the smallest of windows. Fixing these windows was a breeze. For some reason the screens for this room had been removed and were left leaning against the inside wall just below the windows. Since they hadn't been as exposed to the elements they were still in excellent condition so all he had to do was to mount them onto the frame and that task was done. That night he was so pleased when he crawled into bed that he was going to be sleeping in a mosquito free zone.

The next job ahead of him was the wood stove. Gilbert had tried using it when he first arrived at the cottage and was smoked out of the room the minute the fire got started. Shutting down the dampers on the chimney and the lower side of the stove to starve the fire of oxygen he raced outside to catch a breath of fresh air. Using an old ladder that had been leaning up against the wall he went onto the roof and took the top part of the old rusted chimney apart. Sure enough a bird's nest was completely blocking the pipe. Luckily the fire hadn't burned long and he was able to reach into the pipe and fish out the nest without burning his hand on the hot old metal. As soon as he did, the remaining smoke that was trapped in the pipe billowed out and stung Gilbert's eyes making him feel slightly dizzy. Perched on the roof the way that he was, this was not a good thing. Though the chimney was rusty in a few places it was still a solid piece of pipe so he put it back on knowing that if he didn't he wouldn't be able to get enough up-draft when he lit the next fire. He hung onto the pipe till he regained his balance. But, when he started to climb down he ended up putting his foot right through a roofing board that was rotten, tearing three shingles. *It never ends*, he thought, *another task on the list for tomorrow*. He made a mental note to make sure that he purchased a few new lengths of stove pipe to replace the rusted ones. They would be OK for now but once the stone cottage was being used on a regular basis it wouldn't be long before they would deteriorate and become a fire hazard.

After careful examination he decided that the rest of the stove was in pretty good shape all things considered. Sure there were a few rusted spots on the surface of the stove top and the warming closet above but those could be sanded out. The hinge on the door to the oven was slightly bent but it still opened easily and the door still shut tightly. The lid to the water reservoir attached to the side of the stove squeaked when he opened it but a couple of drops of lubricating oil fixed that.

It was several days before he decided to try lighting a fire in the stove again. He missed his morning coffee but he had been making due by drinking the cold fresh clear water that was taken right out of the lake. He was very happy that the next fire he lit in the stove went well. No smoke could be seen or smelled, the oil on the hinges was smouldering a little when it heated up but the smell went away quickly.

Though it was warm out during the day and he didn't need to light the fire in the large stone fireplace in the main room, Gilbert decided it would be a good idea to try lighting one anyway, in the day time, in case this chimney was blocked as well. Doing it during the day was a smart thing to do in case he got smoked out again. At least he could problem solve whatever the issue was in daylight hours rather than in the dark. To his delight, the chimney was fine, the fire burned well and there was no residual smoke in the cottage.

The following morning, the first order of business; a pot of strong black coffee and a couple of toast cooked over the open fire. Gilbert thought as he slowly moved the wire rack holding the bread back and forth over the open flame *Toast tastes great when cooked at home in an electric toaster but there is nothing that beats the taste of a slice of bread toasted over an open flame.* He was really pleased that the stove didn't smoke up the room like the last time he lit the fire. He knew he'd be really disappointed if the nice white mortar he had mixed to chink between the logs was blackened by the smoke from his first fire. Once he had cleaned up from breakfast he got on with his day, checking things off the list he had made as they were completed. *There is something very satisfying about making a list and scratching the items off one by one,* Gilbert thought. *You get a sense of accomplishment at the end of the day, especially when you sit back and reflect on your day and you realize all that got done today.*

*****

June 1927

Gilbert sat on a small stool on the front stoop of the stone cottage and leaned against the smooth stones of the west wall. He could feel the warmth from the stones on his back through his shirt and he pressed his back more tightly to the hard surface for maximum effect. It had been a totally clear and cloudless sky all day and the warming sun had done its job to heat up the stone walls of the cottage. In the slight westerly breeze the air moved warm and gentle upon his skin. He was suddenly suffused with happiness and, as always in these rare transitory moments of peace and quiet was intrigued by the purely physical nature of its joy and its impact on his sense of well being. The warmth from the rocks moved along in his veins with a gentle surge and he felt the tension in his shoulder muscles, hardened after a full day of labour begin to relax. He did not dwell upon it, just enjoyed it for what it was because even to analyze its nature was to lose hold of it. He recognized it for what it was, the first clear intimation that life would be good here, and his thoughts lingered there, while he relaxed and thoroughly enjoyed his surroundings.

Though he often found it to still be a bit cool out at this hour in the late evening it had been an unseasonably warm day, heating the granite rocks from the shoreline right up to the tree line which began about twenty yards from the back of the cottage. The effect on this night was that heat radiating from the rocky granite shore helped to warm the fading breeze as the sun began its decent below the horizon. At this time of year the temperature could drop significantly overnight but luckily the stones that formed the four walls of the main cottage retained enough heat from the daytime that a fire in the fireplace tonight to stave off the chill wasn't really going to be necessary.

Hard physical work during the day, a short swim in the cool clear water of the narrow channel then relaxing on his stool in this spot late in the evening, coffee in hand had. It had become his regular routine. It was the perfect spot to come, sit and think, to reflect on his day and plan his work for tomorrow. From his vantage point he could see a wide expanse of Georgian Bay through a gap in the trees on the island opposite. The stillness of the water reflected the last of the days' light like shimmering pools. Only the cawing of the odd seagull flying low over the water heading towards its overnight refuge on an outer island broke the stillness of the moment.

As darkness deepened the sky and millions of stars so clearly visible on this cloudless night turned to shimmering diamonds, Gilbert was aware of a mosquito buzzing around his head but on this beautiful night it didn't really bother him too much. He paid no attention to it as it hummed near his ear. He was more interested in the sudden appearance of a meteor that was flaming across the sky, the big dipper serving as the celestial backdrop and at that moment he once again realized just how blessed he was to be able to live the life he and Maude had made for themselves. They often spoke with excitement and enthusiasm about their good fortune and in anticipation of being able to raise Ben and Emma in this environment. For Gilbert it was perfect to be so close to nature and to be able to continue to enjoy the things they both cherished most. For Maude it was a way for her to still feel connected to the lifestyle she had known growing up in Granite Bluff Inlet.

Though he was enjoying his quiet reverie on the stool outside the stone cottage, it didn't take long before his mind was dragged back to the many tasks and work that was before him. He had so many things on his mind he was glad for these quiet times so that he could sort through them and prioritize what was most important and what needed to be done next.

There had been a flurry of activities in the last several months. There had been so much to do and so much to get ready before closing up their home in town and move up to the stone cottage for the summer. Maude had become pregnant soon after they were married and he was thrilled, but to have twins, well that took some getting used to. He was so proud of her. She was a natural at handling and caring for the babies. Her maternal instincts were very strong and she embraced the idea of having two new infants to care for with as much enthusiasm and energy as most women have with one. She was not daunted in any way by the fact that there were two.

"Just more to love. I feel like we have been twice blessed," she'd say when asked about how she was managing. "If you are busy with one usually the other is resting or sleeping, and if not, well, then you are busy with two. But…when they are both settled, well that's the time to get other things done."

Gilbert was always in awe of the stamina Maude had for both looking after the children and all the other chores she did around the house on Water Street and now at the stone cottage.

At first, when the twins were born, Madelaine would stop by almost daily on her way home from Dr. Johnson's house. She liked to see if there was anything she could do or help Maude with. Often there were things still needing to be done around the house and she was happy to do them. It wasn't as though she didn't have enough of her own to do but she had to admit it was pretty darn quiet at her house at the far end of town now that Gilbert and Maude had moved out. Stopping by to check on Maude and the twins was her way of staying in touch with what was going on in the busy and at times hectic household. The thrill of holding, cuddling and helping with the twins never got old. Madelaine knew she would cherish this time spent with her only grandchildren till the day she died. It restored her faith in God and his "master plan" as she put it. She had tragically lost both her husband and youngest son at a young age but she firmly believed the twins were a gift from God to help fill that void in her life.

If Maude and Gilbert were going to be blessed with having two children at the same time they were lucky the twins had been such good children since they were born.

"Some people who have twins aren't this lucky," Maude would say. But, Benjamin and Emma fed well, and usually slept well and for the most part did not require a lot of entertaining in between.

"They are that way because you are such a good mother Maude," Madelaine said one day. "You are a calm and peaceful person. You don't get all riled up. Babies can sense that you know. If you were agitated and uncomfortable with going about the activities of daily living and struggling with breast feeding the babies they would be agitated as well. I am so proud of the mother you have become." Maude blushed slightly and didn't really know what to say in response to that glowing compliment so she just humbly, said thank you to her mother-in-law and continued rocking her infants in their bassinet.

Thankfully they almost always slept on their boat rides between Penetanguishene and Cognashene. This was a blessing for Maude and Gilbert in and of itself. Invariably Gilbert was usually kept busy enough just trying to get across the gap without incident as Mr. France's heavy wooden boat plowed through large waves caused by high winds. With a boat motor that was temperamental to say the least it often needed to have the carburettor tweaked prior to and during each trip. As a result Gilbert was always busy on every trip across the gap. He found the engine ran too rich causing a strong smell of gasoline to overwhelm the passengers in the small cabin up in the bow and though, try as he may to adjust the carburettor just right, mysteriously it slipped back to its old settings once underway.

With that as an ongoing challenge during nearly every trip, Gilbert was glad the babies liked their first and subsequent boat rides. Adding crying or fussy twin infants into an already stressful trip across the gap was not something anyone would look forward to. Mr. France on the other hand seemed to be totally oblivious to the problems with the engine as he navigated the familiar channels. He was just glad to have Gilbert along to hold it all together as he manoeuvred the sluggish craft across the waterways. He would sit calmly at the helm steering the boat to its destination and frequently turn to look at Maude holding the twins on her lap. His smile was a warm, friendly, knowing smile. He was happy that Maude was so comfortable on the water and that Gilbert was along to manage the temperamental engine.

Usually the twins slept blissfully through it all, sleep arriving soon after the boat left the dock, the gentle swaying motion of the boat rocking them into a sound slumber. Many times the twins wouldn't even wake at the end of the boat ride since the gentle rolling and rocking of the boat had lulled them into a very deep sleep. On those days that meant that Maude and Gilbert could get them settled into their crib in the cottage and then together unload the boat of all its supplies. There were days however when the children awakened when the boat stopped at the dock and well, that was a different story. Maude became primary care giver and Gilbert was left with the chore of unloading and storing the supplies away. It was more important for Maude to be cuddling and cooing with the twins while she breast fed them than it was to get everything put away quickly.

*****

As Gilbert looked at the shoreline he noticed that the level of the water in the Narrows channel was much lower than usual and an oblique line of foam moved sluggishly among the furthest rocks as it was slowly being carried out into open water by the current in the channel.

Because Cognashene Lake is not land-locked and is, in effect a part of Georgian Bay, with the narrow channel being the only entrance to the lake, there is always a current flowing. Sometimes the current is very obvious and sometimes hardly noticeable at all. When the current in the channel is flowing southerly the water level in the lake beyond is likely to go down. Conversely when the current in the channel flows northerly the water level in the lake will rise. Gilbert often thought of this almost daily flow of water in and out of the bay to be like the tides in the ocean but in reality it is a result of the changing atmospheric pressures. Most days the change in the water level happened in mid afternoon and was very subtle, a couple of inches at most on a day with little wind and mild weather conditions. A very strong west or north wind however could easily raise the level of the water in the lake by seven to twelve inches in a matter of hours. A storm surge or a three day blow was a force to be reckoned with and could wreak havoc with the dock's piers if they weren't properly weighted down with stones or well secured to shore. Many a boater was at risk of hitting free floating driftwood logs and boards, or dead heads as the locals called them, that had broken away from docks or been lifted from the shore when the water rose. Equally, a strong and sustained wind from the east could also lower the water level by almost a foot as the winds blew the waters towards the western shores of Georgian Bay, the Bruce Peninsula and Lake Huron.

Lower levels of water in the bay for the most part weren't a big deal. The local people know where the shoals are and manoeuvre their boats clear of them. The problem with the lower water level that Gilbert was facing was that he was expecting a large barge full of building supplies to be delivered. Supplies much needed for the repairs and the renovations to the main cottage that Dr. Johnson had hired him to fix. When the water was at its usual level the work boat that tows the barge was able to pull up to the dock in the cove in front of the main cottage and the barge could be brought right up alongside to make unloading the lumber, roofing shingles, windows etcetera, much easier. Now that the water level was low it wasn't likely the old inboard tug with a draft of about four feet was going to make it up to the dock. This meant that the barge would have to be secured to shore further down the southern end of the channel and all the supplies would have to be taken over the rugged terrain by hand to the worksite. This in effect tripled the distance it all had to be carried. Though not something that he ever wished for, Gilbert thought a storm surge sure would be handy right about now so that the barge and tug could come to the dock and save him a lot of extra work.

In the end, by the time the work-boat made it to Cognashene from Penetanguishene, the water level had risen just enough to allow the barge to be brought into the cove in front of the main cottage. As luck would have it, the tow boat operator was a man Gilbert had done a number of odd jobs for back at home so he was more than willing to give Gilbert a hand to not only off-load the supplies onto shore but to carry it right up to the main cottage where it was needed. Gilbert looked skyward and mumbled, "Thank you Lord," and thought, *I must be doing something right to have things work out so well.*

*****

A month and a half had gone by and Maude and Gilbert had settled nicely into a cottage routine that worked for them. For the most part, every day began with Gilbert drawing fresh water from the channel in large tin buckets he had brought with him to the cottage from the hardware store. These buckets were then brought up to the stone cottage and used to fill the water reservoir attached to the side of the old wood stove in the kitchen. A fire was lit and as the water in the old stove top coffee percolator began to boil, the aromatic scent of freshly brewed coffee filled the kitchen and main living room. At the same time the water in the reservoir was being heated for the twin's morning baths and the never ending pile of dishes that seemed to accumulate faster than anyone could believe.

Breakfast was usually a simple meal of homemade bread toasted on the open flames of the wood stove where a lid from the stove top had been removed. A daub of Madelaine's homemade strawberry, blueberry or peach preserves on the toast rounded out the breakfast and added just the right amount of sweetness to the early morning. On Sundays as a special treat, once the stove top was really hot, Maude would lather a section of the stove top with lard or bacon grease, and then fry a few onions and slices of potato. This was a treat she had become accustomed to when she was living with her parents up at Granite Bluff Inlet and she had almost forgotten about it until she got to the stone cottage and saw the old cook stove. "Freshly brewed coffee, homemade toast and jam, fried potatoes and onions. You can't get a better breakfast than that up here," Gilbert said to Maude one morning.

Typically once Gilbert had finished helping Maude with bathing, dressing then settling the twins for their morning nap, he would head out to begin the work he had planned for the day while Maude worked on her chores within the stone cottage. Usually this included baking bread and preparing much of the next two meals ahead of time in case the twins were fussy. Another never ending job was washing up the sometimes overwhelming pile of diapers that had to be washed then wrung by hand and hung to dry on the makeshift clothesline Gilbert had strung between two trees behind the cottage.

On a warm day in late June Maude had settled the twins for their afternoon nap and was bent over the laundry tub working on the never ending pile of diapers when she noticed Gilbert coming up from the dock with a few tools he had used to fix a dock ring that had come lose. She said, "if we are going to be at the cottage all summer long every year I think I would really like to get one of those portable hand-crank wringers that you sell at the hardware store." She straightened up her back, put her hands on her hips and stretched slightly backwards to work out a few kinks.

She had been bent over at the wash tub which was located on a small low table on a flat slab of granite just outside the cottage. She had been working in that position for the last ten minutes and was getting tired. "It would sure make life a lot easier you know. My hands get so sore from wringing out these diapers. If I wasn't using bleach in the water it wouldn't be so bad but I can't rinse the diapers since we only have one tub and that chlorine in the water is really starting to do a number on my hands."

"I'll look around for a hand-wringer next time I go to town," said Gilbert. "Seems to me I remember seeing one on a shelf in the back room at Mrs. Beaudoin's house when I was there this winter to replace the switch on her new electric wringer-washer that she bought. If she isn't going to be using it now that she has the new machine maybe I can buy it off of her. It looks like it is still in good shape," said Gilbert."If memory serves me correctly the rollers are still really solid, the rubber on them hasn't hardened or cracked up at all and this one even has a little lever you can use to change spacing on it so that you can adjust it depending on how thick the fabric is you are feeding through the wringer."

"Sounds perfect," added Maude. With having twin infants to care for at a remote location like this without electricity anything that could make life simpler up at the cottage would be a welcome addition to say the least.

"This wringer I am thinking about has a flat base on it. You can use C-clamps to mount it steady on a table or a bench," said Gilbert. "Maybe what I can do is build a nice solid bench from some of the planks I have found under the main cottage. I can clamp the wringer to the bench and that way you can even sit down while you wring out the laundry."

Maude said: "If you can bring back that spare basin we have in the bathroom at home on your next trip to town I could put some clear lake water in it to rinse everything before I wring them out. That will get the soap and bleach out and it won't be so hard on the clothes."

"Using a real wringer will take a lot more moisture out of the clothes too so that when you put them on the clothes line they'll dry faster," said Gilbert.

"This is sounding better every minute," said Maude. "It's the little things in life that make me happy."

"Thank God," said Gilbert.

*****

Once every two weeks Gilbert would go into town with Mr. France and pick up supplies. Since refrigeration was almost nonexistent, meat did not do well. Because of this, for the first couple of days after a trip into town their evening meals included either some beef, a cured ham or a roast of pork that Gilbert was able to pick up from Maude's uncle at the butcher shop. But, after that was used up the main protein they had in their diet was from the fish that either Maude or Gilbert would catch in the narrow channel or from canned meats that were picked up at the grocery store.

At first Maude had also been making the trip into town with the twins. Their routine developed quickly and usually she would drop the twins off for Madelaine to watch. She would then go to their house on Water St and get what was needed for the cottage, pick up the grocery supplies and any other items needed while Gilbert went to the building supply and hardware stores to purchase what he needed for the projects he had underway.

"I used to think that this was a good thing for me to be going back and forth to town with you because it would save you a couple of hours of time. I do groceries and check on the house while you pick up what you need but, we can't leave to return to Cognashene until Mr. France is ready and I find we often sit at the dock in Penetanguishene for a couple of hours while we wait for him to gather what supplies he needs," Maude said to Gilbert.

"If you don't mind Gilbert, I think I am going to try staying behind at the cottage with the babies next time and I think it will be a lot easier on all of us. That trip into town really disrupts the twin's routine and it takes me a day or two to get them back on track. There will be more room in the boat as well and with that motor on the boat acting up the way it does the fewer times I have to smell a dirty old carburettor again the happier I'll be."

"Sounds fine with me as long as you feel comfortable being here with the twins by yourself," Gilbert said to Maude.

"Things don't change too much here from day to day so I am sure that I'll be just fine," said Maude. "I'm not worried about it at all. You forget sometimes that I lived in a very isolated community for the first seventeen years of my life. I'm sure I'll be fine."

"It does make a lot of sense. It is a lot of work for you to take the twins up Main Street, meet up with my mom to have her watch them while you check on the house and then get groceries," he said. "I'm sure my mom doesn't mind seeing the kids for that brief time but then for you it's all the carting of stuff down to the dock, loading it in the boat then returning to Dr. Johnson's house to meet me so there are two of us to bring them and their stuff back down to the boat. That's a lot of work for you. You manage it well but, on the days when the kids are fussy, I don't know how you do it."

"I know it will make extra trips to the town dock for you. It will mean you will have to do double duty but without the twins to worry about it might be better that way."

"We'll give it a try, I don't see how there could be a problem," said Gilbert. "I'm thinking of asking my mom if she'd like to come up to the stone cottage to stay with us for a couple of weeks on my next trip into town. Would that be OK with you?" he asked.

"Oh, I'd love it; a little extra female company up here would be nice. It will be good timing too since it'll be right in the middle of summer and the best weather of the year." Maude said happily. "I'm sure your mom would like to have a little get-away. She never takes any time off and I know she loved the trip up to Granite Bluff Inlet last year when we got married. She still talks about it all the time."

"And I'm sure she won't mind spending some time with the babies either," said Gilbert.

"And us too I hope," said Maude jokingly.

*****

And so it was; their routine was established and life was good. Gilbert's mother Madelaine came to the stone cottage for an extended holiday and with her helping out with the children in the morning and the day time chores around the house it meant that Gilbert was able to focus on getting the restoration work to move along at an uninterrupted and steady pace at the Johnson's main cottage. With Maude's great nurturing, the children were growing like good corn, feeding well during the day and sleeping blissfully unaware of their surroundings all night long. In fact, everyone slept well all night long. It was so quiet and peaceful in the stone cottage and a hard day's work for both Gilbert and Maude meant that by the time the sun went down everyone was ready for bed.

The days turned into weeks and the weeks into months and soon it was the end of September. The number of daylight hours were diminishing and Gilbert found it was cool enough to have a fire in the large stone fireplace every evening in the main part of the cottage. The fire in the wood stove first thing in the morning turned from a way to make the coffee and heat the bath water to a welcome treat to warm the kitchen and its occupants.

As the summer months went by, Gilbert's talents as a carpenter and handyman were noticed by other cottagers in the immediate area. Though he was employed by Dr. Johnson to work on the main cottage during the week, Gilbert was able to find time on weekends to repair temperamental gas powered water pumps used to fill large reservoirs in the more elaborate cottages, repair and replace deck or dock boards and complete other tasks the wealthier neighbours in the area wanted done. The extra money he was paid, which usually included a handsome tip, came in handy and it offset the income Maude and Gilbert had become accustomed to from Maude's work at the hardware store.

As they sat at the kitchen table having their coffee after supper one evening Gilbert said, "Although it seems like we just got here, it looks like we should start making plans to return to our house in town,"

"I know. I just love it here and the kids are doing so well here being outdoors so much and enjoying the fresh air every day but you can tell by the smell of the air and the change in the colour of the water and the leaves that it won't be long before we are into the grips of autumn," said Maude.

"At this time of year in Granite Bluff Inlet the people in our community start to make plans to prepare for winter. They get busy smoking deer meat and fish, harvesting the produce from the garden, preserving what they can and getting in the supplies like flour, sugar, cornmeal they are going to need over the winter. Winter can be pretty harsh up there sometimes, trust me I know," she said with a far away gaze in her eye as she pictured life back home at this time of year. "Though I'm not opposed to spending a winter here, having the option of returning to our nice home in town with a furnace, running water and indoor plumbing is a blessing I'm not too proud to admit to."

Gilbert was quiet for a few more minutes then said, "I have been asked by six of the cottagers in the area if I would close up their places and winterize their boats for the winter" He let that news sink in with Maude then said, "I agreed to do it because I know we need the money."

"But most of those people continue to use their places until the Thanksgiving weekend," said Maude. "Don't you think that waiting until after you close up all those cottages will make it too late for us to leave?" questioned Maude. "I know the gap doesn't freeze over until late November or December but I'm not crazy about waiting around until November when the water is rough and cold. I think to be bringing the twins across in Mr. France's old boat is a bit of a risk at that time of year. If the motor should stop while we are out there, we could be drifting a long time before someone would find us."

"I've been thinking about exactly that," said Gilbert. "I think what we should do is leave on Thanksgiving weekend. Once we get ourselves settled in at home, I'll come back up by myself and get the work done. Mr. France and his family live up here year round so I can hitch a ride with him. I'll be fine at the stone cottage on my own for that extra week or two while I am shutting things down up here."

"Will you need any help," Maude asked. "I think my dad would love to spend some time with you here."

"You know, I'd love to have him join me and he'd certainly be a big help but with the weather so unpredictable at this time of year it gets to be a matter of whether he'd be able to get back home to Granite Bluff safely if the weather turns bad. The Keewatin doesn't run up to Parry Sound after Thanksgiving weekend so he'd have to travel by land from Penetanguishene but then it's a long ride for him in a small boat from Parry Sound to the Inlet."

"You're right."

"Closing up the cottages, putting on shutters, draining water lines and all those things are easy enough for me to do on my own, but I'll admit, it sure would be good to have an extra pair of hands up here though to help me haul out those water soaked rowboats, and dispros. They can get pretty heavy by the end of the season."

"I bet I know someone who would be more than happy to help you," said Maude suddenly.

"Who?"

"What about my old friend Isaac?" Maude asked. "In the last letter I got from my mom she said that Isaac isn't working right now. With winter coming, things have slowed down in the lumber yard in Mactier where he's been working. I bet he'd leap at the opportunity to spend time up the lakes with you. And since he isn't going back to the Inlet for the winter you won't have to worry about him making his way there in bad weather."

"Great idea Maude," Gilbert smiled at his wife's concern and resourcefulness. "Only one thing, how do we get a hold of him?"

"Leave it with me," she said. "As soon as we get back to town, I'll find out the name of the lumber yard in Mactier from the office at the mill across the street from our house. I'll give them a call, and maybe they can give me his contact information."

"I love you for many reasons Maude Valcour but tonight you have just added yet another reason," said Gilbert with a smile on his lips. His face lit up with the thought of having help with the heavy lugging and slugging associated with closing up the summer homes in Cognashene. Though he'd probably be able to do it on his own with the help of a 'come-along' set of pulleys having someone else around was just going to make his life so much easier.

"We even have a spare room at our house," said Maude. "If you don't mind, maybe Isaac would like to board with us, perhaps find work in town for the winter. It would be great to have him around again."

"I could use his help with building canoes in the shop at the back of the house over the winter," said Gilbert liking the idea of Isaac living with them more and more. "We could crank out a lot more of them working the two of us at it than just me alone." He paused, "I bet there would be a good market for them up here next summer if we were to bring some up with us."

"I love it when a plan comes together," said Maude.

"Well don't count your chickens before they hatch Maude," said Gilbert. "Two things; we haven't spoken to him, we don't know if he would like to come up here to give me a hand, and we don't know what his plans are for the winter." He paused. "Let's figure out how to track him down first."

"Your right," said Maude with a bit of a resigned tone to her voice. "I guess I just got a little carried away."

"No, it's a great idea. Let's run with it as far as we can. This could work out for us and him as well." And with that they cleared the dishes and made preparations for bed each kind of lost in their own thoughts. Maude was happy that she and the twins would be returning home soon, and Gilbert was lost in his thoughts of all that had to be done to close up the Johnson's place for the winter. It would be so much better to have help with the six other places he'd agreed to work on as well and was wondering if Isaac would be around to help.

As it turned out, Isaac was easy to track down. True to her word, as soon as they returned home from the stone cottage on Thanksgiving Weekend, Maude went to the office of the lumber mill at the end of Water Street. They did have the phone number for the Mactier Lumber Yard in the office as they were one of the mill's best customers in the northern market. The yard foreman said that Isaac was staying with him for a few weeks while he was looking for alternate work so he was able to relay the message to make contact with Maude that evening. Two days later Isaac was on the bus from Mactier to Penetanguishene. Two days after that Isaac and Gilbert were on their way back up the shore in Mr. France's old wooden boat, Gilbert at the motor tweaking the carburettor as usual. There was a lot for the two friends to talk about. The last time they had seen each other was at the wedding at Granite Bluff Inlet and so much had happened with Maude and Gilbert *and* the twins during that time away from each other.

Both Gilbert and Isaac were genuinely looking forward to spending some time together once again so they could get caught up on the news of each other's lives. Gilbert was thrilled that Isaac was interested in giving him a hand over the winter to build canoes. Gilbert offered free room and board for the winter, Isaac offered free labour.

*****

Gilbert and Isaac were riding in a small outboard motor boat heading toward the stone cottage but Isaac was feeling a bit conflicted. In one way he was in awe at the scenery and the quiet, peaceful surroundings. He was enjoying the views all around him, marvelling at how it was so similar to the Granite Bluff Inlet that he had grown up in. He wanted to just sit quietly in the boat and enjoy the ride and yet at the same time he was curious to find out about what landmarks he was seeing and what he was going to be doing the next couple of weeks. He had a dozen questions he wanted to ask Gilbert but he also didn't want to disturb the quiet reverie he was experiencing as the beautiful scenery slipped by him.

The surroundings, the rocks, the water, the windswept pines, the waves crashing on barely submerged shoals all looked so familiar he felt like he had been transported back to his homeland at Granite Bluff but, there was one very big and very noticeable difference. Isaac had been raised in a very small humble homestead in the isolated community of Granite Bluff Inlet. Many of the homes were very small, often only one or two room dwellings, many looking just like the one next door. When he was old enough to leave the Inlet and travel to "the outside world" he moved to a logging camp and worked as a logger and bushman for a number of years. Initially this was year 'round work for him, felling trees, chopping off the branches, and dragging them either by horse and sleigh over the rough countryside in the winter months or floating them to the mills down the bigger rivers in the area in the summer months.

When that job ended for him he acquired work at the Mactier Lumber Mill not too far away as the crow flies from Granite Bluff. Again he was exposed to the lifestyle of poor and humble hard working men scratching out their existence, living week to week, pay-cheque to pay-cheque just to survive. Honest, assiduous individuals working tirelessly at often backbreaking work to try raising their families in that often harsh environment. His life to this point had provided him with very limited worldly experiences and what he was seeing before him now was a very dramatic culture shock.

Never before, until this moment, had he ever seen what he thought of as such opulence. The cottages he was looking at that were dotting the shoreline were massive by his standards. He found it hard to conceive that one family could own such a large "cottage". He had never been exposed to such wealth. He just sat, motionless in the small boat, mouth open trying to take it all in. Passing by one of the larger cottages in the main channel Isaac stated, "if this is their cottage, can you imagine what their house must look like?"

Gilbert smiled back at him and said, "I can't even begin to imagine what their homes look like. Don't suppose I'll ever find out either."

"These cottages are like mansions. I've never seen a mansion for real, just pictures in books but…" his voice trailed off. He shook his head rubbed his eyes and refocused on trying to take it all in.

"How many cottages did you say we have to close up for the winter?" Isaac asked.

"Well it started off with just the Johnson's main cottage and the stone cottage of course but as soon as some of the other cottagers around Cognashene heard that I might be available to close up their cottage for them the list started to grow, and it grew quickly."

Gilbert was quiet for a moment as he concentrated on navigating around a small but deadly, sharp edged shoal that was just below the water enough to make it invisible but one that could do serious damage to the wooden hull of the boat or the motor if you ran into it.

"What I have lined up will take us the better part of a week and a half my friend," said Gilbert.

"Tell me again. What is it exactly that we have to do?" Isaac was having a bit of trouble picturing himself actually setting foot in some of the cottages he was looking at and couldn't imaging that he of such humble beginnings was going to be of any help in this other world.

"There isn't much work that we have to do to any of the docks at the places we are going to be closing. I had a close look at them at the end of summer but we should still just check them for loose boards, wobbly piers, that sort of thing. We'll just look them over to make sure that nothing comes loose off them over the winter that could end up being a deadhead in the spring when the ice melts.

As far as the docks go, that's pretty much all we have to do." He slowed the boat slightly to make way for a squawking, honking flock of Canada geese that had just landed in his path.

"There is one dock that I know of that was pretty iffy this summer. I think it might suffer some damage from the ice this winter. The water is too cold at this time of year for us to go under it and fix the pier but I think if we can tie off the top of the dock to a couple of trees down by the shore at least it won't float away as the ice melts. I won't be surprised if there is a new dock in their future next summer."

"The rest of the stuff is pretty basic maintenance work really. We have to drain all the water pipes that are in the cottages to make sure they don't freeze; we have to haul out any boats that the owners may have left tied to their docks. I think we should flip them over if we can once we get them on shore just to help preserve the insides if possible. After we get that done then most of the rest of the stuff is indoor work that we will figure out as we go. I have met with some of the cottagers and they have given me the low-down on what they usually do to close up. Others just said, "we'll leave you a note on the kitchen table with your instructions about how we do what needs to be done, but if there is anything we have forgotten to put on the list just do it and we'll sort it out in the spring."

They rounded a point of land soon after they had come out of the Freddy Channel and were both struck by the uniqueness of the cottage that appeared high on the bluff before them.

"That cottage is called Blarney Castle," said Gilbert. "It was built in the early 1900s by the Thomas Bartley family. Thomas is a Native of Ireland and is a Methodist Minister. He and his family visited the area quite a bit in the 1890s and fell in love with the remoteness and isolation up here. It was a great place for him to get away from it all and in 1902 he began to build this cottage. It may be hard to believe but they actually had the cottage built off site and then had it shipped here in sections. There are some good sized windows in this place as you can see and the sea grass that was used to pack the windows for shipping was used by the family to stuff their mattresses," Gilbert said, feeling a bit like a tour guide.

"Look at the roof line on this cottage," he said pointing to the scalloped ridge at the peak of the roof. "It's supposed to resemble turrets on a castle and that's why they call it Blarney Castle."

"It's a very nice place," said Isaac. "I could be happy living there, the view must be amazing from up that high."

"Yes it is, from up there you can see the western shoreline. It's quite pretty."

"Do we have to do any work here?" Isaac asked.

"Not much, they have a small boat that Reverend Bartley built himself a few years back for his daughter. He even carved the oars for it by hand. Anyway the boat is called the '*Kathleen*' after one of his daughters and he is very protective of this boat. It's a "one-lunger" and has a really unique putt-putt sound that it makes once it is underway. Most of the time you can actually tell when it's coming down the bay before you see it. The family have asked us to make sure that the boat is hauled up into the boathouse and put to bed for the winter. This point of land is pretty exposed and they don't want anything to happen to it. The Reverend spent too much time and effort building it to not take good care of it."

"Seems like this area has quite a bit of history to it already," said Isaac.

"A lot of the cottages around this area date back to the late 1800s but most of them have only been built in the last 20 years or so. Most of the families have been coming here for years though, camping in tents on platforms they build to get them up off the rocks. I'm sure those family members have stories they can tell of their early days up here."

"I have a feeling that a lot of these places are well built and are going to be around for a long time," said Isaac.

"They are the type of place that will get handed down from generation to generation I'm sure of it," said Gilbert.

And so it was. Every place had a story. Some Gilbert knew well and had no trouble relating to Isaac. Others he had no idea about but he was sure if he thought about it he could string a story together to tell Isaac. He could make it up to be some fantastic yarn about this or that, but it wasn't in Gilbert's character to mislead anyone, even in jest. But, he smiled to himself as he thought about the possibilities, *I bet Isaac would believe every word I say.*

*****

Each of their days was full and never boring. They went back to the stone cottage every evening tired, cold, hungry and worn out from a hard day of work, appreciative of the fact that their evening would be filled with good pots of strong coffee, homemade bread toasted to perfection on a blazing fire perfect for

The Stone Cottage

dunking in a hardy stew made on the kitchen wood stove. The evenings were filled with playing card games that Isaac had learned in the bush camps, and of course some lewd jokes were repeated without the fear of offending anyone. Gilbert too had lived a somewhat sheltered lifestyle and was often surprised at the stories Isaac shared from his logging days. At the logging camps Isaac had met and worked with a number of men whose past way of life was varied and often quite colourful, to put it nicely. Consequently Isaac was filled with exciting stories of travel and adventure that he loved to share and, Gilbert thought, perhaps embellish a little, though he never challenged him about them.

"Wow, will you look at this one," said Isaac as they motored slowly up to the dock of the last cottage on the list to be winterized.

"It's a beautiful place isn't it?" said Gilbert.

"It looked big from the water as we went by it the other day but now that we are up close to it, it's huge. These people must be millionaires!" Isaac nodded his head as if acknowledging his own statement, "Yup, they're millionaires all right."

"I'm not sure if they are millionaires," said Gilbert, "but I think they don't have to worry too much about where their next meal is going to come from."

"What kind of job does somebody have to have to own a place like this?"

"I think he might be a judge, I think, but I'm not sure."

"Like in a courtroom judge?"

"Yup, like in a courtroom. He and his wife live in Toronto, or Ottawa, it might be Kingston. I only met him briefly and the subject of where he lives and what he does never came up. We'll ask Wilf France when he comes to pick us up tomorrow afternoon. I think he's known this guy for years. An old friend of a friend kind of relationship."

Isaac leaned forward in the boat and whispered to Gilbert pretending that he didn't want anyone else to hear him even though there wasn't anyone around for miles at this time of year, "maybe his wife comes from a family that is really, really rich. They might have pooled their money together and built this place." Gilbert smiled at Isaac's boyish enthusiasm for trying to come up with a story that suited the cottage.

"Well I've saved the biggest for last for a couple of reasons," said Gilbert as they were tying the boat to the dock. "First of all, we only have two days left up here before Wilf comes to get us and I bet it's going to take us at least a day and a half to close this place up."

"Hmpf," said Isaac, a bit nonchalantly. "A piece of cake. We might even get it done today. Then we can have tomorrow off as a vacation day to relax and warm our toes by the fire," he said jokingly.

"The second reason I've saved this place till last is this boat we have been using all week belongs here. The judge knows I don't own a boat and I wasn't about to ask Dr. Johnson if I can use his boat while I'm working for other people so the judge said use this one. No one else is going to be using it at this time of year."

The cottage was massive, one of the biggest on the bay in fact. Gilbert decided to take Isaac on a bit of a tour before they got to work. "See how it has been built on a point of land that juts out into Georgian Bay? The main part of the cottage is facing west to maximize this beautiful, unobstructed view. It's especially nice in the evening with the setting sun over the open water. There are five bedrooms and two indoor bathrooms which is pretty unusual in this neighbourhood."

"Yeah, no outhouse for these guys is there," Isaac commented more than questioned.

They continued the tour. From the large open concept living/dining room, there was a set of French doors that opened to a large wrap around deck that actually went around three full sides of the cottage. There were multiple sitting areas on this veranda each chosen to take advantage of some special view or rock formation or garden. Portions of the veranda were screened in; others were left to open air. All the sitting areas were furnished with white wicker rocking chairs and small wicker love seats with matching nautical patterned cushions.

"They sure have fancy taste," said Isaac rubbing his hand over the velvety softness of one of the cushions.

"I think the lady of the house has spent a lot of time and energy getting the decorating just right."

Beyond the dining area was the kitchen. All the cupboards were free standing but they were all the same except for the fact that some of the upper cupboard doors were solid panels and some of them had glass inserted into the door's frame. Behind the glass doors full sets of depression-ware dishes in light pink clear glass were on display. Other cabinets showcased dishes in a solid sea-foam green. Another cabinet was dedicated solely to housing crystal stemware, dozens of glasses in various sizes and fancy serving dishes.

"Wait till you see this," Gilbert said to Isaac. He led him through the kitchen door to yet another smaller but still functional kitchen.

"What? This place has two kitchens?"

"This smaller one is called the summer kitchen."

"What do you mean?"

"The first kitchen we were in, the one that has the icebox, the wood stove and all those fancy cabinets is the regular kitchen. It's the one that is used most of the time especially in the spring and fall months. It was built as a part of the main cottage. This smaller kitchen was built after the rest of the cottage was built. When we go outside you'll see that it was put on as a small addition to the back of the cottage. It has lots of windows and ventilation and has a kerosene stove for cooking. They call this the summer kitchen because on the really hot days when the owners don't want the wood stove heating up the rest of the cottage, they cook in the summer kitchen and it keeps the rest of the place cooler."

"Well, now I've heard of everything," said Isaac shaking his head in wonder. "Man when I think of all the times my mom made a meal in our little house back home on those hot days in the summer. It would get so hot in the house you could barely stand to be in there. What she wouldn't have given to have a summer kitchen."

Once they had finished checking out the five bedrooms and two indoor bathrooms, one of which held a large iron claw-foot tub, they moved outside. For the most part the property was just one huge flat windswept piece of granite. The cottage was set back from the shoreline by seventy feet and the flat rock sloped gently towards the water. A large gazebo had been built about thirty feet from the water on a small rocky outcropping that was slightly higher than the other rocks around it, again maximizing the amazing view of the open waters of Georgian Bay.

The land was all granite and there was little to no natural vegetation to be seen other than a few windswept stunted pines and some thorny juniper bushes that somehow managed to grow out of the cracks in the rocks. The owners had decided to take landscaping into their own hands. Barge loads of topsoil had been brought in and sunken depressions in the rock formation were filled then rimmed with stones and small boulders from the property to create individual little gardens. Hardy rose bushes, hens'n'chicks flowers and a variety of mosses and colourful annual flowers were added to create a vibrant contrast to the pink granite.

Around the property, strategically placed so that you could always find a place to sit away from the wind, were various seating areas with multiple Muskoka chairs. Some were positioned to take advantage of water views; some were positioned for the view of the nearby channel so that you could watch the boats go by. Some were set up just so you could relax, meditate and watch the rose bushes grow.

Isaac and Gilbert wandered back down towards the dock where their small work boat was tied. "Look at this breakwater that has been built here at the shoreline," said Gilbert. "I don't know who built it but I'm glad they didn't ask me to do it. Look at the size of some of these boulders."

Isaac stopped to look at what Gilbert was pointing at and to appreciate the work that had gone into constructing the breakwater. Huge boulders had been dragged into position such that they jutted out into the water at a sixty degree angle to the shoreline. "This breakwater must be fifty feet long," he said.

"It's been built in such a way that it completely protects the dock and the boats from the big waves caused by the prevailing westerly wind. They must have had an engineer come and figure out how long and at what angle it should be to get it right. You don't want to have to be moving those rocks and boulders around too often."

"I'm speechless Gilbert," said Isaac. "I just can't believe it."

"Let's go check out the guest cabin then the boathouse and then we'll get to work," said Gilbert.

"Lead on my friend, I'm right behind you, that way if we see a rattlesnake I'll be able to turn around and be ahead of you."

Though he'd heard it before Gilbert still laughed because he knew there was a hint of truth to that statement. Isaac had made no bones about the fact that he was scared to death of snakes regardless of what size or kind they were.

The guest cabin was a modest size with a small sitting area, two good sized bedrooms and a decent sized sun deck facing the channel. There was a very small bathroom in the cabin and it had a dry sink, fancy ceramic water pitcher with a matching basin and a gravity feed toilet that emptied into a small holding tank that had been installed directly below the cabin.

"They are talking about adding a small kitchen on the back of the cabin so that their guests can be a little bit more independent when they are staying up for long periods of time. I don't know when they are going to be building the addition but my guess is that when this family decide they want something they just do it."

"I can't imagine what it must be like to be able to live like that," said Isaac. "For me, if I want something, I have to think long and hard about whether I need it or just want it. Then I have to figure out how I'm going to make the money to get it."

"Maude and I are pretty much the same way as you Isaac but some peoples' lives are very different than ours aren't they?"

The judge and his family owned several boats. A nice cedar strip canoe, a seventeen foot row boat that was pointy at both ends with two sets of oarlocks, the small run about that Gilbert and Isaac were using and a large boat the family used to go back and forth to Penetanguishene. Thankfully the large commuter boat was back in town, it had already been hauled out at a local marina and the engine had been winterized by the onsite mechanic. At least that was one boat they didn't have to deal with.

Gilbert thought the small boat they were using was the one that was the most fun to drive. It had a six horsepower outboard motor on the stern and this motor only had one gear and that was forward. In order to go in reverse you had to pull the starting cord, and then quickly turn the motor completely around on the pivot the motor was balanced on. Once the motor was completely facing backwards the driver increased the throttle and the boat would reverse away from the dock. Many an operator didn't have the dexterity to pull the crank cord and then quickly reverse the direction of the motor. In that case the safest way to use the boat was to drive up to the dock, and then manually turn the boat around facing away from the shore so that when the motor was started you could just head straight out. One thing you had to be sure of regardless of who was driving was that all passengers had to be sitting down when the motor was started. Since there was no neutral gear, the boat started to move as soon as the motor was running. Many a non-water-savvy person ended up going for an unintentional swim after losing their balance when the boat got underway before they sat down.

"Well this is quite the place," said Isaac, "where do we start?"

"This is how I think it should go," said Gilbert. "First we will take all the screens off the windows and the veranda and store them. The builder built shelves under the veranda just for the screens to be laid on. All the screens are numbered so we just have to put the screen on the shelf with that number and in the spring it's just a matter of pulling them out and lifting them up into place. After that we will take all the wicker furniture off the veranda and store it in the living room. There are white drape cloths in the linen closet and there are enough of them to cover all the furniture in the living room. In the bedrooms we will turn the mattresses sideways on the beds and fold them in half. I'm not sure why but the judge said that's the way his wife wants it. Under each bed is a metal storage bin. We have to take the pillows and the bed linen off each bed and store them in the metal bins so that the mice don't make their winter homes in them. After that we have to drain the water pipes that go to the bathroom sinks and toilets and make sure there isn't any water in the traps under the sink. We'll have to do the same with the kitchens. Once we know we are finished inside the cottage then we have to install the storm shutters on all the windows. Thankfully they too are numbered so it will be easier to figure out which shutters go on which windows. Once that is done then we have to make sure the doors are locked then shuttered. After that we have to take all the outdoor furniture down to the boat house to be stored in there for the winter. When that is done we have to close up the guest cabin doing the same thing with the bed linens and mattresses, draping the sitting room furniture with drop cloths, draining the water lines and the toilet. Finally we will hoist the canoe onto the rafters of the boathouse and then haul out the rowboat as well. Once they are in position we will haul out the boat we have been using and lay it up for the winter in the boathouse as well.

"Hey, wait a minute. How do we get back to the stone cottage? I should let you know that although I am a really good swimmer, it is almost the end of October and I'm not swimming there," joked Isaac.

"That's the second reason why I left this place until last. Once we haul out the boat, then we tighten our shoelaces and walk along the shoreline back to the stone cottage."

"You're kidding right?"

"No I am not. We can follow the shore for about a mile and then we have to go inland for a little ways so that we don't have to go through the swamp over

The Stone Cottage

there," he said pointing to an area in the distance where the foliage grew right to the shore. "Once we get passed the swamp we make our way back down to the shoreline and just follow it until we get to the stone cottage. As it turns out it is just behind that large bluff near the entrance to the Narrows."

"Ah, I get it. Now I have my bearings."

"OK then, let's get to work."

Though Isaac had joked that they could close up this massive cottage in one day, it actually took nearly the full two days.

As they started their walk back to the stone cottage Isaac said, "I can see why the judge wanted to hire someone to close the cottage. It's a pile of work."

Gilbert clapped his hand on Isaac's shoulder once they had finished with the big cottage, "Well we better get going. We still have some work to do to close the stone cottage and Wilf will be here to pick us up in a couple of hours and it's going to take us nearly an hour to get there."

They headed off along the shoreline, thoughts of hot coffee and toes being warmed by the fireplace foremost on both of their minds but knowing full well that wasn't going to happen.

They busied themselves with closing the stone cottage but found it to be pretty simple work compared to some of the places they had been in the last couple of weeks. Their belongings packed, they shuttered the doors and windows then went and sat on the dock to wait for their ride to come. Late in the season as it was, it was already starting to get dark by five pm and Gilbert was thinking getting home at this hour was going to be like a night-time crossing using the range lights on shore to guide them across the gap.

By seven pm Mr. France still hadn't shown up and with no way to contact him Gilbert said, "I wonder if we are going to get home or not?"

"Maybe he got the days wrong," Isaac offered.

"More likely he couldn't get the motor started," said Gilbert. "The carburettor on that motor floods so easily it's ridiculous. Wilf is pretty good with the motor but once it gets flooded there is nothing you can do but wait it out." By eight pm it had become quite cold outside and the decision was made to move indoors. "Might as well make ourselves comfortable. I think we are here for the long haul," said Gilbert.

"Good thing we still have some food left," said Isaac as he rummaged around in the old wooden crate they had packed to take home. "What are you in the mood for Gil?"

"Salmon steak with a dill sauce, grilled vegetables and warm apple pie with a slice of cheddar," Gilbert joked.

"I admit that would be good but…I think there is still some bread left, a few cans of stewing beef and some potatoes. You light the fire in the wood stove and I'll peel the potatoes."

"The good news is, spending another night here will give you a chance to try to beat me at cards," said Isaac jokingly. "Must be terrible to lose every night," he said teasingly.

"Oh, don't you worry, tonight is the night you are going to lose big time. I've been holding off winning and letting you win because that is what a good host is supposed to do," said Gilbert laughing but not sounding too convincing to either of them.

As it turned out, although Isaac was the better card player Gilbert did win a few rounds.

"You must have cheated," said Isaac lightheartedly as they were getting ready to climb into their bunks for the night.

"Oh, yeah, for sure," said Gil. "Every time you got up to put another log on the fire I was sneaking a look at your hand."

"Yeah, right. I'm not too worried. You're such a lousy card player by the time you got back to your seat you probably forgot what cards I had in my hand."

The night wore on with similar bantering between the two men continuing till the wee hours. The camaraderie they had developed over the last few weeks was strong; teasing each other about every little thing was like second nature to them now.

The fire went out in the wood stove around three in the morning and by first light it was really cold in the cottage. Both men could see their breath in the air as they went about their morning routine.

"It's a cold one today," said Isaac.

"Sure is, when I was coming back from the outhouse there was a hoar frost all over everything. It looked pretty but it feels like it could snow any minute and there is a dark band of clouds on the western horizon."

"What do you think we should do?" Isaac asked.

"First things first, we light a fire and get some heat in here. I'll get a pot of coffee underway and you go out and see how much firewood we have cut in the woodshed. If it ends up that we have to spend another night we will have to put a fire on in the main room."

"Once we've had breakfast I think I'll go out to the point and see if I can see or even hear Wilf coming along. On a clear morning like this the air is really still. I'll be able to hear a boat coming down the Freddie Channel from a long way. If he isn't here by noon we'll go back to the judge's place, put the small boat in the water and go back to Franceville to find out what's going on." Gilbert looked a bit worried.

"Are you OK?" asked Isaac.

"Oh, I'm fine. It's just that I know Maude must be wondering what's going on."

"Yeah, that's right. I guess there's no way to let her know we're alright."

"If we are only one day late she'll probably think we just got delayed but if we are more than that she is going to be worried," Gilbert said pensively. "If she talks to my mom I'm sure she'll remind her of the time my dad and Eli and I got stranded on Beausoleil Island during a three day blow. We had to wait it out that time and there was no way to let mom know we were OK that time either. The weather has been pretty calm but if she starts thinking we had motor trouble crossing the gap she'll know we could be drifting quite a long time before someone would find us at this time of year."

Remaining rather casual about the whole thing Isaac said, "well let's go with plan A. We'll have breakfast then wait till noon. If he doesn't show up then we will go with plan B and put the other boat in the lake." If push comes to shove and Mr France can't get the boat going, then we'll round up some gas and take the little boat into town."

"That'll be quite an adventure but I'm up for it if you are."

The coffee was made, the firewood box had been replenished after the last night's fire and Gilbert was just lacing up his shoes to go for a walk to the point when he said, "by God I think I hear a boat." He ran to the window out of habit but couldn't see anything out of it because they had left them shuttered for the night. He opened the front door and there, rounding the point was Wilf's boat, chugging along as if it was the middle of summer.

"Looks like plan B is going to have to wait for some other time," said Isaac chuckling as he came to stand by Gilbert down at the dock.

"Don't even bother tying up the boat, I'll just hold on," hollered Wilf over the roar of the engine."

"Get your stuff and jump in. I'm not even going to shut the motor off 'cause if I do I'll probably never get it started again," he said as he glanced in the direction of the motor. The engine box cover was off and laying on its side at the back of the boat. "You gotta love old motors. They can be more temperamental than a cranky old housewife."

"Just give us a couple of minutes and we'll be ready."

The two men ran up the rocks to the stone cottage. Gilbert doused the fire in the wood stove while Isaac took the coffee pot outside and dumped the contents on the rocks. The wooden crates had remained packed and along with the bag containing the few clothes they were bringing home, it was placed on the small veranda. Within minutes the door was locked, and the storm shutter installed. As Gilbert made his way to the dock he noticed the sky had darkened even more. It had now turned to a nearly slate grey colour and the whole sky had clouded over casting a dreary hue to everything about him.

"We don't have any time to waste if we are going to beat this storm that's coming," said Gilbert.

The men piled into the boat and as they reversed away from the dock the first wisps of snow began to flutter around them being tossed about by the westerly wind that was starting to blow in from the outer bay. By the time they reached the gap the wave height had reached nearly four feet and the skyline to the west had changed from a dark grey-blue to just about black presaging the storm to come.

"There's a big snow storm coming in those clouds," said Isaac as he sat quietly watching Gilbert crouched on his haunches nursing the unreliable old engine.

"I think we'll be OK," said Wilf glancing to the west as the waves crashed over the bow of the boat. "It's going to take a while for that storm front to move in but I don't think I'm gonna be able to make it back home tonight. Looks like I may have to stay with family in Midland tonight."

Waves continued to crash over the deck of the boat, many of them spilling over the cabin's roof and dripping, often gushing in torrents into the boat itself. The engine continued to be as temperamental as ever and Gilbert had to keep the engine box cover off so he could manually manipulate the stubborn settings on the carburettor while trying his best to shield it from the dripping water. His hands were numb with the cold and yet he dared not put them into his pockets even for a moment lest the settings should suddenly slide and the engine fail. A stalled motor was the last thing anyone wanted right now. Added to this, the cold water that was running off the cabin roof was dribbling down the collar of his jacket and inside his flannel shirt. His back was wet the whole length of his jacket and the cold wind seemed to seep right into his bones causing him to shiver uncontrollably at times.

"Isaac, I think you are going to have to give up your cozy spot in the cabin and get out here with me," Gilbert said over the roar of the wind and the engine. "We are taking on water and it is sloshing around pretty good in the bilge. I don't think it's serious yet but we can't take a chance. See what you can do about bailing some of that water out of there."

"There's a skinny tin bucket under your seat young man," said Wilf. "It fits nicely between the floorboards and the motor. It's perfect for bailing bilge water. No point trying to use the hand pump in this weather, you'd be tossed in the drink in seconds the moment you stand up."

The ride across the gap was what many would consider a nightmare. The wave height increased midpoint at the Ginn Islands to about seven feet and every other wave crashed, over the roof of the boat's small cabin. Only Wilf, sitting at the helm stayed dry. By the time they had reached Pinery Point and took a westerly heading towards Penetanguishene harbour Isaac and Gilbert were thoroughly soaked.

As they made their way down Penetanguishene harbour the storm unleashed itself with all its fury. Sprays of water blew off the crests of the white caps in the harbour and the snow fall had increased to the point that visibility was near zero. The only good thing was that they were no longer taking on water over the deck and it was no longer dribbling off the cabin roof onto Gilbert.

"Just less than an hour or so and we'll be home," thought Gilbert knowing that Maude would be worried sick at this point. "I can't wait to let her know we are OK."

As if reading his mind Isaac said. "It was nice to be away but it'll be great to be home won't it Gil?"

"I can't wait to get a nice hot cup of coffee in me and start warming myself up from the inside out."

"Dry clothes are going to go a long way too my friend. I hope Maude has some woollen socks we can put on."

"I think I'm gonna put mine in the oven first," said Gilbert. "That should work wonders on my toes. Right now they are so cold I can barely feel them."

They tied the boat to the main dock at the harbour and covered the supplies in the boat with a large tarp. "No point in trying to take any of this stuff home in this storm," said Gilbert brushing off snowflakes that had started to gather on his shoulders. "If it's OK with you Wilf, I'll just leave things here and come back to the boat when the weather clears."

"Fine with me," said Wilf as he stuffed tobacco into his pipe. "I'm not going anywhere in this weather except to the taxi stand up the street."

"You are welcome to stay with us if you need to," said Gilbert. "We have plenty of room."

"Nah," Wilf grunted. "I'll be fine, my daughter should be home."

And with that the three men started off up the main street each consumed by thoughts of getting home, and getting warm.

*****

"I'm so glad we were able to track you down and that you were able to come up to Cognashene with me," said Gilbert. He and Isaac and Maude were sitting at the kitchen table in town. "There is no way I would have been able to do what had to be done without help. Having you there made a world of difference."

"I was glad to be there to give you a hand," said Isaac. "I learned a lot, saw a lot and we worked our butts off but it felt good to get it all done. It's great to have those block and tackle pulleys for hauling out the big, heavy boats into the boathouses. They work really well for that." He looked at Maude. "A couple of times I thought we were going to pull the back wall off the boathouse hauling some of those old waterlogged boats out of the lake but it all worked out in the end."

Gilbert said, "I'm just glad you knew how to work them. It was a lot faster and it made our lives a lot easier to do the work knowing you know how to work them. I think we actually saved some time too because I didn't have to take time to show you how to work them."

"I used them a lot out in the bush," said Isaac as he slurped noisily on a steaming hot cup of coffee Maude had just put down in front of him." There were a lot of stubborn old logs that would still be out there if we didn't figure out how to shackle them with chains and use the come-along tied to another tree to get them moving."

Their conversation went on for hours with each of them taking turns relating stories of what they had done, how they had done it and what they would do differently next year. To Maude it was a great way to find out what Gilbert and Isaac had been up to for the last couple of weeks. She envied them a bit for having had an extra couple of weeks up the shore but then she would think about how nice and warm and comfortable she was at home and how much easier it was to look after the twins at home. She was glad she had been in town instead. Every now and then Maude would chime in and add to the conversation something interesting that had happened with the twins or in town while the guys were away. Gilbert was always attentive to what she was saying as he was truly interested in how her time alone without him had been and, though he had been busy, he really had missed the twins and was eager to find out how they were.

"Your mom dropped by every day and most days she stayed for supper," said Maude. "She was such a big help with getting the kids ready for bed." Gilbert smiled as he thought of his mom helping out, knowing she would have been right in her glory.

"She just loves giving them their bath after supper. It gives her alone time with each one of them and I'm sure she gets as much out of it as they do," Maude sipped at the tea she had just poured for herself from the pot. "There always seems to be a lot of cooing and humming in the bathroom while she's at it," Maude added.

"Once the twins are older they'll be able to help you with that work," said Maude. "We can take them out of school for a week or so. I'll go too and Ben can help you with the outdoor stuff and Emma can help me with what needs to be done inside with the beds and the linens and all that sort of thing."

"Sounds like a great idea but Ben had better eat his porridge daily so he is strong enough to do some of that work," said Isaac. "Some of it's hard going."

"Well we have plenty of time to sort that out. Right now, I think all I want to do is have a nice hot bath then to cozy up to my lovely wife in bed," said Gilbert looking at Maude. "It's so good to be home."

"It's so good to have you back home," said Maude. "You know, I'm not prone to worry but let me tell you, I was starting to get pretty concerned when I saw that storm front moving in this afternoon," she paused. "I'm just so glad you're here," she said wrapping her arms around Gilbert and squeezing him in a hug so tight he thought his head was going to pop off.

As friends Gilbert and Isaac were very compatible often anticipating what the other was going to say or ask. As workers, neither of them shied away from a hard day of labour and many times the day's work got done more quickly than Gilbert had thought it would because they worked so well together as a team.

As closing up cottages and winterizing boats and water lines and emptying holding tanks was something that was new for Gilbert, it was great for him to have someone to bounce ideas off of about the best way to do things. Isaac having been raised at Granite Bluff, was no stranger to the water, hauling out docks and boats, the back woods, the isolation. All this real life experience made Gilbert feel more comfortable doing what needed to be done and asking Isaac for his help and his opinion.

"Working together was like it was a match made in heaven," Gilbert told Maude later in a quiet moment. "It's like our friendship was meant to be. I've always been somewhat of a loner, all my life; I never really had any close friends other than Eli until I met you." Gilbert paused. "But with Isaac, well it's just nice to have someone around that I am so comfortable with. I feel like I've known him all my life." He paused then added, "and I think Isaac feels the same way too."

For Gilbert, working closely with Isaac brought back many memories of his brother Eli. Gilbert figured they would have been about the same age and Gilbert often wondered what life would have been like if Eli had not died in the war. Would they still be as close as they had been? Would Eli be the one helping Gilbert to winterize the cottages in Cognashene. Maybe Eli would have moved away in search of some great adventure and Gilbert would have lost track of him? Gilbert knew he could daydream about the possibilities for hours but in the end, it was all just a dream, a guess at best, and he began to believe that he and Isaac had become friends as a way to fill a gap that existed in both of them.

*****

The following morning everyone in the house was up early. The sky had cleared to a deep azure blue, the sun shone brightly and although a couple of inches of snow had fallen overnight the temperature was warming up nicely.

"This snow isn't going to last long," said Isaac as he looked out the kitchen window. "You can see where it is already starting to melt on the street and the sidewalk.

"I guess the first thing we should do is grab the cart and make our way down to the dock to gather our things. That way if Wilf wants to head out early he doesn't have to wait for us to get there."

"I don't think Mr. France knows what 'head out early' means," said Maude smiling. "He is one man who never seems to be in a hurry as far as I can see."

"Well, he is the kind of guy who prefers to have people wait for him instead of waiting for them," said Gilbert. "But he has been kind enough to get us back and forth all season so we should respect that and make sure we don't hold him up....just in case he heads out early."

Isaac and Gilbert grabbed their coats and headed out to the shop at the back of the house to grab the cart they needed. This cart was a homemade affair Gilbert had built a long time ago with four used heavy-duty wheelbarrow wheels on a four-foot-long by three foot wide 2x4 frame. The sides of the cart looked more like fence rails but they were detachable all the way around so that if something longer than four feet or wider than three feet needed to be carted the sides could easily be removed to accommodate the load. Since they didn't have a car for carting supplies, over the years many miles had been put on the cart by both Maude and Gilbert and even on occasion by Madelaine. Every now and then the odd little repair was required but overall it was sturdy and stable and with its long handle was a very useful item to possess.

Once at the dock they moved the tarp and loaded the supplies they had brought from the cottage onto the cart. They folded the tarp and tucked it up under the deck and headed off home towing the cart behind them.

"I'm going to have to do something special for Mr. France next summer," said Gilbert to Isaac. "He has been so good to Maude and me. I really need to repay him in some way."

"If I'm still around next summer, maybe you and I could go over to Franceville and see if there is some work on one of the hotels or other building that we could help him with. I'm sure he'd appreciate that since it looks like a big place to keep up. I'm not sure how many hotel buildings there are at that resort but surely there must be something we can do for him," said Isaac.

"You're right about it being a big place. And, it's been a very busy place too over the years. There is the Franceville House and the Osborne House. The Osborne house is bigger and the more elaborate of the two. It is four stories high and some people say that it reminds them of a wedding cake with that crow's nest that's been built on the top. The second floor has a wrap around balcony. In the Osborne House the dining room sits forty-eight people and if there is an overflow of guests they set up additional space at the family table near the kitchen. For outbuildings there are the horse stables, an ice-house, a planing mill, a chicken house, a cooperage, a machine shop, a smoke house, a root cellar, a family cottage, a windmill, a marine railway and a water tower as well as a post office for the locals."

"It sure is a big business," said Isaac. "Correct me if I'm wrong Gil. We were only there briefly but I think I remember seeing a tennis court there as well."

"You saw correctly," said Gilbert. "The tourists love having that tennis court there. It has a wooden floor which is pretty unique."

Gilbert looked pensive for a moment then said, "I like your idea Isaac. I don't have much money to be buying Wilf anything but I have a strong back and I'm pretty handy so maybe I can repay him with labour."

"Count me in if I'm around. I'd love to get to see more of the area and spend a bit of time at Franceville and that might just be the best way to do it."

"Who knows pal, you might even meet the love of your life while you are there," said Gilbert as he playfully slapped Isaac on the back.

CHAPTER - 8

November 1927

Christmas was just around the corner and one evening after everyone else had gone to bed Gilbert was sitting quietly in the living room deep in thought, but mindful of the wind blowing through the trees in the front yard. Occasionally a strong gust of wind would come up and a low hanging branch would scrape against the window. *I really need to get out there tomorrow and cut that branch down before it does some damage to the window,* he said to himself. It was one more thing to add to his list of things to do but he had to admit, his list had gotten quite short lately. At the beginning of summer his list seemed unachievable, insurmountable, overwhelming in fact and yet somehow he had worked through it, motivated by thoughts of getting things done before heading to Cognashene for the summer. Now that winter had arrived and the pace of life had slowed down, his remaining list of things to do seemed quite attainable.

In his reverie Gilbert's mind started to wander and he began to think about the past year. It had been quite a year, so many things had happened. *There have probably been more changes in my life this year than in all my years put together so far,* he thought. In his dreams he never pictured that his life would have turned out this way but there was one thing that he was certain of, his blessings far outweighed his regrets. He thought about the sequence of events that had changed his life. He and Maude had moved into their home, the twins were born, he had left his full time job at the hardware store to become Dr. Johnson's handyman, he had completed a large restoration to the veranda at the doctor's house in town, he had restored the stone cottage and turned it into a cozy cabin for his small family and he had begun work on the extensive renovations to the Johnson's large main cottage. All in all, it had been a pretty full year. Once back in town for the winter he picked up where he had left off at the hardware store happy to see that the usual customers were glad to see Mr. Fix-it was back.

I wonder what next year will bring? he thought to himself.

*****

Winter came early that year. The fury of the storms at the end of October being only a taste of what Mother Nature had in store for them. By the time Christmas came around there was several feet of snow covering the ground, the snow-plow drivers and crew were working overtime. Everyone had four foot snow banks at the end of their driveway and already the sidewalks and pathways seemed to be narrower because of the height of the snow banks. And if it wasn't bad enough to have a harsh winter it stayed late into the spring as well. Just when people thought there couldn't possibly be any more snow to come, another storm front would come through and dump a fresh load.

Every time a fresh snowfall arrived Madelaine would say, "Well, this is just the snow coming to get the snow that's left." By the time the snow had finally melted at the end of April everyone was ready to shake off their winter melancholy and welcome spring like the arrival of a new baby.

Once all the cottages up the lakes had been closed up for the winter and trips to Cognashene were finished for the year, Isaac decided to take up the offer and live with Gilbert and Maude for the winter and that arrangement had worked out well for everyone. One blustery day in November while he was stashing more hardwood into the wood stove in the shop at the back of the house he thought, *there has to be a way to keep the shop warmer than this.* As he stoked the flames with the poker he had an ah-ha moment. He emptied the cart of its supply of fire wood, put on his winter jacket and made his way down the street to the lumber mill on the next block.

"Any chance I might be able to take some of those off-cut boards off your hands?" he asked the foreman. Having worked in the lumber yard in Mactier he was pretty sure there would be lots of boards the mill would have on hand that were not good enough to sell to the lumber yards and were practically of no use to anyone due to their odd sizes, lengths and irregular thickness.

"Be my guest," the foreman said. "Take as much as you want. I'll just be glad to get them out of the way. I'm getting tired of moving them from one spot in the mill to another."

Isaac loaded as many of the boards as he could manage onto the cart, then made his way back to the house. When he got to the back yard he sorted them into piles by length and width near the door of the shop. Almost all of them were about an inch thick and for the most part the off-cut boards were a variety of lengths that averaged about six to eight feet long and about eight or nine inches wide. Some still had bark on them, others had had the bark stripped off in the milling process but that didn't really matter for what Isaac had planned.

Two days and many trips later Isaac had enough wood to begin his venture. He hadn't told Gilbert what his plan was, but he did tell him he was working on a project that he wanted to be a surprise. He asked him to stay out of the shop and hoped Gilbert wouldn't sneak in after hours to check things out. Isaac thought of it as sort of his early Christmas gift to his best friend.

Gilbert wondered what Isaac was up to with all that lumber he had seen stacked in the back yard. That part wasn't a secret Isaac could keep for long because the piles were clearly visible outside the dining room window. But, good natured as he was, Gilbert had been asked by Isaac to stay out of the shop for a week and though it was difficult he complied, feigning grudgingly. This was, after all, his shop. But, he trusted Isaac had something up his sleeve and he was willing to let him go with it.

There were two outside walls to the workshop and two walls that were shared with the main part of the house. It was the outside walls that Isaac focused his attention on. Cutting the boards he acquired from the mill to the lengths that he needed, he began by nailing the boards like ship-lap siding to the inside walls, starting at the floor and working his way up. The rough cut two by four studs that formed the outside walls, which if measured, were more like three by five were exposed on the inside of the shop and it was to these studs that Isaac attached the boards. Those boards with bark still on them were stripped of their bark where they met the studs so that they would be flat and level. It didn't matter if there was bark on the rest of the board, it would be hidden between the walls. The surface of the boards that faced into the shop was a smooth milled facade that gave a finished look to them. Once Isaac got the boards to a height of five feet he took the wheelbarrow and a shovel and went back to the mill. Once he got there he wandered over to a twelve foot high pile of sawdust.

"Mind if I take some of that sawdust off your hands," he said to the foreman.

"Go ahead, help yourself, the more you take the less I have to pay to ship out to the dump. How much do you need?"

"Lots," said Isaac, "I'll be back and forth all day, maybe all week, if that's OK with you?" he asked.

"Knock yourself out," said the foreman. He walked away scratching his head and wondering just what this stranger was up to.

With his wheelbarrow full of sawdust Isaac made his way back into the shop and shovelled the sawdust into the space between the studs, the outside walls and the newly installed off-cut siding he had attached. When he got to the point where the spaces were full of sawdust, Isaac nailed another couple of feet high of siding to the studs then went back to the mill for more sawdust. It was a slow process but one that kept Isaac busy for a whole week. He was glad Gilbert and Maude didn't live any further from the mill than they did. By the end of the week all the siding had been installed, the spaces filled with sawdust and Isaac's homemade insulation had been completely installed.

*****

"When am I ever going to be able to get into my shop," Gilbert asked one evening at supper? It had been just over a week since Isaac had asked him not to go in there. The curiosity about what his friend had been up too for a whole week was killing him.

"God created the whole world in seven days Isaac; I can't imagine what you've been up to in there all this time."

"Well monsieur, your world is about to change. I think you can go in any time you'd like," Isaac said with a beaming smile on his face.

"Right after supper is done then, I'm going in, I have to get started on my winter orders for canoes," Gilbert said. "I can't put them off any longer or I'll get behind."

Knowing how anxious he was to get into the shop, Maude thought she'd have a bit of fun at Gilbert's expense. She was fully aware of what Isaac had been up to and very supportive of the project. She was over the moon excited about what Gilbert was going to think about what Isaac had done.

"Well," Maude paused to clear her throat. "I am really tired for some reason today," she said stifling a fake yawn. "Before you go into the shop Gil, I'd like a hand to clear up these supper dishes. And after that is done, I told the twins that you'd give them their bath before bed tonight."

Gilbert let out a sigh and his shoulders slumped. He knew Maude had had a busy day and could use the help but he just wanted to get out into his shop see what it was that Isaac had been up to then get himself organized to begin his work.

"OK, I'll do that but right after I am finished bathing the twins I'm going in," he said faking a pout with his lips. He resigned himself to the fact that checking out the shop was going to be delayed yet again.

"I'm just teasing," said Maude laughing. She stood up and pulled on the back of Gilbert's chair, "Go, git, vamoose, get outta here!"

Gilbert and Isaac stood at the same time and pushed their chairs away from the table. They grabbed their plates and mugs and brought them to the kitchen sink, turned on their heels and headed for the shop. Isaac was as anxious for Gilbert to see what he had done as Gilbert was to see it.

Before supper and before Gilbert had come home from his work at the hardware store, Isaac had lit a fire in the wood stove, tidied up the shop, aligned all the tools on the nails he had put on the walls to hang them from then turned off the light in the shop.

Isaac raced ahead of Gil and stood with his back against the shop door, his arms outstretched on the walls barring Gilbert's entrance to the shop. "OK, here goes, hope you like it," Isaac exclaimed as he slowly opened the door and reached inside to flip on the light switch.

"Ta-da," Isaac said with a flourish waving his hands in the air.

Shock and awe is the only way to describe Gilbert's reaction. He wasn't sure just what to say. "I can't believe you did all this in a week Isaac!" He stood in the centre of the shop and looked around, slowly turning checking out each wall, and admiring the fine workmanship he saw before him. "I can't believe you put siding up inside the shop. This has totally transformed the look and function of this shop. That's going to make it so much warmer in here this winter and will keep it cooler in the summer months as well."

"You bet it's going to be warmer. But, I didn't just put siding up, I also filled between the studs with sawdust. You have about 5 inches thick of insulation between those walls."

"I just can't believe it," Gilbert repeated. "This is great." He felt a bit emotional about the work that had been done and a lump rose in his throat. No one had ever done anything for him or surprised him in this way before. He had always been the handyman doing things for other people. He never expected that Isaac would do this for him. It was something that he had thought of doing when he purchased the house but he didn't expect to get to it for several years, when he could afford to do it.

"This must have cost you a fortune," he said to Isaac.

"Not a red cent my friend." Isaac explained what he had done. "The siding I used is off-cuts from the lumber mill down the street. The foreman was happy to get it out of his way. The only cost for the sawdust was a few bandages I had to get from Maude for the blisters I got on my hands carting that bloody wheelbarrow back and forth from the mill a hundred times."

"I just can't believe it!" Gilbert exclaimed as he turned slowly to gaze around the room. "You truly are a great friend. Thank you so much."

"I lit a fire in here about two hours ago and look at how warm it is still." Isaac smiled, pride at his accomplishments bursting from his every pore.

"I sure am going to save a lot on firewood this winter," said Gilbert.

"So," said Isaac rubbing his hands together anxious to get started. "Just what work do you have planned for tonight sir?"

"Well, I was going to get my mould for the 14 foot canoe up on sawhorses and start making some ribbing for it."

"OK, I can help you with that," Isaac said enthusiastically.

"Isaac, I think you can take tonight off. You've more than earned your keep for this week." Gilbert moved over to where Isaac was standing, embraced him with a gentle hug and said, "Thanks once again."

Isaac turned to leave the shop. Though he was thrilled with Gilbert's reaction to what he had done, he did feel a little dejected because he wanted to spend time in the new shop as well. His shoulders slumped slightly and as he was about to reach for the door knob he heard Gilbert's voice.

Gilbert had seen the hurt look in Isaac's face when he told him he didn't need his help and noticed the slow pace to his steps as he moved towards the door, "Before you go, can you give me a hand with lifting this mould up onto the sawhorses? It's heavier than I remember it being." Always eager to help, Isaac turned and said, "Anything you say boss."

"I think I *am* going to need your help in here tonight after all," Gilbert said, "I may not be able to find all the tools I'm going to need and you certainly know where they are." Isaac turned and smiled.

The two men stooped to pick up the canoe mould and got busy securing it on the sawhorses so that it wouldn't collapse. Their first night in the new shop had begun.

*****

Isaac had never done any boat building before. He had been a labourer all his working life, first in the forests up north as a lumberjack then as a yard man in the lumber yard in Mactier. The type of work he was used to was hard and back breaking but from it he developed a good work ethic. In the past, he had had the opportunity to fix some small boats at Granite Bluff Inlet and at the lumber camps, replacing the caulking between the lap-strake boards of a hull and ship-lap planking but he had never done anything challenging like replacing a transom in a rowboat or shaping the ribbing for a canoe hull. His calloused hands were no strangers to hard work and he was eager to learn all that he could. All of this type work in the shop was very new to him and he was happy to be doing work that, while tedious and time consuming, resulted in a finished product that was of some value. The precision work needed to build a canoe was not something that he was familiar with and it took him a while to get used to the idea that he was making something from scratch where there was a sequence to the steps that needed to be taken.

"You can't rush it when you are building something like this. You have to take your time to shape and gently bend this ribbing," Gilbert said demonstrating how to take the slender pieces of wood and shape them to the mould. "If you try to rush this, the wood will snap like a twig and you will have to start over from scratch which will end up taking more time in the long run."

Luckily Gilbert had a lot of experience at the Boatworks, and had taught quite a few guys how to mould and bend the inner ribbing of boats so it was nothing new for him to teach Isaac in his own shop. Isaac as it turned out was an eager and enthusiastic student.

*****

As the winter wore on, several new canoes had been completed but there were still more orders to fill. Gilbert's reputation as a boat builder was widespread in town so he also had a slew of older canoes stacked in the yard that needed to have the seats repaired or the gunwales replaced. Gilbert was happy to have Isaac's help because he had never had such a demand for his canoes and his repair work seemed to be taking over all his free time.

He was thrilled that some of the orders were from people from out of town who had cottages up in Cognashene, people who had heard about Gilbert's talents as a craftsman. "What a great market to get into," he said to Isaac. "At this rate I could have work for a couple of years by the looks of it."

"Have you ever thought of building something other than canoes?" Isaac asked.

"Not really. I have a great mould for a very stable and seaworthy canoe and the people who try them really like them so I have just stuck with it," Gilbert replied.

"What about row boats?"

"What about them?"

"Have you ever thought about building any rowboats? A lot of them are made pointed at the bow and the stern, very similar to a canoe, they are just wider and with a higher free board out of the water," Isaac said.

"I know the style you mean but I just never thought about making them. Besides, I don't have a mould for that and if you are going to make a lot of them the same style, you definitely need a mould. Once you make the mould and make your first rowboat from it you have to water test it to see if it is stable, that it has the right centre of gravity, that the seats are the right height and in the right position in the boat. I can go on and on about it. I just don't think that I have the time to start on a new project like that right now. Maybe if the market for canoes slows down I can consider it but right now I'm just too busy."

"The shop is big enough," said Isaac glancing around the room. "Do you mind if I try to make a mould for a rowboat in my spare time?"

"Looks like you have been thinking about this for a while. Tell me what you were thinking."

Isaac thought about it for a few moments then said, "well I think I would make them about 12 or 14 feet long. I'd for sure put the ribbing in them the way you do with the canoes. I think I'd like to use cedar cut into strips and apply them to the ribbing in a lap-strake pattern." Isaac thought for a moment then added, "and I'll put floor boards in them over top of the ribbing to give it extra strength. I'll add a foot rest so the person rowing can use that for balance and it will give them thrust with the oars."

"Sounds good," said Gilbert. "What about the hardware, things like cleats, the oarlocks and even the oars for that matter. Any ideas about where to round those up?" Gilbert asked. After a brief pause in his thinking he added, "With a canoe, you just make the canoe and sell it. The buyer is responsible for getting their own paddles."

"There is a guy I know in Mactier who makes oars and paddles, maybe I could buy them from him and sell them with the rowboat as a package deal."

"That's an option for sure but you know, you are getting to be pretty handy here in the shop. What about making your own oars?" Gilbert asked. "It might take you a little bit to get into making them but that way you can cut out the middle man, you don't have to buy oars and then sell them."

"I hadn't thought about that but I guess if I could get the right kind of wood, probably maple or maybe mountain ash right down the street at the mill I could try my hand at it."

"Well you are welcome to use the lathe that I have here in the shop, that will help with rounding them, and I just bought a new draw knife with sturdy handles for heavy work on hardwood so that will help too."

Isaac nodded then said, "What a unique idea to help sell the rowboats to be able to say the oars are 'hand crafted' by the boat builder himself."

Gilbert was quiet for a few moments as he gently tapped some finishing nails into the gunwale of the canoe he was working on then said, "Let me think about it Isaac. I won't say no right away. I have orders for four more canoes for this spring so that has to be the priority for us, but maybe you are on to something."

"I can't ask for any more than that," said Isaac. "We will complete the canoe orders and in my spare time I'll do my research and see if I can figure out how much material it will take and what it will cost to build a rowboat from scratch. That way I'll know if it will be worth getting into this or not."

"I take the profit from the sale of the canoes that you and I build. I know that you work on them too but that was the agreement we made, free labour for free room and board. If you get into building rowboats that will be your project. I'll give you a hand whenever I can and I'll certainly help you to get you started with making your mould but I don't think I'll have a lot of time to help you with the rowboats on an ongoing basis. So, I guess what I'm saying is you can keep all the profits you make for yourself."

"It's a deal," said Isaac as he applied a thin coat of varnish to the seats of a canoe he had been working on. His hands were busy with the work of the canoe but his mind was now miles ahead of himself thinking of all the tasks he'd have to sort out to start his own rowboat building company.

CHAPTER - 9

June 1936

Cut as a slice of wood from a fallen oak tree the seats of the two wooden stools were roughly twelve inches in diameter and four inches thick. Most trees aren't perfectly round, so the outside edges of the stools were irregularly shaped, one stool being more oblong than round the other though closer to being round had three inches of a branch that had not been cut off protruding from one side where the log was cut. Four round oak legs, exactly one inch thick had been meticulously whittled for each stool and they were straight as a poker. They had been fitted into holes drilled into the bottom of the wooden seat on just the right angle to give broad support to the stool without sticking too far beyond the edge of the seat but still affording the stool the proper balance. Two one inch laths mortised into an X pattern were affixed to the legs ten inches from the floor to make sure the legs remained stable when someone sat on the stool.

The backrests of the stools were a simple H pattern rising twelve inches from the seat and were made from one inch square oak. A top piece that extended two inches beyond each side of the top of the H was also made from the same square oak. Multiple coats of varnish with a careful sanding between each coat had ensured that the finish on the stools gleamed as though they had been highly polished. They looked more like a work of art than a functional piece of furniture but in reality they were incredibly sturdy and could bear the weight of an adult with no problem.

Gilbert was very proud of the stools that he had made and couldn't wait for the children to get home. Today was their last day of school and he wanted to present them to the twins as a gift for finishing grade 4 at their primary school.

"I love it daddy," cried Emma when she saw the stool for the first time. "It's so shiny I can see my face in it. It's like a mirror."

"This is a great gift dad. Thanks" said Ben. "They are the perfect height for Emma and I to sit on too. look, our feet can touch the ground when we sit. You figured it just right."

"Your dad worked long and hard on these stools," said Maude. "They are going to be a keepsake for sure. Make sure you take good care of them."

"Can we bring them up to the stone cottage with us for the summer?" asked Emma. "I think they will be the perfect height to fit at the table in the kitchen and they won't take up as much room as the other chairs"

"Sure, we can bring them up with us," said Gilbert. "They are pretty rustic looking. I'm sure they will suit the décor up there just fine," said Gilbert laughing as he thought of all the mismatched furniture that was at the stone cottage.

"Tomorrow is the big day guys," said Maude. "School is over and I have just about everything packed that we are going to need up at the cottage for the summer. Tomorrow we'll be on our way." With that the kids got so excited they started to jump up and down and sing, "We're going to the cottage, we're going to the cottage."

"OK kids, settle down, it's not like you haven't been there before. I am going to start getting supper ready," said Maude, "and while I'm doing that I want you two to go to your rooms and sort through what you want to bring up to the cottage."

"I can't wait to get up there," said Ben.

"Me too," said Emma. "It seems like it's been forever since we've been to the cottage." The children were so happy to be finished school. Going to the cottage for the summer was going to be a real treat. They had been talking about going for weeks on end and this last week in school had been pretty hard to bear. It seemed like the last week of school would never come to an end and now, getting there was so close they could hardly contain themselves.

The twin's conversations about going to the cottage and being at the cottage went on for the rest of the afternoon, each of them sharing memories of things they'd seen and done in previous years. While Maude busied herself in the kitchen with supper preparations Emma and Ben spent the rest of the afternoon going up and down the stairs from the dining room to their bedrooms taking down all the little things they thought they wouldn't be able to live without for the summer. Each stacked their precious valuables in neat piles on the dining room table ready to be packed once the boxes were brought in from the shed.

*****

With his arms loaded with empty heavy-duty cardboard boxes, Gilbert made his way into the dining room just before supper was to be served up in the kitchen. "Whoa, hang on there," he said a little gruffly when he saw the pile of toys and books and stuffed animals the kids had brought down from their rooms. "What's all this?"

"Mom said we could bring what we want up to the cottage so that we have things to keep us busy up there during the summer," said Emma.

"I didn't mean that you could bring everything you have in your bedrooms," said Maude as she came into the dining room and saw for the first time what had been keeping them busy all afternoon.

"I think you are forgetting that we have to cart all of this down to the boat, load it into the boat and then when we get to the cottage find a place to put it all," said Gilbert. The children stared blankly at their father, a somewhat hurt look on their faces.

"I understand why you want to take all this with you but we just don't have room for it all," said their father. Then, in a kinder tone, he said, "So," he paused, "while we are having supper you have to think about what you really, really want to pack. We have enough space under the bed for each of you to have one box with your things in it, so after supper, I want you to go through the piles you made here in the dining room and make sure that it will all fit in the box. Remember, you each get only one box."

"Even your dad and I are making sure everything we want up there will fit into one box," said Maude. "And that includes our clothes."

Emma looked a bit teary at the thought of not being able to bring all the dolls, and stuffed animals she had selected. "Don't worry Em," said Ben, "we are going to be so busy swimming and fishing and diving for shiny clam shells we won't have time to play with most of this stuff anyway."

Maude and Gilbert looked at each other and smiled at the effort Ben was making to help his sister feel better. "Oh, and don't forget we have a lot of blueberries to pick," said Emma as she started to think about other ways to keep busy at the cottage.

"Once we pick the blueberries we can give them to mom to put in our pancakes in the morning," said Ben.

"Oh Ben, you are always thinking about eating," said Emma.

"Well, as mom says, I'm just a growing boy, and I'm usually always hungry," he replied as he rubbed his belly. "Hey mom," he called to his mother who had once again returned to the kitchen, "is supper ready yet? I'm starving."

*****

The boat was so loaded down with supplies both Maude and Gilbert were glad that it was a calm day for crossing the gap. The amount of free-board had become greatly reduced with the load they had packed on board. It was not at a dangerous level but still, a rough chop in the gap could mean some water might have to be bailed out of the boat during the ride. Luckily most of the food provisions such as flour, canned goods and some root vegetables such as a 50 pound bag of potatoes and a hamper of carrots had been brought up in an earlier trip several weeks before. Almost a month ago Gilbert and Isaac had gone up to the cottage to prepare it for the summer and to start opening the cottages they had closed for the winter in the late fall. Still, the load with the remaining supplies, the perishables, the stools, the children, the linen, and the tools that Gilbert needed for his ongoing renovations to the main cottage weighed heavily in the boat.

"At least we have a reliable motor in this boat," Maude said as she looked at the engine box in the centre of the boat. "I never liked the way the motor in Mr. France's boat ran. It just wasn't reliable and the smell of the gasoline, ugh. It used to make me feel sick. I'm so glad that we have our own boat now and don't have to rely on Mr. France to get us back and forth."

"I have to say, I don't miss nursing that motor to life. Continually tweaking the carburettor on some of those perilous trips across the gap was pretty stressful at times," admitted Gilbert. "I'm still grateful to him for all the trips we made with him over the years but you're right, it is good to have our own boat. We can come and go as we need to without feeling like we are imposing on his good nature or taking him away from his business at Franceville."

The boat that Gilbert had purchased was not new by any stretch of the imagination. It had belonged to an older fellow from town who just could no longer handle looking after hauling it out of the water in the fall and launching it in the spring. Not to mention the ongoing repair work it needed each year to keep it afloat. The boat was twenty six feet long, with a lap-strake hull. It had a small four person cabin with two wooden bench seats and was powered by an old Ford inboard motor. When Gilbert first saw the boat it looked like it was in good shape but on closer inspection he saw there was some serious dry rot issues in the transom as well as in a few of the boards in the lower part of the hull just below the water line. Gilbert saw the potential the boat had. It was the right size for crossing the gap and there was plenty of storage space. He was not overwhelmed by the work he knew needed to be done to get the craft sea worthy and he was confident he could make it work for his family. He offered to purchase the boat for $75 and the old fellow jumped at the chance to sell the boat. The deal was struck and Gilbert was the proud owner of a fixer-upper.

"I should be able to get myself a nice little fishing boat with this money," the old fella said to Gilbert. "Maybe a nice little rowboat or something that I can just knock around in Penetanguishene Bay with on the nice days"

"Well if you are looking for a rowboat and want to buy a new one, I know a guy who makes them. His name is Isaac. He has moved back up to Mactier for the summer but I see him every now and then. I'll let him know you are looking for something."

Gilbert quite liked the boat but the only problem was that it was too big to bring to his back yard to work on. Because of this he had to bring his tools and the lumber he needed to make his repairs to the marina where the boat had been hauled out of the water for the winter. Gilbert was well into the repairs when Maude walked over to the marina one day to bring Gilbert a sandwich for his lunch. It was then that she saw the boat for the first time and she nearly shrieked with horror at the sight of it.

"What were you thinking?" she asked as she stared at the transom and saw that the entire lower half of it was missing. She could literally see right into the inside of the boat.

'I hope you know what you're doing," was her other comment as she slowly walked around the boat and looked at the spot where Gilbert had removed the boards in the hull where there had been dry rot.

"Don't worry my love, I'll get it all rebuilt and it will be as good as new," Gilbert paused, "Well sort of."

"I hope so, because if you think I'm going to cross the gap in a boat that leaks like a sieve you can think again."

"It's just like the transoms I've replaced in all those rowboats and the other small runabouts but only on a larger scale," he explained. "The transom has a lot of stress on it. Typically there is a lot of vibration from the motor and so the transom is usually the weakest spot on a boat after it has been used for a long time." He smiled at her and said, "By the time I'm finished you won't even know there was ever a problem. I'm even going to reinforce the new transom to make sure it remains sturdy."

"I sure hope so," said Maude as she turned and walked back towards home.

"Hey Maude," Gilbert called to her. "We need to come up with a name for the boat. I think I'll put you in charge of that." Maude didn't respond verbally but he could tell her mind had already started churning away.

"Thanks for the sandwich," he called out to her. Without turning around she raised a hand to wave to him acknowledging that she'd heard him thank her.

As he got back to work on the boat he was grateful that he had so many years of boat building experience under his belt from the Boatworks. He wasn't worried about what needed to be done. He knew his confidence in his ability to fix the boat was a great comfort to Maude even if she didn't seem to show it at this particular time.

*****

"The bigger the load the slower we go," said Gilbert as he pushed on the accelerator once he had pulled away from the docks. "You might as well make yourself comfortable everybody because this looks like this is as much speed as we are going to be able to draw out of this old tug today."

Maude looked around the boat to find a bag she knew she had packed a few pillows in for the cottage. Once she found it stashed under the deck she pulled it out and fluffed it up. She sat on it with a smile and as she settled onto the softer seat and leaned back on the backrest she said, "That's much better." looking at the scenery out the window of the small cabin she said, "I'm good for the rest of the trip now, doesn't matter how long it takes."

Gilbert turned and looked at her and smiled, content that he was heading up to the cottage for the summer with the love of his life and his two great kids. "Thank God the kids like being up there as much as they do. It sure makes our life a lot easier," he said to Maude. She turned and looked at the stern of the boat and saw that each of the twins had made themselves comfortable on the covered wooden tool boxes that were stacked along the transom. Each of them were looking over the edge of the boat to see how big a wave and a rooster tail the boat was throwing with this heavy load. The wake was big but the rooster tail was pretty much nonexistent. "They love it up there as much as we do. I think we are going to be in for a good summer."

The trip up to the cottage took well over an hour and a half, closer to two hours in fact. The old Ford engine purred smoothly along but the boat was heavy and the load they were carrying only added to the overall weight the engine had to push along.

The gap was calm, the sky was blue, seagulls and ducks flew in low lazy circles around the boat as they motored along as if to say "come this way." Everyone on board had settled in for the ride and the peaceful calmness of the trip gave Gilbert time to reflect on how perfect his life had become. He was a man who was truly happy right down to the very fibre of his being.

It was late afternoon when they pulled up to the dock at the stone cottage and secured the ropes tight to make unloading easier and reduce the chance of something getting dropped into the water between the boat and the dock.

"Come on Emma," Ben called as he ran up the dock. "Let's go explore and see if anything is different from when we were here last year."

"I think I want to go for a swim first," replied Emma. "Can I mom?"

Maude replied, "There will be plenty of time for you guys to go exploring, and swimming and all of that fun stuff later. First we could really use your help with taking this entire load up to the cottage. You are nine years old now and you're big enough and strong enough to help. Once we are all unpacked and settled then you can have a swim before supper if you'd like but I can't take time to sit and watch you right now."

Getting unpacked and settled was actually quite a process that over the years Maude and Gilbert had worked into a routine that worked well for them. Once everything had been brought up to the cottage from the boat, Gilbert and Ben filled the kerosene lamps and trimmed the wicks. Maude had taken out a couple of her soft flannel rags and with Emma's help they polished the lamps' glass chimneys.

"This one is really pretty mom," said Emma as she looked at the lace-like pattern that had been etched into the glass.

"Yes it is pretty isn't it? This chimney fits on the lamp with the square bottom and it goes on that special bracket on the wall. See how there is a mirror on the bracket behind where the lamp sits. That reflects the light and makes the lamp twice as bright," said Maude. She carried the delicate glass chimney over to the lamp and pressed it into place between the upright brackets. "This is a very special lamp for me. My parents gave me this as a present many years ago and I have taken very good care of it. Hopefully nothing ever happens to it."

"Why do we always have to do the lamps first?" Emma asked.

"Well, in case something comes up, or we are interrupted and we don't get everything done before the sun goes down, then at least we can light the lamps and keep working at getting settled in and unpacked even after its dark."

"Ahh," sighed Emma. She understood what her mom meant but she still thought that there would have been time for a swim before all this unpacking and 'settling in' stuff was done. She knew better than to say anything to her mom about it but still the child in her really would have preferred to be out playing in the water on such a hot and sunny day.

Next on the list was to make sure there was enough wood in the old tin wood box next to the stove in the kitchen. "Do you want to bring the wood in to fill the wood box or do you want to make the kindling?" Gilbert asked Ben.

"I think I'd like to try making the kindling this time," Ben answered. "Last year I was pretty clumsy using the hatchet to cut up the firewood into small pieces but I'm a lot older now and I think I can handle it." Ben took off running to the back of the cottage where the hatchet and axe were kept in the wood shed. Gilbert smiled as he walked around to the back of the cottage to the wood shed. He could see a lot of himself in Ben, the way he spoke, the confidence he demonstrated, the way he had become so tall and slim. *He's going to be a big help around here in the coming years*, Gilbert thought.

As Emma helped her mother pull the sheets onto the beds she said, "These bunks don't seem to be as high this year as they were last year. In fact everything seems shorter and smaller than last year."

"That's because you've grown so much since the last time you were here," Maude said. "And next year everything will seem even smaller again."

The unpacking and settling in continued on. Canned foods were put on the shelves, the boxes of personal belongings were stowed away under the beds, water was fetched from the end of the dock to fill the reservoir on the stove, a bucket of water was placed on a small table under the kitchen window next to a wash basin to make clean up easier. Before long just about everything was done.

As luck would have it, Philippe Dagenais from up in the lake beyond the Narrows channel went by. When he saw Gilbert's boat at the dock he stopped to say hello and welcome everyone back for the season. The family hurried down to the end of the dock to greet their visitor, a friend they hadn't seen for almost a year.

Philippe tied his bow rope to the cleat on the dock then sat on the deck of his small runabout. He let his bare feet dangle in the water. "Ahh," he said, his French accent very prominent in everything he said. "The water is so refreshing. It's just perfect for cooling me down after this long hot day."

He didn't bother to tie the stern rope to the dock but just let it drift slowly away from the dock into the small bay. The little bit of current from the channel pulled on the boat and held it in almost a perfect position. Gilbert, Maude and the twins sat on the end of the dock dangling their feet over the edge and in that friendly "cottage way" settled in for a pleasant casual visit with their neighbour from up in the bay. The old wooden dock was high enough out of the water that Gilbert's feet were just barely skimming the surface without touching. Though still not even a teenager yet, Ben's feet dangled above the water not very much higher off the surface than his father's. Gilbert looked at his feet then at Ben's and once again thought of how tall his son was getting.

As the conversation passed Philippe got caught up on the news from town, and Gilbert and Maude got caught up on the news from around the bay. The adults chatted amicably about how their respective winters had gone and soon the twins started to get restless and made noise once again about going for a swim.

Just as Philippe was getting ready to leave, Gilbert asked him if he could deliver a large block of ice for the ice-box.

"Sure thing. When would you like it?" he asked.

Gilbert replied, "This evening if possible. We just brought up a big load of supplies and it will be great to have ice tonight."

"Happy to oblige. Its been great to see you guys again." Then added, "especially you Maude," as he winked at her. Philippe cheerfully waved goodbye as he sped off towards his house, the old outboard engine sputtering away spewing a thick cloud of grey smoke smelling of a bad oil/gas mixture as he accelerated.

Depending on how hot the days were, a block of ice stored in an insulated icebox usually lasted about four to five days. Things that needed to be kept really cold like milk or fresh meat where placed alongside the block of ice in the upper compartment, the rest was put in the "cool" compartment below. A drip tray at the bottom of the icebox collected the melt water and needed to be emptied almost daily during the hot summer months. Not all iceboxes were made the same, some had very good insulation and kept the ice frozen solid for a week while some had hardly any insulation at all and the ice melted almost as fast as if it were sitting on a rock outside. After years of doing this job Philippe had a pretty good idea about how long the block of ice would last in each family's icebox. He made his rounds delivering fresh ice to those who needed more and often it was timed so perfectly that the customers didn't even need to ask him for a new one.

Philippe was one of a handful of people who lived up in Cognashene year round. Once the water in the bay froze for the winter he would cut two foot square blocks of ice from the bay and drag them on a sleigh to his well insulated log ice-house. Next he would cover the blocks with sawdust to prevent them from sticking together. This also prevented them from thawing too quickly. Layer after layer of ice would be piled into the ice-house in this fashion providing him with an endless supply of product stored over the winter to be distributed slowly over the summer months to those in need of ice. In an average year with average temperatures Philippe usually had blocks of ice to sell to the tourists and other full time residents right up until the end of August. It wasn't an easy job, it was darned hard work in fact but it was a good way for him to make a bit of extra cash during the summer months.

It was also a really good way for him to keep in touch with all his neighbours, especially the pretty ladies who often spent the summer months at their cottages while their husbands stayed in the city to work. A lot of women were attracted to the blue eyed, curly dark haired, perfectly tanned man who magically showed up at their dock week after week. Philippe was a handsome, often shirtless man, who's English was broken by a strong French accent softly spoken with that sexy dulcet tone of his that could make even the most faithful woman feel, even if just for a moment, that she was in his eyes, the only woman on the face of the earth. Philippe liked his job, and he really liked the "tips" that he collected along the way. There was more than one woman in the area who had to explain to their husbands when they arrived at the cottage for their vacation that the price of ice seemed to be skyrocketing.

Once Philippe left, everyone started to walk along the dock onto shore and up towards the stone cottage. Maude said, "OK guys. I'm sure we've all worked hard enough and it's time to relax. I'm sweating buckets and I think a dip in the lake is just what I need to cool me off. How about it, anyone care to join me?" she asked knowing full well that the kids had been pining to jump in the water since they'd arrived.

Maude added, "After we've had a swim, it will be pyjama time and we can have a nice supper and sit on the rocks and watch the sunset."

"You've got my vote," said Gilbert as he made his way back up to the cottage to change into his swimming trunks. Ben and Emma raced ahead each wanting to be the first to get into the cottage to change.

Maude linked her arm in Gilbert's as they walked up the path that was lined with junipers, pine trees and sumac. "Did you notice anything unusual about Philippe today?" Maude asked.

"Unusual in what way?" Gilbert questioned.

"Oh, I don't know. It was just in the way that he was looking at me. It made me feel uncomfortable. It was almost like he was trying to send me a message through his eyes. He even winked at me a couple of times."

"Philippe is a very charming man. I think he looks at people that way to try to engage them in conversation. I bet there are a lot of women who like it when he looks at them that way and winks," said Gilbert.

"Well I don't. I know he's a ladies' man for sure. A real Casanova if you know what I mean."

"I'm sure he gets a lot of attention being like that."

"He sure does. I'm just glad you are always around when he delivers the ice. Some women in the bay are here alone or with just their kids and I've heard talk about some "special deliveries" at night."

"I'll have a word with him if you want me to."

"No, not at this point. But, if he makes a move on me, I hope he's a good swimmer because he's going in the lake."

Gilbert laughed. Maude felt a bit better for having told him about how she felt when Philippe had stared and winked at her. She couldn't believe he would act that way in front of her husband and children. *He must have had a long, cold winter,* she thought.

Not wanting to think about it anymore she said, "I have a special treat for you tonight Gil." Maude paused as she bent over to pick up a branch that had fallen across the pathway. "I made your favourite fried chicken before we left home today."

"And," she said playfully tugging on his arm, "I made a big potato salad and sweet vinegar coleslaw just the way you like it. And," she paused adding drama to her statement, "as a special celebratory treat I have two bottles of beer for us that I brought from town. I wrapped them in several towels to keep them cold. Once Philippe comes back here I'll put them alongside the block of ice to keep them that way."

"WHAT," Gilbert nearly shouted. "Beer! I haven't had a beer in a couple of years." He was delighted. "How did you manage to get a couple of beer up here without me knowing about it?"

"When I went to the butcher shop to get my supplies my uncle was there and I asked him if he could get me some. He said he had some beer in his apartment at the back of the shop and so I got two bottles from him. I tried to pay him for them but he wouldn't take anything from me. He said you've always been so good to him when he goes into the hardware store that the treat was on him."

"This is turning out to be the best day of my life so far," said Gilbert.

*****

Later that evening after their refreshing swim, the celebratory meal and the lazy evening enjoying the beautiful sunset, Maude got the kids settled in bed and then joined Gilbert out on the bench that was along the west side the stone cottage. As they relaxed and sipped on the beer they chatted quietly about their plans for the summer. Gilbert told her about what still needed to be done at the main cottage and about the requests for handyman work that he had received in the fall while closing up the tourist's cottages.

"I think I'm going to have enough work to keep me busy all summer again this year Maude."

"Let me know if there is anything you will need my help with," she replied, "I can't leave the kids and go to the other cottages with you but I can certainly be a good pair of hands and a helper if you need me at the main cottage. That way I can still keep my eye on the twins."

"You'll have enough to do around here as it is. What, with keeping up with the twins, making bread a couple of times a week, doing the laundry by hand and helping Mrs. Johnson with the main cottage if they have guests up for a visit. I'd feel badly asking you to do more."

"If I can help I will," she paused. "The kids are older now and pretty much amuse themselves. They just need supervision for the most part, and besides, I'm a big girl now," she said as she gently squeezed his hand, "If I'm too busy or don't have time, I'll tell you, don't you worry."

Gilbert moved over a little nearer to her on the bench and put his arm around her shoulders and pulled her closer to him. "I love you so very much Maude. You are the best thing that has ever happened to me." He hugged her tightly. "I don't know what I'd do without you. I can't imagine my life now without you."

He leaned into her and with his free hand he gently turned her face towards his and pulled her even closer to him and kissed her softly on the lips. As the kiss lingered that old familiar stirring in his loins caused him to smile and he slowly drew away from her and asked. "Do you think the kids are asleep yet?"

*****

The next morning as Gilbert was taking a bucket down to the dock to get a fresh pail of water he noticed that clouds had started gathering on the north western horizon. It had started off being a warm and sunny morning with the promise of a great day ahead of them but there seemed to be something ominous about the blue-grey cloud formation. Maude came out of the cottage to dump a dishpan of water and she too noticed the sky and the clouds.

"I think there is a storm coming," she said to Gilbert. "The birds have stopped singing and there seems to be a pretty strong current in the Narrows. Look how it's swirling around that big rock on the far shore."

Gilbert turned and looked in the direction Maude had pointed. "You're right. In fact, all morning there has been a chipmunk in the tree near the kitchen squawking at us like a banshee and even he has stopped as well."

Gilbert looked up at the sky, "The sky doesn't look so good but maybe we'll be lucky and it'll blow over us."

"I don't think it will, I think we're in for something," said Maude as she watched the rapidly advancing storm front moving in their direction.

"We'd better make sure there is nothing left outside then. I'll go over to the main cottage and make sure all the windows are closed. I opened a few of them yesterday to air the place out a bit. Get Emma and Ben to do a walk around and make sure they haven't left anything lying around that might blow away."

"I'd better take our towels from last night off the clothes line as well," said Maude as she rubbed her arms with her hands to stave off a chill that had settled in her. "Boy, the temperature seems to be dropping pretty quick," and as she said that large droplets of rain started to fall from the sky.

"Mom. Look at how big the raindrops are!" Emma shouted. "They are leaving great big wet blotches on the rocks."

"Go in the cottage and get Ben. Tell him to come out and help us pick up anything that shouldn't get wet or might blow away. I think we are in for a big storm," she said as she ran around to the back of the cottage to take the towels off the clothesline that had already started to flutter in the wind.

The rain continued to fall, slowly at first in large droplets like Emma had noticed but soon it turned into a regular rainfall. Gilbert returned from the main cottage and noticed that the wind had picked up. It had gone from being calm to a slight breeze to a strong wind. All this had happened in a few minutes and now the clouds were completely covering the sky. He looked up and noticed there wasn't any blue sky anywhere to be seen, it had been completely replaced by the navy blue, almost black clouds that were rapidly advancing from the northwest, a sure presage of a bad storm. He made his way down to the dock and checked the ropes on the boat and the way they were tied to the cleats on the dock. After tying each one of the ropes with an extra knot and making sure the bumpers were in good placement to keep the boat from banging against the dock in the wind he made his way up to the cottage. By the time he got there he was completely soaked. His shirt was so wet it was stuck to his back as if he had fallen in the water. As he stripped it off, he glanced through the window and said, "I think we are in for a doozy."

The wind continued to gain strength and the rainfall intensified into a driving rain that was coming in white sheets across the water.

The Stone Cottage

"Look Dad," said Ben as he stared out the window. "It looks like it's snowing out, it's raining so hard and the wind is blowing so strong it looks like snow drifting across the bay."

Maude came over to the window facing the Narrows channel then said, "Emma, can you get me the towels we used last night after we had our swim. I need to put them on the windowsills. The rain is just driving in through any cracks it can find."

As the roof of the cottage was not insulated but just the roofing boards covered with shingles the sound of the rain hitting the roof was very noisy. Though it was hard to believe it could happen, the wind gained even more strength and the rain turned from sheets of water to a deluge being forced across the bay. Within minutes the rain turned into hail and then it was so noisy in the cottage it was hard to hear each other speaking.

"Now I can't even see across to the other side of the Narrows," said Ben. "It's hailing and raining so hard it's like a white out."

"I'm not scared," said Emma trying to put on a brave face and looking up, "but I think the roof is scared. It's shaking."

Gilbert looked up and noticed that Emma was right. There seemed to be a slight tremor to the frame of the roof. As the wind howled outside and the water drove in under the front door it was pretty obvious that they were in the midst of one of the worse storms to hit the area in a long time. Then suddenly there was a large crack, like a gunshot and Emma screamed. Maude rushed over to her and cuddled with her drawing her tightly into her arms.

"I think the roof is going to blow off the cottage," Emma said.

"No, I don't think it will. It's just when there are strong gusts of wind it causes the roof to shake but it doesn't shake when there aren't any gusts. When I was up on the roof to fix the shingles it seemed solid to me," said Gilbert trying to reassure his daughter.

"I don't know what that loud noise was but trust me little one, we are safe in here. We have fifteen inch thick stone walls. Nothing will ever blow those down."

"It's so noisy with all that rain hitting the roof and the wind howling like that," said Ben. "Now all we need is thunder and lightning and we'll have had all the weather Mother Nature can send us."

"I think I can do without the thunder and lightning," said Maude as she wrung out the towels in a bucket and placed them back on the windowsill. As she leaned over the table to replace one of the other towels she felt water drip on her head. looking up she noticed the roof was leaking about ten inches higher than where the water had dripped on her. The rain drops had forced their way in and were running down the inside of the steep roof and dripping off one of the ceiling rafters. Gilbert was summoned and he got a roast pan from the kitchen and put it on the table to collect the water. "It's the best I can do for now," he said to Maude. "I can't go out there to fix it in this weather."

"That'll do just fine."

The storm raged on for the better part of the morning. Ben continued to watch the storm from the window at the front of the cottage. The waves in the bay turned into whitecaps and then the wind started to churn the water even further and blew a white spray of water off the tops of the white caps. With the strong west winds blowing the water in from the greater Georgian Bay to shore it caused quite a high storm surge. The water level had risen over a foot so far during the storm.

"Mom, Dad, come and see this," said Ben.

The wind was blowing waves in the Narrows from north to south but the storm surge was forcing water into the Narrows to fill the lake beyond from south to north. The water appeared to be going in two directions at the same time and there were occasions when the two directions would clash, the waves would collide and they would lift straight up together into an even greater wave.

"I've only ever seen that once before," said Maude. "I remember a big storm up at Granite Bluff Inlet when I was a child. It was just like this. The wind was pushing the water into the inlet but the current was forcing the water in the opposite direction. The waves crashed together just like that."

"Look at the boat," said Gilbert. "The storm surge has raised the water so high that the boat ropes are straining at the cleats on the dock. The boat is about a foot higher at the dock than it had been. That's causing the boat to lean towards the dock like it's getting ready to flip over. I've never seen anything like it in my life."

"I'll be happy if I never see anything like it again either," said Emma who had sneaked in between her parents to peer out the window.

Knowing they were safe and secure behind the thick stone walls it was awesome to watch Mother Nature at her best tossing every bit of weather she could muster at the bay and the cottage. But, even though it was interesting to watch, everyone in the cottage was glad when the storm started to subside. First the rain seemed to slow down, it wasn't quite so noisy on the roof, then within about twenty minutes the damaging wind gusts stopped almost as abruptly as they had arrived. It was incredible how much quieter it was in the cottage. Within the hour the rain had stopped altogether but the wind continued to blow. Though still fairly strong at least there weren't any further forceful gusts. Emma was happy to see the roof had stopped shaking and she felt a lot better and repeatedly voiced her opinion about that.

Once the rain abated and there was just the wind to contend with Gilbert decided it would be safe to go outside to take a walk around the properties and do a damage survey. The first thing that he noticed was that there were several shingles that had blown off the roof on the west side. *Ah, the cause of the leak. That will be easy enough to fix,* he thought. He still had a few shingles left from when he fixed the roof a few years ago so he knew that would be OK. Otherwise, after a careful checking around the rest of the place there was no damage to the stone cottage that he could find. *That was quite a storm,* he thought, *and this old place held up pretty well, everything looks good.*

He leaned upon the post supporting the front veranda and the bottom edge slipped from its base. When he looked down at it he noticed that cement that was packed around the bottom of the post affixing it onto the solid granite rock had cracked and become dislodged with his weight against the post. He kicked the bottom with his boot and it dislodged from the cement completely. He reached up closer to the roof of the veranda and wrapping his strong hands around it gave the post a good shake. It didn't budge up top but the cement on the bottom cracked further and broke into small pieces. The posts had had quite a job to do holding the roof from flying off in that wind. He wasn't surprised the posts had been stressed. Chipping away the broken cement and packing a new batch around the base of the post was all that it was going to take to fix it good as new. Thinking the other four posts could also be lose he walked over to check the integrity of each one of them and he was pleased to see they were all intact, top and bottom.

Satisfied that was all the damage he could find he opened the front door and said "We got off pretty easy Maude. There are just a few shingles missing on the west side and one support post has broken lose at its base here by the door." When he got no response from either Maude or the kids he looked into the main part of the cottage and saw the room was empty. He could hear chatter coming from the kitchen so Gilbert called out Maude's name then repeated his earlier findings hoping that she'd be able to hear him above the noise of the wind. Still no response. They must be washing up the breakfast and lunch dishes he thought. He didn't really feel like taking his wet boots off so he closed the door and thought, he'd just tell her about everything he found once he went back in.

As he started to walk down to the boat to begin the job of bailing the water out of it he noticed the large stately pine tree that had been about forty five feet tall. Now it was snapped in half and was lying across the path that led to the dock. *Ah-ha. That must have been that loud, gunshot-like noise that we heard,* he thought.

This was going to be a big job cutting the rest of the tree down and clearing it out of the way, the trunk was almost two feet in diameter. As he looked around he noticed a couple of other trees on the property that had either lost their top or their branches, or in a few cases had blown over completely, exposing their entire root system to the air. As the whole property was granite based, the root system of most of the trees was pretty shallow so it was no wonder he could see so many overturned trees with the near hurricane force winds they had just experienced. Looking across the Narrows channel to the far shore he noticed there were a number of large trees that had been blown over and or had snapped in half as if they were twigs. *Such devastation in such a short period of time,* he thought.

As he scanned the damage on the island opposite the stone cottage the optimist in Gilbert thought, *Well, the good news is our view of the outer islands has just improved significantly.*

Soon Ben joined his father at the fallen tree that was blocking the path to the boat. "Well son, looks like we have our work cut out for us this afternoon don't we?"

"I'm pretty good with the hatchet now, I'll get started on the branches," said Ben and he turned around and ran to the back of the cottage to get it.

When he returned Gilbert said, "This isn't going to be easy work Ben."

"I know dad, but if I work hard maybe I'll get to be as strong as you are and I'll be able to build and fix things and drive a boat and maybe in a few years I can even get a job up here in the summer time and make some money working for the tourists like you do."

Gil smiled and thought, *I hope he never loses this enthusiasm.*

*****

Luckily Gilbert was able to make his way around the tree and get down to the boat so that he could start to bail it out. This was his priority. It wouldn't do to have the boat, their only means of transportation, sink at the dock. As there was only the small cabin close to the bow of the boat, the entire back of the boat from the engine box to the stern was completely open to the elements. Without a tarp to cover this open area, the boat was exposed to the weather and it took on a fair amount of water during the deluge of rain the storm had delivered. Bailing a boat this size was no easy task and Gilbert was glad that he had left open areas in the floor boards near the transom for just this purpose. Always thinking about the best way to do things he had designed a hand pump that turned out to be incredibly efficient. At the hardware store he had purchased three lengths of six inch wide stove pipe and a T-piece. He fitted the T-piece onto one pipe then attached a second length. On the short end of the T-piece he attached a shorter piece of pipe. To bail the boat he stood the long length of pipe up in the transom and directed the shorter end of pipe off the T-piece over the gunwale of the boat. Next he took an old string mop that he had been saving for just this purpose and put it down the pipe. Pulling it up quickly it acted like a plunger and drew the water from inside the bilge and out the end of the pipe into the water. When he had initially assembled it back home he hadn't had time to check it out to make sure it worked. When called into service though he was quite pleased with how well it worked. It took less than five minutes to bail the boat with almost six inches in diameter of water flowing out of the pump into the water with each up-stroke. Ben wasn't sure what his father was using to bail the boat and came down to see for himself. As he was finishing up Gilbert thought, *I should patent this pump. It looks funny but it works amazing. I could be rich.*

"What are you doing?"

Gilbert looked up to see Ben standing on the dock staring at him. "I'm bailing the boat."

"With a stove pipe and a mop?" Ben asked incredulously.

"Yup, look how well it works," Gilbert said and did a short demonstration to show how well it brought bilge water up and out of the boat.

"When I saw rain falling sideways during the storm I thought I'd seen everything but looking at this pump I have to say, now I've seen everything."

Gilbert laughed. Seems Ben was developing quite a sense of humour.

*****

Though the rain never returned, the sky stayed cloudy and the wind continued to howl throughout the night. The stone cottage got off easy with just a few shingles to be replaced on the roof and one veranda pillar to reinforce but, as the wind persisted, Gilbert and Maude's sleep was restless to say the least. Every now and then as gusts blew in from the north they could hear more tree branches snapping like twigs being trodden upon. At one point it sounded like a few more shingles were lifted from the roof.

"I'm glad it stopped raining. At least if we lose more shingles we won't get wet."

"I'm pretty sure there is going to be a lot more work to do outside after the wind goes down," Gilbert whispered to Maude as she snuggled closer to him in the bed.

"The weather has been just awful today. Let's hope it clears by morning," she replied.

"I hope so too," said Gilbert as he rolled slightly onto his side to find that sweet spot between the springs in the old mattress. Once comfortable he finally dozed off.

*****

The cleanup of that big pine tree took a long time even with Ben helping. With nothing for cutting trees but a Swede saw and his axe, cutting up the part of the pine tree that had broken off and blocked the path took the rest of that day and the following morning. It was a big job. Gilbert surveyed the damage and noted that six trees had been damaged with either large branches broken off or the entire tree uprooted and toppled over. Luckily none of the trees that fell had landed anywhere near either cottage.

Though the stone cottage had only lost a few shingles, the main cottage however did not fare so well. On the west side of the cottage near the loft's dormer windows, many of the shingles and the metal flashing in the valley where the two roof lines met had been ripped off with the fierce winds. As a result, the rain had just poured into the open areas. It had soaked through not only the loft but down into the main part of the cottage as well. The mattresses in the loft that were located just under the windows were completely saturated and by the time Gilbert had made his way into the room they had already started to smell musty. These were old mattresses that had been in the cottage for years before the doctor had bought the property. Gilbert was sure it wouldn't be a great loss for the Johnson's but just the same, he had to drag the mattresses, soaked and heavy as they were, out to the access ladder and down to the main room and out of the cottage completely. Not an easy task and he was glad Maude was able to help or he'd have never been able to do it on his own. Left up in the loft the entire cottage would have reeked with the smell of old wet mattress.

A huge puddle had formed in front of the large stone fireplace and the linoleum flooring was buckling and bubbling with the moisture. The area rug in front of the couches flanking the fireplace was drenched. It was pulled outside as well and laid on the granite rocks to dry.

As the couple dragged the heavy carpet off the veranda and onto the rocks Maude said, "Hopefully the wind will be able to speed up the drying process." She looked up at Gilbert a smile broadening across her face.

"On second thought, since its wet anyway I think I'm going to take this as an opportunity. I'm going to get a bucket of soapy water and my broom and I'm going to scrub it. Then I'll get the kids to rinse it by throwing buckets of water from the lake on it. That'll keep them busy and they'll find it fun to throw buckets of water on the carpet." Then she added, "I hope," and the two of them laughed.

Gilbert added, "Knowing those two I wouldn't be surprised if there is an occasional bucket of water that is thrown at each other as well. Make sure they are wearing their bathing suits then they won't need a bath tonight."

In the kitchen, the windows facing the channel had blown open at some point during the storm. They were large windows, each one being almost six feet high and two feet wide. They were designed so that they opened on hinges like French doors and laid flat against the walls to allow for maximum airflow. They closed upon a frame in the centre of the two windows with a latch that held them shut. The latch however was no match to the force of the wind and due to their size, the strength of the wind bent the metal latch and the windows had blown open. The one on the left had been blown in with such force that three of the panes of glass had been broken as it slammed against the wall. Not only was there a massive amount of rainwater that had poured into the kitchen through the open window, but there was broken glass everywhere with shards that had landed as far as the kitchen table five feet away.

"Oh my, what a mess," said Maude as she surveyed the damage and leaned forward to pick a few shards of glass that were stuck into the oilcloth covering the table. "We have our work cut out for us for sure."

"I'm going to have to make a list of things we need and make a trip in to town to get supplies," said Gilbert. I've got some small boards I can put over the broken window panes for now but I don't have any glass. There are a few bundles of shingles under the cottage I can use to fix the roof near the loft but I don't have any metal flashing."

"Make a list for sure," said Maude, "it would be a shame to get back up here and realize you've forgotten something."

"I'll stop in and talk to Dr. Johnson as well and let him know about the roof, the windows and the mattresses. It's nothing that can't be fixed but I think he would want to know about it."

Maude picked up the broom and dust pan and started to sweep up the glass on the floor. "I bet you're glad you hadn't gotten around to putting up all the screens on that huge front veranda you built. They'd probably be torn right off the frames the way the wind was howling last night. I'm sure they'd have been wrecked."

"I'm not usually one to brag, but if I have to say so myself, that veranda and roof I built last year survived the storm very well. I must have built it pretty strong to withstand that storm," said Gilbert.

"You're a good carpenter," agreed Maude. "I don't think anyone will ever dispute that." As she continued to sweep the broken glass on the floor of the kitchen another thought occurred to her. She turned to Gilbert and said, "The cushions for all the new wicker furniture on the front veranda are still laying on the bed in the front room. Thank goodness I hadn't gotten around to putting them out yesterday morning either or they'd be ruined too or worse yet, blown away with the wind."

"Don't get too hopeful. I haven't checked out that room yet," said Gilbert. "It could be a mess in there as well. Replacing that whole window in the room was one of the things on my to-do list." With that, Maude's shoulders slumped noticeably at the thought of the new cushions being ruined as well. Gilbert turned and left the kitchen to check for damage in the bedrooms.

The Stone Cottage

"We're in luck Maude," Gilbert called from the front of the main cottage. "That old window held tight. I'm not sure how, but it did and those new cushions for the wicker furniture and the mattress on the bed are still dry too."

"Is there any damage to the other bedrooms at the front of the cottage," Maude asked.

"I don't think so but give me a minute and I'll check." As he went from room to room he opened the bedroom doors and the windows in each room to air them out as there was already a musty smell that was developing throughout the cottage. The last thing Gilbert wanted to deal with was mould developing anywhere. With the brisk breeze that was still blowing it wouldn't take long to dry things up.

A couple of minutes later, Maude heard a loud thumping noise, like the sound of something large falling on the floor at the front of the cottage. She ran from the kitchen where she had been busy trying to straighten out the curtains that had become tangled in the broken window frame. "Gil, are you all right?" she asked as she went from one bedroom to the other trying to find him. "I heard something crash on the floor."

"I'm fine," he said kind of laughing to himself.

Maude pushed open the door to the largest of the bedrooms at the front of the cottage. This door had a tendency to swing shut on its own if there wasn't a door stop in place and there she found Gilbert sitting on the floor. He was leaning up against the bed and rubbing the top of his head with a sort of a half smile, half frown upon his face.

"What are you doing on the floor?"

"That window that faces north," he pointed with his free hand, "had blown in and the screen is torn. Since the screen is torn, I went over to close the window and a squirrel jumped off the window sill and onto my shoulder. I was so surprised I spun around trying to swat it off of me and I lost my balance, I tripped on the floor mat and landed on my rear."

"Why are you rubbing the top of your head?"

"Well, that's the funny part. I went to stand up and didn't realize the window had blown open again and when I got up I banged my head on it and it knocked me back down onto my butt again. I hit it hard enough that I think I'm actually seeing stars."

It struck her as kind of funny that Gilbert, who always seemed to be so in control of things, had pretty much lost it in this room over a squirrel and seeing that his pride was really what hurt the most she turned to leave. Trying not to laugh at the situation Maude said, "Ah, the attack of the killer squirrel," then teasing him said, "looks like you're going to have to replace that bottom hinge on the window, it looks pretty bent."

"I'm not surprised it's bent. I hit my head on it hard enough to tear it right off the frame."

"Well at least the glass didn't break."

"Yup, that would have been yet one more pane of glass to bring up here if I had."

"I'll go finish up in the kitchen," said Maude. "You take your time and get up only if you're not dizzy." Then she smiled lovingly at Gilbert, "Maybe you should crawl out of the bedroom on your hands and knees. It might be safer," she said taunting him. As she turned and walked out of the room, a bit of a giggle welled up inside her but it didn't last long.

Suddenly Maude reappeared at the bedroom doorway. "Wait a minute. What happened to the squirrel?"

"I haven't a clue."

"So you think it's still in here?"

"I didn't see it go back out the window," Gil said.

"Oh, my God," said Maude resignedly. "We have to find that squirrel before we do anything else. The last thing we need is to have it tearing up the mattresses or chewing on the cushions or getting into the food in the cupboards." She turned and left quickly to go get the broom she had been using to clean up the broken glass in the kitchen.

By this time Gilbert had managed to get to his knees. He used the bed frame for support to stand up and though a bit wobbly with his steps he made his way to the bedroom window to shut it properly. Once that was secured he headed for the bedroom door to begin his search of the cottage. He paused half way. A thought occurred to him at the same time as Maude shouted from the living room.

"Check under the bed and the chest of drawers of the room you are in. If that varmint isn't in there shut the door so he doesn't go back in there." It was like she was reading his mind as that was the exact thing that he was thinking.

And so the search began. There were six bedrooms to check but it only took them a few minutes to check them all. The search pattern they established was the same for each room. look under the bed, check in the closet, under the dresser and the pillows near the headboard. Once the room was checked they would shut the door. Though Maude wasn't afraid of the squirrel, she used the handle of the broom to aide in her search banging it loudly on the floor and walls while she checked in those hard to reach or see places. The little critter could be hiding anywhere, like under the living room couches or the free standing cupboards in the kitchen. Ten minutes later they still hadn't found it. They'd searched all the bedrooms, the bathroom, the kitchen, living room and even the loft upstairs all to no avail. It is a big cottage and there are a lot of places the squirrel could hide out.

"Are you sure that he didn't leap back out the bloody window," a frustrated Maude asked as she flopped down on the couch, her hand resting on her chest. Her heart rate was racing from scurrying around the cottage, lifting mattresses, moving furniture and getting up and down off stools and chairs and whatever was handy to check the high spots. Gilbert walked in the door after checking the front porch when she added, "My heart rate is banging away as if I just swam across the bay in a race."

And, just as she said it, she let out a blood curdling scream the likes of which Gilbert had never heard in his entire life. As he twisted to see what was wrong with Maude he immediately saw what the problem was. As Maude sat on the couch the squirrel dropped down off the wagon-wheel lamp that was suspended from the ceiling directly above her and landed on her head. In one fluid motion it leapt from her head onto the coffee table in front of her, bounced off the table and raced for the front door that Gilbert was just about to close. With lightening speed Gilbert swung around, grabbed the doorknob and shut the door right behind it. The speed that he turned was such that he immediately became dizzy, partly from his head injury he suspected. He flopped down onto the couch beside Maude and half groaned, half sighed.

"It's gone," he said as he turned to look at Maude who had both arms raised above her head, her hands rapidly brushing her hair as if the squirrel was still there.

"Oh my God that scared me," she said. "Oh my God," she repeated. "If my heart was racing before you should check it now. It feels like it's going to beat right out of my chest."

"We must look like quite the pair right now," said Gilbert rubbing the goose egg that was forming on the top of his head where he'd hit the window.

"I'm sure we do," said Maude. She turned to look at Gilbert and suddenly the two of them burst out laughing. "I'm sure we do."

"Ah, the attacks of the killer squirrel. We could write a book."

*****

It literally took them days to clean up and clear away the mess and debris that the storm had caused. The priorities had been to replace the missing shingles on the roof of the stone cottage and the main cottage in case it rained again, replace the broken glass in the windows that had shattered, repair the window screens and apply a new batch of cement to the veranda post. Additionally they had to fix the old wooden walkway that bridged a large crevasse in the rocks leading to the water's edge. It had sustained broken boards from a large branch crashing onto it rendering it unsafe until it was repaired. As this was a part of the path to the water it was something that had to be fixed right away as the alternate route was pretty long, especially when carrying buckets of water for the kitchen. They worked from early morning till suppertime for nearly a week.

Ben and Emma where commissioned to help with whatever they could, sometimes being an extra pair of hands outside helping with clean up and sometimes they were commissioned to make lunch or supper while Maude helped Gilbert with some of the more challenging repairs. The twins were learning very quickly that life isn't all about having fun, there is also a lot of work involved as well.

Gilbert had made a trip into town with Ben the day after the storm to pick up supplies and have a chat with Dr. Johnson about the damage the storm had caused. It was hard to put a dollar value on the damage that had been done as some of those things that were destroyed, such as the mattresses were very old.

"I don't think it will be worth putting in an insurance claim for this," Dr. Johnson said to Gilbert. "Many of those things we had planned to replace in the near future anyway. So, pick up what you need and just tell the stores to put it on my tab and I'll go in and pay for it all at once when we have everything we need."

By the time Gilbert had picked up all the supplies he needed to make the repairs and loaded the boat with two new mattresses for the loft he had quite a boat load to bring up.

"This could be another slow ride back to Cognashene," Gilbert said to Ben as they left the town dock.

"That's Okay with me," added Ben. "Any day I get a boat ride is a good day in my books." Gilbert smiled thinking about how much Ben was growing up to be like him.

Luckily for Gilbert, Dr. Johnson was so appreciative that Gilbert was looking after things he insisted that Gilbert accept a bonus of $50 to pay for gas for the boat. It would be a good way to compensate him for his extra trip into town. As it turned out that bonus more than covered the cost of the gas and Gil tucked the remaining money in a small jar on the shelf in the kitchen of the stone cottage.

"There is enough money here that we will have our ice for the icebox covered for quite a while this summer. If it gets really hot towards the end of July like it sometimes does maybe we can even get some extra ice to keep things cool," he said to Maude.

"That will be so nice," she replied.

CHAPTER - 10

July 1937

"Everything looks amazing Gilbert," said Dr. Johnson. "I can't believe it but you have made my dreams come true." Gilbert could tell his friend and boss was pleased.

The two men were standing on the dock and looking up towards the main cottage. The doctor stood with his hands in his pockets jiggling the lose change he always seemed to have an abundance of and simply smiled as he took it all in. He hadn't been to the cottage since early in the summer the year before when there was still so much work to be done. A side trip to Europe to visit distant relatives had consumed most of his time last summer. With him being away for almost a month it took him forever to get caught up with his own work and he never made it back up even in the fall. He, and his wife, who hadn't seen the cottage since the week they bought it several years earlier and had never stayed at the cottage for more than a few hours at a time. They certainly had never stayed overnight.

The cottage, built on the highest point of the twenty acre lot to maximize the view, now thanks to Gilbert's hard work, possessed a large covered porch that had been added across the front of the entire cottage. This addition gave the cottage an added sense of old world grandeur and beckoned people to come "sit for a spell and have something cold to drink". Gilbert smiled at the compliments being lavished upon him and had to agree, the fresh coat of paint that he had applied to the entire outside of the cottage early in the spring did truly transform its overall appearance. Gone was the drab beige/brown siding. The tongue and groove ship-lap siding had been painted a crisp, brilliant white, the frames around all of the windows and screens were painted a dark evergreen to match the roofing shingles and the steps leading up to the front porch were painted a soft dove grey. All in all, now that Gilbert had weaved his magic on the place, it looked like a brand new building. Even he had to admit, the old place did look pretty good.

"This is fantastic," raved the doctor. "I just can't believe you have transformed an old run down cottage into something that my wife and I can enjoy and share with our friends for years to come."

"Well it has taken a few years for me to get it to look this way but I think in the end it was well worth it," Gilbert said.

The men started down the dock and stopped at the small pump house that Gilbert had built about thirty feet from the shoreline. Once electricity was available in the area, the doctor had agreed to have power lines run to the cottage. While the electricians and power company personnel were at the cottage to install the hydroelectric power, an additional line was extended down to the pump house to power up the water pump. A couple of extra outlet plugs were also installed in case at some point in time it was necessary to have power down at the dock. Running a series of extension cords from the main cottage would be a cumbersome thing to do considering the distance the cottage was from shore.

The pump house, painted white and green to match the cottage was a small six foot by six foot square shed that was barely tall enough for Gilbert to stand up in, but that was Okay, he wasn't planning on spending a lot of time in there. The shed housed a brand new Briggs and Stratton water pump that Gilbert had ordered special delivery to the hardware store. Once the pump was installed it was used to take water from the lake up to the main cottage's kitchen and bathroom.

"So this is the beast that cost me so much money," Dr. Johnson joked as he stooped to examine the motor on the water pump. "I can't believe we had to have it brought in as a special order. You'd think with electricity being run to so many cottages these days, water pumps would become a stock item."

"Well, there may be a lot of people getting power to their cottages but the pumps can be finicky and pretty time consuming to set up and manage. They're great when they are working but as soon as they lose their prime and water backflows towards the lake they can cause a lot of heartache. A lot of people can't be bothered with them at this point."

"Why would a pump lose its prime," the doctor asked.

"Most of the pumps don't have a back-check valve in them to keep the water from going backwards. You'd think they would but they don't. After that you are wrestling with gravity," said Gilbert. "Even with this pump, new as it is, I bet I spent about two and a half hours getting that thing primed. Just when I thought I had it working… uhh, it was so frustrating. I ended up having to get a water pitcher and a bucket from in the kitchen and pouring water into the pipes to fill them so that the pump could muster up enough suction to prime itself. Once this one got primed though, it has been working like a charm. But…I won't say that out loud too often," smiled Gilbert as he winked at his boss and patted the pump tenderly as if it were a delicate item. "This pump has its work cut out for it too considering the elevation the cottage is at. It takes a pretty strong pump to get the water up that high."

The doctor looked at the pump for a few more seconds, obviously deep in thought then said, "Now that it's finished we can actually make some plans to stay here. My wife will be so pleased, I hope. The thought of bathing in the lake or sponge bathing from a basin of water heated on the stove did not really make her very happy. Now with running water and a hot water tank, well…" he suddenly stopped talking and looked back at the dock nearly losing his balance as he turned.

"Gil, I'm so sorry. I was so interested in the cottage I didn't even notice the new top you put on the dock. That must have taken you quite a while. All that lumber that you had brought up here for the dock. Did you have to cut it all by hand?"

"No, I got lucky. The dock is sixty feet long and eight feet wide. The four log piers that are supporting the top were still in pretty good shape. Over the years the ice had done some damage to them but overall it wasn't too bad. I was able to straighten them up, square them to the best of my ability and drive some two foot spikes into them to keep them that way. With the top off it was easy to fix the piers and while I was at it I added more rocks to them to keep them weighted down and grounded."

The two men stooped at the shoreline and looked under the dock at the pier closest to the shore. The logs of the pier were straight and squared off and it was easy to see the pier was filled to the brim with some pretty big rocks and boulders. Gilbert continued, "Because the dock is so long, rather than order the wood from the building supply company I went directly to the sawmill and told them how many boards I was going to need and asked if they would cut them all at eight foot lengths. As it happened the barge delivering the lumber arrived just as I was finishing up with the frame for the top so it worked out perfectly. Instead of unloading the wood onto shore and then having to move it into position on the dock, we just lined up the boards right there and then. It couldn't have worked out any better."

"Now that's a lot of work Gil. I know one thing for sure, I wouldn't have even attempted to do that. My back is sore just listening to what you went through to rebuild it," said the doctor as he arched his back backwards and rubbed his flanks. "I can't believe you were able to get some of those boulders into the piers. They are huge."

"It was a lot of work, I won't deny it. I think that dock is going to outlast all of us though. It's been built pretty strong and you are lucky. In the wintertime, the water in the Narrows channel doesn't really freeze because of the current. I was checking with some of the local people who live up here year round and they said that typically there is only a thin skim of ice on the bay right here around the dock so," he paused, "it should last a pretty long time."

With nothing more to be said about the dock the men started towards the cottage.

Dr. Johnson said, "I don't know if I told you yet but I have decided to call this cottage 'My Shangri-la.'"

"Actually you did tell me when you first bought the cottage. That reminds me; I have another surprise for you. Come with me up to the cottage. Maude and your wife are in there looking things over inside so it will be good to show you both the surprise."

As the two men followed the stone granite path from the dock to the cottage Dr. Johnson kept stopping along the way and taking long hard looks at his newly restored cottage, complimenting Gilbert with each new thing that he saw. It was obvious to Gilbert that the doctor appreciated the work that had been done and could appreciate how difficult some of it had been. It made all his hard labour worthwhile.

As they neared the steps to the front porch they could hear the two women inside. A short stop on the steps and they could hear Maude's voice quietly explaining how a certain something had been fixed or refinished or replaced.

The dulcet tones of Maude's voice were intermittently replaced by the nearly shrill ooing and ahhing sounds made by Mrs. Johnson as she took it all in.

When she noticed the two men on the front veranda Mrs. Johnson said, "Oh, Doc. You've got to get in here and see this. It doesn't even look like the same place."

Inside the cottage the first thing that they noticed was that the multitude of random patterned kerosene lamps that had previously seemed to dot every flat surface in the living room were gone. The kerosene lamps had been placed in storage in the butler's pantry off the kitchen, easy to retrieve in case there was a power failure. All the former lighting fixtures had been replaced with antique looking electric Tiffany lamps. Some had patterns depicting cottage lifestyle pictures etched into clear shades while others bore multicoloured leaf and flower motifs painted on delicate white shades. Still others bore actual stained glass shades, in the classic Tiffany style. There was even a small brass lamp perched on the top of the piano with a dark lime coloured shade that Mrs. Johnson had sent up from home earlier in the season to illuminate her sheet music.

All six bedrooms had received a fresh coat of soft pastel coloured paint and new larger closets had been built into the corner of each room. Patchwork quilts adorned the beds and delicate eyelet lace curtains bedecked each window. As the gentle breeze blew in the windows the curtains fluttered in a welcoming wave inviting the passerby to gaze at the awesome view beyond. The doors and trim to each bedroom were painted a brilliant glossy white and this feature helped to brighten up the living room which had been painted a very light powder blue. Those colour choices were key in updating the look of the living room and brightening it up. It only has windows at one end and in the past had a tendency to be a bit dull inside save and except for the muted light that filtered down from the loft.

"I have to admit, when I first saw the cottage it was in pretty bad shape but things did turn out pretty well," acknowledged Gilbert.

"I wish I'd brought my camera with me," said the doctor. "The view from the front porch is spectacular. I think next time I come up, I'll take a picture and have it enlarged. I'll hang it in my office waiting room. And maybe I'll take a picture of the cottage from the water and have it enlarged as well so everyone can see what a beautiful place Gilbert and Maude have turned it into."

"Well, I thank you for the compliment Doctor," said Maude, "but I really didn't have much to do with how this has turned out. It was all Gilbert's vision."

"Maude is being modest," Gilbert said to the Johnsons'. "She was a big help in picking out the colours for the bedrooms, finding just the right quilt for each room and she made all the curtains by hand at home over the winter."

"Everything has come together so well, I just can't believe the transformation," said Mrs. Johnson.

"Now tell me Gil," the doctor said. "What is this surprise you have for us?"

Gilbert bent down in front of the long couch that faced the fireplace and once on his knees he reached under and pulled out a large slab of wood that was about four feet long, and fourteen inches wide.

Gilbert explained, "One day last fall, I was down at the slab docks at the Saw Mill in Musquosh and I came across this battered old piece of wood. It had a few twists and turns in it and it didn't come out of the mill in very good shape. Not good enough to be sold as a piece of lumber that's for sure, so I asked them if I could have it." He paused in his talking while he got up off his knees and started to straighten up. "I brought it back here to the cottage and sanded it down to the best of my ability, just on one side mind you 'cause it wasn't easy going." As he stood up to his full height, he turned the piece of wood over to reveal a beautifully sanded surface with "MY SHANGRI-LA" carved into the centre of it. On each side of the lettering he had relief carved images of cottage life. On one side, a picture of a man standing up to his knees in the water fishing, on the other side was a carving of a hammock strung between two pine trees."

"Oh my God," cried Mrs. Johnson as she rushed over to Gilbert's side to rub her hands across the carvings. "It's beautiful. It's perfect. It's says everything about being at the cottage all in one piece."

Dr. Johnson walked slowly over to Gilbert. Putting his hand on Gilbert's shoulder he said, "Gilbert, I have no words, I am speechless. To say thank you seems so insignificant for the amount of work you have put into this place. Everything is simply perfect."

"I am so glad you like it." Still with the piece of wood in his hands he walked towards the front door and stepped outside. "I thought that the best place to hang this carving would be to mount it here above the front door. That way you and your guests will see it when they come up the front steps. It will be protected by the roof of the porch so it shouldn't be affected by the weather."

"I love it! A great idea once again. You've thought of everything."

"I'm glad you agree with where I thought it should be hung because I've already mounted some sturdy hooks into the wall above the door," said Gilbert a little sheepishly.

"That will be just fine," said Mrs. Johnson. "It will be a perfect focal point to the cottage entrance."

Dr. Johnson rubbed his hand over the finely sanded and glossy finished carvings. "I had no idea you were so artistic. Where did you learn to carve so beautifully?" he said as he continued to examine the carving. "look at this grain in the wood, the way you have finished it, it just makes the carvings pop out."

"I have built a lot of canoes, and boats over the years. When I worked at the Boatworks in town, the owners asked me if I would carve the surname of the purchaser into the dashboard of the custom built boats. I got pretty handy with my set of carving chisels and soon I was carving boating motifs into the dash for boats that were not custom ordered. Just to give them a bit of flare. I thought it might make them more attractive and they would sell better. I guess I just developed it from there," said Gilbert humbly.

The doctor turned to his wife and said, "I think this calls for a celebration. I'm going to run down to the boat and get our cooler and picnic basket that we packed." He turned to Maude and said, "we brought a fine bottle of Chardonnay with us and some cold cuts. We also packed some fancy breads and rolls with flavoured cheese I picked up at the bake shop just this morning."

"That's a great idea," said Mrs. Johnson. "I'm starved. Maude, why don't you go over to the stone cottage and round up the twins. I'm sure they'd like to join us as we celebrate our new, old cottage."

Maude started for the door but stopped when Mrs. Johnson asked, "Do you know if there are any wine glasses in the kitchen china cabinet?"

"I don't think there are," said Maude. "I remember seeing about eight small juice glasses in the cupboard but no wine glasses though."

"Well," said Mrs. Johnson. "I guess that will be the first thing to go on my list of things to bring up to the cottage. Wine glasses. A person can't do without wine glasses."

Maude smiled to herself as she took off out the door in search of the twins. She knew all too well about how much wine the doctor's wife drank. She'd seen her pretty tipsy a few times at home. Maude truly believed that Mrs. Johnson had a drinking problem, but she also knew that she hid it very well.

The wine flowed freely and everyone enjoyed the picnic lunch the Johnson's had brought from town. The new wicker furniture on the front porch provided the perfect setting for the celebration. The conversations were friendly and came easily between the adults and though Dr. Johnson's 'station' in life was a little higher than Gilbert's he certainly treated him as an equal and afforded him the respect Gilbert deserved for a job well done. The two men had become very good friends in the last couple of years and cherished each other's company in the short and infrequent times they had together.

*****

As the sun slowly began to set in the west and the mournful call of the loon echoed in the granite rocks, a slightly slurred and barely audible voice was heard coming from the oversized wicker arm chair in the corner of the porch. "I've made a decision and I don't know if you are going to like it?" said Mrs. Johnson to her husband.

"And what decision would that be my love?" he replied.

"I think that when we get home tonight, I am going to pack my bags and move up here for the summer. I just love this place so much I don't really want to leave."

"Oh. I had a feeling you might say that," moaned Dr. Johnson. "What about your work in my office and around the house? If you're not there who is going to do it?"

"Gilbert's mother does most of the work around the house already. Most days I just have to put the supper she has prepared for us in the oven. I'm sure if you sweet talk her, she'll stay until your patients are gone and then get your meals for you."

"And, what about the patients? You're not just my wife but my office nurse as well. I depend on you to keep things going in the office. I don't think I can manage it alone."

"Maybe you can hire that nurse that used to work at the hospital. I can't think of her name right this instant but you delivered her triplets a few years ago and she never went back to the hospital because she couldn't do the shift work anymore. Last time she was in the office with the kids she said working in your office would be perfect for her. The hours would be better for her especially since she has all those children to take care of."

"Oh, I know who you mean. Her name is Lydia. Yes," he paused as he contemplated what his wife had just suggested. "Yes, Lydia would be good. I'll give her a call. I do seem to remember her asking me if she could fill in for you if ever you wanted a day off."

There was an awkward silence for a while, each of them deep in thought and then, "You have your own boat so you could come up to the cottage whenever you want," said Mrs. Johnson. "Maybe you could come up every Wednesday afternoon. You typically have that time off already. That way I can give you my list of the things I will need for the next week and you can bring it up when you come for the weekend."

"Oh my, oh my. You've got this all figured out don't you."

"I think I'd like a week or two up here alone, with just Maude and Gilbert and the twins and you of course when you come back and forth. That way I'll be able to get settled in and get used to the place. Then maybe in August we could plan to start bringing some of our friends up for a weekend here and there."

"Sounds perfect. It's pretty well what we had talked about when we were in the process of buying and renovating this place."

"Oh, I have another idea!" exclaimed Mrs. Johnson excitedly as she straightened up in the chair. "You can bring our friends up with you on the weekend, and then the wives can stay up here with me for the week to keep me company, and the husbands can go home with you on Sunday evening,"

"It sounds like a plan," he said, thinking about the logistics of what his wife was talking about. "It all seems a bit rushed but, umm...summer is short so if we're going to do this, we'll have to get started,"

"The sooner the better as far as I'm concerned," his wife replied. They both stood up at the same time and started to collect the items they were going to bring back home. Once the picnic basket and cooler were ready to go, Doc took them down to the boat and started the engine. Mrs. Johnson brought the used dishes into the kitchen and placed them in the sink knowing full well that Maude would be over in the morning to wash them up and put them away. Mrs. Johnson was very used to having people do things for her. "Wine glasses," she said to herself, "I must remember to bring wine glasses." She opened the kitchen cupboards and took stock of the dishes that were there. "And some good sized tumblers and brandy snifters as well."

*****

True to what she had decided to do, Mrs. Johnson did go home that night and pack her suitcases, carefully wrapping her favourite crystal stemware in items of clothing that she thought would protect them from being broken while in transit or while being handled in the boat and on the docks. It took a couple of days for her to get everything organized at home and in the office but she was a motivated woman and by Wednesday afternoon that week she was ready to head to the cottage for the remainder of the summer.

The doctor had planned to drive her up to the cottage but as luck would have it one of his patients had gone into labour that morning and the baby was taking its own sweet time being born.

"You know I can't leave now. I have to stay until the baby is delivered," Dr. Johnson said to his wife who was sitting pouting in the sun-room of their large house on Water Street.

"Well I'm all packed and I have nothing else to do today," she said despondently. "Now that I've made up my mind that that's what I want to do, I just want to get to the cottage and get settled in so I can enjoy the summer."

"I'll see what I can do. I'll make some calls and see if I can find someone to drive you up there," said the doctor. Secretly he was quite happy that his wife was going to be spending the summer at the cottage. He needed a break from her. He loved her dearly but she had been drinking quite a bit lately and all his efforts and pleading to try to get her to cut back on the amount that she drank fell on deaf ears. He worried about her being up at the cottage without him but knowing that Gilbert and Maude were merely a couple hundred feet away at the stone cottage was reassuring.

After a few phone calls a friend of his who had gone fishing up the lakes with him on many occasions before the cottage had been purchased, agreed to drive the good doctor's wife up to her new summer home. It was just coincidence that he had taken the day off work to get a few odd jobs done around his house but the opportunity to go for a boat ride trumped anything he had planned to do. He arrived at the house within the hour and loaded the car to the roof with all the bins, boxes, grocery bags and suitcases Mrs. Johnson had packed.

When she arrived at the cottage her first order of business once the suitcases were brought up from the dock was to unpack a special bottle of Merlot that she had been saving at home for a special occasion. She opened the suitcase that had the stemware in it carefully so that nothing would fall out in case it had become dislodged in transit. Satisfied that all of the glassware had survived the trip from town and that there weren't any other boxes that needed to be brought up from the dock she bade goodbye to her husband's friend and wandered slowly back up to the cottage appreciating the beauty of her surroundings. *Ah, the peace and quiet of Georgian Bay,* she thought. The only sounds to distract her were those of a few seagulls calling out to each other in the distance and the faint whispering of the light breeze in the pine trees.

She placed the crystal in the china cabinet, the groceries in the fridge and then went back to the kitchen to find a cork screw. She searched around in the drawers one by one but...nothing. She rummaged through each drawer again, slamming them in frustration. She couldn't believe she hadn't thought to pack a corkscrew just in case. She should have left the one they had brought from home in the cooler on the weekend here at the cottage. *Lord knows we have enough of them at home,* she thought.

Mrs. Johnson heard a light knocking at the kitchen's back door. "I heard some rattling around and drawers slamming on my way down to the dock to fetch a pail of water," said Maude. "Is everything OK?"

"Oh, thank goodness you're here. I wanted to open a bottle of wine to celebrate my first day at the cottage and I can't find a corkscrew. Do you have one over at your place?"

"No we don't," said Maude.

"Maybe Gilbert has one in his tool box," said Mrs. Johnson hopefully.

"I'm pretty sure he doesn't," said Maude.

"Can you ask him?"

"He's not here right now. He's gone to do a small job for a couple down in the Freddie Channel. He won't be back till supper time."

"Oh," said Mrs. Johnson, with disappointment and frustration building in her voice.

"I'll go over to the stone cottage though and see if I can find something that will help you out." She left the kitchen the way she had come in and as she was walking over to the stone cottage she felt saddened by the fact that the doctor's wife was so consumed by her addiction to alcohol that she couldn't go an afternoon without a drink.

She returned to the main cottage shortly after and offered up what she had found. "It's not really a corkscrew but I think it will work," said Maude as she handed over a long brass screw, a screwdriver and a pair of pliers.

"This is perfect Maude. What's that old saying? 'Necessity is the mother of invention.'"

"Well, I think if you can use the screwdriver to get the screw into the cork nice and straight, then you can use the pliers to pull it all out."

"I won't be able to do this on my own," said Mrs. Johnson as she started to screw the screw into the bottle. "Here, you hold the bottle so it doesn't tip over."

Maude gripped the bottle tightly and soon said, "There, I think that's in far enough."

"Okay. You hold the bottle down, and I'll pull with the pliers."

After a couple of minutes of grunting and groaning, pulling and tugging the two women were successful. Even Maude thought that the sound of the cork popping out of the bottle was exciting.

"Thank you for your help Maude," said the doctor's wife. "I couldn't have done it without you. Here, I'll pour you a glass of wine and we'll drink a toast to being here and settling in."

"That's very generous of you to offer but I really have to get going. I have bread in the oven and I can't stay a moment longer or it will be ruined," said Maude, grateful that she had an excuse not to drink with her new full-time neighbour. Once again she hurried out the back door of the kitchen and followed the path to the stone cottage all the while thinking, *I wonder how she is going to get the next bottle open?*

*****

"Gin, with tonic water. It's good for what ails you," said Mrs. Johnson to Maude. "Trust me, I'm a nurse, I know these things."

Maude smiled a rueful smile. At least the gin bottle has a screw cap top she thought. It means I don't have to come over every afternoon and help open her bottle of wine.

The Stone Cottage

"Here Maude, have a seat on this lovely wicker settee. I've been here for over a week now and you and I haven't had an afternoon yet where we just sit and chat. You stay put, I'll get you a drink."

"I think I'll just have some lemonade if you don't mind," said Maude as she sat on the well stuffed patterned cushions of the loves-seat. "I'm not really very much of a drinker and I do have the twins I have to keep my eye on."

Mrs. Johnson disappeared into the living room but returned momentarily with a tall glass of lemonade. "I'm sure this'll be good for what ails you as well on this sweltering hot summer day."

"I'm sure it will." Maude took the tall glass from Mrs. Johnson and noticed that a light bit of moisture was forming all around it. The lemonade was right out of the fridge and was very cold. She hadn't had a really cold drink in a long time and it sure was delightful.

"Who is that young man that I saw over at the stone cottage this morning?"

"That's Philippe. He delivers ice once a week."

"I thought that was what he was doing. I didn't see him go into the cottage but I saw him come out with a big pair of ice tongs. When he got down to the dock he rinsed them in the lake. I'm not sure why but he did that but then he put them under the seat and took off."

"I think he was probably rinsing a bit of sawdust off the tongs. He packs his ice in sawdust over the winter and it keeps the blocks from thawing too fast and sticking together." Maude took another sip of the chilled lemonade. "Usually when he grips the block of ice with the tongs, he lifts it over the side of the boat to rinse it off in the lake before he brings it in. I guess there must have been a bit of sawdust left on the tongs."

"Humph. Well I did notice he sure is well built. He isn't really very tall but he is very muscular. It must be from carting all those big blocks of ice. They can't be light," said Mrs. Johnson. "And he's got quite a tan too. Does he ever wear a shirt? I've seen him go by in the channel often but I didn't know what he does for a living." Mrs. Johnson was babbling away like a young school girl smitten by a boy she liked in her class. Maude was trying hard not to laugh at her as she thought of that analogy.

"Well sometimes he wears a shirt but he says he is more comfortable without one. Riding around in the boat all day with all that ice must keep him cool on the hot summer days."

"You really will have to introduce me to him seeing how we are neighbours and all. You never know when I might need a bit of ice for my gin and tonic." Maude and her hostess both broke out in a laugh at the same time but for different reasons.

*****

"I don't know what to think Gil," Maude said to her husband that evening after supper. The children had gone to the inland lake which was about a quarter mile behind the stone cottage to look for frogs to use as bait for fishing the next day. The couple were alone sitting at the kitchen table enjoying a leisurely cup of coffee and a bit of quiet time without the chatter of the twins.

"She's a nice person, we get along just fine and she has been so good to me but I just don't know what to think about her."

"What has happened that makes you worried?" Gilbert asked.

"Well, she is always offering me something to drink. Finally I told her that I'm not much of a drinker and she was OK with that but I think she wants me to have a drink with her so she isn't drinking alone."

"Maybe she feels guilty having one by herself and if you have one with her then it's more of a social drink," he said.

"I can see your point but once she's had a few drinks she starts saying silly things."

"Like what?" Gil asked.

"She saw Philippe today, and was asking a lot of questions about him. She has noticed him going by in the boat every day and she really wants to meet him. I got the feeling that she was having romantic thoughts about him."

"Oh, that's not good."

"I've met Philippe quite a few times in the last couple of years. He always seems really nice to me, and is pretty chatty but I just realized I don't know very much about him. I don't even know if he's married."

"Well he isn't," said Gilbert "I don't know much about him either but what I do know is that he lives with his mother up at the very farthest end of the lake. I'm not one to repeat gossip but I have also heard that Philippe is quite the ladies man. He's handsome and he knows it." He paused and took another sip of his piping hot coffee. "His father is quite old and has been really sick. Last winter his

The Stone Cottage

father stayed with his daughter in Penetanguishene and he hasn't come back up yet this summer."

"After all those years of living up here, he must miss being here."

"When you aren't feeling well I don't think it matters too much where you are living."

"It's not my place to say anything to Mrs. Johnson but I hope that she doesn't keep going on and on about him. She's a married woman, it's embarrassing."

"You're right about that." Suddenly their quiet was shattered.

"Mom, Dad, look at what we caught," Ben shouted as he rounded the corner from the living room into the kitchen. Gripped in his hands was a huge bull frog, its long legs dangling between his arms, his hands barely big enough to ensure a good grip on the frog. A deep croak that sounded more like the word "har-rumph" emanated from the bull frog as the soft tissue below his head swelled with air.

"You don't need to bring that into the kitchen Ben," said Maude. "Let's go outside and you can tell us all about it. Where's your sister?"

"She's coming," Ben said with a sigh. "She has a couple of small frogs that we caught in a pail and they keep jumping out of the pail so she has to stop and catch them. I guess we should have brought a lid for the pail."

Just as Ben said that, Emma rounded the corner of the living room and came into the kitchen as well, lifting the pail up and saying as she entered the room, "look at what we caught for fishing tomorrow."

As if on cue a frog leapt out of the bucket and landed right on the table. "Get those out of the kitchen," Maude said. "Reptiles belong outside not inside." Gilbert quickly stretched out his hand and grabbed the runaway frog and put it back in Emma's pail.

All four of them filed out of the cottage and stopped on the large flat section of granite that was used as their front sitting area.

"That's a marvellous bull frog you have there," Gilbert said to his son.

"I know, and he was actually pretty easy to catch too." Gilbert and Maude could tell that Ben was pretty proud of himself for being able to get a hold of it and keep his grip on it. "I don't want to let him go. Just before I caught him, I saw him jump and he can go about three feet in the air," Ben said excitedly.

"Ben was a bit afraid to catch him," said Emma. "It took him a while to work up to grabbing it but now that he has his hands on it he won't let go."

"Can we keep him Mom?" asked Ben.

"Keep him if you want to, I don't care but just don't bring him back into the cottage. I don't want it getting lose and leaping on my bed in the middle of the night."

"What can I put him in?" he asked.

"There is an old laundry tub behind the cottage, use that for now," said Gilbert. "I'll round up a piece of plywood to make a cover for it."

"Put some water and a few rocks in the tub as well," Maude added. "That way he'll be happier."

"He's too big to fish with," said Emma. "Maybe we could eat him instead."

"Maybe we could," said their father. Maude rolled her eyes.

"Dad, can you do me a favour?" Ben asked.

"Sure, what is it?"

"Can you hold the frog for me while I get the wash tub and put water and rocks in it?"

"How about if I get that stuff together for you? You've got such a good hold on that frog and it looks like you guys are getting along real fine. It would be a shame to interrupt that."

Ben sat down cross legged on the rock and stared at his new pet. Every now and then he would risk letting go with one hand and would stroke the soft pad of skin in the frog's neck. Occasionally he'd be rewarded with another "harrumph" and Ben would giggle. "Mom, I think he likes me."

"I'm sure he does but you'll have to remember that you've taken him from his home so you'll have to be sure you find things for him to eat and keep his water fresh."

Gilbert returned with the tub and a bucket. He set it up on the veranda in front of the stone cottage then went down to the lake to get a pail of water. On his way back he picked up a couple of flat stones and one round one to put in the tub. "There, that ought to do it," he said to Ben. "Just give me a minute to get a board to cover this with and then you can put him to bed for the night."

All the while this was going on, Emma was wandering around with her pail and the three frogs she had in it. She too wanted to put some water and stones in the pail but was afraid to go to the water to in case the frogs jumped into the lake. Maude seeing her dilemma offered her assistance and soon the pail, with a small board for a lid and the laundry tub with a large plywood lid were sitting side by side on the veranda.

"Tomorrow we'll go fishing in the Narrows with our frogs," Emma said.

"I'm going to catch a nice big northern pike and maybe we can have that for supper tomorrow night, right mom?"

"Oh for sure, we haven't had fish for a while now, so I'll make you guys a deal. You catch them, I'll clean and cook them."

The twins lifted the lids of their respective prized possessions to peek inside one more time to make sure all was well. As Emma lifted her lid one of the frogs leaped out and landed right in her lap. She shrieked, not because she was afraid but because she was startled.

Maude and Gilbert both laughed at the same time, then Maude said, "OK you guys, time to go into the kitchen and get washed. And scrub really well. I don't want you getting in bed with any inland lake pond-scum on you."

*****

"I thought that I heard your boat land at the dock," Mrs. Johnson said to Philippe as he was walking up from the dock with a large block of ice for the stone cottage.

"Yes, I'm here, in person, right on schedule," said Philippe, his French accent seemingly more pronounced to Maude than it usually was.

"My name is Ronnie Johnson."

"Pleased to meet you," Philippe said politely.

"And your name is Philip, I understand."

"Actually it is pronounced like Phil-leap, it's the French way."

"Well my name is really Veronique but everybody calls me 'Ronnie' because I don't like my first name very much. It sounds too, I don't know, sophisticated."

"Veronique is a lovely name," he said letting the 'r' roll a little on his tongue, his French accent maximizing the sound of it.

"It does sound better when you say it but uh, you can just call me Ronnie."

"If you prefer," he said and gave her a little wink as he hoisted the block of ice a little higher in the air so it wouldn't drag on the ground and knock chips off. Shirtless as usual when he lifted the block of ice higher his biceps flexed and strained with the weight of the ice block and his shoulder muscles tensed as well. Mrs. Johnson couldn't help but notice and smiled, glancing at Maude to see if she too had noticed.

Maude led the way up the path and "Ronnie" fell into pace up the path behind him admiring how well "Phil-leap" filled out his dungarees.

Maude was a little shocked listening to this exchange of names down at the dock. In all the time that she had known Mrs. Johnson, she never knew what her first name was. Mrs. Johnson had certainly never volunteered her first name to either her or to Gilbert that she knew of, preferring to be referred to as Mrs. Johnson, or the doctor's wife.

"There you go Maude, you should be good for another week," said Philippe as he closed the door on the ice box.

She handed him the money and as she was about to say thank you Mrs. Johnson interrupted and said, "Philippe, I have an electric refrigerator over at my place. The freezer in it is very small and I can't make ice very well because I have stored some meat in it."

"Ah, I see," Philippe said as he listened attentively his hands resting on his trim waistline.

"Would you come over and have a look at it to see if you can sell me a piece of ice that would be just the right size to fit. I like to have ice with my drink in the afternoon and it would be so nice to have some."

Maude thought, *flirting seems to come naturally to her*.

"Certainly madam," Philippe said. "I'd be happy to go have a look."

The two made their way out of the stone cottage and headed down the path towards the main cottage. Maude followed them as far as the front door and stopped there. She rolled her eyes skyward and thought, *Should I go, should I follow, make sure they*... and she stopped herself. *They are grown adults. They don't need a chaperone.*

Maude slowly made her way back to the stone cottage wondering just what Mrs. Johnson's motives were. Not long after that Maude noticed Philippe down at the dock and thought that it seemed to be taking him a long time getting ready to leave. When she looked closer she noticed that he seemed to be cleaning off a space in the front seat and wiping it with a towel that he had taken from under the deck of his small runabout.

"I'll be down in a minute," Mrs. Johnson shouted to him from the front porch. "I just have to talk to Maude for a minute."

"Oh boy, I wonder what's going on," Maude thought.

Almost instantly Mrs. Johnson was in the path to the stone cottage. Maude left from her front veranda and walked towards Mrs. Johnson on the path. The first thing Maude noticed was that her neighbour had changed her clothes. Now she was wearing a white cotton halter top with the ends tied into a big bow behind her neck and a big bow in her lower back. Her midriff was showing pale, white flesh between her top and the pair of very brief white cotton shorts that she had put on. A matched set if ever there was one. A large straw hat covered her head and white sandals protected her feet from the hot rocks. *She looks stunning in that outfit, like a movie star in fact,* Maude thought. *Tall, slim and very attractive, the muscles in her long slender legs tensing as she climbed the path.*

"Do you need something Mrs. Johnson?"

"Oh no, I'm fine. I was just mentioning to Philippe that I am new to the bay and other than you, Gilbert and the twins, I don't really know anyone else. He said that he has quite a few deliveries to make today and said that if I wanted to come along, he'd be happy to take me. It'll be a great way for me to get a chance to see the sights and learn my way around. He said he'll introduce me to some of the other women in the area too."

"That will be nice," said Maude. "This is a beautiful area we live in and I'm sure Philippe will be a terrific tour guide. He certainly knows his way around."

"Oh well, I'm off then. I just wanted to let you know where I was going in case you were looking for me. See you later."

"Yes, see you later. Have a nice time." Maude watched as Mrs. Johnson rushed down the path to the dock. Philippe had already started the motor. As she got to the boat, there was a brief conversation about where she should sit and then he lifted his hand to help guide her off the dock, into the boat and onto the seat he had cleared for her. He untied the ropes and as he started to reverse away from the dock Maude could see her looking back up the path. She waved with one hand as she clutched onto her straw hat with the other and then they were gone.

*****

Maude had been sitting on the dock watching the twins swimming in the small cove near the Narrows when Philippe pulled his boat up to the dock. As he helped Mrs. Johnson out of the boat Maude could tell by the way she was moving that she was in pain. As Philippe pulled away from the dock she turned to wave goodbye and immediately Maude could tell that the pale, white flesh on

Mrs. Johnson's back was not only just a bit pink but actually a very angry looking red colour.

"I can't believe I have such a bad sunburn. We were only gone for about two hours," said Mrs. Johnson to Maude as they made their way up to the main cottage.

"You look like you have a pretty nasty sunburn on your back Mrs. Johnson," called Emma from the water's edge. She waved to her mom and then dove under the water again.

"My back is so sore Maude. I must have been sitting in the boat in a peculiar position. There aren't any back rests in that boat so I had to lean against the side of the boat the whole time." She tried to do a few shoulder rolls and stretch her arms forward and back. "I'm so stiff," she grumbled. "Gosh, look at my legs," she said as if noticing them for the first time. "They are burnt too, but in a weird pattern," said Mrs. Johnson.

"It's probably from the way you were sitting in the boat this afternoon," said Maude trying to reassure her friend. "It's surprising how fast you can get sun burnt when you are near the water."

"I was sitting on that front seat the whole time and had my legs curled up under me for the most part."

"When you are on the water on a calm day like today, the sun beats down on you from the sky but it also reflects off the water as well so you kind of burn twice as fast," said Maude.

"I'm not sure if I have anything to put on it," said the doctor's wife, "and it's starting to sting already."

"Well, there are two home remedies that I know of," said Maude as she followed Mrs. Johnson onto the front porch. "First of all we'll try the easiest one. Do you have any vinegar?"

"Vinegar!" she said surprised. "No, I don't."

"You just wait here, I'll go over to the stone cottage and get some that I have over there," offered Maude and with that she backed down off the porch steps and headed to the stone cottage.

She returned within minutes with a small hand basin. The clear liquid was sloshing around the edges as she walked up the steps and Maude had to slow her pace a bit so that she didn't spill any.

"I've mixed equal parts of cool water and vinegar," said Maude. "I'll get a couple of facecloths from your linen closet and soak them." She returned within just a few moments and put the cloths into the basin to soak.

"Just lean forward on your chair and I'll drape the cloths on your back," instructed Maude.

Mrs. Johnson complied and as soon as the cool cloth was applied she felt immediate relief from the burn. "Oh, that feels so good," she said.

"The trick is to use cool water, not cold water. That will shut the pores of your skin to quickly and nothing will absorb in. It won't take long for these cloths to heat up with a burn like you have but at least I can keep dipping them in the basin and reapply them."

"I was such a fool wearing a top that had no back on it," said Mrs. Johnson.

"I could tell when you left the dock that your back was pretty exposed. The way you were leaning with your back against the gunwale, I thought you might get a sun burn today. You are so fair skinned, you are going to have to be careful if you are going to be on the water all summer."

"Your skin tone is pretty dark Maude, do you ever get a burn or do you just tan?"

"Oh yes, Mrs. Johnson, sometimes I get a burn, but not too often. I'm kind of lucky that way. First of all, I don't expose too much of myself to the sun for long periods of time. When I'm wearing a bathing suit it usually means I'm going in the water and when I get out, I usually put on a light blouse if I'm not getting dressed right away. My face, hands and arms are always exposed to the sun and are pretty brown but being Native I have more of a tendency to just tan rather than burn. But it has happened."

"Maude that feels so good," said Mrs. Johnson as Maude replaced the cloth with a new cool one. "In all my years of nursing and helping Doc in the office I've never ever heard of anyone using vinegar and water to soothe a sunburn."

"Well Mrs. Johnson, this will be one remedy for you to remember. With a burn like you have you aren't likely to forget it soon either."

"Please Maude, just call me Ronnie. Since we are neighbours I hope that we will become good friends to. I don't think you need to be so formal. Just call me Ronnie," she repeated.

"OK, if that's what you prefer. Ronnie it is," said Maude letting the name kind of linger across her lips a bit as if testing it out. She continued to periodically replace the cloths on Ronnie's back as they warmed. After about twenty minutes of friendly idle chatter between the two women, Maude telling her about her day, Mrs. Johnson describing where she had been and whom she had met Maude said, "although this has been nice to sit here and chat, I do have to leave you. The kids have been in the water way too long. I've been able to keep my eye on them from here on the porch so I know they are just fine but they have been in the water for almost two hours now, diving for clam shells and an old silver tea spoon they keep retrieving and tossing back into the lake. They'll be waterlogged if I don't make them get out. If it were up to them they'd probably stay in the lake till supper."

"Thanks again Maude," said Ronnie. "You've been really helpful. You are very good to me, you always have been. I don't know if I deserve it but…" she paused as if she were going to say something more about their relationship then changed her mind. "I think I'll take these cloths off my back now and let them soak on my upper thighs for a while. They are really starting to sting as well."

"I don't know how long you will get relief from that mixture but if later this evening you are still really uncomfortable maybe we can try my home remedy number two," said Maude.

"And what would that be?" asked Ronnie, a broad smile parting across her perfectly white teeth.

"Oh, a girl can't give away all her secrets at once," joked Maude. "You'll have to wait and see." She stepped out of the porch and shouted towards the dock as she descended the stairs. "OK you guys time to get out of the water before you start to grow fins and gills." She turned at the bottom of the porch steps and walked towards the dock gathering a couple of towels she had left lying on the rocks near the pump house.

*****

Philippe's hunger for a beautiful woman was returning and quickly. It had been way too long since he had been with a woman. It had been a very long and lonely winter. Just thinking about Ronnie made his pulse race a little bit quicker than normal. He wasn't at all disappointed when she had mentioned that she didn't know anyone in the bay other than Maude and Gilbert. Taking her in the boat with him as he made his deliveries was a perfect way to spend the day with such a pretty woman. *Oh, those legs,* he thought, *so milky white, so smooth and slender.*

How he'd love to rub his hands along the curves of her thighs. It was all he could do to keep his hands off her as they rode along in his small boat. He could have easily leaned forward and reached out to touch her but he didn't. He didn't want to seem too needy, he didn't want to scare her off. *Slow and easy, let her get to know me a little, let her see how charming I can be,* he thought. He rubbed his hand across his bare muscular chest, fingering the thick coarse chest hair and twirling a few strands on his fingers. *I think she liked seeing me without a shirt on.* He smiled as he thought of her leaning against the gunwale of the boat, her elbows slightly flexed for support, her back arched just enough to push her breasts out forward, straining the thin cotton of her halter top. He could almost feel the quivering of her muscles as he imagined his hand pressing into the small of her back.

Yes, he thought, *I will have to make sure that we become very good friends.* He smiled as he thought of the two of them together. *She is one of the most beautiful women I have ever met. Maybe she would like to go on a picnic on one of the outer islands. Maybe she likes to swim. I could take her over to the bluff in the Freddie Channel and we could hold hands as we jump from the highest point into the distant water below. Maybe we could…*

Suddenly Philippe was startled by how close he had come to hitting one of the shoals sticking out of the water. He pulled hard on the tiller arm of the engine and steered the boat away from the dangerous rocks. He chastising himself for daydreaming about a woman as he navigated the narrow spaces between the shoals that protected his dock from the bad weather. *I've only known this woman for a few hours and already she has some kind of power over me,* he thought.

He pulled up to the dock. After shutting off the motor he tied the ropes to the dock rings and easily leapt onto the dock. He hoisted the waistband of his jeans a little higher and sauntered up towards his house whistling a merry tune. *One thing I know for sure,* he thought, *I'm going to like delivering ice to Mrs. Johnson.*

*****

The persistent knocking on the front door of the stone cottage was soft but loud enough that Maude heard it from the kitchen table where she sat by the dim light of a kerosene lamp. She was deep in thought as she worked on a cross-stitch pattern she had brought up with her from home and was a bit startled by the sound. As she crossed the floor of the front room Maude heard her name being called softly.

"Maude, Maude, are you still awake?"

She opened the door to see a rather haggard looking Mrs. Johnson. Gone was the stylish straw hat, white shorts and halter top from earlier in the day. All she was wearing was a simple nightgown of a very thin material with a finely printed pattern of delicate looking tiny roses. She seemed to be slightly winded as if she had been rushing and the smell of gin on her breath indicated that she had probably had enough to drink that she didn't really care too much about how she looked right now or who saw her dressed like this. Maude was glad that Gilbert had gone to bed already. She wasn't sure it would have been too appropriate for him to see her dressed this way, her short nightgown exposing most of the upper thighs, her breasts rising and falling with her heaving chest visible through the sheer material.

"Maude I can't stand the pain of this sunburn anymore. My back is so sore I can't bear it. I can't even tolerate wearing any clothes. Even this light night gown seems like a lead weight on my shoulders." She stood motionless in the doorway her only movement was the wringing of her hands together in front of her as if unsure what to do.

"You sure do have a bad sunburn Ronnie," said Maude as she glanced at the brilliant red tips of her friend's shoulders visible through the sleeveless nightgown. "I'm not a doctor but I wouldn't be surprised that if your husband were here he would diagnose a second degree burn."

"I wanted to put those cloths with the water and vinegar on my back again but the water had become warm. When I tried to put the bowl in the fridge to cool it off I spilled what little bit there was left on the floor." Ronnie seemed devastated. "I'm sorry to bother you so late but I could see a light was on in the kitchen and I hoped you would still be up." She dropped her hands to her side and said, "I think I'm ready to try out remedy number two."

Maude smiled. "I thought you might come to see me later. In fact, I was so sure of it that after supper I made several pots of tea that..."

Ronnie interrupted "I don't think having a cup of tea right now is what I need," she said with panic in her voice.

"Oh, you don't drink it. I made it extra strong and have had it sitting on the table to cool. Just like I did with the vinegar and water, I'm going to put some of it on your back as a compress." She turned and walked toward the kitchen. "I'll just get a few rags that I can use to soak in the tea. I don't want to use any good cloths because this tea is so strong it will stain them for sure."

Within a few moments Maude returned with another large basin in her hands. This time it was filled with a dark amber liquid. She had a few rags draped over her shoulder. She said in a whispering voice, "How about if we go back to your place? That way our talking won't wake the twins." As they moved off the veranda and started down the path Maude thought to herself, *and, if Gilbert wakes up he won't see you dressed like this.*

"Maude I really can't believe that you know all these home remedies that are so simple yet so effective," said Ronnie as she sat leaning forward on a kitchen chair, her elbows on the table, her hands cupped under her chin.

Maude thought for a moment then replied. "You must remember Ronnie, I grew up in a very isolated community many miles up the shore from where we are right now. We didn't have a doctor. My people hardly ever saw a doctor unless they were very ill and even then they had to travel by canoe to Parry Sound to see someone. Many people were too sick to make that journey and had to rely on the support of people in our village. Our next door neighbour, Mrs. King was an elderly woman who had what we called 'the gift of healing.'" Maude chuckled a little at the thought of her then said, "She had a whole slew of home remedies up her sleeve and she could treat most illnesses with just herbs and medicines she made from berries and certain types of bark. She would make lotions and potions from special plants she would find in the forest behind her home. She was a very talented woman but she didn't share her knowledge very often except with people she really trusted. My mother was one of those people so I learned a lot from her." Maude removed a tea soaked compress from Ronnie's back and replaced it with another sliding it up under the nightgown carefully so as not to scratch the tender skin. "In fact... our neighbour also delivered babies and I'm happy to say she brought me into this world and I think I turned out all right."

"You sure did." Ronnie sighed at the relief from the cool compress. There was a lull in the conversation then Ronnie said, "It must be the tannin that is in tea that is making this feel so much better."

"I don't know much about the science behind this. All I know is that it works," said Maude.

The two women were silent for a few minutes each deep in thought when Ronnie broke the silence saying, "Tell me more about your childhood Maude." She paused briefly and before Maude could answer she added, "It seems I haven't given much thought to what life was like for you before you moved to town."

The two women chatted amiably, like old friends. Maude was happy to share the details of her past life with someone other than Gilbert and the twins. She didn't really have any friends in town so she never got a chance to share her story of what life was like living on the reserve. Though life was very different for her now, she never forgot where she had come from. Her race and culture was something she felt very strongly about upholding and being able to talk about it with Ronnie that evening reinforced in her that she was still very proud of her upbringing, her heritage and the life she had before she met Gilbert.

"And what about you Ronnie?" Maude said. "I heard you tell Philippe that your real name is Veronique but you prefer to be called Ronnie. That sounds like a very French name to me."

"You're right. It is a very French name. In fact my full maiden name is Veronique Marie St. Onge. I was born and raised in Montreal. I bet you are surprised by that," said Ronnie with a laughing lilt to her voice.

"Actually I am surprised. I can't detect any kind of French accent when you speak."

"Though my father is French, my mother is English and when I was growing up I learned the two languages fluently at the same time. My dad spoke to me only in French my mom spoke only in English." She laughed, "A person learns two languages pretty quickly in a household like that."

"Tell me more," said Maude not wanting to stifle the conversation.

"When I was finished high school I decided that I wanted to go into nursing and so I enrolled in nursing school at the Royal Victoria Hospital in Montreal. In those days the nursing students lived in a residence that was attached right to the hospital. Lucky for me, I knew how to speak both French and English so I was able to communicate with all my patients and the doctors regardless of their mother tongue."

"That must have been handy."

"It was. There were quite a few nurses who had to quit because they struggled with the languages. But not me. I just marched right along." Maude changed the compress again then Ronnie continued. "That's where I met Dr. Johnson."

The Stone Cottage

"I thought he was from Toronto."

"He is but in his final year of med-school he decided to move to Montreal to study under one of the doctors there that specialized in orthopaedics. He is quite famous in the medical world."

"What's that?" Maude asked.

"Oh sorry, that's a doctor who does bone work. Doc knew that he wanted to practice medicine in a small town and that if one of his patients broke an arm or a leg, he wanted to be able to set it properly, put a cast on it and do whatever was needed. Because I could speak English I was assigned to work with Doc almost exclusively, kind of like his interpreter shall we say. We got to know each other pretty well. After that semester was over Doc moved back to Toronto to finish med-school and he asked me to go with him. And," Ronnie waved her hands in the air, "the rest is history. We moved around and worked in a few small towns and villages before we finally made it to Penetanguishene. We liked it so much we stayed. C'est la vie."

Maude wondered if that is why Ronnie felt such a strong attraction to Philippe when she met him. Maybe it's the kinship of being French or maybe not. Oh well, it wasn't her place to worry about that. Her focus was to find some way to make her boss and new friend comfortable. And if strong tea compresses on a very red sunburn where what it took, then that is what she would do.

It was late when Maude crawled into bed next to Gilbert. He had obviously been up while she was gone because the kerosene lamp had been turned down very low, giving off just enough of a glow to allow her to move in the rooms without running into things. Maude didn't know what time it was exactly but she did know that morning was going to come early.

*****

The first thing that Maude did when she got up in the morning was run over to the main cottage to check on Ronnie. She was worried about her. Maude knew that Ronnie had had a few drinks in the evening before she came to get her for remedy number two. She also knew that while she was there applying the tea laden compresses Ronnie had asked her to mix her a double martini stating that perhaps the gin would help with killing the pain. Maude had put her off by saying that she didn't know how to mix a drink like that but she was pretty sure that as soon as she left to go back to the stone cottage Ronnie would be in the butler's pantry mixing herself a stiff one.

When she got to the main cottage, much to her surprise Ronnie was sitting at the table drinking a coffee. She had an old battered copy of National Geographic opened before her.

"You look pretty perky this morning," Maude said.

"I woke up early. Typically I prefer to sleep on my back or my side but with this sunburn I was only able to sleep on my stomach and that didn't work out very well for me so I got up and made some coffee. Would you like a cup?"

"You know what, I think I will." Maude walked over to the stove and took the old fashioned coffee perk off the range and poured herself a cup.

"If you want milk or cream there is some in the refrigerator."

"No, that's OK. I just take it black. We don't have very good luck keeping milk in that old icebox we have at the stone cottage so I've grown accustomed to having my coffee black."

"You know Maude, if ever there is something that you want to be sure is kept cold, just put it in the fridge here. For the most part it's just going to be me here and I don't need to take up the entire fridge. You really are welcome to store things here."

"That's very kind of you to offer." Maude smiled at this change in attitude from Ronnie. She had known her for a number of years now and Mrs. Johnson had always seemed to be a little distant with her, keeping that social class distinction between them as a barrier to getting to know one another. But, it seemed Ronnie had turned a new leaf. Perhaps because Maude was the only other woman around her these days or perhaps she just liked Maude's company and her competent way of handling things, like how to manage a sunburn. Whatever the reason, Maude liked the new Ronnie a lot better.

When she joined her at the table Ronnie looked at her and sighed. Maude could tell that something was weighing heavily on her mind.

Finally Ronnie said, "Doc is coming up tomorrow. I don't know what I'm going to tell him about how I came to get such a bad sunburn on my back and legs."

"It wouldn't hurt to tell the truth," Maude said. "You went for a boat ride with the man who delivers ice as a way to get to know the people who live around here. There's nothing wrong with that that I can see."

"Well that's the truth but I have to admit, I kind of asked Philippe to take me along because I thought it would be fun to spend the afternoon with a handsome devil like him." Ronnie paused as if she was reluctant to say more than added. "I've always maintained that it's OK to look as long as you don't touch but I'm afraid I may have pushed the envelope on this one a bit."

"Did something happen?" Maude asked.

"No, nothing happened but it could have. You should have seen the look in his eyes when he was driving the boat. I think he spent more time looking at me than where he was going, and do you know what? I kind of liked it."

Maude sat quietly and said nothing mostly because she was not quite sure what to say. She'd never been in a situation like this where another woman confided in her, especially about something like this.

"Maude, I have to tell you. It's something very personal. I hope you don't think badly of me but..." she paused as if not sure if she should actually say anything. "I've never told anyone else this but... things aren't very good between Doc and I. We've been having some problems."

Maude said nothing. She just sat quietly and reached across the table and took Ronnie's hand in hers. This simple gesture bridged some sort of hidden gap between the two women and suddenly Ronnie began to cry, the tears running down her cheeks and dropping silently on the flimsy nightgown she was still wearing from the evening before.

"I think that Doc is having an affair with one of the nurses at the hospital."

"What makes you think that?" Maude asked.

"I'm not just his wife, I'm his office nurse and secretary as well. I have to keep track of all that he does in the office and I also have to keep his files and records of his hospital visits straight too. He's gone a lot more often and for longer periods of time than what he is recording in his notes. He's getting in late almost every night."

"Have you asked him about it?"

"I have and he always seems to have some lame excuse about what took him so long. So I got to the point where I thought, I'd just wait up for him. I got into the habit where I'd pour myself a drink and sit in the sun room. When he would get home we'd chat about the day, the evening and other things. I'd try to keep it casual and friendly hoping he might slip up and spill the beans about what he'd really been up to but...." She didn't finish her sentence.

"But he never did," said Maude.

"That's right. It's been going on for a few years now. I've kind of gotten used to it. I think it's one of the reasons why I like being up here at the cottage. I don't have to worry about what time he's going to get home. We don't have any children you know. And mostly it's because we aren't together in that way very often. He usually makes excuses about that as well saying he's too tired, or too stressed but I think he's been seeing someone else and that's why."

Maude was beginning to see the big picture now but was having a hard time with it all. She had known the doctor for a long time now and found it hard to believe that he would be cheating on his wife. He just didn't seem to be the type. She also knew that Ronnie was drinking a lot and had been for several years now. What she couldn't figure out was whether the doctor having an affair because his wife was drinking a lot and their marriage was shaky because of it, or whether Ronnie was drinking because she believed her husband was having an affair and it was her way of coping with it. Maude let go of her grip on Ronnie's hand and realized that her own palms were sweating. She could also feel beads of sweat forming on her forehead. She was starting to feel pretty uncomfortable and wasn't really sure what to do or say.

"What do you think I should do Maude?"

"This is quite a lot for me to process Ronnie. I don't think I'm the right person to be giving advice about it. I've just never known anyone who has had this sort of problem to cope with. I'm kind of at a loss for words."

"Oh, I know. I guess I didn't really expect you to have an answer but it's just that I really had to tell somebody and …"

"I get it," said Maude taking Ronnie's hand in hers again. "I'm just glad you thought enough of me to tell me. Just know that your story is safe with me. I won't tell a soul."

They sat at the table for a few more minutes neither one of them speaking then Maude said, "I guess I have to get going. Gilbert will be wondering where I am and the twins will be up soon and looking for breakfast."

She stood to leave and as she did Ronnie reached out and gripped her hand once more and said, "Thank you Maude. I trust you and I appreciate you listening to my sad story. I just hope I didn't scare you off. Can we still be friends?"

"We will be friends. Maybe even better now. Remember, I'm just down the path so if you ever want to talk, I'll be ready to listen."

"I'm so lucky to have met you."

*****

Dr. Johnson arrived the following afternoon a bit later than he had planned. He apologized to Ronnie for being late but he explained that he had been tied up at the hospital in the operating room since early in the morning trying to patch together what remained of the arm of one of the labourers who worked in the lumber yard at the end of Water Street. The man had gotten his shirt sleeve caught in one of the rollers of the conveyor belt the logs ride on towards the mill's main saw. Before he could get his shirt off his arm was nearly sliced off by the big saw blade.

"It was pretty messy," the doctor said as he stood on the porch looking out at the view and jingling a handful of change in his pocket. "I did the best I could with what was left but I'm not sure he's going to be able use that arm ever again. He may even lose it."

"What a terrible thing to have happen," Ronnie said. She felt guilty for thinking that the reason he was late getting to the cottage was because he was with someone.

"Yup, it sure is, he's lost a lot of blood and we had to transfuse four units to replace his volume." After a short pause he continued, "You know what Ronnie? It's been kind of a tough day and I think I could use a good stiff drink. Would you care to join me?" he said knowing full well that she would.

After the drinks had been poured they went to sit side by side on the comfortable porch swing and idly rocked back and forth appreciating the magnificent view before them.

Doc said, "So tell me. How do you like living up here? Are you finding enough things to keep you busy?"

"I love it here. I can't believe how lucky I am to be able to wake up each morning to this," she spread her arms wide open before her encompassing the view.

"It's not too hard to take is it?"

"And I have been spending a lot of time with Maude. We've become pretty good friends. I know it's only been a couple of weeks now but I feel like I've known her all my life."

"Well you did know her from town as well."

"I did," she agreed, "but we seem to have connected on a different level here. It's been really nice. She's so sincere."

"I'm glad to hear that. I was afraid you might find it lonely up here so far from town and the friends you play bridge with."

"I have to admit, I haven't spent much time thinking about them. It's been a nice break from that routine."

Ronnie thought it was time to come clean about getting her sunburn in case Doc noticed it later. "I did get a chance to meet some of the other women who live up here during the summer as well."

"Oh, did Gilbert introduce you to them?"

"No actually. It was kind of funny the way it happened. There is a guy who lives up at the far end of the lake who delivers ice. He had a boat load of ice with him and when he stopped to deliver some to Gilbert and Maude I got a chance to talk to him a bit. When he told me what he was doing that afternoon I sort of invited myself along for the ride. He knows everybody so well it was great to go for the boat ride see the sights and get to meet some other ladies as well. You don't mind I hope."

"It does seem a little unusual but you've always been a pretty spontaneous person so I can understand how it would have all worked out."

"I think the next time he comes to deliver ice to the stone cottage I'm going to give him a job to do. I'm going to have a party and I'm going to invite all the women I met the other day."

"That sounds like a nice thing to do."

"I'll write notes to each of the women and ask Philippe to deliver them while he is delivering their ice."

"It seems like an old fashioned way to do it but without a telephone up here I don't really see that there is any other way. As long as Philip doesn't mind you imposing like that."

"I don't think it will be too much of a burden for him. He's pretty easy going," she paused as if trying to decide whether to say something else and then decided to go ahead with it anyway. "He pronounces his name Philippe," she said, her French coming out well in the pronunciation.

They were quiet for a short while rocking slowly back and forth on the porch swing. "This is so nice," Doc said. He reached his arm and out and draped it across her shoulders drawing her in to him.

She lifted his arm off her shoulders and said, "Oh, that's a pretty cozy thing to do but I've got a pretty good sunburn on my back and shoulders the other day when I was in the boat and it's still pretty sore."

He put his arm back down by his side and looked a bit quizzically at her. "I thought you'd know better, being a nurse and with all that you've seen. Someone with delicate white skin like yours needs to be protected from the sun."

"Maude said that when you are near the water the sun reflects off the water as well as from above so you can burn twice as fast." She smiled. "I've learned that lesson the hard way but Maude was there to save the day. She put vinegar and water together and made compresses in the afternoon and then later that night she made compresses with some strong tea that she had made. Old home remedies but do you know what? They worked."

"I'll have to remember that."

They continued to swing back and forth enjoying each other's company. Doc broke the silence by saying, "This party that you are going to have is a good idea. It's a great way for you to meet the other ladies. You will have to make me a list of all the things I'll have to bring up from town. And don't leave anything off. I want this to be a success for you."

Ronnie gave an inward sigh of relief. Maude had been right. Just tell the truth. She had and Doc hadn't been upset at all. She'd have to be sure to thank Maude for the good advice.

*****

Ronnie lay naked on the bed, the thin cotton sheets barely covering her body. Philippe too was lying on the bed admiring the long and slender beauty that lay entwined with his. He was on his back, his free hand slowly caressing the curves of her hips and the outline of her body partially draped over his. Her head was resting on his muscular shoulder, her free hand casually roaming over his powerful chest.

"I don't think I've ever met a man with such strong muscles. It must be from hauling all those blocks of ice." She rubbed her hand across the far side of his chest pinching his nipple slightly. He twitched with the sensation, his pulse quickening with her every movement. Casually she slid her hand up the side of his neck allowing it to linger there for a moment. She raised her hand a little higher and gently rubbed his earlobe.

He groaned and said, "oh, that feels so good."

"I know something else that will feel even better," she said.

She let her hand slowly wander back across his chest then she brought it down further and let it rest on his belly. "You have absolutely no fat on you. You are all muscle, I like that in a lover," she whispered in his ear.

He smiled, appreciating the compliment. Her hand dipped even lower and she tenderly caressed his scrotum then gripped his shaft, tugging slightly upward as she did so. She was surprised at how soft and delicate it felt in this flaccid state. She gripped tighter and was even more amazed at how quickly it became rigid in her hand. She continued to stroke him and the more she did, the more rigid and larger he became.

"I have a better idea," he said. He leaned up on his elbow and rolled her over onto her back. He slowly moved on top of her taking the majority of his weight on his elbows and gently eased himself into her moist and welcoming body. Her sigh as he slowly dipped further into her proved her eagerness to continue.

She moaned with the joy of having him in her and soon her hips were moving to the rhythm of his lovemaking. She shuddered with a spasm of pleasure and dug her fingernails into his muscular back.

"Oh, I can't hold back any longer!" he cried out. He collapsed on top of her, their panting breaths matching their delight.

He awoke suddenly soaked in sweat with a painful and throbbing erection. He was disappointed when he realized that it had all been just a dream.

"She really has a hold on me," he thought. "I can't stop thinking about her during the day and now I'm dreaming about her at night. I must go back and see her."

*****

It had been a week since he had pulled up to the dock to deliver ice to the stone cottage but the memory of him meeting Ronnie that day was still as vivid in his thoughts as if it had only been yesterday. He had driven by in his boat several times since that day and slowed down each time he passed in the hopes that he might see her on the porch, or the dock, or perhaps sunbathing on the rocks in her swimsuit. He knew that she was a married woman but after spending the afternoon with her he got the impression from the way she spoke about her husband that her marriage to the doctor was on shaky ground. If there was one thing that Philippe had learned over the years was that he was good at detecting when a woman was interested in him or just being polite. By her flirtatious behaviour that day in his boat, he was pretty sure she was more interested in him than sightseeing or meeting the other ladies in the bay.

He pulled up to the dock, shut off the motor and tied the ropes to the dock rings. Stepping carefully as he moved, he reached under the front seat to retrieve the heavy cast iron ice tongs he used to lift the blocks of ice from the floor of the boat. He pulled the heavy canvas tarp off the corner of the ice blocks beneath and with two hands opened the tongs and gripped a large block. The sawdust he had used to insulate it and keep it from sticking to the other blocks was still thick on its surface. He closed the tongs carefully so as not to split the block in two and held them tight until he had a firm grip on the block then hoisted it up from its resting spot and over the side of the boat to dunk it in the lake, rinsing the sawdust away.

Ben and Emma came running down from the stone cottage to greet him. "Boy we sure are excited to see you Philippe. Mom said that after you brought us fresh ice she would make us some cold lemonade. We can't wait."

"It's good to see you guys too," he said to them as he walked up the dock. Ben was following closely at his side and said, "how heavy is that anyway? I bet I could carry it, I'm getting to be pretty strong you know."

Philippe stopped and lowered the block to the dock. "It is pretty heavy but maybe you can lift it." Ben gripped the handles of the tongs with both hands, his legs straddling over each side of the ice. He lifted with all his might and was able to get it about 4 inches off the ground but wasn't quite able to take a step. Philippe laughed and playfully scratched the hair on the top of Ben's head and said, "maybe next year you'll be strong enough to carry it all the way to the cottage but for now I guess it's up to me."

Emma said, "I knew he wouldn't be able to carry that and I told him but he had to try anyway."

"No harm in trying," said Philippe. "He'd never know for sure unless he tries," and with that the twins raced off up the path, Emma shouting to Ben, "bet you can't catch me."

He made his way to the stone cottage and just as he was about to knock on the door Gilbert opened it, "I thought I heard some chatter out here. Hope the twins weren't bothering you."

"They never do," replied Philippe. "It's good to see such happy kids."

"Come on in. I think that Maude is just about finished wiping out the icebox so you can just put it right in."

When that task was completed the two men moved back outside and standing in the shade of the porch roof, chatted casually about the weather, fishing and outboard motors. Gilbert was interested in how Philippe liked having a small boat with an outboard on it. He was thinking of buying one so that he didn't have to take his big boat every time he had to run out to do an errand or a small work project for one of the many people who hired him as a handyman. Both men agreed it was the most practical way to go and was a lot more fuel efficient as well.

Philippe promised to keep his eyes and ears open for a good used boat and motor and the two men parted ways, Gilbert going back into the stone cottage to check with Maude while Philippe headed down the path that led to the main cottage.

"I'll just check in with Ronnie," he thought. "Maybe she'd like to come for another boat ride." The thought of her riding in the front of his boat on this beautiful afternoon smiling and chatting away making small talk like a schoolgirl put a bounce in his step. He loved to flirt with women and it was obvious she enjoyed it too.

It was a hot summer day and he had put on just a pair of shorts when he got up this morning rather than jeans. He knew his lady customers liked to see him like that. As usual he wore no shirt and even at this time of the day his body glistened slightly with the faint musky scent of his sweat. He knocked on the kitchen door at the back of the cottage and Ronnie answered it right away. She had seen his boat pull up to the dock and had hoped he'd come by to see her.

"Come in. Please sit down. Can I get you something cold to drink?"

"I don't really have time for a visit," he said. "I still have several deliveries to make and on a hot day like today the ice melts pretty quickly. Would you like to come with me for the ride?"

"I'd love to but last week I got such a sunburn that Maude had to keep putting cool compresses on my back all evening to ease the pain of it." She was wearing a similar halter top to the one she had on the first time he saw her but this one was pink with white pinstripes. She wore matching pink shorts. She reached into the fridge and pulled out a bottle of cold water. Taking a glass from the open shelf in the kitchen she poured herself a small amount and sipped slowly on the refreshing water as if contemplating her next statement. "Well…Maybe if I put a light blouse on over top what I have on it would protect me a little better from the sun. I'm so fair it seems it doesn't take much time when I'm on the water to get burnt."

"It would be great to have you come with me."

"I have a small favour to ask of you," she said.

"Anything for you Ronnie." He smiled and winked one of those flirty little winks he was known for around Cognashene.

"I want to have a little party next week and I'd like to invite all the ladies from around the bay. I've written invitations to them. Do you think that we could deliver those on your rounds?"

"I'd love to do that for you."

"That will be really helpful. I have six people on my list."

"All women I suppose."

"Yes," she said coyly. "It's a girl's only party."

She gathered her things and the two of them headed off down to the dock. She didn't bother to let Gilbert and Maude know she was leaving. She knew they'd figure it out if they went to find her and she wasn't there.

As they pulled away from the dock she looked back at the cottage and thought. *This truly is My Shangri-la.*

CHAPTER - 11

July 1938

It was a beautiful sunny summer day on Georgian Bay. As beautiful a day as anyone could possibly hope for. It was hot without being oppressive and for the first time in days there was no noticeable humidity. The clear blue sky was totally cloudless, the winds were non-existent, the flag on the pole by the main cottage hung limp, not even attempting to be stirred by the faintest of occasional breezes. The outlines of the trees on shore were reflected so perfectly in the mirror-like waters that a person could even distinguish the individual branches and various shades of green that differentiated the evergreens from the deciduous trees.

On a day like this it was impossible not to enjoy the beauty and wonder of endless pink and grey granite shorelines and the never ending views of the water as it stretched out to meet the sky in uninterrupted majesty. Gilbert and Maude, appreciated how lucky they were and how fortunate the twins were to be able to celebrate the wonders of nature in its entire splendour and its simple magnificence?

"There is a majesty in simplicity," Gilbert said to Maude as they made their way towards their destination. "There is nothing out here but simple beauty," Maude agreed.

The outer island they had chosen for their picnic was fondly known by the locals either as Cranberry Island or Lizard Island depending on who you spoke to. A long low slab of mostly pink granite, the island is quite narrow, perhaps only one hundred feet at its widest point, but is nearly a quarter mile long with undulating rocky outcroppings and small protected coves. There are multiple spots where the water over the years has worn away some of the softer rock to form small cliff like structures and some even have eroded away perfectly round holes in the overhanging ledges ideal for tying the ropes of your boat to, and that is exactly what Gilbert did.

Once he had navigated the narrow passage between the banks of rocky outcroppings known as the Newton Islands and followed the eastern side of Cranberry Island for about two hundred feet, Gilbert pulled into one of the small deep coves. After passing the bowline through one hole in the rock he pulled the runabout alongside the face of the small cliff and secured the stern line to yet another perfectly located hole in the rocks.

Pleased that the length of the boat matched the distance between the holes in the rocks so closely Gilbert patted the rocks with the palm of his hand and said to Maude proudly, "There, we could get gale force winds right now and this boat wouldn't go anywhere." Standing back and admiring how perfectly Mother Nature had created this mooring Gilbert looked over the stern of the boat to check the depth of the water under the outboard motor. "It's perfect. Lots of water under the boat and the motor."

"It's like it was meant to be," chimed in Ben who was itching to get out of the boat and start exploring.

"Let me help lift you up onto the gunwale Ben so you can climb the cliff a little easier," Gilbert said.

"Dad, I'm not little anymore. I'm eleven now. I can do this. Watch how easy it is," said Ben as he nearly vaulted himself clear of the boat and onto the rocks.

Following Ben's lead Emma climbed out of the boat and onto the shore. Maude reached down into the boat and passed the picnic basket, blanket and cushions she had brought from the cottage for them to sit on.

"Just put all those things over there on the rocks," Maude pointed to a flat surface where some previous visitors had had a bonfire. There were remnants of charcoal and unburned sticks still evident, neatly packed inside a ring of small rocks that had been used to contain the bonfire. It was a perfect spot for a fire because it was protected from the winds by a small outcropping of solid rock.

"I think I'd like to go for a walk before we eat," said Gilbert. "I feel like I haven't had much exercise lately and a good brisk walk on this island will get me limbered up.

"It's just what I need too," admitted Maude.

Once Maude and Gilbert had secured all their picnic supplies into one area the four of them headed north along the eastern shoreline. The children quickly made their way towards the far end of the island running and jumping playfully into puddles to see who could make the biggest splash. Within minutes the twins were well ahead of them and soaking wet.

"Be careful where you step if you are close to the edge of the water. Where ever you see the rocks look black and shiny it's really slippery," shouted Maude to the twins. "These rocks don't get much foot traffic to wear the slime off of them," Maude continued. The children who were currently stooped at the water's edge were trying to count the number of tadpoles they had found in a small puddle just above the waterline and seemed to pay no heed to what their mother had said.

"There are too many of them to count," Emma said to Ben. "I think there must be a hundred but they won't stay still long enough for me to count them."

"We just have to guess," said Ben poking a small stick into the puddle to agitate and stir the water just enough to keep the tadpoles swimming. "My guess is there are probably fifty."

"There are not," said Emma defensively as she got on her knees for a closer look.

"OK you two," said Maude as she got close to where they were and bent over to look into the puddle. "It's just a guess and one guess is probably as good as another. Let's keep going. Let's go explore right to the north end of the island."

Together the four of them set off once again, the kids skipping ahead of their parents. Maude, still in her bare feet gripped Gilbert's hand for better balance as they made their way around a rather large algae filled puddle. "That looks pretty yucky," she said, "you can't even see to the bottom."

"One big rain storm or a heavy wind and this puddle will be rinsed clean," said Gilbert.

They made their way to the farthest point of dry land where the children had found a cache of small pebbles in the crack of a rock. They were tossing the rocks into the calm water and competing with each other to see who could skip the rocks the farthest. Sometimes they had trouble counting how many times the rocks that Ben threw skipped across the surface because they were thrown with such force they went too far to discern individual skips before they sank.

"He has quite a throwing arm on him," Maude said to Gilbert. "Maybe he should think about a career in baseball when he's older. He could be famous."

"He's eleven years old already, and he's been working hard around the cottage cutting and splitting wood, moving rocks, not to mention the miles and miles he has covered swimming this summer. All that builds up his muscles."

The couple stood on the shore each with their pant legs rolled up to their knees letting the cool water wash over their feet. "It's so beautiful here," said Gil. "The water is so calm, the horizon looks so far away. It looks endless," he paused. "You can barely tell where the water meets the sky. And look," he said pointing his finger to the west, "you can clearly see the shoreline on Giant's Tomb Island and you can even make out the lighthouse on Hope Island. You don't see that very often from here."

"It is such a clear day. I love it," said Maude. "But it can't last forever." She paused as if deep in thought then added. "We've had really great weather for the last couple of weeks. It's been perfect but I just have a feeling it isn't going to last."

"Let's just enjoy it while we can," said Gilbert as he turned and started to walk back.

"OK you two. We're going to head back to where the boat is tied up and have our picnic before the food spoils in this heat," Maude called to the twins.

"I'll race ya," Ben said to Emma as he scooted around his parents and headed down the long ribbon-like island.

Emma gave chase but soon stopped and walked back to her parents looking down at her feet. "Dad, why is there so much yellow stuff all over the rocks here. I noticed that it's just at this end of the island too. I didn't see any down where we parked the boat. It looks a lot like moss but it looks like it has gotten old and rusty."

"It is a type of moss but a little different from the green spongy moss we have around our stone cottage Emma," Gilbert bent down to try and scrape a bit of the crusty clump off the rock with his thumb nail. "See how it just breaks off in small little bits. This is called Lichen and they aren't really a plant like other mosses are. These are really a fungus because they can't survive without algae. A plant can live on its own, a fungus needs to feed off of something." He held up a small scraping of the lichen and brought it closer to her for inspection. "See how they have tiny leafless branches that just lay on the rock. When they dry out they look like they are paint flakes that are peeling off the rock. When they don't get enough algae to live on then they dry up and turn this rusty yellow colour."

"Why do they grow here then?" Emma asked.

"Well this part of the island is pretty low and when it gets really windy the waves wash right over these rocks we are standing on. There is always algae in the water and when the wind stops and the waves settle down, then the surface of the rocks dry up and any algae that was on the rocks dries out and it feeds the lichen that made these rocks their home years ago. "

"How old do you think this lichen is?"

"Some people say that lichen fungus is some of the oldest living organisms on the whole planet."

"Hum," Emma said thoughtfully. "I'm going to talk to my teacher about this. Maybe we can study this in science class."

"Great idea Emma," her father said. "And you'll have the advantage of knowing about it and seeing it in its natural environment. That's something most of the other kids in your class won't ever get a chance to see."

"I'm going to tell Ben," she said and scooted ahead once again.

"I'm glad she asked you about that," Maude said to Gilbert with a smile on her face. "I'd have probably just told her it was orange moss." Gilbert laughed then said, "I just read an article about Lichen in an old issue of National Geographic I found in the main cottage when I was doing the renovation or I'd never have known about it.

The couple ambled along holding hands, enjoying the peace and quiet watching the kids jump from one rocky prominence to another. When they got back to the picnic area Maude spread the blanket out and arranged the cushions in a semi-circle while Gilbert went back to the boat to check on the ropes and retrieve the small cooler they had packed with the remnants of ice that was left in their icebox. He also retrieved a jug of ice tea Maude had made earlier in the day and without even realizing it he rubbed his tongue over his lips thinking about how refreshing a cold drink was going to be on this hot, hot day.

"Mom," Ben asked. "This island has two names doesn't it?"

"Well actually three."

"I can understand why some people call it Lizard Island because when you stand at the far northern end and look towards the south the long ribbon of rock looks like a lizard crawling in the water.

"Uh-hmm," Maude mumbled as she continued to set up the picnic.

"But why do some people call it Cranberry Island?"

"Come with me for a second," Maude said. They climbed a bit of a bluff and looked towards the southern and wider end of the island. "Look over there," she pointed as she spoke. "Some people call this Cranberry Island because of the narrow stretch of swampy ground that runs through the centre of the lower southern end. That swampy area is full of cranberry bushes and in the late fall you can pick the berries once they are ripe and they are good for cooking and eating. Maybe you remember me making cranberry sauce to go with the turkey dinner we eat on Thanksgiving Sunday?"

Ben didn't respond to his mom's comment about the cranberries. Instead he asked, "You said the island has three names. What is the other name?"

"The formal and legal name for this island is Esh-pa-be-kong. Some say the name is Ojibwa for 'where little berries grow.' But, I'm not exactly sure."

"Humph," Ben said almost dismissively as he turned to walk back to the picnic site. "I'm hungry, can we eat now?"

"You betcha!" said Maude. "I'm hungry too. Let's go. I'll race ya," said Maude knowing full well it was a race she'd never win but giving Ben the chance to shine anyway.

*****

It was a most pleasant afternoon. Probably the best afternoon they'd had together as a family in a long time. The weather was perfect, the food was delicious, and the ice tea was as sweet and refreshing as everyone had hoped it would be. A slight breeze had started to blow out of the west and a ribbon of dark cloud formed on the horizon, defining exactly where the sky ended and the water began. The cloud bank stayed in the distance and didn't advance but Gilbert kept his eye on it just the same.

Everyone was stuffed and once the picnic dishes had been cleared up and the basket repacked they all decided to just relax and lie on their backs and let the warmth of the rocks seep into their bodies.

After about twenty minutes Ben said, "Mom, I'm getting pretty hot, can we go for a swim?"

"Sure, just be careful near the edge." She sat up and looked directly at Ben and said, "and no diving off the shore. There could be some rocks hidden in the water. I don't want you to bang your head," Maude said.

"You wanna come Emma?"

The Stone Cottage

"No, I don't think so. I'm so comfy lying here on the blanket I'd like to just stay here forever."

Ben swam for what seemed like an hour. No one was actually timing him but swimming for him was effortless, his long slender body slipped through the water like an eel as he swam back and forth doing lengths parallel to the shore line. When he got bored swimming lengths he dove for clam shells which he proudly presented to his mom each time coming up to her soaking wet and purposefully shaking his head, rubbing his hands through his hair so as to sprinkle Maude in a playful game they enjoyed nearly every time the children swam at the stone cottage.

"I hate to put an end to this perfect afternoon but I think we should pack up and make our way back to the cottage," said Gilbert as he gazed off to the western sky again.

"Aw, this is so nice," said Emma. "I don't want to go so soon, can't we stay longer."

"I don't really want to go either sweetie, but we've been here for hours already and if you look over there," Gilbert said pointing to the west, "you'll see there are some pretty heavy and dark looking clouds that are building and they are moving our way."

Maude sat up and looked at what Gilbert had pointed to. "Is it coming quickly?" she asked.

"Well at first it wasn't. It seemed to be just hanging around on the horizon but in the last half hour it started advancing pretty quickly."

"Well we better get going," said Maude as she started to gather the picnic paraphernalia and folding the blanket. "I've got a full load of clothes on the line that I washed this morning. I don't want them to get wet."

"Come on Ben," Gilbert called to his son, "time to get out."

Ben nodded to his father to let him know he'd heard him and he gracefully swam a perfect front-crawl to shore.

The wind continued to get stronger and Gil was glad the boat was so securely moored to the shore. Ben came alongside his dad on the edge of the small cliff and slid down off the rocks onto the gunwale and then dropped softly onto the floor of the boat. "Here dad, hand me the picnic basket and the other things," he offered. He had sensed there was an urgency in his father's tone and mannerisms and he was eager to help.

"Thanks Ben, good to have your help. Once we are all in the boat I'll get you to untie the bowline from the shore and I'll do the one on the stern and then we can push off from the shore at the same time. "

Gilbert adjusted the angle of the engine and was happy to see that it started on the first tug of the pull cord. "Glad I tinkered with the carburettor when I bought this boat," he said to no one in particular. The engine sputtered to life and once the ropes were in the boat, they shoved off from shore. Gil put the motor into reverse and began backing away from the protected cove into the channel that was already beginning to get choppy.

"I'm glad we live pretty close to here," said Maude as she glanced at the skyline to the west. "This storm is moving in pretty fast."

*****

Everything was working out perfectly for Philippe. Just the way he planned it. He knew that Maude and Gilbert were gone for the afternoon with the children and he was desperate to see Ronnie again. Rather than leave his boat at the dock for the world to see that he was visiting yet again, he had pulled his boat up on shore in a small inlet just on the north end of the Narrows channel. Hardly anyone ever went by there and so it was the perfect place to hide his boat.

A short jaunt overland and soon he was knocking lightly on the back door to the kitchen of the main cottage. Through the window in the door he could see Ronnie was dressed in a light, nearly transparent chiffon house dress. It was multicoloured, was gathered at her slender waist and showed off her figure perfectly. She answered the door in an instant. It was almost as if she was expecting him to come. She glanced out the kitchen window towards the dock and then back at him.

"Ahh, mon Cheri. You make my heart race," Philippe said to Ronnie as he flashed that million dollar smile at her again.

Is he trying to be irresistible, or, does it just come naturally to him, Ronnie wondered? *He was trying,* she decided, *though he doesn't have to try very hard.*

"Where's your boat?" she asked a bit puzzled that he was there but his boat wasn't. "I didn't hear you pull up to the dock."

Philippe walked over to Ronnie and drew her into his arms, kissing her tenderly on her neck and nibbling gently on her earlobe.

"I pulled it up on shore just inside the bay," he said tilting his head in a slight nod to indicate just at the north end of the Narrows. "I don't want anyone to see that I'm here right now."

"Why not," she asked playfully pulling away from his embrace and spinning around in a circle making her skirt billow outwards like a schoolgirl would do.

"Because, I'd like to spend the night and I don't want anyone to know."

She moved slowly towards him and this time it was her turn to pull him into her embrace. They stayed that way, motionless, breathing in each other's scent for a few moments then she placed her hands on his muscular bare chest and slowly pushed herself away.

"I guess if you're going to be here that long you could get thirsty. I think I'd better make you a drink." She sauntered over to the liquor cabinet and as she opened the glass doors she turned to him and asked, "What would you like?"

"I'll have whatever you're going to have," he said as he tugged slightly at the swelling that was developing inside the crotch of his jeans.

"I'm having a gin and tonic with lots of ice. That always cools me down on a hot day like this."

"That'll be perfect," he said as he turned away from her slightly so that she couldn't see he was adjusting himself and making room in his pants for his ever growing erection.

Ronnie glanced up from the drinks she was making and said, "You look like you are very hot. I can see beads of sweat forming on your forehead that weren't there a few minutes ago when you came in." She lifted chunks of ice out of the bucket and dropped them loudly into the crystal highball glasses. Then she poured a good measure of gin into each tumbler not using a shot glass but just eyeballing the amount. "Hmm, does that look like enough to you?" Then without waiting for an answer she tipped the gin bottle over the glasses once again and poured a bit more in each. "There. That looks about right." She splashed a bit of tonic water in each glass and dropped a couple of olives into the mix.

"Here you are. I hope you like it this way," she said as she handed him his drink.

He took a long slow sip of the ice cold drink and then held the glass to his forehead allowing the cool crystal glass to linger there. He took another sip, smiled and said, "I think it's perfect."

"There's nothing like a good stiff drink to put hair on your chest." She laughed then added, "My dad used to always say that when he poured himself a drink."

She slowly walked over to him and using her index finger coyly twisted it in the jet black matting of hair on his chest circling around and around his right nipple. He groaned and put his drink on the table afraid he might spill it if he held it much longer.

"I see you must have already had a few stiff drinks in your lifetime."

He winked at her and said, "Indeed I have," and in one smooth and effortless motion he scooped her into his arms and carried her to the bedroom, laying her gently on the bed and climbing on top of her.

Leaning over her he looked deeply into her eyes and said, "I've been waiting to do this from the moment that I saw you that very first time." Stealthily he undid his belt buckle and the zipper of his shorts with one hand while supporting his weight on the other. He slid his hand down towards her knees and pulled her skirt up to her waist surprised to find that she wasn't wearing anything underneath. He quickly slid his shorts down to his knees then began to caress the perfectly trimmed thatch of hair that covered her groin.

She was already moist with anticipation and he slipped into her gently and slowly allowing them both to enjoy the moment to the fullest. Soon their hips were rocking in the motion of their love making and she whispered, "I love a man who knows what he's doing." He smiled that million dollar smile once again and eased himself further into her allowing himself to penetrate to his full length, her vaginal muscles gripping tightly against his shaft to give both of them the pleasure they'd been seeking for a long time.

When it was more than he could bear he erupted into her. She dug her fingernails into his back, wrapped her legs around his and clenched even tighter joining him in orgasmic delight.

Panting to catch his breath he rolled off her and onto his side. "Ah, Ma-Belle, you are so beautiful." With the back of his hand he rubbed his forehead to remove the beads of sweat that were dripping into his eyes, the salty fluid stinging them slightly.

"I have never met a woman as beautiful as you," he said, his French accent even more pronounced than usual.

She too rolled over onto her side and faced him. "Thank you Phil. It's been a long time since I've heard those words." For a brief moment he thought she was going to cry. He reached over to her and brushed away the hair that had fallen into her eyes, "Is something wrong?" he asked.

"I think my husband is having an affair," she mumbled. "He heads off to Toronto twice a week. He doesn't say what he is doing there and I've noticed there is money missing from our bank account every week. He doesn't pay much attention to me anymore and he has even missed coming up to the cottage on a few weekends. I know he loves it up here so he must be having an affair, I can't think of any other reason." Her sadness waned slightly and then slowly a smile formed on her lips. "But two can play his game."

She moved a little closer and rubbed herself against his now flaccid penis. Almost instantly he responded and she gripped him tightly in her hand and began to stroke him, slowly at first, then more quickly. Once he was fully erect she pushed him over onto his back and straddled him. She reached down to the waist band of her dress and in one fluid motion pulled it off over her head and tossed it onto the floor beside the bed. Philippe reached up and cupped her ample breasts in his hands slowly rubbing her nipples with his thumb until they were hard. She rocked back and forth. Using both hands she rubbed him against her. Slowly and deftly she guided him into her and their lovemaking resumed, both of them hoping the moment would never end. When it was over they lay back on the bed their energy spend, and fell asleep, unaware the temperature in the room was dropping quickly and that a storm was rapidly moving in.

*****

The Stalker was fifty feet long and was a gaff-rigged, top-sail sloop. Though it was long enough to be classified as a cutter which typically has two foresails and one mainsail this particular sloop had been rigged with two masts, the shorter foremast with a jib and a taller aft mast which carried the single mainsail. The advantage to this design was that it could easily be handled by a small crew of two to three men. The brilliant thing about how this boat had been engineered was that its sails were large and designed in such a way as to catch enough wind to give it the speed and agility of a smaller vessel even though it was large enough to be a cargo vessel.

It had been built forty years earlier by a master shipwright named Frank Galbraith in a small town on the eastern coast of Canada and over the years had served as a supply boat that could transport an amazing load in its cargo holds. As trading and supply needs increased over the years and the cargo loads became too big for her holds it was sold, then commissioned as a fishing boat plying the waters of the Atlantic near the south shores of New Brunswick. More recently, it had been re-commissioned again then outfitted as a passenger vessel shuttling passengers from St. John, New Brunswick to Digby, Nova Scotia.

The rigging was complex but pleasantly logical having evolved over the last few years to maintain function without any unnecessary or redundant lines. The vessel also had a small diesel engine that was designed not for speed but more to assist with taking the vessel into narrow harbours, navigating tricky shoal riddled channels and to facilitate smooth landings in ports where she was allowed to pull up to the docks. A small fourteen foot, six person mahogany life raft with two sets of oars and locks was hung from a series of pulleys with one inch hemp ropes on a set of sturdy oak davits fastened on the stern to complete the topside equipment. The life raft was used routinely to tender passengers from ship to shore and back at times when the ship was at anchor.

It was an incredibly well-built sailing vessel with the hull constructed from two inch cedar planking on bent oak frames. Including the keel, the draft was ten feet and the beam fifteen and a half. It possessed a small but efficient galley, three cabins and one head and it easily slept six passengers. The crew quarters aft of the main cabin were much smaller but were pragmatically designed to take advantage of every square inch making them as comfortable as possible. As it was beginning to show its age five years ago, it was brought up on dry dock in its home port where it had been built. There the craftsman in the shipyard sistered eight of the oak frames with new ones to provide the needed support. This was a timely repair as three of them were beginning to show signs of dry rot. The other five were cracked as a result of its time in rough seas in the Atlantic ocean and threatened the integrity of them as support for the hull.

Once it was dry docked numerous planks were identified as also showing evidence of the beginnings of dry rot as well, so they too were removed, replaced, re-caulked. The seams were reefed out, puttied over and then long boarded, affixing them to the hull with four inch brass screws. The masts were lowered, stripped of its old varnishes and refinished. The mainsail was replaced with a strong tear resistant canvas and the jib was replaced with a colourful canvas of brilliant red, yellow and gold.

When it was re-launched the vessel looked like a new boat ready for its next great adventures as a passenger vessel eventually destined for the somewhat calmer waters of the Great Lakes.

Though it sat idly in port for over a year in 1934, The Stalker was purchased by a sawmill owner from the town of Penetanguishene who was looking to diversify his interests. Taking advantage of the ever growing tourist trade he felt a restored sailing vessel with all the character and charm associated with a turn of the century sailing sloop would be an attractive and novel venture in the area. Commissioned to take tourists on one, two and three week sightseeing cruises between Penetanguishene and Sault Ste. Marie the sailboat was perfectly suited for its new role.

On the recommendation of the owners of the shipyard where the vessel had been restored the mill owner hired a crew with knowledge of sailing around both the eastern coast of Canada as well as the St. Lawrence River. Once in Montreal a different crew would take her down the remainder of the St. Lawrence to Lake Ontario, through the newly restored Welland Canal with its eight marine locks to Lake Erie. There from its southern end of this, the shallowest of the Great Lakes, it would head northwest through Lake St Claire, to Lake Huron and eventually to Georgian Bay.

*****

The air was warm and clear and was stirred only occasionally by a faint, gentle breeze from the southwest. Leaning casually against a bench seat built onto the side of the cockpit of the sailing sloop, the captain lost himself for a moment in the beauty of the scene; the azure arms of the bay encircled the ancient islands of granite, the far horizon blending almost seamlessly with the lighter blue skyline. There was no mistaking it; Georgian Bay possessed some of the most beautiful scenery he had ever come across in all his years of plying the lakes, rivers and bays of his great province.

By late afternoon the mirror-like calm waters of the bay he and his crew had been enjoying had disappeared. For over two hours now the gentle breeze that had lulled them into a peaceful carefree demeanour was beginning to fetch a greater force. As the winds began to mount the slight chop turned to waves that pounded against the hull of the boat. They considered raising the remaining sails to take advantage of the new wind which could help them navigate into a safe harbour sooner but a glance to the western sky changed their mind. A storm was quickly mounting to the west and raising the sails might prove to be disastrous.

"We'll continue to motor on," the captain said somewhat to himself but loud enough for his first mate to hear.

"Perhaps we should just raise the mainsail to a halfway point to keep us on a steady course," called out his second mate. "Not right now my friend," the captain replied.

Though clouds had mounted on the western horizon and were quickly overtaking the sky, directly above them a brilliant cloudless blue sky still shone brightly giving a false sense of security to the passengers who had gathered on the decks earlier in the day to enjoy the beauty that was surrounding them.

The winds continued to mount. "We are too far from any landfall or protected bays to outrun the storm," the captain said, "we're going to have to prepare to see this squall through, out here in the open water."

The captain spun the helm to starboard and pointed the sailboat directly to the west while the second mate prepared the sea anchor in case it was needed to slow their progress in the wind. The first mate secured the main sail to the boom with the canvas straps to prevent unwanted winds gathering in any part of the lashed canvas.

The water was ugly and beautiful at the same time. What remained of the sunshine was shimmering on the waves highlighting the white crests of the water as the waves rolled over onto themselves in a sharp contrast to the darkened water. In the distance lightening streaked through the purple black clouds and the thunder came like the roll of a thousand drums. Occasionally they could hear the echo of the thunder as it bounced off the distant granite cliffs but the wind was whipping up enough of a storm that the noise of the waves slapping against the hull and the wind in the rigging was getting to be louder every minute and drowning out all other sounds. Even the seagulls, that had been accompanying the vessel for the better part of the day meandering in slow even circles hoping for any kind of food scraps that might be tossed over the side of the boat, had mysteriously disappeared.

Suddenly the sun was consumed by the overpowering clouds and the furors of the rain fell upon them without pity making navigation nearly impossible as the visibility diminished before their eyes. The full force of the gale was now upon them and was accompanied by torrential rain, a drenching downpour that blocked out the sky and turned the water around them into a boiling broth of foam. The noise of the large drops hitting the hull and cabin of the boat as well as the noise of it slamming into the waves was deafening. The raindrops, whipped by a wind that howled like dozens of banshees through the mainstays pelted the crew so hard it stung their faces and hands and pressed their shirts to their back sticking the fabric to their skin as though it were glued to them. Spray was hurled at them from wave crests that had risen in no time to six and eight feet above the troughs.

"Get all the passengers below deck," the captain instructed his second mate, "and secure all the hatches. Check the staterooms to make sure all the port holes have been closed and secured," commanded the captain.

The second mate quickly ushered those passengers who had remained on deck to witness this storm down the companionway, a stair-like ladder that led from the cockpit to the galley below. One elderly gentleman who had just recently retired from the banking world on Bay Street in Toronto, had been enjoying his first adventure cruise until now, but as he was making his way down the steep steps his arthritic hands did not have a firm enough grip on the single banister and as the boat heeled over to the port side, he was tossed like a wet rag to the floor of the galley. The second mate rushed down the stairs to aid the passenger but even his seasoned sea legs that were used to a boat that pitched and heaved in the water were not enough to be of any help. It was impossible to help the man to his feet so he settled him onto a bench then crumpled to the floor himself. Even though the boat was heeled over to port at about a thirty degree angle he finally managed to stabilize himself enough to climb the rungs of the ladder and close the hatch cover, effectively sealing the cabin off from any water that was splashing into it. The slippery floor of the cabin was slick with rain and lake water and it was nearly impossible for the mate to move from cabin to cabin to check the portholes without crashing into the walls like a drunken sailor saturated with rum.

All too quickly the wind gathered even more strength unleashing yet a greater fury the gusts causing the waves to become broken and confused and striking the boat from one direction and then another. The captain gripped the helm with such fervour that his knuckles were white and ached but he vowed not to loosen his grip as he blindly tried to hold the boat steady in the waves.

The storm increased its shrieking violence as the waters doubled their frightening onslaught against the boat, its passengers below deck clinging to anything that didn't move to keep them from being tossed around like ping-pong balls. The boat was heaving and began corkscrewing violently as the wind tossed it from crest to crest before plunging it down into seemingly bottomless troughs.

As the sky darkened and nighttime took over the cloud blackened sky there was no sharp dividing line between the air and water. It was now impossible to tell where one left off and the other began. A massive grey wave curled down upon them smashing the hatch to pieces and filling the boat's interior with churning foam soaking them all thoroughly to the skin and tending to pull the centre of gravity of the boat further and further downward into the water. The next wave of nearly equal force ripped the life boat from its davits with a single blow. The noise of the solid oak davits being torn from the transom of the hull was barely audible over the wind screaming through the halyards and stays. Water continued to pour into the cabin unchecked with nothing to stop it.

The next twenty four minutes passed like twenty four hours and the crew hung on grimly to stay alive. They were so overcome with the fear of losing their lives no one spoke; all being overwhelmed by the fury of the sudden onslaught of the storm that had, for all intents and purpose come out of nowhere. Had they tried to speak, their voices would have been carried away by the unrelenting winds only to fall on ears deafened by the howling gale. So there were no words and therefore no description for their misery.

The never ending walls of water poured into the boat leaving them choking and gasping, vomiting mouthfuls of water and straining the ropes they'd tied to themselves as lifelines to keep them from being swept overboard never to be seen again. There could be no chance of rescue in the writhing waters where visibility was reduced to just a few feet.

In the flashes of lightening the pain and agony on the faces of the passengers was evidence of the suffering and misery they were enduring. Several of them prayed to God that if this was to be the end of life for them that he would take them quickly and release them from the horror of this Georgian Bay storm.

The captain and first mate, two lifelong friends who had owned several boats together for the better part of ten years, braced themselves with their feet against the sides of the boat's cockpit for added support. Straining together for all they were worth they tried to hold the helm steady as the boat was tossed in the waves. Giving up hope their strength would last they lashed a rope to the spokes of the helm then secured it to a bollard on the gunwale leaving the two men free to cling to the stays along the gunwales, their knuckles white with the grip they had upon the lines.

The captain looked at his friend and knew there was no end to the man's endurance. He knew he would push himself beyond his limits before he would loosen his grip on the boat and surrender himself to Georgian Bay. This unending resolve to hang on reinforced in him the notion that if there was a chance they *could* make it, they *would* actually make it, if they could just tolerate the tempest for one more minute and then another. It became their path to survival, thinking of surviving not in the long term but minute by minute. It was more bearable that way.

CHAPTER - 12

It is said that a mother sleeps with one ear open at all times. Always on guard. Always mindful of where her children are sleeping. Always sensitive to the children's noises of the night. The noises that, even in sleep are unique to them. The soft sigh as they roll over adjusting bed sheets, their grunts as they struggle to untangle themselves from their twisted nightclothes. It is a well known fact, that even in sleep when there is a change in the usual sounds of the night, a mother is aware.

Maude awakened with a start. Her eyes opened in the darkness looking side to side, ears straining to hear what it was that had awakened her. She knew that she had heard something, but just what it was, she couldn't quite tell. The sound wasn't something she heard very often but her mothering instinct kept her tuned at all times for something just like this.

She was now fully awake and sat upright in the bed. She glanced over at Gilbert who was lying beside her soundly asleep and blissfully unaware that something was wrong. The noise had not come from him. Then she heard it again, still faint but clearer this time. It sounded like a cry for help. She clambered out of bed in a near panic thinking one of the twins had gone outside while she was sleeping and she was not aware they had left. There was just a faint light that came in through the kitchen window but it was enough for her to see around the room. She stretched, leaning forward in the darkness and looked at the children. Both were sleeping peacefully in the upper bunk. The noise was not from them.

Maude made her way to the kitchen window, lifted the sash and placed her ear against the screen. The howling wind that had accompanied the storm from earlier in the day had subsided; in fact, there was no wind at all. The moon had poked its way through the clouds and a thin silvery beam of light was splayed across the water from the far shore to near the dock where the boats were parked.

Initially Maude tried to reassure herself and thought that perhaps it was just a breeze whispering in the pines behind the stone cottage, but this sound...it was very distinct. She stayed bent, leaning into the window frame, motionless, ears straining, listening. Then she heard it again. It *was* a cry for help. Her mouth went dry as she stood frozen in place, still straining to hear.

"Gilbert," she called out. "Gilbert wake up."

"What is it?" He sat up in bed, "What's wrong Maude, why are you out of bed?"

"I hear someone calling for help."

"Are the children in bed?"

"Yes, yes they are. Come over to the window, hurry."

He slid out of bed pulling his tee shirt that had bunched up around his waist down to cover his bare bottom and made his way across the room.

"Bend down here and listen at the window." She moved out of his way. "It's a very faint sound but listen closely and you'll hear it. Someone is in trouble."

He stooped down at the open window and placed his ear to the screen. After a few moments he said, "I don't hear anything." He listened again, "maybe it was just a raccoon or a muskrat down by the dock."

"I definitely heard someone calling for help."

"Let's go stand out on the veranda at the front of the cottage. Maybe we'll hear it better there."

They made their way through the front room. Gilbert opened the heavy wooden front door then slowly pushed the screen door open. He stood on the stones just off the front veranda and Maude joined him at his side.

The two stood there side by side, motionless, silent. Ears straining, eyes peeled, looking for anything that might be different. Searching for a sign that something was wrong. Then suddenly they both heard it, more clearly, more distinctly.

"Help!"

"It sounded like it came from the main cottage. Maybe Ronnie has fallen and hurt herself. We have to go over and check," said Maude.

The Stone Cottage

"Wait here just a minute; I have to go put some pants on. She may be a nurse but that doesn't mean I can show up half naked," Gilbert said as he turned and made his way back through the screen door. In less than a minute he was back.

"Okay, let's go," he said as he came through the doorway. He was holding his new flashlight that he had picked up at the hardware store during his last trip to town. The beam of light was brilliant in the night and illuminated the stone pathway between the juniper bushes perfectly.

The main cottage was in complete darkness. There wasn't a sound coming from anywhere near it.

They heard the call again.

"Help." It seemed fainter to them now. Like the person calling was getting more tired.

"Maybe she fell outside at the front. The steps are steep and if she has been drinking she could have lost her balance," said Maude.

They made their way to the front of the cottage. Gilbert cast the beam of light in a wide arc around the bottom of the steps and onto the path that led to the dock.

"She may have fallen inside the cottage. What if she broke a hip and can't get up."

Gilbert opened the screen door on the front veranda and made his way to the glass door that opened onto the living room. He shone the beam of light onto the floor in front of the fireplace and couches. Suddenly Philippe appeared naked in the bedroom doorway one hand rubbing the sleep out of his eyes, the other pushing the door fully open as he tried to figure out what the strange light in the living room was from. He looked at the front door and saw Gilbert standing there with the flashlight. Immediately his hands dropped to his crotch to cover himself and he spun on his heels and disappeared into the bedroom returning to the doorway within seconds pulling his pants on.

"What is it Gilbert?" he said as he zipped up the fly on his jeans.

"We heard someone calling for help, we thought it might be Mrs. Johnson," said Gilbert a bit sheepishly as he stepped into the front room, trying not to think too much about why Philippe was here at this hour.

"Nope, not here," said Philippe. "We've both been sleeping. We're fine."

He winked at Gilbert and nodded his head. "Really fine."

Maude made her way into the front room from the veranda, where she had stayed to listen in case there were any other calls.

"Phil," she gasped surprised. "What are..." she stopped herself from saying anything further by putting her hand to her mouth. She had pieced the reasons together quickly.

"I heard it again Gilbert," said Maude. "Someone is definitely in trouble out there."

All three of them went outside and stood on the front veranda. By now the clouds had completely disappeared and the moon was casting an eerie glow as it settled a bit lower on the horizon partially hidden by the tall pine trees on the island opposite them. What bits of light that did peak through the branches on the trees caused a shimmering of silver in the water and made the whole scenario seem spooky.

"Help!"

"Yes, there it is, it sounds like a man's voice," said Philippe.

"Help!"

"It's a bit louder now," said Gilbert. "It seemed stronger this time."

"It sounded different from the voice before," said Maude. "Maybe there's more than one person out there."

"Help. Please. Somebody help."

"It sounds like it is coming from the shoals out on the outside," said Gilbert. He handed the flashlight to Maude.

"Philippe, get your shirt on, Maude run over to the stone cottage and get some blankets. We have to go find these people."

Philippe rubbed his hands up and down, across his chest, looked at Gilbert and embarrassed said, "I, uh, I don't have one with me."

"Maude," he called after her. "Bring one of my shirts for Philippe to wear too. And bring any sweaters you can find and meet us down at the dock."

By the dim light of the moon, Philippe and Gilbert made their way from the main cottage down to the dock. "We'll take the runabout rather than the big inboard," said Gilbert. "That way we can get closer to shore if we find someone," he explained.

Just as the outboard engine was sputtering to life Maude appeared at the ramp that led to the dock. Her arms were full of bundles of blankets, sweaters and an old beat up flannel shirt.

"Can one of you come and take this from me? I can't see the edge of the ramp with this load in my arms."

Philippe leapt from the boat and onto the dock with his arms extended to take what Maude was carrying. "This is the best I could do on short notice," said Maude as she handed Phil the flannel shirt.

"It's perfect. Thank you," he said as he slipped on the shirt. "It will be cooler at this hour on the water. This is great," he said as he buttoned it up.

Gilbert donned a sweater Maude had brought down to the dock and then began to untie the ropes.

"Can you please go up to the cottage and tell Ronnie what is going on?" said Phil looking up at Maude from the bow of the boat. "I'm sure she must be wondering."

Maude nodded to Phil to let him know she had heard his request and then asked Gilbert, "How are you ever going to find them in the dark?"

"We have this new flashlight and it has a pretty powerful beam," he splayed the beam across the Narrows channel and lit up the rocks and trees on the far shore. "I'm going to drive out on the outside and head in the direction of Go Home Bay. Once we get out in the open water I'll turn off the motor and listen for anyone calling. Hopefully we'll see them on shore or on a shoal and we can pick them up."

*****

At full throttle Gilbert steered the small runabout out of the Narrows and into the bay. The large bank of outer islands looked ominous in the darkness, the water between them and the shoreline a steely dark grey. With the last vestiges of moonlight the sky was somewhat lighter but that lighter shade was fading quickly. The islands that formed the line of the horizon between the two appeared as a streak of blackness slashing through the middle. What was that old saying Gilbert thought, *'It's always darkest before the dawn.'* Tonight he discovered it really was true.

Gilbert navigated the small craft out of the shelter of the outer islands and headed into open water heading north towards the flashing light on Red Rock at the entrance to Go Home Bay. Though the winds from the storm earlier in the day had diminished the remnants of the storm could still be felt in the swells of the dead-sea that tossed the small boat to and fro. Gilbert had to slow the engine to a fast idle as the spray from the swells was coming into the boat and water was already gathering at their feet.

"Phil, there is a small bucket under the back seat. Move back here from the bow and start to bail or we'll be the next ones a search party will be looking for."

With the stealth of a person who was raised on the water and spent endless hours in a boat, Philippe moved from the bow to the stern in an almost cat-like slither so as not to rock the boat unnecessarily. He found the small bailing bucket, an old used coffee can and quickly began dipping it into the water that was sloshing over the floor boards around their feet.

When Gilbert figured he was half way between the Newton Islands light and Go Home Bay he shut down the engine and let the boat drift. He flipped the switch to turn on the flashlight and the interior of the small boat was illuminated as if it was the middle of the day.

"We took on a fair amount of water in a pretty short period of time," Philippe said.

"It was hard to tell in the darkness just how much water was splashing in but when I felt it gathering at my feet I figured we'd better slow down and bail."

There was no wind to speak of, there were no white caps in the bay, but the small boat bobbed up and down in the swells just the same.

"It must have been a heck of a storm to cause such big waves to still be around at this hour."

"You didn't hear the storm?" Gilbert asked incredulously.

"Didn't hear a thing," Phil admitted. "Ronnie and I were dead tired after..." he stopped himself from going any farther. Now was not the time to be bragging about his affair.

Gilbert shone the light outside of the boat. Amazingly the bow was still facing north and he scanned the water on the starboard side of the boat in search of the shoals he knew to be along the eastern shore.

"Gil, I hope it doesn't bother you that Ronnie and I..."

"Phil, let's just be quiet for a while and listen for someone calling for help. The fact that someone probably capsized their boat today in the storm bothers me more than anything else right now."

Not another word was mentioned. For five full minutes the pair sat silently, Gilbert continuously moving the arc of the beam of light from the flashlight steadily back and forth, scanning the water, searching for shoals that a boat might be perched on.

After five minutes Gilbert started the engine and slowly moved a little bit farther north. Again he shut off the engine and the pair sat perched on their seats eyes straining in the darkness, ears perked for the slightest of sounds.

"I think you may be too far north," Philippe said. "I don't think we would have heard anything at the cottage from this far away."

"That's a good point."

Gilbert started the engine and at a slow, near idle speed, headed towards the eastern shoreline. Philippe with flashlight in hand, panned the water in front of the bow of the boat. "There are a lot of shoals right around here. I often come out here to fish."

Gilbert continued to navigate in an easterly direction until they were about a quarter mile from shore and then he turned the boat and headed south keeping the shoreline on the port side of the boat. After a few minutes he again shut off the engine and they listened. All they could hear was the sound of the dead-sea waves crashing on the shoals and the rocky granite shoreline.

Again Philippe panned the light in front of the boat in a slow and steady left to right motion, the two men scanning for anything they could see.

"I feel like we should move a little farther south again Gilbert," Phil said. "I deliver ice to that cottage over there," he pointed to the faint outline of a large old, plantation style cottage perched on a high outcropping of rock. "There is no way we'd have heard anything from this far."

Gilbert agreed and again started the engine. Slowly they made their way, keeping the shoreline five hundred yards to the port side. Gilbert steered the vessel based on hand signals from Philippe who was able to see the outline of some of the submerged shoals in the light of the flashlight.

After a few minutes he shut the engine down and again the two men sat motionless, looking, listening and...

"Help! Please help us!"

Philippe raised the level of the beam of light and scanned the water as far along the surface as the beam of the flashlight would allow. Nothing.

"We're over here," the voice said. "We can see your light."

It was so disorienting in the darkness to be searching, constantly being fooled by the motion of the waves, the sound of them crashing on the shore or swelling up and then receding from the underwater hazards. It was impossible to home in on where the voices were coming from. The only benefit that existed was that on the eastern horizon a faint lightening of the dark grey sky could be seen as the sun was beginning to make its way to the surface.

"Over here. We are on your right, about a quarter mile away."

Gilbert cautiously steered the boat to starboard, again at idle speed. He remained cognizant of the numerous shoals that dotted this area like a barrier reef between them and mainland and inched forward slowly but surely in the direction he thought the voice had come from.

Philippe shouted, "I think I saw someone. Over there," he pointed almost directly in front of the boat.

"Keep the light on the water Phil, when it shines in the boat or on the gunwales I can't see anything beyond the boat."

Philippe moved right up to the bow of the boat leaning his elbows on the small deck to steady himself and held the flashlight as stable as he could. "There," he shouted pointing with his hand, "there are two men. They are in the water. Looks like they are up to their waists."

The ongoing swells made navigating towards that shoal almost impossible. Afraid the engine would hit bottom Gilbert shut it down and tilted it on its mounts till the propeller was completely out of the water. He quickly grabbed a paddle and continued in the direction he had set, his strong arms forcing the paddle into the water, stroke after stroke a motion his muscles remembered from years spent in a canoe.

"Do you have another paddle?" Phil asked.

"I do but I'd rather you keep the light shining on those men, if I can see them, I can paddle us to them."

It seemed like the minutes dragged on into hours, Gilbert's arms and shoulders ached from this sudden burst of exercise, but in reality it took only a few minutes for them to reach the shoal. The air was filled with a tangible kinetic energy in part from Philippe and Gilbert for having finally found the men they had been searching for, and partly from the men in the water who were ecstatic for having been found.

"How deep is the water there?" Gilbert shouted to the men.

"We are standing on the highest rock, it isn't very big, the rest of the shoal is flat and smooth."

By now the sky in the east was considerably lighter. Gilbert and Phil could easily make out the outline of the two men standing in the waist high water.

"We'll come straight at you. That way you can reach out and grab the bow. Once you have a grip on the bow I'll steer the boat to the side and we'll help you aboard," instructed Gilbert.

As soon as the boat was near enough to them the two men clutched onto the bow with an iron grip and slowly pulled the boat to the port side. From there the first man tried to climb into the boat. His arms felt limp and his legs were weak with exhaustion from his ordeal in the open water. It made him clumsy and awkward as he tried to get his leg over the gunwales of the boat. He tried several times to lift his leg that high but couldn't quite make it. Exhaustion was getting the best of him. He tried to grab onto the side of the boat and pull himself in but his arms no longer possessed the strength needed to haul his body aboard. He sank back down into the water sinking up to his neck.

"I can't do it, I'm too weak," he sputtered as a wave washed over him and he unwillingly swallowed a mouthful of water.

"You can do it, I know you can. Try once more." encouraged his friend.

He reached out and gripped the gunwales again, this time managing to half pull himself aboard and rest his belly on the side of the boat. He tried to kick with his feet into the water hoping to propel himself further but his efforts were useless. The boat rocked precariously with the extra weight and motion and the side of the boat dipped very close to the surface of the water.

"Wait a second," Gilbert commanded, "you'll tip us over." The man stopped his attempt to climb into the boat but left his legs dangling in the water. He waited, trying to catch his breath but did not loosen his grip on the gunwale.

"Phil, you and I have to get on the starboard side so we can balance the boat while they climb in."

With Gilbert in the stern and as far over to the right as the seat would allow him to get, Phil moved to the middle seat and he too sat right up alongside the edge. Slowly the first man reached into the centre of the boat and grabbed onto the bench seat. The second man still clutching the gunwale with his left hand, used his right hand to gently lift his friend's right leg over the edge, then the left leg. This effort successfully hoisted him into the boat. The small boat rocked side to side for a few moments as it adjusted to the added weight and when it was steady, the second man repeated the action of the first and slowly pulled himself over the gunwale and slithered like liquid mercury to the bottom of the boat. No one said a word. They were all in shock. They looked at each other and nodded as if to say, "We made it," and a broad smile flashed across Philippe's face, the fine row of pearly white teeth evident in the gathering light of dawn.

The two new passengers settled onto the middle seat, the look of relief evident on their faces even in the dim light. "Here are a couple of blankets. Wrap yourselves tightly. You must be near frozen," Gilbert said as he handed each man a blanket. They gratefully accepted his offering and pulled the blankets around their shoulders clutching the edge of the homemade quilts at their neck.

Philippe stayed at the bow with the flashlight shining into the water and Gilbert carefully stood at the stern. Using the paddle he pushed the boat off the shoal and away from the dangerous rocks that were threatening to scrape the bottom of the small vessel in the endless swells.

"We are in deep water again," said Philippe as he scanned the water with the flashlight from side to side.

Gilbert let the engine down on its mounts and pulled out the choke. After priming the engine with the priming bulb in the centre of the gas line, he gave a quick tug on the pull cord and the engine sputtered to life.

With the added weight of the two men, the boat rode much lower in the water. Cautiously Gilbert increased the speed from idle urging the throttle to speed them up but then he was forced to slow down when he realized that even at this speed the waves were splashing over the sides. At idle once again the boat bobbed like a cork but with Philippe guiding them around the shoals they were soon within the leeward shelter of the outer islands that had seemed so ominous at the beginning of this rescue. The dead-sea swells subsided as they reached the protected waters of the bay.

"I don't need the flashlight anymore Phil," Gilbert said. "I can make my way home from here just fine now that it is starting to get brighter."

Philippe extinguished the light and suddenly the sky seemed brighter. Within minutes they were inside the Narrows channel and Gilbert steered the boat expertly to the dock.

"We'll tie up the boat and go into the cottage. I'll light a fire and we can work at warming you guys up. I'll ask my wife to make some coffee and that will warm you from the inside out as well. Maybe then you can tell us how you came to be standing on a shoal in the middle of the night in Georgian Bay."

The Stone Cottage

Maude, hearing the runabout's engine from a long way off had already lit a fire in the stove and had put the kettle on to boil water for coffee. As the group of men made their way up the path from the dock she rushed out to greet them ready to offer any help they might have needed. Once they had all made it to the stone cottage, she held the door open as the soaking wet, bedraggled group of men lumbered past her. Gilbert quickly moved into the main room and gathered kindling and paper to start a fire in the large stone fireplace.

"This is no time for modesty gentlemen, strip off your shoes and clothes and wrap yourselves in these blankets," Gilbert said as he handed them new dry blankets that Maude had brought in from the other room. "If you stay in those wet clothes much longer you're sure to get hypothermia." Turning his back on them to give them privacy, he busied himself with building the fire. Philippe went into the kitchen with Maude to help with the coffee and the two men stripped down then wrapped themselves tightly in the dry blankets. Each took a seat at the table.

Sensing they were settled, Gilbert stood up and made his way over to the pile of soaking wet pants, shirts, underwear and socks that were already making small puddles on the floor. At first he started to drape the items over the backs of the chairs but when Maude came out with a tray loaded with cups of steaming coffee she said, "Just leave those for a minute Gilbert, I'll wring them out then hang them on the clothesline. The sky is clear and the sun is coming up. These clothes will be dry in no time."

As she busied herself with gathering the clothes Philippe came into the room with a plate that had some warm biscuits and jam. Gilbert got up and gently closed the door between the kitchen and the main room. "The twins are stirring a bit. I think they might settle if we aren't too noisy."

Grateful to be alive, the two men looked appreciatively around the stone cottage. Neither man spoke. Both had a very sombre, vacant look upon their faces. Both were silent for the longest time as they sipped at the piping hot coffee, clutching the cups in their shaky hands trying to bring warmth to their stiff and injured fingers. One man inhaled deeply as if trying to catch his breath but instead started to weep as a wave of sadness overcame him.

"I can't believe we are alive," he sobbed. "The others. I don't know." He paused looking at his friend. "I can't stop thinking about them. They could still be out there. But where? How far did we drift? How long were we in the water?

Where are we now? How would we know where to look?" His short staccato sentences were abrupt, broken by his efforts to get his sobbing under control. They seemed to echo what his partner was thinking. Again he sobbed, his entire upper body heaving with his gut wrenching sadness and feelings of guilt.

His friend reached out from under his blanket, the skin on his arm appeared translucent, with a pale bluish tinge. The extended limb seemed so frail yet it firmly gripped the man's shoulder and gave it a heartfelt squeeze demonstrating the warmth and friendship the two men shared. In a soft caring voice he said, "We *are* lucky to be alive my friend. We have to take comfort in knowing that we did all we could."

Gilbert and Philippe joined the men at the table. For a long time no one said anything, each man lost deep in thought while trying to come to grips with the seriousness of the night's events. These were harsh experiences they had just been through and it would take a while to sort it out.

Finally Gilbert got up, added more wood to the fire then brought the coffee pot over to the table. "Here, let me refill your cups and then we'll start at the beginning."

Philippe and the two others slid their cups to the centre of the table to make it easier for Gilbert to refill them. Once he had added the remaining coffee to his cup, he pulled his chair up closer to the table so he could rest his outstretched arms and grip his coffee mug in his two hands. He looked at the two men, smiled slightly and quietly cleared his throat.

"I'll go first," he said trying to set the men at ease and orient them to their surroundings. "My name is Gilbert Valcour and this is my friend Philippe Dagenais. My wife's name is Maude. In the other room there is our children and they are still asleep. Their names are Ben and Emma. This cottage is in Cognashene and we live here for the summer. We live in Penetanguishene in the winter. Philippe's home is about a mile away and he lives there year round. The town of Penetanguishene is about an hour to an hour and a half away from here." He paused and smiled, "depending on how fast your boat is and what the weather is like when you are crossing the gap." He took a long slow sip of his still steaming coffee then blew gently into the cup to try and cool it down a bit then said, "so guys, tell us who you are and what happened."

"My name is Jean-Baptiste LeTard and this is my best friend Napoleon LaVasseur. We have been friends for almost our entire lives. We grew up together in a small town just outside of Montreal." The two men were near the same age but Jean-Baptiste looked considerably older than the other. When he spoke again he said, "I was just wondering Gilbert, do you smoke? Could I get a cigarette from you, I could really use one right now."

"I'm sorry, I don't smoke and neither does my friend Philippe."

"Oh well, I just thought it would help calm me down." He twisted in his chair a bit and pulled the edge of the blanket back around his legs where it had fallen open slightly.

"The little town we grew up in near Montreal is right on the St. Lawrence River so Napoleon and I have been on the water our entire lives," he said as if trying to justify being on the water tonight.

Napoleon spoke up and added, "We have worked on many boats and have sailed in the Atlantic and up and down the Great Lakes. We have been in some pretty bad weather but this storm we were in last night. It was the worse one we've ever seen."

"OK, so how did you come to be where you were tonight?" Gilbert asked.

Jean-Baptiste answered. "We work for Mr. Gauthier in Penetanguishene. He owns a small sawmill in town." Gilbert nodded and said, "Yes, I know him well."

Jean-Baptiste continued, "Anyway, he decided he wanted to get into the tourist business so he bought a boat called The Stalker. This boat is fifty feet long and is a sailboat..." Napoleon cut in saying, "I think you better say *was* fifty feet long. I don't think the boat survived."

Jean-Baptiste gave his friend a desolate glance, swallowed hard then went on. "Mr. Gauthier had set up the business so that it was like a tour boat, you know, a pleasure craft for the people who can afford to take a two or three week holiday and sail from Penetanguishene to Sault Ste. Marie and back again." He stopped, took a fairly heavy gulp of coffee and then said, "Napoleon and I have been working on the water for years. We have lots of experience and when we saw this job advertised we thought it would be perfect for us. We had been working for three years on the big Great Lakes steamships that go back and forth between The Sault, Penetanguishene and Midland and we know the route pretty well. So we applied. We were thrilled to have a smaller boat to look after and to be, you know, kind of like our own boss with just a few passengers to look after. This was just our third trip in the sailboat."

"But we've worked on lots of sailboats before this," Napoleon added, reinforcing what Jean-Baptiste had said. "We worked out east for a while and worked on fishing boats, and cargo boats on the St. Lawrence River so working on this boat was like a dream come true. We get to do what we love to do in the most beautiful part of the world."

"Three nights ago," Jean-Baptiste said, "we were in the little port of South Bay Mouth on the south east end of Manitoulin Island. She's a pretty fast sail boat. We had a good wind and we made it from there to Parry Sound yesterday. We picked up a new passenger there and first thing in the morning we headed off on our way back to Penetanguishene."

Napoleon picked up the story. "Then the wind died completely. Even though we had the sails up there was no wind at all. The sky was clear blue and we were just drifting for the longest time so we decided to start the little diesel engine on board and motor sail for a while. The passengers loved it. It gave them a chance to just sit up on deck and look at the scenery. Then the storm hit."

"And what a storm it was. It was the worst storm we've ever seen," said Jean-Baptiste.

"Yes it was quite a bad storm. We got it here as well," said Gilbert. "So tell us what happened next,"

"I am the captain," said Jean-Baptiste. "I take full responsibility for what happened." He took another long drink from his coffee cup then put it down slowly. The pain of the tragedy of the storm was written across his face. "The storm came up really quickly. Napoleon wanted to put the sails up so we could quickly head to shore to find shelter but I didn't think there was time. I thought it would be better if we kept the sails down and just motored into the bad weather to ride out the storm in the open rather than take a chance being too close to shore and smashing the sailboat up on shoals or the rocky shoreline." He tried to continue with his story but he was too choked up. Again he became very emotional, his breathing became very shallow and he seemed to be having trouble catching his breath. Though he was trying to speak, nothing would come out. He rubbed his hands briskly across his face a couple of times trying to calm himself.

Napoleon said, "The storm was so bad. It was more than the boat could handle."

"How many people were on the boat," Philippe asked.

Napoleon lifted his hands to count on his fingers as he named each person. "There was Jean-Baptiste and me, and there was Jacques our second mate, and then there were five passengers. That makes eight."

Jean-Baptiste by now had a better grip on his emotions and was finally able to speak again. He continued saying, "the boat was doing well. Since it had been so nice out before the storm hit I thought that it might just be a squall that would be short lived. When the storm hit, it started raining pretty hard so I got Jacques to take the passengers down below deck and get them settled in. I got him to close the hatch because the rain was pouring in through the hatch. The wind was mounting and the odd wave was splashing into the cockpit and the galley below. Then it started to rain really hard and the waves got to be about eight feet and the boat was pitching and heaving badly. One huge wave crested and broke right over the cockpit and it smashed the hatch and the roof of the cabin. We started to take on a lot of water. I was just about to get Napoleon and Jacques to help me get the life raft ready when another wave smashed into us and tore it from the davits and washed it away. It was like a nightmare. It was all happening so fast. The boat was nearly impossible to steer at this point so we lashed a rope around the helm to hold it on a steady course as much as possible and Napoleon and I hung on for dear life. By now the boat was riding very low in the water. We had no idea how Jacques or the passengers were doing. The storm just raged on around us and the waves just kept battering the boat to pieces. It just kept getting lower and lower in the water. I couldn't tell what was happening below deck. It was so dark and stormy I couldn't see anything. Napoleon and I tied ourselves onto a large piece of the oak davit from the life raft that had not broken off earlier. We did this so that we wouldn't get washed overboard but it was no use," he choked a bit and swallowed hard trying to get a grip on what he was saying. He stared into the fire that was burning in the large fireplace, tears rolling down his cheeks. Unashamed he wiped them with the back of his hand. He gathered himself and slowly in a much softer voice started to speak. "But it was no use, that piece broke off on the next big wave and was swept away taking the two of us overboard with it." He sat still for a long time clutching his coffee mug like it was a lifeline. "We were tied to that big piece of oak but the waves were so strong it washed us away from the boat quickly and we couldn't swim over to the boat. The last time I saw the boat it was barely floating. It was heeled over onto its side. The mainsail had broken lose and when a gust of wind came the boat heeled over so far the sail filled with water and held the boat on its side. Napoleon and I just hung onto that piece of oak davit for all we were worth. The waves pushed us farther and farther from the boat." Jean-Baptiste sobbed uncontrollably, guilt written across his pale and ashen face, his hands trembling, his head nodding up and down.

Finally he spoke, "I don't know how long we were in the water, how far from Parry Sound we had made it before the storm hit or how far the storm blew us off course." Napoleon reached across the table and once again placed his hand on his friend's shoulder. His grip was firm, his intent was reassuring and comforting. Jean-Baptiste's shoulders sagged with the weight of the responsibility that was bearing down on him. He leaned slightly towards his friend drawing strength from the consoling hand that remained on his shoulder. He dropped his head into his hands and rested his elbows on the table.

"What are we going to do? What are we going to do?" he kept repeating.

"We need to get out there and see if we can find the boat," Napoleon said to Gilbert and Philippe. "It has to be out there, it's made of wood, it might not have sunk," he said hopefully.

Gilbert spoke up, "I think it would be impossible for us to mount an effective search for the boat ourselves. Not that we can't help but we need more people and boats than just us." He stared into the fire for a few moments as if seeking inspiration and the right words of encouragement. "As soon as your clothes are dry and you have warmed up I will take you into town. We'll go to the police and tell them what happened. They'll know what to do. For sure they'll be able to organize a search party a lot better than we can. Also we have to let Mr. Gauthier know. He must have been expecting you to arrive last evening. That was a pretty fierce storm that hit yesterday and I'm sure it went as far south as town so maybe there is already a search party being organized."

Philippe said, "Gil, while you take them into town, maybe I can go out in my boat and comb the shoreline to see if I can find anything or anyone." He buttoned Gilbert's shirt that he was still wearing up to the neck and stood up. "In fact it's pretty bright out already. I'll run home, get some extra gas for my motor and I'll stop at my cousin's place next to me. He can help I'm sure. I'll get him to head north along the shore between here and Go Home Bay and I'll head straight up past Go Home towards Indian Harbour and start looking there. That will give us a head start on searching," he said enthusiastically. Without another word or waiting for approval he opened the front door and jogged down the path.

Maude came into the main room and started to gather the coffee mugs. She stopped when she noticed the tray that had the homemade biscuits. It sat untouched in the middle of the table. "You men need to eat something. You've had a really bad thing happen to you and that has probably stolen your appetite but..." she paused and looked into their pale, worried faces. "But... It's been a long time since you ate. I'm sure you aren't hungry but it could be a long time before you get another chance to get some food in you. You'll be no good to anybody if you don't have the energy to stand up." She leaned over the table and officiously started to smear some jam on a biscuit. She smiled as she handed the biscuit to Napoleon and said, "I'm not your mother but I can say, 'Now eat up.'" Gratefully he accepted the food and was surprised at how quickly he swallowed it down. She smeared a healthy amount of jam on another biscuit and handed it to Jean-Baptiste. "This one's for you. I put extra jam on it 'cause you look like you need it."

"That's mighty kind of you Maude. Thank you for all you and your husband have done for us. We really appreciate it."

After the men had each eaten a second biscuit Gilbert stood up and poked what remained of the fire. He didn't bother to add any more wood, the room was plenty warm enough. He stood up slowly, a look of grave concern on his face and went outside. A few minutes later he came back in with an armful of clothes. "They aren't completely dry but at least they aren't soaking wet." He handed over the clothes and went into the kitchen, quietly closing the door between the two rooms.

Jean-Baptiste and Napoleon quickly dropped their blankets and struggled into their clothes. Their bodies were dry and warm but the damp clothes stuck to their skin as they pulled them on. Shortly thereafter Gilbert came back into the main room and said, "I've told Maude that I'm taking you into town now. She is going to wake up the children and then she and Mrs. Johnson next door are going to go out and start searching the outer islands close to where we found you. Perhaps more than just the two of you washed up close by."

Jean-Baptiste said, "That is such good news. The more people out there looking, the better. Be sure to thank her for helping." He bent down to tie up his shoes and when he straightened up he said, "I want to be hopeful that the boat didn't sink and the passengers are still alive, but I am fearful that it may have smashed up on some of those shoals and there will be nothing left but planks and a keel."

"Let's not give up hope," said Napoleon. "Hope may be all that we have left."

Gilbert gave the men a few more minutes to finish getting dressed. "If you guys are ready, let's head out," he said as he held the door open. "We have a full day ahead of us. It's not going to be a pleasant day but we'll get through it. We just have to try to be optimistic and think positive." As they made their way down the path to the docks Gilbert tried to encourage them further by adding, "Take comfort in knowing that you did nothing wrong. Mother Nature unleashed her fury upon you and she won. It doesn't sound like there is anything else you could have done to save The Stalker or the passengers that were on board."

"Thank you for saying that. You are a good man Gilbert," said Napoleon as he headed down the path towards the dock.

In the distance Gilbert could hear the high-pitched whining noise of Philippe's outboard motor revved at full throttle as he made his way down the bay towards his cousin's house.

At least those guys know the water around here really well, he thought. *In the daylight they'll be able to steer around those submerged shoals much better than we did in the dark last night. It will be a lot easier to see if there is anyone or anything floating too.*

Soon, Gilbert and his two rescued souls were motoring down the bay towards Penetanguishene. All three men were silent, deep in thought as they scanned the surface of the water around them hoping to see some evidence of a survivor or some bit of flotsam that would indicate 'The Stalker' had drifted this far south.

*****

The newspaper article read:

Six People Dead in Marine Tragedy

Five passengers and one crew member are missing and presumed dead after a fatal storm sank the 50 foot pleasure craft The Stalker. Touted as being a very seaworthy vessel it had seen active work in the Atlantic as both a fishing trawler and cargo boat. The craft had been completely restored and outfitted as a passenger boat and was currently commissioned to usher tourists on the popular sightseeing cruises of Georgian Bay sailing from the ports in Sault Ste. Marie to Penetanguishene.

Captain Jean-Baptiste LeTard and first mate Napoleon LaVasseur are devastated over the loss of life and the tragic sinking of the vessel that was under their command. The two men had remained topside during the storm in an effort to steer the boat through the maelstrom however they were washed overboard just as the boat began to sink. The two men were rescued by local Cognashene residents Gilbert Valcour and Philippe Dagenais in the middle of the night Thursday. The men were found clinging to a shoal near the outer islands of Cognashene in Georgian Bay after spending approximately twelve hours in the water.

Though an extensive three day search for survivors ensued, all five passengers and one crew member are still listed as missing and presumed drowned. No evidence of the boat has been found as of yet.

Mr. D. Gauthier, owner of the vessel said that it was a very seaworthy boat and he is distraught over what has happened. In an interview he stated, "A very capable and knowledgeable crew did all they could to try to ride out the storm but the weather was too extreme and the vessel was torn apart by the powerful storm. I hold no one responsible for this tragedy but Mother Nature."

Families of the deceased have been notified.

CHAPTER - 13

Maude was standing at the kitchen table, hands deep in a basin of steaming hot soapy water. She was washing up the remaining dishes that were left from supper. Her hands were moving through the practised motions of scrubbing dishes but she wasn't looking at what she was doing. She was staring out the window, a far-off look on her face.

Gilbert made his way over to where she was standing and quietly came up behind her tenderly wrapping his arms around her waist and squeezing. As soon as he touched her she jumped slightly, reflexively. She turned to look at him.

"You startled me," she said in a matter of fact tone but not angrily. She turned back again to look out the window. Gilbert rested his chin on her shoulder and with his head beside hers he too looked out the window. He gave her another embrace then said, "I saw you staring out the window, like you were looking at something but not seeing anything. You looked like your mind was off in a different world."

"I was just thinking about those poor people who lost their lives in that horrible storm a couple of weeks ago. Every time I look out at the open water I can't help but think of them. I shudder to think of how terrifying their last moments of life were and how frightened they must have been. I can't imagine what it was like for them."

Gilbert lifted Maude's hands out of the basin of water and slowly turned her to face him. He could see the anguish in her eyes. This time he gave her a proper hug, holding her in his arms for a little while longer than usual. He said, "I'm surprised this is staying with you so long. There have been other boating accidents in the past and they didn't seem to bother you as much as this one has."

"I have thought about exactly that," said Maude. "I struggle with trying to understand why this accident has saddened me so much but I think that it is because this one was personal."

"Personal in what way?" he asked.

"Well," she paused, "we had been out on Cranberry Island and having a wonderful time. Probably the happiest day of the season so far. You noticed that the weather seemed to be changing, that storm clouds were rolling in pretty quickly and you got us home safely, just in time. We were out of harm's way." She raised her open palmed hands upwards motioning towards the ceiling and said, "this old stone cottage protected us from yet another vicious storm. We really were lucky we got in when we did. I'm grateful to you for being such a conscientious person, always keeping an eye on the sky. Always protecting your family."

"You make me sound like some sort of hero but I'm not. I'm just a man who loves his family and looks after them in whatever way he can. You do the same."

"I know. But here we were, safe and sound and pretty well oblivious to the world around us as a storm raged on. When the storm was over we went to bed and slept soundly. You know, just another day in paradise. And then I heard the calls for help. It frightened me to know that someone was out there in danger. You and Philippe risked your lives to rescue them." She paused, went to the icebox and with the ice pick that always sat atop the icebox, chipped off a small sliver of ice to put in her mouth. She sucked on the ice chip letting the cool liquid wet her dry, parched mouth and throat. "You did what you had to do to save those men. You *are* a hero of sorts."

"I just did what anyone else would have done."

She walked over to the table again but rather than doing more dishes she pulled out a chair, sat down and looked at Gilbert. "I guess this tragedy is more personal because we were involved. Not responsible but involved. When you came home with Jean-Baptiste and Napoleon and I saw how tormented they were, how distraught and helpless they felt, I wanted to reach out to them and hug them and tell them everything was going to be okay. But I couldn't because I didn't know that it would be."

Gilbert walked over to where she was sitting. He crouched down in front of her and took her hands in his. "It was personal for me too," he squeezed her hands. "I have wrestled with similar thoughts in the last couple of weeks too. I didn't know any of those people who drowned that day but I feel a connection to them in some odd and unusual way. I've been in some pretty bad storms on the water and thought that I was going to meet my maker a few times, but I've survived, I've been lucky. We both have." He shifted his weight on his knees and gripped Maude's hands more firmly. "It wasn't that way for them. It's hard to accept that life can be taken away so quickly sometimes without notice. Death is hard to accept in whatever form it takes.

"When someone has been sick for a long time, when they die it isn't easy for the family to accept but it is something that you have known is coming. You are able to prepare yourself for it. But, when there has been an accident and life is lost so suddenly, so tragically, there is no time to prepare yourself for it. There are thoughts of 'what if' and second guessing and wondering how things could have been changed in some way. All that is for naught, there is no turning back the hands of time, to do things differently. Hard as it is we must just accept what happened to those people, learn from it and be helpful to those who have been left behind." He looked deeply into her eyes and smiled, "I think we did that. We helped when help was needed most. For those who survived this terrible accident, they will be forever grateful to us and we can rest knowing we did all that we could at the time."

He stood up slowly and pulled her to him. He kissed her gently and hugged her again. "We've been through a lot of things Maude, mostly good things but some bad things to. This is something that will probably stay with both of us for a really long time. We just have to thank God every day that we have each other and our children and be grateful for the life we have. That night proved to us just how precious life is and how quickly it can all be taken away. You and I are sensitive to that sort of thing and maybe that is why we are still bothered by it."

Maude put her hands back in the still soapy but somewhat cooler water and said, "thanks for talking with me about this. It makes me feel better to know we are both feeling the same way."

He started to walk into the main room but turned to look at her, a smile forming on his lips, he said, "and I'm sure that Jean-Baptiste and Napoleon are grateful to you for many reasons but mostly that you have been blessed with one heck of a good set ears."

*****

The next day Maude's life was back into its same old routine. Life at a cottage can become pretty ritualistic at times. You start with fetching water in a bucket to fill the reservoir for bathing and the kettle for coffee. You light a fire in the old wood stove to heat the water to make coffee, toast the bread or warm the biscuits. Then you wake the children, serve them breakfast and assign them their chores for the day. There is always laundry to do, dishes to wash and put away and tidying up the space that, as the children got older and bigger, seemed to be getting smaller all the time.

Then there is the work next door at the main cottage. Tidying, washing floors, changing the bed sheets, washing them by hand then hanging them out to dry. Additionally there always seemed to be an endless list of things to help Mrs. Johnson with to get ready for her next set of company.

The guests and company were coming and going from the main cottage regularly now. The number of trips Gilbert was making into town to pick up guests or return them to Penetanguishene was steadily increasing and he found it was starting to interfere with his ability to get his work done in a timely manner. But, he always made it work. It was his job after all to be the caretaker, maintenance man, fishing guide, canoe paddling instructor, tour guide, taxi driver and to fit in any other duties that were asked of him. Doctor and Mrs. Johnson appreciated his flexibility and his ability to do it all.

It seemed that almost every week there were new people roaming around the property. At one point Maude made the comment to Ronnie that she didn't think it was possible for anyone to have so many friends. From her perspective, having been raised in an isolated community, there were very few people she knew. Then Ronnie explained. When she went to nursing school in Montreal, she lived in a large dormitory type nursing residence attached to the hospital. There she met and became friends with about twenty women who were enrolled in the same nursing training that she was. She explained that living in such tight residency quarters the nursing students became very good friends. For them it became like a large sisterhood. Many of the women who were now guests at the cottage were her former room-mates from that time in Montreal. At first Ronnie had invited a couple of women who were her closest friends from that time to come for a visit at the cottage. However, now the word was out. Those friends told their closest friends about the amazing vacation retreat they had experienced at Ronnie's and the letters of 'self-invitation' started pouring in. Years had gone by since Ronnie had seen many of these nurses and so for her it was a chance to get caught up with what was happening in their lives. It was like a school reunion of sorts but only a couple of people at a time. She was quite happy to entertain, have a visit with her friends and show off a little of the lifestyle she was enjoying on Georgian Bay.

For Gilbert, once breakfast was over his days were usually pretty full as well. His morning routine of daily maintenance included keeping the pathways free of debris such as dried pine needles, pine cones, broken branches and any toys or fishing gear the twins may have left out from the day before. Next on the list was filling the kerosene lamps and trimming the wicks, cleaning the shad flies off the windshields and decks of the motor boats and doing any repairs to the docks, stone cottage or main cottage that were needed. And then there were always cobwebs to sweep and brush away. Living next to the water as they did, Gilbert and Maude had resigned themselves to the fact that life on Georgian Bay meant sharing their space with the over abundant population of spiders that crawled around and nested in every nook and cranny jettisoning their sticky, tenacious webs across any opening they could find in the hope they would catch the ever present nightly batch of mosquitoes, shad flies, fish flies and humans. Each morning, as sure as the sun would rise in the east a barrier of cobwebs could be found strung across the doorways, windows, pillars, posts and trees. The cobwebs were everywhere. There was no point in getting upset about them, it was a fact of life, the morning routine included cobweb removal duty for whoever was the first one out the door, which in this household was usually always Gilbert.

As the area's resident handyman his afternoons were usually spent heading off to work on whatever project the neighbours had lined up for him to do. Add to those daily activities multiple trips into town to either pick up or drop off guests, groceries, building supplies, tools etcetera and his day was usually pretty full. He often didn't get in for supper until about seven in the evening and by then he was pretty much physically done for the day. But, he always seemed to have enough energy saved to play with the children for a short while and help Maude with the supper dishes. When their lives had become so busy with the countless activities of daily living it had become a family rule that they would always eat supper together. Many times they were off in different directions, the children went out fishing, berry picking or playing, Maude had her endless work at the stone cottage and main cottage and Gilbert's work often took him away from the property all together. Because of this scattering of family members it was important to Maude and Gilbert that they at least commit to eating the supper meal together as a family in order to regroup, share their activities of the day with each other. It was their way to stay connected as a family.

One thing that Gilbert and Maude insisted was that at each meal, everyone had to share at least one thing that was a positive experience for them that day. They believed it was a great way to teach the children the importance of not letting the negative things in life overtake the positive.

*****

"It sure seems quiet around here," Gilbert said to Maude. "I'm away most afternoons but you are here all day every day. You must find it really quiet too."

"Oh you are so right," said Maude smiling. "They are my children and I love them dearly but sometimes in these small quarters I find there are times when they just seem like they are underfoot and right behind me whenever I turn around. I've had times where I almost tripped over one of them. I send them outside and they are good about finding things to do but even when they are outside I have to keep eyes and ears open for them."

Gilbert added, "It was a good idea to have them go spend a week at my mother's place. With them being up here all summer long I know she really misses them. It gives all of us a much deserved break."

"They are eleven years old now and are good kids but they are really busy. I'll bet after a week she'll be glad to get her house back to herself."

"Actually, I forgot to tell you. Mom said that if it's alright with us, she'd be happy to have them with her for a couple of weeks."

"Humph, maybe she has something special planned for their visit."

"I don't think so but I told her that I go into town every week and that I'll check with her at the end of the first week. If she still wants them for another week, well, we'd talk about it then.

"I'd hate to have them wear her out."

"I think that with Ronnie up here all summer long, there is less for her to do at the doctor's house so she is looking for some way to fill up her days."

Maude laughed then added, "Well, they'll be full all right. The kids are old enough to keep her amused rather than the other way around."

The Stone Cottage

There was a knock at the door. "Maude, are you there?" Ronnie's voice echoed throughout the main part of the stone cottage. "Maude?"

"Yes, Ronnie, I'm here. Come on in." Maude crossed the room and opened the screen door. "Gilbert and I were just talking about how quiet it is around here without the twins."

"I've noticed the same thing. Those little rug rats," she paused, "well they aren't so little any more are they, anyway" she paused again while she adjusted the waistband on her skirt, "they are pretty good kids, but, when they aren't around it does seem quiet. Even I miss their endless chatter and playful antics jumping off the docks and splashing around." She took off her sunhat and tossed it casually on the dining table then pulled a chair out and sat down.

"Oh," she sighed leaning back on the chair. "I'm just exhausted. Having this much company week after week is starting to wear me out."

Though she didn't say it, Maude thought, *you're worn out! I'm the one who's been doing the cleaning, the tidying, washing all that linen and those bed sheets by hand and making half the meals.* But…what she did say instead was, "can I offer you some cold iced tea?"

"Oh, no thanks. I've just finished some lemonade and later the girls and I are going to have ourselves a little picnic out on one of the outer islands. I'm fine for now."

"I have a small job to do down in the Freddy Channel. I'm leaving in a few minutes but I'll be back in about an hour and a half. Do you want me to take you and your friends out for your picnic then?" Gilbert asked.

"That would be perfect. I was thinking there is a long low island just north of Cranberry Island. It looks more like a large shoal really. I thought that maybe you could drop us off there for the afternoon and then come and get us before suppertime. That way we can have time for a swim, a bite to eat, some sunbathing and just plain old relaxation."

"That will work fine for me," said Gilbert. He walked over to Maude, gave her a quick peck on the cheek and said, "I'm off. I'll be back soon," and left the room.

"Maude, the reason I came over here was to ask you a favour." said Ronnie.

"What would you like?"

"I was wondering if you'd mind taking my friends out in the rowboat and showing them the lake beyond the Narrows. The three of us walked over to the far end of our property where you can get a pretty good view of Cognashene

Lake and I was telling them about how the lake is actually a lot bigger but is divided into two lakes by those islands that are in the middle. Try as I may to explain it, they couldn't picture what I meant."

"Umm, well, the twins aren't here and my work is all caught up so I guess I have time to take them for a ride."

"Oh, you are such a doll. Thanks so much. That will give me a bit of time to myself." She tilted her head back slightly and rolled her eyes skyward, "Lord knows I haven't had much of that lately." She picked up her hat, placed it gently on her head so as not to crush the silk flowers that were sewn around the brim. She made her way to the door. "Any time you are ready, I 'm sure my friends will be ready." She turned and walked out the door but then poked her head inside the screen and said, "oh, their names are Anne and Beatrice."

*****

"You seem pretty comfortable in a rowboat Maude," said the tall, blond, lanky woman named Beatrice. She was sitting on the right hand side of the back seat of the rowboat and aimlessly dragging the fingers of her right hand in the water.

"I grew up living next to the water, so canoes and rowboats are nothing new to me," said Maude as she pulled on the oars taking two quick, strong strokes in a row.

"You grew up around here?" asked Anne who was sitting next to her friend.

"No, I was raised in a small community called Granite Bluff Inlet. It's north of here by about fifty miles."

"Well you sure know how to work those oars. It takes a fair amount of coordination to pull on both of them with the same amount of force at the same time."

"If you don't then you'll find that you go off course or go around in circles," Maude explained. "Here let me show you. See, if I take both oars and pull on them with the same amount of force you go straight. But," she pulled hard on the oar on the left and barely pulled on the right oar, the boat turned slightly, "but if you don't, then see how the boat turns to the right?" Maude pulled on the right oar to make a course correction and then resumed her natural rhythm.

"I don't think I have the strength in my arms to row a boat," said Beatrice pulling up her sleeve and flexed her bicep. Glancing at it she added, "Nope. Nothing there." She laughed at her own joke.

"It does take some practice and it's an excellent exercise. This rowboat is pretty light and neither of you two ladies are very heavy so that makes it a lot easier for me to row," said Maude. "If this was a bigger heavier boat, I'd have to pull a lot harder on the oars to get anywhere."

"And there isn't any wind right now. I bet if it was windy it would be pretty hard to row then."

"You're right," said Maude, "that can be a real challenge especially if you are heading into the wind."

They rowed on in silence for a while all three of them enjoying the peacefulness and amazing scenery. It was a calm, clear, cloudless day and the water reflected the shoreline like a mirror. Within about ten minutes Maude passed by the four large islands that were situated right in the middle of the lake hiding what was beyond. As she steered the boat north of those islands, the lake opened up again, the shores on each side seemed to be farther away from each other making this part of the lake wider than the one before and it appeared that the end of the lake was about another mile or two away.

"Wow, this lake is big. I see now what Ronnie was talking about. When you stand on shore near her cottage and look in this direction, you see land but it looks like a solid shoreline because the islands kind of jut in and out. But when you get past them you can see the lake is really huge."

"The lake is really wide and long. I don't think I'll take us all the way to the end but I can tell you there are several families that live down at the far end of the lake," said Maude. "They live here year round."

"They must go stark raving mad living in such an isolated place in the winter time. Who would come to visit and what on earth do they do all day?" exclaimed Anne.

"Well there are a couple of families and in the winter time they still find plenty of things to do. Sometimes they go fishing or hunting. One of the families harvests the ice from the lake and they store it in log ice huts. Between each layer of ice they spread a layer sawdust. That acts like insulation so the ice doesn't melt and the blocks don't stick together that way. Then they sell the ice to the summer residents and usually have enough to last all season long."

"Well I'll be damned," said Beatrice. "Imagine that. Making a living selling ice."

"It's actually pretty hard work. Those blocks of ice are almost two feet square and are very heavy," said Maude thinking of Philippe and how his muscles strain with the weight of the ice when he is carrying the blocks up to the cottage. Not wanting to go too much further she slowed down her pace and added, "The other family have a fair sized boat house and in the winter time they build small run-about boats. Some people put outboard motors on them or use them as rowboats. It all depends on what they want. Most of the people on the bay own one of their boats."

As Maude reached the middle of the lake she pointed out a few of the more prominent spots along the shoreline where the granite turned from pink to black or sometimes it faded to a beige-grey colour. In other places there were prominent veins of brilliant white quartz that ran down from the tree line right into the water bifurcating the granite in half with its shimmering crystals. It looked like it was placed there on purpose to highlight the otherwise drab tones of the granite.

Maude rowed on a little further then said, "We've been gone for over an hour now so I guess I should turn this ship around and head us back to home port," joked Maude.

The two passengers barely noticed as the boat made a slow and gentle arc in the middle of the lake and Maude started homeward.

"This scenery is just spectacular," said Beatrice who was once again dragging her hand in the warm water.

"It is so clean, so peaceful, so untouched by anything but nature," said Anne. "The water is so clear you can almost see to the bottom of the lake." She too leaned over the side and dragged her hand in the water. "I can understand why Ronnie wants to live here all summer."

"Oh, look," Anne said pointing to an opening between mainland and one of the islands, "it looks like a hidden channel."

"I can take you that way if you'd like. It's actually a bit of a short cut back to the cottage," said Maude. "The channel gets quite narrow and shallow at one spot maybe only about twenty or twenty five feet wide but we can certainly fit the rowboat through." Maude rowed on occasionally turning her head to check out her position in the channel. "There are some really beautiful granite bluffs down at the end as well. They would make great photos if you have a camera."

The passengers looked at each other then started to laugh. "You know Maude, both of us brought cameras with us for our vacation and neither one of us remembered to bring film so the cameras are pretty much useless to us on this trip." Both women laughed at their faux pas.

Maude continued to row down the channel occasionally turning her head to see where she was going. Every now and then she would make corrections to her steering so she would not hit the shore as she rowed.

"Look," Beatrice said pointing to the bluff that was soaring sixty feet in the air in front of the boat. "I think I see a bear on the top of that rock up there."

Maude turned quickly and looked. Sure enough a small black bear, about a year or two old was standing on the edge of the rocky outcropping watching the boat come closer into his view. Periodically he would raise his nose into the air and sniff trying to catch their scent. The ladies were now only about fifty feet away and had a perfect view of him from there.

"Maybe we should turn around," suggested Anne.

"He looks so majestic up there on the rock. He looks like he's the king of the castle looking at us like we are the dirty rascals," said Beatrice.

Maude continued to row at a steady and even pace hoping that the splashing of the oars in the water would not attract too much attention from the bear. "This is the narrowest part of the channel right here," whispered Maude, "and then as soon as we round this bend it opens up into the first part of the lake," she rowed on steadily moving the small craft forward. "Let's just be quiet and maybe he'll lose interest in us and wander off." Maude quickened her strokes.

The two passengers were fixated, staring at the top of the bluff and the black bear that was looking down at them. Neither said a word but Maude could tell by the look on their faces that this was a scene they would have permanently etched in their brain for years to come.

Anne leaned forward and said quietly "You were right Maude, he has left the top of the rock. looks like he's probably going away."

Maude breathed a silent breath of relief and thought, *That's good news. The last thing I needed is to have these ladies scare the bear.*

As she pulled on the oars Maude turned once again and looked ahead of the boat to make sure she had steered the rowboat in the right direction and not to close to shore. Beatrice and Anne were once again quiet taking in the sights and looking at the rock formations and the interesting shoreline. Both were amazed at the number of painted turtles that had crawled up on the warm rocks to sun themselves.

Suddenly and without any warning Maude noticed the bear had appeared from the dense underbrush and was running along the shoreline. Bears run quickly and this one was wasting no time catching up to them, roaring as he ran. Once he was even with the little boat he jumped into the water and began to swim after them. With the channel being so narrow in this spot it took no time at all for the bear to catch up to them."

"Row! Maude row!" shouted Beatrice.

Maude didn't need to be told what to do. She dug the oars deep into the water and pulled hard on them doubling, then tripling the speed she had been rowing before.

"Its gaining on us Maude, he's coming after us really fast! I didn't know bears could swim that fast."

Maude dug deep and pulled on the oars as fast as she could till her arms ached but the bear kept advancing. "I can't believe how fast he can swim," she said breathlessly.

When it looked like the bear was going to win the race Maude suddenly stopped rowing and pulled one of the oars out of the oarlock.

"What are you doing," shouted Anne, "he's going to swamp us."

"I need one of you to move to the front of the boat right now so I can get on the back seat," ordered Maude.

"Are you going to club him with it?" asked Beatrice as she hurried to the front of the boat. Anne scampered to the middle seat where Maude had been sitting to free up the entire back seat.

"I'm afraid that might be too risky, I might break the oar. Or I might tip the boat when I swing at him," said Maude as she got on her knees on the back seat.

Just as she was saying this the bear was now close enough to the boat that with one swipe of his front paw he could have overturned the boat. Maude gripped the oar with both hands and waited just a moment longer. When the bear was within just a few feet of the boat she took the oar and using the blade-like wider end pushed the bear's nose underwater. She pushed with all her might, shoving the head as far under water as she could. This slowed the bear's advance. He stopped paddling. He raised his head above the water and gave it a shake to clear the water from his snout. With a loud snort the bear started to close in on the rowboat. Again Maude, gripping the oar for all she was worth, pushed hard on the bear's snout half way between his eyes and nostrils. This time she was able to hold it under longer than the first time.

The bear seemed to disappear under the water for a moment and when it raised its head above the water it growled baring its large yellowed teeth in anger, it's sharp curved fangs just inches away from Maude's hand. Just as it was about to blow out the water from its nostrils Maude anticipated this and didn't wait. She immediately pushed the bear's head under the water again not giving it a chance to catch its breath. Again she held it under for as long as she could. She could feel the bear shaking his head under water to free the blade of the oar that was holding him down. Maude struggled to keep the blade positioned on his snout. She lost her balance in the small boat and her foot slipped. Her ribs smashed into the transom and she crashed onto the floor but never lost her grip on the oar.

When the bear's head re-surfaced it seemed to be a little disoriented and shook its head like a dog would shake when it has fallen in the water. The boat was now almost on top of the bear. One swipe with its paw and the boat would be overturned. Maude regained her position on the back seat and just as she was about to push its snout under again, the bear stopped its advance and seemed to drift back a bit. Then it turned and headed for shore snorting loudly as it paddled trying to clear the water from its nostrils.

Maude quickly put the oar back in the oarlock and, taking her seat in the middle of the boat, dug both oars into the water with lightening speed. Soon they saw the bear crawl up on shore and shake to shed the water from its fur. It turned and looked at them, growled a long low menacing growl then turned and lumbered up into the forest.

"I think I've wet my pants," said Beatrice.

"I know I wet mine," said Anne. "I've never been so scared in all my life. I thought we were goners." The two women returned to their places on the back seat and hugged each other. Neither said a word after that, both of them were in shock about what happened and thought of what could have happened.

*****

By the time they reached the dock at the cottage Maude was exhausted. She had rowed the boat at double time across the bay and through the Narrows channel. She was glad her passengers had been quiet for the rest of the ride home. She needed time to collect her thoughts and steady her nerves. The adrenaline rush she felt at the time she was tangling with the bear had given her the energy to row the boat like she had never rowed before but now that she was near the dock she started to shake, her whole body trembling as if she were cold and shivering. Her arms fell limp at her sides and she had a hard time moving in her seat. That was by far the scariest moment she had ever had in her life and she was glad the outcome was as positive as it was. Things could have turned out a lot worse.

As the rowboat drifted in towards the end of the dock Anne said, "Maude that was the bravest thing I have ever seen anyone do in my whole life. I was so scared I was going to die. That bear was so close to tipping the boat over. You saved our lives. I'll never ever forget this. Not ever,"

"I don't know what to say Maude other than you were amazing. We will all have quite the story to tell of how you fought the bear and you won," said Beatrice. She moved to the middle of the boat to give Maude a hug and noticed that she was trembling. "I know you must have been scared too, but you knew what to do. You are the best."

Ronnie came ambling down to the dock wearing a brightly coloured summer frock and the fancy hat with the flowers around the brim.

"Look at you guys," she said as she leaned over the edge of the dock and grabbed the bow line to tie the boat to the cleat. "You've been sitting here at the dock for a couple of minutes now and not one of you seem to have the energy to tie up the boat," she said jokingly.

When she got no response from any of them she sat on the dock and put her brightly painted toes on the gunwale of the rowboat. She looked at the three women and said. "My God! You guys look like you've seen a ghost."

At the same time Anne and Beatrice started talking. They started to tell Ronnie what had happened. One would start the sentence, the other would finish it. Ronnie's mouth fell open and remained agape the whole time. She was barely breathing as she listened to the story of what had happened. She moved her hand to her throat and took a gasp of air. She was having a hard time breathing. She was shocked and for once had nothing to say. She just listened, shaking her head as the details of the battle with the bear were relayed to her.

All the while Maude just sat still on the middle seat of the boat, listening as the story unfolded. She couldn't believe what she had just done. She couldn't believe she had saved these women and herself from near death. She thought back to how quickly it all happened. It seemed so surreal but, as she heard the details being spoken out loud, it became very real and she knew it wasn't just a dream. At the time it seemed like the struggle with the bear had gone on for hours but in actuality it was only about three or four minutes. But, those were four of the longest minutes in her life. She knew one thing for sure, it was an experience she'd relive over and over again in her mind. It was an experience she never wanted to repeat again for as long as she lived.

"I have to go up to the cottage and change my clothes," said Beatrice. "I must smell to high heavens, what, with wetting my pants and all."

"I'm the same," said Anne. The two women clambered out of the boat on their hands and knees. Beatrice tried to stand but toppled over onto her side. "I'm still so upset by what happened I don't know if I can walk."

Ronnie stood up and helped the two women to their feet. "You guys go on up to the cottage, I'm going to stay here for a few minutes and talk to Maude."

Maude leaned forward and grabbed the stern rope and tied it to the cleat at the end of the dock. She tried to stand up to get out of the boat but her legs were too weak to carry her weight. She sat back down. "I think I used up all of my energy fighting that bear and racing this boat home," she said to Ronnie.

"You just sit right there were you are. I'll be right back. I'm going to the cottage and I'll get you a nice cold glass of lemonade with extra sugar in it to give you some strength back," and with that she quickly stood and ran up the dock.

Within moments she was back with two glasses. One filled with water, the other with lemonade. "You are sweating like crazy Maude," said Ronnie as she handed her the glass of water. "Here, take this first to re-hydrate yourself then you can take your time sipping on the lemonade."

Maude gratefully accepted the offerings. As she raised the glass of water to her lips she noticed she was still shaking and spilled a bit on her blouse. "My arms feel like they are made out of rubber," she said brushing at the water spots.

"They will probably be like that for a couple of hours till your adrenaline level drops back down. Tomorrow your arms will probably feel like they are going to fall off right from the shoulders after the ordeal you put them through today."

The two women sat silent for a few minutes while Maude sipped on her lemonade then Ronnie said, "Maude, I always knew that you were special in so many ways, you are kind, you are caring, you are hard working. You never complain, you just go about doing what needs to be done and somehow you always get it done. I never thought I'd have to add to the list of your qualities that you are a bear wrestler as well," she joked.

Maude burst out laughing, appreciating how Ronnie had made her feel better so easily.

*****

The two women were still sitting when they heard the familiar sound of a boat motor. Both turned to look out in the bay and saw Gilbert's boat idling in towards the dock. He pulled up alongside the dock, and effortlessly jumped out onto it, the bow line already in his hand. He stooped to tie the rope and made his way to the stern and grabbed that rope. He turned to look at Maude and Ronnie who were sitting on the dock with their feet dangling over the side resting them on the gunwale of the rowboat. He said, "you guys look comfy." He bent down on one knee, tied the rope and then said to Maude, "Hey is that lemonade? Can I have a sip, I'm parched. You wouldn't believe what I've been up to for the last hour or so."

Maude raised the glass towards his outstretched hand and he noticed that her hand was trembling. "Are you alright Maude," he asked. "Have you been out in the sun too long?"

The two women started to laugh. "I wish that was all that it is," said Maude.

"OK, what's going on?"

"We can tell you what's going on," said Beatrice and Anne in unison as they arrived at the dock.

They recounted to Gilbert the story of what had happened, not leaving out a single detail and emphasizing how Maude had saved their lives. They had nothing but praise for her.

"I don't know if I'd have been that brave," he said shaking his head back and forth. "I'm not sure what I would have done in that situation either, so I'm glad you figured it out. If ever that happens to me, I'll know what to do."

"I hope and pray that never happens to you," said Maude. "And I hope and pray that never happens to Ben or Emma. They might not have the strength to push a bear's head underwater like that."

"Well we'll have to be sure to tell them the story and I think for safety sake, we better tell them that taking a row boat or canoe through that narrow channel is not permitted."

"I think I want to go up to the cottage and change my clothes," said Maude to Gilbert. "I'm pretty sweaty."

"I should say. You worked up a sweat," said Anne. "You rowed that boat like an Olympic athlete today. In fact I think you probably set a new world record."

"What, for the fastest time getting away from a bear?" joked Maude as she made her way to the end of the dock.

Gilbert turned to the three women on the dock and asked, "Do you ladies still want to go on your picnic?"

"I think we'll pass on that Gil," said Ronnie. "I think we'll just settle in for the afternoon on the front sun porch and maybe have a nice cold gin and tonic." She winked at Gilbert then said, "when you get up to the cottage, tell Maude she is welcome to join us. In fact tell her I insist that she join us. She deserves a good stiff drink."

"I have a feeling she might just do that," he said.

And she did.

CHAPTER - 14

Word of Maude's 'adventure' with the bear spread around the lake and the neighbouring channels like wild fire. For the next week whenever Maude met up with anyone she knew they would ply her for details about what and how it happened. They would pat her on the shoulder or shake her hand and praise her for saving the lives of Mrs. Johnson's friends. Many people passing by through the Narrows would slow down and point at the stone cottage. Sometimes they could be heard to say, "that's where she lives." If Maude was outside at the time they would shout a greeting to her and give her a thumbs-up gesture of congratulations or shout "way to go Maude." As a genuinely shy person Maude found all this attention to be somewhat embarrassing. She would simply say thank you or wave back and try to be as indifferent as she could be.

Maude and Gilbert were both surprised at the stories they were hearing by the end of the second week. It seemed that the more often the story was told, the more the story was embellished. By the end of the third week, the bear was a large full grown male who hadn't eaten in many days. In this new version the bear jumped from the bluff into the water, the wave he created nearly toppled the boat and Maude fearing for their lives had clubbed the bear over the head with the oar sending the bear to its premature death. In the story it seems the trail of blood from the bear's fatal wounds could be seen flowing in the water being carried away towards the shore by the wind. It was this same wind that had taken the scent of the ladies perfume up to the bear and caused him to go after the women in the first place. Soon the seagulls and turkey vultures common to the area began circling the carcass looking for the free meal they knew was to come before long. Maude and Gilbert were quick to set the story straight whenever they heard details that were not correct but sometimes when all was said and done, they had to laugh at how bizarre some of the stories sounded.

Ben and Emma however, though they knew the true story, sometimes weren't so quick to set the story straight. Instead they sometimes let the people tell them the story while they basked in the radiant descriptions of their mother, the heroine. When Maude heard the twins repeating some erroneous details of the story one day to a couple of new guests that were staying at the main cottage she pulled them aside. Maude being the humble person that she was, used it as a learning opportunity to teach the children about how stories can become utter gossip that can sometimes get people in trouble if it gets told to the wrong person or repeated in a malicious way.

By the end of the fourth week the story of Maude and the bear had become old news and for the most part people forgot about it. Maude was quite happy when the attention and stories shifted to other people and other events.

*****

On a hot and humid day in the beginning of August, Maude went over to the main cottage to check with Mrs. Johnson about when the next group of company would be coming. Though it was still early in the afternoon, Ronnie was reclining on the wicker love seat in the front porch and was obviously enjoying the beverage she clutched in her hand. Maude could tell it was not her first one of the day by the slurring of her speech and the almost imperceptible sway to her body even when sitting still. Ronnie was very happy to see Maude at her door and welcomed her inside. She was still in awe of what had happened weeks before and had recited the story to her friends over and over. To her credit, even though she was not always sober when she was telling it she always got all the details straight and was certain to give all the credit to Maude whenever anyone asked about what had happened.

Ronnie looked down into her glass and smiled while absentmindedly swirling the liquid in the bottom of the glass. Maude thought it was interesting to see that Ronnie had an enviable capacity for enjoying the familiar things in life like a cold drink, but at the same time she felt sorry to think that Ronnie had such a dependence on alcohol to get her through the day.

"Come and join me Maude. It's a hot summer day and a nice cold drink will make your day just a little brighter."

"No thank you. It's kind of you to offer but I need to get back, I have a pot of fish chowder on the stove that I have to watch closely."

"Mmm, I love fish chowder," said Ronnie.

"I'll send some over for your supper with one of the twins."

"You look like you were going to ask me something," Ronnie added.

"Yes. I was going to ask if you will be having company this week or this weekend. I was thinking of taking a week and going up to Granite Bluff Inlet to visit my parents. I haven't seen them in a couple of years... but if you're getting company I'll put the visit off for now."

"Don't be silly, take the time, don't worry about me. Go see your parents. I'm sure if you haven't seen them in a couple of years they must be pining to see you as well. Are you bringing the twins with you?"

"No. I'd love to but they'll be staying behind with Gilbert. I can't afford to pay for three tickets on the Keewatin."

"Rubbish, you should take them with you." She reached for her purse that was on the credenza by the front door. Digging out a wad of bills she counted out fifty dollars and handed it to Maude. "Let me pay for you to have a vacation with your children. I'm sure there is enough here to cover the cost."

"No, I couldn't let you do that. That is way too much," said Maude trying to give the money back to Mrs. Johnson. "Just getting the time off was all I was looking for."

"Nonsense. For all that you do, for all you've done and especially for the bravery you demonstrated a few weeks ago, I can't think of anyone else who deserves a holiday and this money more."

"Really," said Maude looking at the money, "that is too much. I don't feel right about taking the money." She walked towards the credenza and placed the money on it.

"I insist," Ronnie said picking up the cash and thrusting the money into Maude's hand, "and I don't want to hear another word about it."

"This is so kind of you," Maude said graciously. "My parents have never even met the twins. The twins have never been to my homestead at Granite Bluff so they've never seen or experienced what life on a reserve is like. I've dreamed about taking them up there since they were born but never thought I'd ever be able to do it." She looked down at the bills in her hand. "Thank you so much," said Maude, a lump forming in her throat making it difficult for her to speak. "This will be a trip of a lifetime for me and the twins."

Slightly embarrassed by what had just transpired and not used to receiving such a generous gift she turned and started down the path to the stone cottage. Then she remembered what she had originally gone over to see Mrs. Johnson about and turned around. She knocked on the door.

"Come in," shouted Ronnie who was now back in the cottage mixing another drink at the liquor cabinet.

"I never got an answer from you about whether you are getting company this week."

"I am. Doc is coming up on Wednesday afternoon this week and if you can believe it, he's taking a few days off work and staying until Sunday." She dropped some lemon slices in her drink then added, "I can't believe it myself."

Maude said, "that will be good for him to get some time off and away from town. He works so hard day after day. He deserves to get a chance to enjoy the cottage."

"He's bringing two couples up with him and they are staying until Sunday as well. Both of the men are friends of his from medical school." She stopped talking for a minute and went to the kitchen to get some ice from the fridge. When she returned she added, "I don't really like these guys. They are both pretty arrogant but, I can't really say anything because Lord knows Doc's put up with enough of my friends coming up here over the last couple of years."

Maude reassured Ronnie, "The cottage is big and the property is massive so I'm sure if you need some space from them there should be some opportunity for you to make yourself scarce if you have to."

*****

Maude returned to the stone cottage and was immediately aware of the smell of something burning before she had even opened the door. She raced to the stove glad that she hadn't stayed visiting with Ronnie any longer than she had. The wood in the firebox had burned a lot more quickly than she had anticipated and the stove top was glowing red. The fish chowder that she had so painstakingly prepared had boiled over and seared onto the surface. The whole kitchen smelled of burnt milk and overdone fish.

Maude grabbed a T-towel to protect her hand, reached down and closed the red-hot dampers at the bottom of the firebox then closed the damper on the chimney hoping to quickly choke out the fire. She knew throwing water on it to cool things down would surely crack the stove top and warp or irreparably damage the firebox. Grabbing some well used oven mitts she lifted the soup pot off the stove and carefully set it down on the stone hearth of the fireplace in the main part of the cottage. The windows were already open but she propped open the front and back door to let a breeze blow through and create a draft. She untied her apron and using it like a fan, tried to cool things off in the kitchen manually.

I can't believe it, she thought. *I just had some of the best news of my life five minutes ago and here I am playing fireman in my own kitchen. Kind of sucks the joy right out of it.*

Once the stove top was cooled enough she took a flat metal spatula that looked more like a putty knife and started to scrape at the burnt chowder that was stuck to the stove. It wasn't long before she had amassed a small mound of dark brown to black soot on the stove top. Emma came into the cottage just at that point and said, "Mom, why are the doors propped…" she paused, "wow, what's that smell?"

"That was going to be supper. I was making fish chowder and it boiled over."

"Can I help you with what you are doing?"

"Sure. You can take the soup ladle and another pot and see if you can salvage any of the soup that is in the pot on the hearth. Be careful not to scrape the bottom of the pot, I'm pretty sure that part will be scorched and taste horrible."

Emma took the ladle and as instructed began to spoon out the soup into another pot. She was three quarters of the way to the bottom of the pot when the colour of the soup started to change from milky white to a beige-brown shade. That is when she stopped. Bringing the pot of soup back into the kitchen she showed what remained in the pot to her mother. "I left the good soup in the other pot on the hearth for now but what do you think I should do with this?"

"That's a good question," Maude paused while she thought about it. "I think the best thing to do is to take this spatula," she said handing it to her daughter, "and scrape the bottom of the pot as well as you can. Then take it to the outhouse and dump it in there. If you dump it anywhere else it might attract some animals we don't want to have around." Emma turned her nose up a little at the thought of what she was being asked to do but did what she was told.

When she returned with the now empty pot Maude thanked her for her help and told her that she really appreciated her help. Taking the pot from Emma, she filled it with soapy water to let it soak. "I think I'll be scrubbing on this pot for a week," she said to her daughter laughing. Slowly her good mood started to return as her thoughts strayed from the task at hand to making her vacation plans.

At supper time that night, there wasn't enough fish chowder for everyone to have a second bowl but that was OK, it did have a bit of an unusual taste to it anyway. At Maude's suggestion everyone took an extra slice of homemade bread with a thick coating of butter instead.

As was tradition at supper there was a round table sharing of something positive that happened to each person that day. As usual the sharing started with the children.

Emma said, "Mom had a bit of an incident in the kitchen this afternoon. I asked her if I could help her and she said I could. When everything was all cleaned up she thanked me and told me that I had been really helpful and that when people work together they can make a bad situation better."

Gilbert thanked Emma for being there for her mother then said to Ben, "OK, young fella, what good thing happened to you today?"

Ben cleared his throat, took a last bite of his bread then said, "You're not gonna believe this but there was a man who was fishing in the Narrows today. I've never seen him before but he looked like he was pretty new to fishing. I could tell because when I was watching him he would take a worm out of his bucket and lay it across his hook and then drop it in the water. Of course the worm would float away and he was using up his worms pretty fast. I went over to him and said, "Hey mister, if you don't mind me telling you this, you have to pass the hook through the worm to get it to stay on the hook." Well he tried a couple of times but I could tell he wasn't too comfortable handling the worms. I offered to show him how to do it and as God is my witness as soon as he dropped the line in the lake a nice small-mouth bass bit his hook. The man was over the moon excited." Ben cleared his throat and straightened himself up in his chair to make his story seem more impressive. "That was when we realized the fish had swallowed the hook. Then I had to show him how to reach in and grab the top end of the hook and pull it out. We were even able to save half the worm. That man thanked me over and over again. He even tried to pay me with a couple of quarters that he had in his pocket but I told him it was my pleasure to help out a city slicker like him." Maude and Gilbert glanced at each other a frown forming on their faces. Gilbert thought about cautioning Ben about his language around strangers but within seconds they burst out laughing and everyone joined in.

Gilbert then said, "Maude, what about you? What is your positive experience from today?"

"I'd like to go last this time. Why don't you tell us how your day was?"

Gilbert started by taking a small sip of his coffee then said. "A really good thing happened to me today." He took another sip of his coffee and paused for a while waiting to be urged to continue.

"Well, go on. Are you going to tell us or not," said Emma.

"Last week I did some work for Mr. Thibbeault in the Hangdog Channel. I put a new floor down in his kitchen and with what was left over; I had enough to redo the floor in his bathroom. He was really pleased with what I did and now he wants me to build him a screened in porch on the side of his cottage so he can get away from the bugs at night and watch the sun setting over the gap."

"That's really good news," said Maude.

"The best part is he is going to pay me half of the cost of my labour up front as a retainer then he'll pay me the rest when the job is done." A broad smile erupted on Gilbert's face then he continued. "This is great because it's a big job that is going to take me quite a while to do. This will give us some extra cash in our pockets in the fall when you guys," he looked at the twins, "head back to school. The taxes and insurance are due on the house at the end of September too and usually we have a hard time coming up with the money for that but we won't this year."

Maude smiled, thinking that what Gilbert had said was such good news she thought that maybe she should hold off on sharing her news so that it didn't take away from his good news story but… she was so excited to tell everyone she blurted out. "Wait till I tell you what happened to me." Everyone looked at her. She was so energized by what she had to say she could hardly sit still.

"Mom, come on, what is it? You look like you won a million dollars," said Ben.

"Well I kind of did. Not quite a million but I feel like I did." She took a sip of water, sat up a little straighter and said to the twins. "I'm taking you guys for a ride on the Keewatin and we are going to go up to Granite Bluff Inlet to see my mom and dad. It's been years since I've seen them and I can't wait for them to meet you and see how big you've grown."

"Maude that is a really great idea but I don't think we can afford to have the three of you go all the way up there. I'm not opposed to it but Mr. Thibbeault hasn't paid me yet and as I said, I sort of had plans for that money."

"Don't worry about that. I've got it covered," Maude said as she pulled five, ten dollar bills out of her apron pocket.

Emma's eyes bulged. "Mom, did you rob the bank or something?"

"Here's what happened. This afternoon I went over to see Mrs. Johnson to see if she was getting any company in the next week or so. I told her I'd like to take a week and go up north to see my parents. She asked if I was bringing you guys and I told her that although I'd love to I couldn't afford it so I would be going alone. Well, she wouldn't hear of it. She took fifty dollars out of her purse and gave it to me. I tried twice to give it back to her because that is so much money but she refused to take it back. She said after all we've been through this summer nobody deserves to take their children to visit their grandparents more than I do."

Ben and Emma were so excited they pushed the wooden stools Gilbert had made them away from the table and grabbed their mother by the hands. Pulling her to a standing position they each took turns giving her a giant bear hug. Emma said, "I can't wait, I can't wait. This is going to be so much fun. We've never been to Granite Bluff."

"OK, OK," Maude said hugging each one of them in turn.

Not to be left out, Gilbert stood, put his hands out to Maude and said sheepishly, "Can I have a hug too?"

Soon, all four of them were embracing in a group hug and bouncing up and down. Gilbert whispered in Maude's ear,

"This really has been a good day all around hasn't it?"

"Well the bad news was I burned the chowder today but...our positive news sure outshines the bad news."

*****

Though the sky was a clear indigo blue the wind was blowing, nearly howling, from the west at about thirty five knots. It had been since early that morning. It was Wednesday afternoon and Doc had just arrived with his guests. Due to the wind, it was a challenge to park at the dock and Dr. Johnson had to make several attempts, backing up and correcting his direction a couple of times before he actually pulled up alongside the dock. He was very glad Gilbert was on the dock to help catch the boat to prevent it from crashing into the dock or the rocks on shore.

"That was an awful landing," Doc said as he moved out from the driver's seat.

Smiling, Gilbert replied to the Doc's comment as he reached for the bow line, "Any landing you can walk away from is a good landing." The two men started to laugh at the humour in that comment.

The ropes weren't even tied yet when a slender, well put together woman, leaped out of the boat and bent over the other side of the dock and vomited. Her husband was quickly at her side, passing her his handkerchief so she could wipe the spittle from her lips. When she turned around Gilbert noticed she was an unusual shade of green.

"Oh my God," the woman proclaimed, "the only thing worse than feeling this seasick is thinking that I still have to go back though that awful gap again to get off this island." She looked like she was about to cry.

"Maybe you can stay here until the water freezes in the winter time and you can walk home," said her husband joking. If looks could kill the daggers that were shot from her eyes towards him would have flattened him on the dock right there and then.

"Too soon to be joking about this?" he smiled weakly.

"Too soon," she said still holding the handkerchief to her mouth.

She turned to face Gilbert and tried to smile at him but was immediately overtaken by yet another wave of nausea and she once again rushed to the other side of the dock vomiting a yellowy bilious fluid. By this time Ronnie had come down to the dock and grabbing her guest by the hand said, "Come with me Honey, I've got some Gravol up at the cottage. Or, if you'd rather I can make you a nice cold gin and tonic."

"I better stick with the Gravol. Giving up alcohol was one of the things I bargained with God about if he would just deliver me to this dock safely."

The two women headed off the dock and up the shore. The other couple, who had by this time climbed out of the boat were gathering the luggage that Gilbert had placed on the dock. He said to them, "Why don't you guys just go up to the cottage and I'll bring all this luggage and the coolers up in a minute."

Relieved the work was going to be done for them everyone smiled and started walking up the dock. Gilbert could hear Doc Johnson saying, "and that is the front porch that I was telling you about that Gilbert built." Gilbert smiled and thought, "one thing about the Johnson's. They always give credit where credit is due."

He made his way to the front of the boat to pull the remaining pieces of luggage out from where they'd been stowed under the deck to keep them dry. He heard water gurgling about in the bilge and the boat seemed unusually tippy as he moved from side to side. He raised the engine box to look at the bilge and noticed there was quite a bit of water sloshing about. He flipped the bilge pump switch and immediately water started to pump out. The bilge pump ran for a full five minutes before it stopped. *It must have been one heck of a rough ride across the gap for them to have taken on that much water,* he thought.

*****

With Maude and the twins away for a week Gilbert had the stone cottage to himself. While the cottage was beginning to seem a bit small when the whole family was there, once his outside chores were done he found himself wandering from the front room to the kitchen and back again, aimlessly moving around, as if looking for something. He thought, *this place is big enough for us.* He strolled over to the window and looked at the boats tied up at the dock checking to make sure none of the ropes had come undone in the wind and then he settled himself on a chair at the table. Looking around the room he realized after a while that he wasn't really looking for anything, he just missed his family being there.

He got up and lit a small fire in the wood stove and put a kettle of water on to boil. He started to add the usual amount of coffee grounds to the pot and realized he was making enough for him to share with Maude. He scooped some of the grounds out of the pot and added them back into the coffee can. *Old habits die hard,* he thought.

Once his coffee was ready he went outside and sat on the bench that was against the west wall facing the Narrows. He could feel the warmth of the rocks through his shirt and was comforted by their soothing effect on his aching muscles. He was also comforted by the idea that some things never change, such as this quiet time on a favourite bench with a hot coffee and a good view. This was his happy place for sure, but at this moment he was missing being able to share it with his beloved wife.

*****

The Stone Cottage

The next morning Gilbert was up with the birds. He couldn't believe how well he had slept throughout the night. The room was quiet, the bed seemed huge and there was no tug of war with the covers like there usually was.

He picked up the empty water pail that was by the stove and put it on the porch by the front door. After a quick stop at the outhouse he took the pail and went into the Narrows. Standing on a flat rock that was close to the edge of the water he scooped up a pail full of clean, clear water. Getting the water from this spot was tradition because this was where the current was the strongest and it ensured that there would be no debris, or pollen or other impurities that could usually be found floating closer to the docks and the nooks and crannies along the shore.

Once in the kitchen he again lit the stove and put the kettle on to boil for his morning coffee just as he had the night before. He thought about how making coffee was a part of Maude's daily routine and till this moment never appreciated what she went through, like the tedium of some repetitive tasks such as making coffee. He took it for granted that if he wanted a coffee Maude would make it happen regardless of what time it was. He thought to himself, *I must remember to thank Maude for all that she does so naturally, incorporating these sorts of things into her day.* He pondered for a moment deep in thought. *What a shame it is that as we fall into the rituals of daily living we end up taking each other's work for granted. I must try to be more mindful of that and thank her.*

With breakfast out of the way and the dishes neatly stacked in the wash basin Gilbert made his way outside to begin his daily routine of sweeping cobwebs, cleaning the paths and washing the shad flies off the decks of the boats. Soon after he got to the dock he was joined by Dr. Johnson, alerted to his presence by the jingling of lose change in his pockets.

"Our guests are all still asleep. No one is up but me. I guess it's so quiet here they are sleeping like babies."

Gilbert turned to face Doc and said, "I slept really well too. Maude and the twins are away for seven days visiting her parents and I have the cottage to myself. I didn't think I'd sleep very well because it was so quiet but even the strong coffee I had just before I hit the sack didn't keep me awake."

Doc stood at the end of the dock and peered into the water. "How deep is the water right here at the end of the dock Gilbert?"

"It's at least eight feet. I haven't really ever measured it but I can tie a stone to a rope and drop it down to give you an exact measure if you'd like."

"Nah, don't bother with that." He walked over to the other side of the dock opposite to where his boat was parked. Here the water was obviously more shallow, deep enough only for a canoe or a rowboat. He moved and stood in the middle of the dock looking side to side deep in thought, the change in his pocket clattering away. Occasionally he'd take a step back and look at the width and length of the dock apparently sizing it up in his mind.

"I bet it would be a really big deal to move this dock further into the bay so that it is deep on both sides of the dock."

"That would be a huge job," said Gilbert. "The dock is built on piers that have been built not to move even with the force of the winter ice. To get deep water on each side of the dock we'd have to move the dock over by about ten feet. That would mean taking the top off, dismantling the piers, removing all the rocks holding them in place then rebuilding it from the bottom of the lake up. The piers will be deeper in the water too so they will need to be built higher and that will take more rocks to fill them as well."

Gilbert was feeling a bit weak in the knees at the thought of the potential job ahead of him. "It would be a lot easier if we were to leave the dock where it is and add an extension onto it. We could either go straight out or make a T-shaped dock at the end."

Doc considered what Gilbert was saying. "There's room here in the bay Doc said motioning to the little lagoon the docks were in. I think we should just build another dock. We can leave this one the way it is." Gilbert breathed a sigh of relief. "It is pretty high up off the water which is good for when the water level rises and falls but I think I'd like a new dock built that is at least twenty feet long, no, make that twenty five feet long and I'd like the top of it to be closer to the surface of the water. How about if you make it about a foot off the water."

Gilbert was puzzled by the dimensions and description he was hearing. "You know, if the dock is built low, when the water rises, say with a storm surge for example, it will end up being underwater pretty quickly."

"Not if you make it a floating dock. Then it will go up and down with the height of the water."

"Are you thinking you want a dock that is lower in the water so that it is easier to get in and out of the rowboat or the canoe?"

"No, not a small boat. I'm thinking I want to get something really fast. I'm tired of this business of taking over an hour to come up from town, or on a windy day nearly swamping in the gap. No" he paused and looked over the side of the dock once again, "I want to get here quickly and for what I have in mind, having the dock lower will just make life easier."

Gilbert knew that Doc could sometimes be naïve about things related to cottages and boating. If he wants to get here quicker the only way is with a speed boat. Those are low to the water but not very practical in windy weather. It would definitely be easier to get in and out of a speed boat at a low dock rather than climb up onto the main dock like they have to do currently. Gilbert wondered what Doc had in mind and was just about to ask him when Dr. Johnson asked, "Can you build a floating dock?"

"Yes, I guess so. It's not something I've ever done before but I think I could figure it out. The hardest part would be to find someone who can supply us with enough logs. We'd have to confine them in a frame and then add a top to it. I'd have to figure out how many logs and how big they'd have to be but I'm sure I can find some…" He stopped mid-sentence as if suddenly a light came on in his head. "A brilliant idea just popped into my head. I'll go to the sawmill in Musquosh and get the logs floated or barged up here from there."

"You're a genius my friend," said Doc clapping Gilbert on the shoulder. "In fact the guy who owns the sawmill owes me a favour," he leaned in a little closer to Gilbert and whispered, "I helped him out of a bit of a sticky situation a few months ago and he insisted that if ever there was anything he could do for me, and he repeated *anything*, he'd be happy to oblige."

Gilbert was quiet for a few minutes sizing up the space in the small lagoon where the docks were and trying to figure out how he would attach a floating dock to shore. "Well," he said eventually, "I can make it happen. When do you want me to start on this?"

"The sooner the better." He turned and started down the dock. "Oh," he said turning back to face Gilbert, "If anyone asks, just tell them I wanted another dock for the rowboats and another runabout." He laughed then added. "Tell them I'm going to start collecting a fleet of boats and need more dock space." Smiling at the thoughts of what he was planning he turned and started towards the cottage the change in his pockets jingling with each step.

*****

The long weekend with the two couples from the city went by without a hitch. Ronnie thought it would have been a lot easier for her if Maude had stayed around but when she thought of how important it was for her to go visit her parents, the inconvenience of not having her around was a little more bearable.

Not having Maude's help with meal preparation and clean up gave Ronnie the perfect pretext to excuse herself from the group and disappear into the kitchen for long periods of time. During the day the men were off fishing with Gilbert as their guide and that left Ronnie to entertain these virtual strangers who had invaded her cottage. The first day she took the women for a walk to show them the property and the lake beyond the Narrows. The second afternoon, she took them to a large flat slab of granite located next to the inland lake about a quarter mile behind the cottage. This rock was a favourite of Ronnie's as it was very secluded and private and was a perfect spot for sunning herself and working on her 'all-over tan.' Though slightly embarrassed at first by Ronnie's lack of modesty the women were soon talked into sunbathing in this way. The thermoses of cold gin and tonic that seemed to go down pretty smoothly helped to loosen their inhibitions and soon the three of them were laying topless on their towels giggling like school girls.

By the third day she realized that it wasn't that she didn't like the women who were her guests but she found she didn't really have much in common with them. She could only listen to stories about their 'perfect' children for so long and then got bored with the conversation. Being alone in the kitchen gave her time to think about Philippe. She hadn't seen much of him all summer long. He came to deliver ice at the stone cottage every week, but his visits were limited to him poking his head in the door to say "bonjour ma-belle," and then he was off again. It was, after all, his busy time of the year and if he stayed too long, the ice in the boat would melt. Summer was drawing to a close and soon a number of the families would be heading back home to prepare for the new school year. *Maybe things will slow down a bit for him in a week or so,* she thought. *Then he'll have more time to visit rather than just popping in to say hello.* Just thinking of Philippe made her feel better and put a smile on her face.

*****

This was the first time she had spent five days in a row with Doc in a long time and she found he was still more than a little cranky. Even though they had guests and he was putting his best foot forward he still seemed to be quiet, slightly withdrawn and very detached. *Maybe he knows about Philippe and me*, she thought. *No, how could that be possible. The only ones who knew she was having an affair were Maude, Gilbert and Philippe and she knew none of them would tell Doc.*

Late Saturday evening she decided to ask him about his seemingly detached attitude but his answer did not provide any more clarity. He just blamed work. He said he was busy, said he'd be glad when summer was over and the tourists went home and the office and hospital quieted down a bit. He said he missed having her in the office because although Lydia was working out OK it wasn't like having Ronnie working with him. He felt there was so much that wasn't getting done the way Ronnie did things and he missed her. Though that was the kindest thing he had said to her in a long time, to her, it still didn't seem to account for his demeanour even after all this time away from town.

Ronnie thought that if Doc was trying to lay a guilt trip on her for not being around home and the office, it wasn't going to work on her. She was loving being at the cottage for the summer. She had become quite close to Maude, Gilbert and the twins and she had made some really good friends here in Cognashene. And then there was Philippe. She certainly couldn't leave him out of the equation. He made her feel like a sexy, vibrant, beautiful woman for the first time in a long long time and that alone was enough to make her want to come back to the cottage year after year.

The three couples enjoyed an early supper on Sunday evening, Doc and Ronnie played the part of gracious hosts right to the end of the weekend and the guests seemed to be very relaxed in their company. When dinner was over and the last of the wine had been consumed, slowly and without much fanfare the guests helped clear the final dishes from the dining table then went to their rooms to pack their bags and prepare for the ride home. When the entire load of luggage was gathered on the front porch Gilbert was summoned to give a hand and like a flock of ducklings following each other they all headed down the path toward the dock.

Luckily, the winds had subsided. It was a calm clear evening and showed promise of a wonderful, uneventful boat ride from Cognashene to Penetanguishene. And it was. Much to everyone's surprise no one got seasick and the camaraderie and cheerful banter between Doc and the passengers continued for the duration of the trip. Doc was happy to see his friends having such a good time and made promises when they arrived in town to "do it again sometime."

Once everyone was gone, Gilbert returned to the main cottage to see if Ronnie needed any help with cleaning up after the guests. Knowing that it was going to be another few days before Maude returned Gilbert felt he should pick up some of her duties and lend a hand if needed. Ronnie didn't mind having Gilbert help with the dishes but once they were stored away in the butler's pantry she immediately went to the liquor cabinet and poured herself a double.

"Would you like to have a drink Gilbert?" she asked. "You've done double duty this weekend you certainly deserve one."

"That's kind of you to offer but I'm more in the mood for a cup of strong coffee and a bit of peace and quiet if it's all the same to you." He thought about how busy his weekend had been and how much he'd been looking forward to watching the sunset sitting on his bench while sipping his coffee. His happy place was calling his name.

"Have it your way. But if your coffee doesn't do it for you come back over. There is still plenty of booze in the cabinet and I'm happy to share."

*****

The sun set as a bright red orb on the horizon. It never failed to amaze Gilbert as he watched the sun setting how quickly it disappeared once it touched the horizon. From his vantage point on his bench his view was of the open water of Georgian Bay. When the sun set it looked like it was sinking into the water. He had timed it many times before and was always surprised that it only took three minutes and forty two seconds from the time the sun touched the horizon until it was completely consumed and had disappeared below the surface. Over the years there were a number of times he had one or both of his children sitting on his lap to watch the sunset and he would say to them, "Listen, I think we'll hear it sizzle when it touches the water." It was one way to get the kids to sit quiet even if for just a few minutes, but it was a few minutes he cherished, and tonight he longed for it in their absence.

With nothing else pressing for him to do, Gilbert stayed on his bench enjoying the stillness of the evening. He had just about dozed off leaning against the wall of the stone cottage when he heard a loud clattering noise which startled him. Fully awake he sat there for a moment listening, wondering what it was that he had heard. He knew there was no one in the stone cottage but it didn't mean that some animal, a raccoon perhaps might have made its way in. Wondering if the noise had come from within the stone cottage he quickly got up to check things inside. The screen doors were closed, the window screens were intact and cottage was clear. The only thing it could be was something had happened in the main cottage. Putting his coffee cup on the table, he grabbed his flashlight and made his way down the path towards the main cottage.

What he found wasn't really much of a surprise. Ronnie had dropped the crystal pitcher of gin and tonic she had made for herself on the floor of the front porch. It had shattered to pieces and when she stooped over to start picking up the pieces she had fallen in her drunken stupor against some of the wicker furniture and that had overturned the patio table. The entire porch looked like a disaster zone. He hurried into the porch and helped her to her feet. Sitting her down on one of the wicker settees he quickly checked her bare feet to see if she had stepped in any glass. He didn't see blood anywhere on the floor but it didn't mean she didn't have a glass shard stuck in her foot somewhere. Confident she was not injured, he went to the pantry and gathered the broom, dustpan, mop, rags and started cleaning up the mess. Stretched out on the settee with her head tilted back and her eyes closed Ronnie was too dazed to even realize what she had done. Gilbert was nearly finished cleaning up the mess and straightening the furniture when she roused a bit and immediately sat up a little straighter. She said to Gilbert, "I see you've come over for a drink. What can I get you?"

"It's not my place to say this Ronnie but I think you've had enough for the night. Maybe you should just call it a day and head for bed."

"Nonsense, just a little nightcap and then I'll go to bed. Are you sure you don't want one?"

"I'm positive."

She got up from the settee and made her way to the cabinet. "Gilbert," she called. "Have you seen the crystal pitcher that I usually make my drinks in?"

"I've seen it and I've swept the broken pieces of it up and tossed it in the garbage can out back."

"What do you mean, the broken pieces, what happened to it?"

"Ronnie," he questioned, "are you so drunk that you don't even remember falling in the porch and breaking the pitcher?"

"I don't remember that at all, I guess I must be more drunk than I thought."

"Well like I said earlier, maybe it's time you call it a night and go to bed. Your memory may be better in the morning."

Ronnie closed the liquor cabinet door and said, "Oh, all right. I'll just get a glass of water from the kitchen then go to bed. A girl gets thirsty having all that company you know."

A moment later, Gilbert who was washing the floor in the porch for the second time to get rid of some of the sticky mess Ronnie had made heard the outside kitchen screen door slam shut.

"What the heck?" he said out loud. He dropped his mop and raced through the dining room and into the kitchen. Ronnie was nowhere to be seen. He went to the door and looked out. There was Ronnie, bent over the trash can reaching down into it trying to grab a few pieces of the broken crystal.

"Ronnie, its pitch black out here, you are going to cut your fingers on that glass in the garbage. I really think you should go back inside, wash your face and hands and make your way to bed."

Grudgingly she agreed, though she really wanted to follow the path that led around the cottage from the back to the front so that she could go in the front door. He helped her up the steps, guided her to the bathroom and stood outside the door while she washed up. When she came out, she looked like she had just been through the wringer, water dripping from her hair, the front of her dress splattered with watermarks. He could see evidence of toothpaste smeared across her upper lip and though she had brushed her teeth, her breath still reeked of gin.

"That bastard never even kissed me goodbye when he left. I tried to talk to him about why he doesn't seem to care about me anymore but I got nowhere." She moved her hands to her face as if she was going to rub her eyes then started to cry. "I'm sure the marriage is over Gilbert. It isn't working. What am I going to do?"

Always the pragmatist he said, "There is nothing you can do about it tonight. Just go to bed and maybe when you wake up you might see things a little differently and you'll be able to make more reasonable decisions."

"I guess you're right." She brushed at the water stains on her dress, looked at herself in the hallway mirror and said, "I am a frightful mess. I'm sorry you have to see me like this." She turned and headed for her bedroom.

Once she was settled and Gilbert, who had been sitting in the living room thought he could hear her snoring, got up from the couch and made his way to the back door. He stepped outside then turned the latch on the screen that kept the door from opening in the wind, in the opposite direction. "There, at least she can't get out the back door tonight" he said to himself. He made his way around the cottage following the same path the two of them had taken earlier and let himself into the front porch. He closed the door between the porch and living room but not before he had grabbed the homemade afghan Maude had made that was always lying across the back of the couch. Though the settee was too small for him, he made himself a bit of a nest of pillows and cushions, pulled the afghan around himself and settled in for the night. It wasn't an ideal way to spend the night but he thought, *she can't get out the back door and if she tries to get out the front door I'll hear her.*

*****

The floating dock was one of Gilbert's bigger challenges in his building career. He had a lot of experience with building decks, porches and docks that were supported on piers but the floating dock was another thing all together. As requested, he built the dock twenty five feet long using eight-foot-long logs supported in a rough hewn four inch by twelve inch frame. The logs were lashed together with twelve inch long spikes that Gilbert drove with a sledge hammer through the frame and into the logs. Next a deck-like top was made from planed two by six beams. The dock looked great at a glance but as soon as more than just Gilbert stood on the edge of it things weren't so great. With his weight and the weight of Maude and the twins all on one side, the dock would tip and the edge would quickly become submerged. He thought about removing the deck top and adding another row of logs in the opposite direction to give it more height but he knew that Doc wanted it to be low to the water's surface. Instead he added another three feet to the overall width, again driving spikes through the frame to secure the addition to the existing dock. As it turned out, adding extra logs and lumber to the width of the dock increased the water-dock surface tension making it heavier in the water therefore harder to shift and raise out of the water and therefore less tippy. Everyone's toes stayed dry. Success again, but, it was exhausting work.

Once the upper decking was extended Gilbert then had the challenge of figuring out how to keep the dock floating in one spot. He had to find a way to make anchors that he could build on the dock then drop over the edge into the water. His solution; on his next trip into town he brought back four large used truck tires and multiple bags of cement. Cutting boards to fit as a base inside the tires Gilbert then added rocks to fill the space between the boards on the bottom edge and the top edge. A large iron ring was then added to each tire wedged between the rocks. The remaining spaces were filled with cement. Once the cement had cured heavy chains were secured to the rings in the tires and their free ends secured to the frame of the dock. The next time Philippe delivered ice to the stone cottage Gilbert commissioned his help. With the two of them grunting and sputtering they were able to lift the tires up onto their side, roll them out to the edge of the dock and drop them into the water. One large anchor at each corner of the dock was enough to keep the dock secured into the same spot. Gilbert then built a twelve foot ramp made of two by ten planks and the access to shore was complete.

In the end Gilbert was quite pleased with the look and function of the dock. It definitely sat lower in the water than the pier dock and to his amazement even when the wind got up, though the cove was well protected, the positioning of the dock relative to the shoreline remained stable and didn't drift in one direction or the other.

*****

It had been two and a half weeks since Doc and the guests had returned to town and no one had heard from him. Ronnie didn't mind; it gave her a bit of cooling off time. A chance to gather her thoughts. She was drinking a little less this week and seemed to have better clarity of thought. Things didn't seem so bad after all. She reflected, *Maybe it was just the booze talking that night that Gilbert spent the night on the porch. He did that so that I wouldn't escape and do something stupid like fall off the dock.* She gave her head a little shake as if to clear some cobwebs from her hair. *Maybe that's all it is.*

When Gilbert went to town he checked at the doctor's house and office to see if he was there. His nurse said he had been in the office but had gone up to the hospital to deliver a baby. She said she'd be happy to take a message but Gilbert said he didn't really have one. He just wanted to check in with Doc and let him know about the progress he was making with the new floating dock. After gathering the supplies that Maude and Ronnie had requested and making his usual stop at the hardware store to pick up what he needed, Gilbert headed back up to the cottage confident that Doc was OK but just busy as always.

*****

The next morning Philippe came over to deliver ice to the stone cottage and instead of just poking his head in the back door of the main cottage to say hello, he knocked and then went in.

"Ah, Ma-Belle, you look as radiant as ever." He flashed her that million dollar smile of his and made his way to her. Wrapping his arms around her slender waist he hugged her tight lifting her slightly up in the air. Putting her down gently he lifted his hand and rubbed her cheek with the back of his fingers.

"Oh, Philippe," she moaned, "I've missed you so much." She opened her arms and returned his embrace. Slowly she raised herself up on her tippy toes to give him a quick kiss on the lips then backed away from him slightly. "How's business, do you still have more ice to deliver? I could go with you," she blurted out.

"Things are really starting to slow down. We are more than half way through August and a lot of the tourists have started to pack up and head back to the city. I only had three ice blocks to deliver today and so I made the stone cottage the last on the list so that I could hang out here for a little while." He winked at her then added, "Hope you don't mind."

"If I don't mind?" Ronnie exclaimed her eyes widening with her excitement, "If I don't mind?" she repeated. "I don't mind at all, in fact, I'd have been disappointed if you didn't want to stay for a while."

They made their way out onto the front porch and sat together on the settee facing the water. He placed his hand on her knee and rubbed it gently. Ever so slowly he started to inch his hand up her thigh.

Ronnie sat motionless for a moment enjoying the feeling of being touched, goose bumps breaking out on the back of her neck. After a moment or two she put her hand over top of his and said, "Not here, not now. The twins are just on the other side of the cottage picking blueberries. If they come around the corner and see us there will be lots of questions I'm not ready to answer right now."

"I get it. I understand. As much as it pains me to think about it, I do have to remember that you are a married woman and I am just the guy who has hopelessly fallen in love with you."

Ronnie was shocked by Phil's comment. Though she too was as much a part of the affair as he was, it surprised her to hear him say he was in love with her.

"How about if we go for a picnic somewhere, just the two of us, where there is no one else around. We can say and do whatever we please and don't have to worry about any prying eyes or ears."

"I know just the spot," Philippe said. "Just on the other side of Cranberry Island is this small island. I think it only has one tree and a few low shrubs on it. It has quite a steep bluff to one side and a very long low flat area on the other side. It would be a perfect spot to spread out for a picnic. Even if someone were to go for a walk on Cranberry Island we'd be completely hidden by the bluff."

"It's almost lunch time now. How about if we go this afternoon?" Ronnie urged.

"Works for me," said Philippe rubbing his hands together. "I'll just take a quick ride home, wash up a little and get rid of the tarps in the boat that I use to cover the ice. I can be back in about twenty minutes, maybe a half an hour at the most."

"That's perfect. It will give me enough time to put some things together in the cooler for us to munch on and a few drinks too wet our whistles."

"Sounds perfect," he said as he got up to leave.

"Oh, and Phil, do you think you could round up a bit of ice for the cooler. It seems I'm right out of it."

"I'll see if I can find some," he joked then disappeared out the door and down the path to the dock.

*****

True to his word Philippe returned in twenty minutes. His dark curly hair, slicked back with Brilcream glistening in the sun. Shirtless as always it appeared he had put some sun tanning oil on his chest and arms and they too glistened highlighting his biceps, flat abs and muscular chest.

Carrying a small tarp about the size of a bath towel he slowly made his way up the path to the cottage careful not to spill the chunks of ice he had wrapped inside. He had rolled up the cuffs on his cut off jeans and his muscular thighs rubbed together ever so slightly with every step.

When Ronnie saw him her mouth dropped open, agape. If a film crew had been on site they would have surely photographed him for the cover of 'Perfect

Man Magazine.' She had always been attracted to him knowing he was a very handsome man with a killer French accent but today it was like she was seeing him for the very first time and her heart skipped a beat when she thought, *I'm going to be spending the afternoon alone on an island with this Adonis! The Gods are in my favour today.*

Ronnie too had dressed for the occasion. She had put on her favourite white silk sundress that had hand-painted flowers around the bottom hem. The strapless halter top seemed to defy gravity as she walked but every now and then she did hike it up under her arms just a little, feigning modesty as she did so.

They gathered the cooler, Ronnie's sun hat and some sun tanning lotion. She didn't want to make the same mistake about being out in the sun too long like she had done before. Once settled in the boat, Phil untied the lines and pushed off from the dock. He started the engine and going no more than trolling speed, steered the boat around the outer shoals to the far side of Cranberry Island. While still about a mile away he pointed out the island with the bluff to Ronnie and asked if she thought that it would be alright to have their picnic there. She agreed that it was and said she was surprised that for all the times that she had been out this way she had never noticed that island before. Then she thought, *Phil didn't seem to even hesitate when it came to choosing a spot.* She wondered if perhaps he'd brought other women out here before her but quickly chased that thought from her head. It didn't matter. What mattered was they were here now, together and for this blissful afternoon nothing else mattered.

*****

She straddled him, his naked body firm and fully aroused beneath her. Slowly with both hands she guided him into her. She moaned with the pleasure of feeling him inside her and she rocked slowly back and forth eliciting maximum pleasure for both of them. She reached up and touched her hard nipples then grabbed Phil's hands and cupped them around her breasts.

Phil could hardly contain himself any longer, "I'm going to …" she cut him off saying, "No, wait just a little longer." She rocked slowly forward and back feeling the full length of him inside her and after a moment she felt his warm release within her and it washed over her in wave after wonderful wave.

Fully spent she collapsed in his open arms and snuggled into his firm embrace. "I don't ever want to let you go," he said and squeezed her more tightly.

The sun beat down on her bare back and she could feel the tingling of its rays burning her skin. "I have to move," she said breaking their embrace. She rolled off of him and covered herself with the blanket they had spread out for the picnic. Phil rolled over onto his side, his limp and flaccid member nearly touching the rock. "You'd better be careful," Ronnie said. "You don't want to get that sun burned."

He rolled back onto his back and stared up at the clear blue sky. "This has been the most perfect day of my life." He propped himself up on his elbows and stared out at the calm waters of the gap. A small flock of seagulls was soaring on the thermals above them aimlessly floating in mid air barely moving their wings as they went.

"I'd like to be as carefree as those seagulls are," he said. "I have always wanted to fly. Perhaps someday I'll get the chance." With that he stood up and walked naked towards the shore. Effortlessly he slipped into the water letting it cool his overheated body. "Come on in." He reached down trailing his fingers in the calm clear water. "Come and join me."

She dropped the blanket and stood. He had turned to look at her as she made her way to the water's edge and once again marvelled at how beautiful her naked body was. Instantly he was hard again. "Have you ever made love in the water?" he asked.

"Never," she said as she playfully splashed him.

"Prepare to be amazed Ma Belle. There is nothing like it." And true to his word there wasn't. She couldn't believe the stamina and strength he had. He pulled her close to him and she could feel his erection rubbing against her inner thigh. He grabbed her under the arms and lifted her onto him, the natural buoyancy of the water making her feel like she was floating but somehow tethered to one spot. This time it was his turn to provide the pleasure. Once inside her he lifted her slowly then brought her down closer to him, over and over again. She felt like she was going to explode and after a while they both did at the same time. Clutching onto each other tightly, their bodies entwined as one, he felt her entire body shudder as she began to relax.

He took her hand and slowly guided her across the slippery rocks at the water's edge. Once they were out of the water he bent down and straightened the blanket on the rocks and sat down. For a few moments they were silent each deeply languishing in their own thoughts, comfortable on the blanket, thoroughly spent and perfectly content.

"It has been a very long and hot summer and I feel as though I have barely seen you," Ronnie cried softly as she nestled into his open arms. "Soon summer is going to be over and I will have to leave and go back to town, back to my husband, back to my boring, hum-drum life." She wiped her hands across her face to brush away the tears that were forming. "I don't know if I can do it."

"Of course you can." Taking the tanning oil from the handbag he poured a generous amount into his palm and reached out towards her and started to rub the oil onto her back. Slowly, methodically, he rubbed the oil into her skin using firmer strokes as he rubbed the knotted muscles near her shoulders.

"We have been through this before," he said. "You come up for the summer, we have fun, we go places, we make love and have incredible times together and then it is time for you to go." She turned and looked at him, a puzzled look on her face.

"You make it sound so casual, like it means nothing to you."

"It means everything to me. You are the most beautiful women I have ever met, the most generous and caring person I know and I love you for that. When I am not with you I think of you all the time, but, you are a married woman and I know that I can't have you all to myself." He stopped, added more tanning oil to his open palm then said. "Here, turn around so I can rub the tops of your legs, they are getting pretty red." She turned slowly towards him. He paused, gathering his thoughts then added. "It has taken me a long time to come to grips with this. I know I have to share you. I hate it but that is the way it is. I've thought about it a lot and I know I'd rather have you some of the time than not at all."

Ronnie turned fully to face him and pulled herself up onto his lap. Placing her arms around his neck she pulled him closer to her then gently kissed his open mouth, her tongue darting quickly across his teeth. He put his hand behind her head and pulled her closer still and returned her kisses, gently at first then with a ferocity as though he was never going to see her again.

He said, "I know it is going to be hard for us to part at the end of the season. For me, it's like we were meant to be together. We have to think about what we *do* have, cherish that and hope that our memories will hold us over until we meet again next summer, and the summer after that."

"Oh, Phil, I love you so much. I just want to be with you all the time. I don't know what to do?"

"We will do what we've always done. We will go back to the cottage and act like we were just two people out for a picnic and having fun. I'll wink at you as I leave and you will know that secretly I'm saying 'I Love You' and no one will be any wiser."

"Gilbert and Maude know. They've known for a couple of months now. I just don't know how much longer I can keep this from Doc."

He stretched his naked body out on the blanket, placed his hands together behind his head and looked up at the clear, cerulean blue sky. "You will know the time is right when it comes. Till then I am happy to have what we have."

She lay next to him, one leg draped casually over his, her head resting on his shoulder her hand slowly caressing the hair on his chest. "I guess you're right. I'll know when the time comes. But for now… I just want this day to never end."

They lay motionless for what seemed like an eternity, both deep in blissful thought, the warm late August sun beating down on them. Finally Phil gently moved her off of him and sat up. He grabbed his shorts and pulled them on. "I have to take you home. It must be well past supper time and Gilbert and Maude will be wondering if we are OK."

Reluctantly she sat up, ran her hands through her tangled hair to straighten it out a little then stood and pulled on her sundress.

"We have to go. I will cherish today forever Ma-Belle. It has been the best day ever."

Ronnie said nothing. Though there was plenty she wanted to say, she was unable to speak because of the huge lump in her throat. She knew that if she could speak, she'd start to cry and she didn't want to spoil this perfect moment.

CHAPTER - 15

Gilbert was laying flat on his belly on the floating dock with his arms outstretched as far as he could reach into the water. He was in the process of adjusting one of the anchor chains when he heard the plane. The low even dulcet tone of the plane's engine hinted at a motor that was well tuned. There weren't many airplanes that flew over this way. Usually they stayed closer to the towns like Penetanguishene and Midland where there was a landing strip nearby. The sound of the airplane continued to grow louder, closer. Gilbert looked up to see if he could spot the plane as it drew near. He had heard it in the distance before he saw it but the engine noise seemed to be getting louder, the sounds coming closer and closer all the time. Finally he saw the plane coming across the sky just above the tree tops the wing tips maybe only one hundred feet above the tallest of the trees.

It was a small single engine plane with two flotation pontoons attached to the struts rather than wheels. It flew past the stone cottage, over the main cottage and towards the north end of the lake. The sound of the plane's engine seemed to be fading in the distance and Gilbert wondered who on earth would be flying a plane so low. It was almost as though the pilot wanted to land but decided at the last minute not to.

Ben, Emma and Maude came out of the stone cottage when they heard the plane flying by so low and watched it in the sky until it was hidden by the trees on the north side of the property.

"I wonder who that was?" said Maude. "It scared the living daylights out of me. I thought it was going to take the roof off the cottage."

By now Ronnie too had come out of her cottage and made her way down to the dock.

"I can't believe that plane was flying so low to the ground. I wonder who it was? I hope they aren't having engine trouble."

"Maybe it's some rich guy checking out the property that is for sale down at the end of the lake. It's one way of getting a good look at it and the surrounding properties all at the same time," added Gilbert.

Just as Maude and the twins were about to head back into the cottage the low, monotone sound of the plane's engine seemed to be getting louder again, suggesting that the plane had circled at the end of the lake and was heading back. When the plane returned the sun glinted off the pontoons like a brilliant silver wink and then the plane descended fully, landing perfectly in the bay. It coasted across the water towards the stone cottage, the roar of the engine nearly deafening as it approached the dock. The plane taxied to the floating dock and the engine was shut down. The pilot removed his hat and aviator sunglasses and opened the door. Dr. Johnson climbed from the pilot's seat and gracefully slid out of the plane landing lightly on his feet on the pontoon. He turned, grabbed a rope from the cockpit and handed it to Gilbert and smiling said, "Bet you're surprised to see me today."

Gilbert was stunned. He couldn't believe what he was seeing before him. He had a look of utter shock on his face that said it all. Then all the pieces of the puzzle came together. This was why Doc wanted a floating dock built. The specifications for the dock were exactly what were needed for the plane to park at. The pontoons were about twenty feet long so they fit nicely against the dock with a little bit of dock at each end to spare. The height of the dock was perfect as well. It was so easy for Doc to just step off the pontoon and right onto the dock with ease. He didn't want another boat for crossing the gap on windy days; he wanted an airplane so he could fly over the gap and arrive in a fraction of the time it took to cross by boat.

For once Doc just stood there not jingling the change in his pocket. He was getting too much pleasure looking at the shock and awe on the faces of those gathered on the dock. Ben and Emma of course were the first ones to speak. They had dozens of questions. "Is this your plane? How fast does it go? What does the ground look like from up there? How big is our lake really? Can you take us for a ride?" The questions were coming so fast Doc couldn't answer them all. Ronnie came and stood by Doc and stared at the plane. She was speechless.

Doc went over to her, put his arms around her and gave her a warm and tender hug, something he hadn't done in over a year.

"Ronnie, honey, I hope you don't mind but I'm thinking of buying this little gem. A friend of mine has owned it for a couple of years now. He keeps it in mint condition and he has decided to sell it so he can get one that is a little bigger, a little faster and can take extra passengers."

Ronnie didn't know what to say. She stood motionless fighting with the emotions that were competing for attention in her mind. Reflexively she hugged Doc back then stepped away from him. She stood about three feet away, jammed her hands into the pockets of her shorts and shook her head. She pulled her hands from her pockets and ran them through her hair, a look of total exasperation on her face. She turned and faced the cottage as if contemplating going there, running away but she didn't. Instead she turned and looked at the plane then to her husband.

"I can't believe…I didn't know…" she was having trouble figuring out what to say first. Everyone was looking at her.

"I didn't know you knew how to fly a plane!" she finally said.

"I didn't," said Doc. "When you and I went to England a couple of years ago, we went for a plane ride, remember?" He started to jingle the change in his pocket, the nervous habit returning. He then repeated, "Remember? You and I. We went for a short sightseeing ride just outside the city limits of Cambridge."

"Yes I remember that."

"That was the day I decided I wanted to learn how to fly a plane. We already had this place by then and I kept thinking how much fun it would be for you and I to own a plane so we could fly up to the cottage whenever we wanted regardless of the weather. I fell in love with the idea that we could go sightseeing by air. It's beautiful up there, getting the birds-eye view. I feel so carefree when I'm flying."

"When did you learn how to fly a plane?"

"Remember, for the last year or so, I kept going to Toronto a couple of times a week?"

"I remember that very well. All those evenings sitting home alone wondering what was so special about going to Toronto."

"Well… I was taking flying lessons."

"Why didn't you tell me?"

"I wanted to surprise you. I wanted it to be the biggest surprise of your life. I didn't want to lie to you and say that I was taking a night course in some specialty of medicine. You'd have caught on pretty quickly when you didn't see me studying or writing term papers. I wanted to just show up at the dock some day and say, hey, want to go for a ride?"

"Well you sure as hell surprised me," Ronnie said a little bit too forcefully. She started pacing on the dock. A million thoughts were screaming through her head. *He wasn't having an affair, he had a reason for going to Toronto that had nothing to do with another woman. I've had an affair with Philippe out of spite, out of loneliness, out of anger at my husband when all the while he was just learning to fly a stupid airplane.*

Doc could see that she was visibly distressed. He noticed the colour had drained from her face and she was trembling slightly. He moved closer to her but she pushed him away. Backing away from her slightly he said, ""Honey, what's wrong you seem more angry than happy about this?"

"What's wrong? What's wrong?" she stammered. "Everything is wrong." She was feeling plagued with guilt. What had she done? Why hadn't she pushed him harder for answers about what he was doing in Toronto? Was it because deep down she didn't really want to know what he was up too in case he *was* having an affair? What did this mean for *her* relationship with Philippe? Just the day before, she had professed her love for him. This changed everything, absolutely everything. Her husband had been faithful. She turned and ran from the dock towards the cottage.

Maude and Gilbert who had been standing on the dock the whole time said nothing. Both felt pretty uncomfortable with the scene that had just unfolded in front of them. Both knew what was behind Ronnie's outburst. It was as if they could read her mind.

Maude, always the rock, always the peacekeeper looked at Gilbert and he knew by her look what she wanted to do. He nodded to her and she turned to Doc and said, "I'll go and see if she's OK."

"I thought she'd be happy about this," Doc said to Gilbert. He lifted his hands towards the plane, palms up, a questioning look on his face. "I just don't get it." He was quite surprised by Ronnie's outburst and really didn't have a clue about why she was so upset. They had never been a couple to quarrel over money, he had always made a very good income and they had never had to scrimp or save for anything in the past. Buying a plane was going to be pricey but he knew they could afford it.

"Maybe she is just having a hard time processing all of what's going on in her mind right now," said Gilbert.

Doc added, "She seemed to be really upset about this. More than just a bit, I mean *really* upset." Doc looked puzzled then asked Gilbert. "Is there something going on that I don't know about?" He looked at Gilbert, stopped jingling the change in his pocket then looked Gil straight in the eye and said, "You'd tell me, right? You'd tell me if there was something that I should know?"

"Doc, you and I have been good friends for a long time now and we talk about a lot of things but there are a few things that you may have noticed over the years. We have never talked about politics, we have never talked about religion and we have never talked about relationships and I don't think that's about to change now. If you think there is something going on, it's up to you to have that conversation with Ronnie, not me."

"You're right. I'm sorry, I shouldn't have put you on the spot like that. It's not fair. I'll go check things out with Ronnie myself." He started to walk up the dock toward the cottage then slowed his pace. He turned around saying, "Maybe I'll give Maude a little more time with her though. Sometimes women relate better to other women."

Ben and Emma who had been present for the entire conversation between the adults still stood on the dock looking at the plane. They hadn't been paying too much attention to the adult conversation because they were too busy arguing among themselves about the features of the plane; the pontoons, the size of the propeller, how fast it probably goes, how big Cognashene Lake really looks from up in the sky. Finally Ben worked up enough courage and went to stand beside Doc. When he and his dad stopped talking Ben asked, "Do you think you could take Emma and I up in the plane for a ride sometime? I bet Emma that our lake looks bigger from the sky than from shore and she doesn't agree. It would be great to see it for ourselves."

Doc looked down at him and smiled. Rubbing the top of Ben's head he said "That's a great idea but I can't say that I can take you unless your dad says it's OK."

Immediately Ben turned to Gilbert and asked, "Can we dad? Is it OK? Can we?"

"If Doc wants to take you for a ride I guess it's alright with me. That's a lot to ask of Doc though, he just got here." He turned to Doc and said, "I hope they haven't put you on the spot Doc?"

"I'm a big boy now," said Doc jokingly. "I'd tell you if they had," he winked at Gilbert then looked at Ben and Emma and said, "It's fine with me too. This will be fun."

He turned towards the plane, opened the cockpit door and moved a few things around on the seats. He turned to face Ben and Emma and stooped slightly so that he was at their height. "Just give me a few minutes to get this set up for passengers. This is serious stuff here. You will have to do exactly what I say. You will have to wear a harness that is attached to the seat and the frame of the plane and…" he said pointing his finger at both of them warning, "You *have* to remain sitting. If you can promise me that, then I'll take you."

"We'll do exactly what you say won't we Ben," said Emma. "This is going to be so much fun," She excitedly made her way closer to the edge of the dock near the plane's pontoon, "I can't wait to tell the kids at school about this, they are never going to believe it."

Doc turned to Gilbert and smiled at the twins' enthusiasm. "Once I take them for a ride, I'll come back and give you a turn. I know you know this area like the back of your hand but it looks so amazing from the air. Your whole impression of the area will change. Your perspective about the size of the lakes, the islands, the distance between channels will be different. You'll recognize everything. It all looks the same but somehow it all looks different."

Gilbert rubbed his hand on the strut that supported the wing then said, "I really appreciate you taking the twins up for a ride and I'm looking forward to going myself."

"It's quite alright. I get the feeling that Ronnie doesn't really want to see me right now anyway."

"Yup, I get that impression too," Gilbert agreed.

*****

By the time Maude got to the cottage Ronnie was already standing in front of the liquor cabinet. She poured a stiff measure of gin into a highball glass and before putting the bottle down took a long swig right out of the bottle.

"You want one?" she asked Maude offering her the bottle.

"You know what?" Maude paused briefly, "I think I will. I think that will be just perfect right now." She rubbed her hands together feigning excitement then added. "I prefer mine in a glass with some ice and tonic water though," she said jokingly trying to lighten the tension in the room a little.

Ronnie took a second glass from the cabinet, poured a healthy amount into the glass without measuring then took it into the kitchen to get some cold tonic water from the fridge. "Do you want a lemon wedge?" she called from the kitchen.

"Sure," said Maude. It was a pretty warm day and a cold drink would be good but she had seen how much gin Ronnie had poured into the glass and thought, *I'd better sip this one slowly.*

Choosing the living room over the sun porch for more privacy Ronnie sat down on the couch and let out a long slow sigh, exhaling fully. She took an extended deep breath in, held it for a few seconds then let it out slowly clearly trying to force herself to relax a bit. It was only then that she took a sip from her glass. She sighed again a little less dramatically than before, raked her fingers through her hair then lifted her legs up onto the couch and tucked them under herself, sitting on her feet.

Looking over towards Maude she said, "Can you believe it? An airplane! Not in my wildest of dreams did I ever think that I was competing for my husband's attention with an airplane. I can't believe it. I've been a total ass." Her hands had a visible tremor to them and she started to shiver as if she was chilled to the bone. "I've made a complete mess of things." She took another sip of her drink then put it down on the table in front of her. In an effort to try and steady her hands she once again ran her hands through her hair, pulling tightly on the strands between her fingers as she did it.

Maude didn't quite know what to say so she sat quietly on the armchair facing the couch and just looked at Ronnie, hoping that her silence would encourage her friend to say more. *Best to let her just talk and vent, and let it out,* she thought.

Finally after a few moments of silence Ronnie said, "Oh Maude, I don't know what to do. Yesterday Philippe and I had the most wonderful day. We made love a couple of times on one of the outer islands. We told each other over and over how much we loved each other. I was convinced that I was going to leave Doc for Phil and let Doc go to whatever woman he was seeing. But I was wrong, all wrong. I love Phil but how can I give all of this up," she waved her hands in front of her in an all encompassing gesture to take in the contents of the cottage and the property. "I was prepared to leave all of this for Phil because I thought Doc was having an affair." She dropped her head to her chest and started to cry, sobbing so heavily it seemed to be taking her breath away.

"What am I going to do, what am I going to do?" she repeated over and over again.

Finally she stopped crying and brushed her hands through her hair one more time. She rubbed away the remaining tears on her cheeks with the back of her hand, her makeup smearing across her face as she did so. She leaned forward picked up her glass from the coffee table and took a long slow drink. She looked up towards Maude a questioning look on her face, hoping to find inspiration and guidance from her friend.

Measuring her words carefully Maude started, "Ronnie, you've known me for a long time and you know I've never been one to give out a lot of advice but I really think that as difficult as this will be you should come clean with Doc. You can't go on living a lie. You've known for a long time that this day would come." Suddenly her throat was dry. She took a sip from her drink, the cool liquid giving her some relief and giving her a moment's reprieve from the tension in the room. "You have to tell him. You have to tell him everything. He has a right to know."

Maude moved from the armchair and sat next to Ronnie on the sofa. Taking both Ronnie's hands in her own she looked at Ronnie and with as kind and gentle a voice as she could muster she continued. "Tell him what you were thinking all those nights that he was gone to Toronto. Tell him your fears that he had found another woman. Tell him about how you have found him to be so distant and detached that your heart was breaking. He has to know. You have to trust that he loves you enough that he will see things from your perspective."

Ronnie sat silently on the couch listening to her friend. She wished she could turn back the clock and this horrible situation would just all go away.

Maude continued, "And, as hard as this is, you will have to choose between the man you married, the man who has provided you with more than everything you've ever wanted, and the man who makes you feel loved and important for only three months of the year."

Sullenly Ronnie mumbled, "I know what you are saying is the right thing to do, I know I have to tell him," her shoulders drooped visibly as she spoke.

Maude added, "You say that Phil loves you but your affair has been going on for quite a while now and from where I sit, it's been nothing more than a fragmented relationship for a few months at a time for a couple of years. Do you think Phil really loves you? Do you think that Phil would actually have you come and live with him and his mother at the end of the lake year round? Has he ever said he wants you to leave Doc and live with him? If he hasn't after all this time, maybe he is happy with this on again off again kind of relationship."

"Maude, are you trying to make me hate Phil?"

"No, but I think that you have to think about the fact that a relationship is more than just going to bed with someone because it feels good. You've been married to Doc for a long time and though maybe he doesn't make you feel special anymore, you both have invested a lot into your marriage, your home, the medical practice. Are you prepared to throw that all away because Phil is a good looking guy who is good in bed?"

"You're right. Doc and I have been married a long time. Over the years we have had a lot of good times. We've both worked hard to get to where we are and there is a lot more to a relationship than just crawling into bed with someone," said Ronnie, repeating what Maude had said as if to help confirm in her mind that Maude was right.

Maude asked, "Think about this. Has Phil ever mentioned that he'd take you in? Do you really think you could live up here year round? You and Doc have always led such an active and lively social life, do you think you could give that up to live in isolation for months at a time during the winter. These are all things you have to think about. Things that you'd be giving up."

"But..." Ronnie started to cry again as the gravity of her actions started to sink in. "But what if Phil doesn't want me to live with him and Doc is so mad and angry that he wants to divorce me? What then? I'll have nothing. I'll have no one. I'll have nowhere to go. I don't even have any family left in Montreal to go to. What have I done?" she sobbed.

Maude didn't really have an answer for this. She didn't know what to say. She thought it best to let Ronnie mull this one over for herself knowing that she didn't have any answer that Ronnie would want to hear right now.

*****

Ben and Emma, belted onto the passenger bench seat sat as quiet as church mice. Doc had been sure to strap the harnesses around them tight enough to make sure they were secure but with enough slack in the shoulder strap that they could lean forward slightly to look out the side windows.

Gilbert untied the mooring ropes from the cleats on the pontoons and coiled them onto the dock. With Doc's help the two men slowly manoeuvred the plane away from the dock and turned it so that it was facing out towards the bay. Doc climbed into the pilot's seat and did the routine pre-flight checks of the fuel gauges, oil pressure gauges and other safety checks that needed to be done. Satisfied that all was as it should be he then turned to the twins and said, "OK guys, I'm going to start the engine now. It's going to be pretty noisy here inside the plane and when I start to speed up the whole plane is going to shake and vibrate but that is normal so don't be afraid." He leaned forward, pulled out the gas throttle lever and turned the key. The engine started immediately.

"Are we your first passengers Doc?" Emma asked the concern audible in her voice.

"Well, in a way you are. I have had my flight instructors up in the plane with me many, many times and after I got my pilot's licence a few of the fellas that did their training with me came for a ride and then I went for a ride in their plane. But you guys are the first passengers that I ever take for a ride who have never been in a plane before."

"I'm not scared, are you Emma?" Ben asked in a voice that was a bit tremulous.

"I'm not scared either, I'm just …" Ben couldn't hear the end of Emma's comment because Doc had pulled out the throttle lever to accelerate away from the dock and the noise inside the plane was deafening. Soon the plane had taxied to the far end of the bay and Doc gently turned the nose of the plane into the slight breeze that was blowing from the west.

Keeping his eyes on the gauges and the bay before him, Doc turned slightly towards the back of the plane so he could be heard above the roar of the engine. "OK kids, here we go. This won't be like any boat ride you've ever been on. When I pull out the throttle the plane is going to speed up really quickly and you will see how fast we are moving. Sit still because the plane has to stay perfectly level until we get lift-off. Once we are in the air and I tell you it's OK to move around then you can lean forward to look out the windows."

"Aye, Aye Captain," said Ben.

As the plane accelerated across the surface of the water, Emma turned her head and looked out the side window. She could see her dad standing on the dock watching the plane take off. She wanted to wave at him but didn't want to move. She could tell that her dad was waving at them and she smiled thinking about how this was going to be such a great story to tell at supper tonight when everyone got a chance to share the best part of their day.

As Doc accelerated even more the plane started to shake and they could feel the plane trying to escape the clutches of the water as it tried to get airborne. Ben had his hands at his side and had lifted himself up slightly on the seat to get a better view. Emma reached across the seat and grabbed Ben's hand. It was trembling slightly and she wasn't sure if Ben was shaking with fear or whether it was just the vibration of the plane. Again Doc pulled on the acceleration throttle, the plane sped up even more and finally they had lift off. Suddenly there was less noise, and the twins experienced a sense of weightlessness for the first time.

"This is incredible Doc," shouted Ben. Turning to Emma he said, "Wow, look how high we are. I think that's Hangdog Channel"

Emma shouted, "I can see the stone cottage and the Narrows from my side of the plane."

Doc carefully monitored his flight instruments for a while and when he reached 500 feet of elevation he pushed back on the throttle slightly and levelled the plane by pushing the yoke forward. Not until he had fully and carefully scanned the skies around him did he take the chance to turn his head to check on the twins. The combined look of shock and awe on their faces was worth a million dollars and he regretted, not for the first time in his life, that he didn't have children of his own to share this with.

"Well kids, what do you think?" he shouted over the roaring engine.

"This is just the best ride we've ever had, ever," said Ben.

"Yeah, nothing can compare to this," agreed Emma.

Doc pulled back on the yoke and rose to 1,000 feet of elevation then levelled the plane off again. "I don't want to go too much higher or else you won't see as much detail but from this height you can still make out pretty clearly what you are looking at."

"Emma, look over there, I can see the entrance to Go Home Bay," said Ben pointing his finger at the starboard side of the plane. Doc was impressed with Ben's ability to distinguish the landscape so clearly for his first time up in a plane.

Often it takes a person new to flying several times in the air before you recognize what it is you are looking at.

"You're right Ben, that is the entrance to Go Home Bay," said Doc. "I'll fly over the channel and maybe we can follow it eastward for a few miles so you can see the waterfalls at the end of the bay."

"I can't believe how narrow the channel is," said Emma leaning forward as far as her harness would allow. "The water looks like a pretty silvery-blue ribbon winding between the green trees of the forest. The forest is so dense it's a wonder any animals or people can even get through it"

Once they had passed the waterfalls at the eastern end of Go Home Bay Doc banked the plane in a gentle turn and headed west towards the open water of Georgian Bay. The ride continued for about another twenty minutes with Doc pointing out certain landmarks along the way that he was sure the twins would recognize. The islands looked so small from this height and they were glad when Doc identified Giant's Tomb Island, Hope and Beckwith Islands. They marvelled at how different it looked from up high.

Finally he turned the plane in a slow, lazy arc back towards mainland and began his descent. "I'm heading back to the cottage now," he said to his captivated audience. "When I get close to landing you are going to feel like the plane is tipping backwards a bit but I have to get the back of the pontoons down onto the water before the front of the pontoons. We might bounce a bit as we land on the water before we are levelled off but that's normal. Don't be worried."

As the plane descended through the small air pockets the plane seemed to sink like it was falling and then it would feel like it was floating again. The noise of the engine was nearly non-existent as Doc decelerated but once they were floating gently on the waves and taxiing towards shore Doc had to rev the engine to get enough thrust to steer the plane. Soon the engine was cut, and they could feel the plane tip slightly with Gilbert's weight as he stepped onto the pontoon to secure the mooring rope from the dock.

Gilbert reached forward and opened the passenger door. Immediately his ears were assaulted by the loud almost unintelligible chatter of his children. "Hey guys. You don't have to yell. There is nothing wrong with my hearing."

"Oh dad, this was so much fun. It was so noisy. Everything looks so different from the sky. This was the best thing ever," they shouted competing for his attention.

"Not so loud!" Gilbert repeated.

"That's pretty common to talk that loud after you've been in the plane," said Doc. "You'll see for yourself. It's so noisy in there that everyone talks loud in the plane just to have a normal conversation and when you get out you just keep speaking loudly."

After sharing some of the details about their ride Ben and Emma raced off to the stone cottage to find their mom and tell her about it.

"Are you ready for a ride?" Doc asked.

"I'd love to go if that's all right with you. It's not too much for you to do back to back rides I hope."

"Gilbert, I think I could fly this baby all day long," Doc said patting the belly of the fuselage like a proud parent. "I'm happy to go up again. Do you think Maude would like to come too?"

Already excited himself about his first plane ride he quickly said, "I'll go ask."

He quickly turned and was soon trotting towards the end of the dock and the path to the main cottage knowing that Maude was still there.

Within barely a few moments both Gilbert and Maude came down to the dock. "Maude is going to pass on the plane ride for now," said Gilbert but she'll give us a hand turning the plane around and head us in the right direction.

"Are you sure you don't want to come for a ride?" asked Doc.

"I'd love to go but uh … I had something to drink a little while ago and it isn't sitting quite right with me so I think I'll pass. Maybe next time." Maude wondered if Doc picked up on the fact that she had gone to the main cottage to chat with Ronnie and the drink she had had was what was causing her to feel a little queasy.

Doc repeated his pre-flight check as if the engine hadn't been run at all that day. He went through the same routine, taxiing to the end of the bay and pointing the nose of the aircraft into the wind. The wind had gotten up a little since his last departure so it took a little less time to get lift off but soon the small plane was soaring through the air. From the front passenger seat Gilbert had a spectacular view of the land, the water, the cloud formations in the distance and all things around him. He marvelled at how easy it was to distinguish the landmarks and agreed with Doc about how different it was to see them from on high. A few boats were crossing the gap between Cognashene and Go Home Bay and from this height Gilbert could easily pick out the driver, passengers and pretty much figure out an approximate length of the boats. He was shocked at the clarity and details he could determine.

"Oh man, I sure wish that we had had your airplane to search the shoreline after the big storm. Philippe and I searched this area for hours looking for survivors and it was so time consuming because we had to check out each and every nook and cranny. But from up here," he waved his hand before him, "you can see every rock, crevasse, and little bay at a glance. It just shows up so much more clearly."

"Don't ever beat yourself up for not being able to find any other passengers or debris from the shipwreck," said Doc. "It was amazing that you were able to find the two men that you did and under the conditions that you found them."

"Yeah, I guess you're right," agreed Gilbert. "I still believe that God had a big hand in us finding those guys. I can't see any other way than a bit of divine intervention playing a part in it."

The aircraft flew on, Doc circling around different features of the landscape below to afford Gilbert a better view of what there was to see from above. Neither man said very much, both sobered by the thoughts of the marine disaster that was still so fresh in their minds as well as taking in the pure serenity and beauty that lay before them.

The deep blue cobalt coloured waters of the gap lay open before them for as far as the eye could see. Small ant-sized formations appeared every now and then on the far horizon signalling that they were approaching another small island, some of which had manned lighthouse stations on them such as Double Top Island, the largest of the Western Islands. Others appeared from this height as just merely rocky shoals and outcroppings that could be fatal if your navigation skills were off.

After nearly an hour of flying along the shoreline from Cognashene to Indian Harbour, out over the outer islands and then heading southward towards Honey Harbour, Doc guided the plane in a lazy slow arc and flew over mainland for a while, the two men taking in the wonder of the landscape with all its small inland lakes, ponds that were completely covered in lily pads and more often than not, the large granite rock outcroppings where no vegetation was ever able to grab a hold, not even in the cracks between the boulders. As the sawmills of the Musquosh River came into view Doc leaned over the centre console and said to Gilbert, "I think I've seen enough sights for one day, I guess it's time to head back to the cottage." Gilbert nodded his approval and sat up a wee bit straighter in his seat preparing for the water-landing that would be coming soon.

"I sure hope we've given Ronnie enough time to get over the fact that I'm planning to buy this airplane," said Doc as he began the descent. "I hope she is in a better mood than when I left."

He looked at Gilbert and smiled. Gilbert, who had not made any comment either way looked over when Doc said, "You know, I said I'd seen enough sights for today, but if Ronnie has cooled down a bit and says she's ready for a ride, I guess I'll be taking in a bit more scenery before the day is over."

"Yup. Perhaps a ride in the plane will be just what it takes to make her feel better."

*****

The plane landed as smoothly on the water as it would have if the pilot had had thousands of hours of flying time.

Once the pontoons hit the water's surface Gilbert relaxed and said, "You're very good at this flying and landing stuff." Doc was serious for a few moments checking gauges and dials as they taxied towards the dock then said, "Thanks, I appreciate the compliment. Glad I didn't scare you or your kids." He shifted the yoke into neutral position as the plane neared the lagoon. "In order to be licensed to fly a plane with pontoons you have to have a certain number of hours of flying time and landing with regular landing gear on airstrips. Then there is a special training you have to take for flying with the extra weight of pontoons. Then there are flight instructors who teach you how to land with pontoons because it is quite a different approach landing on the water and landing on dry land. I was lucky enough to get all that time in with my training in Toronto so it has worked out pretty well for me."

As they approached the dock they could see Emma, Ben and Maude all coming down from the stone cottage to help with the landing and tether the plane to the dock. As soon as the ropes were secure and the cockpit door opened the twins were chattering away asking their dad about his flight, where did they go, what did he see, what he thought of flying, did he think things looked really different to him from way up there?

"Hey guys, I know you are excited but maybe you can calm down just a little. I'm happy to tell you about my ride but just give me a few minutes to thank Doc for giving us these rides and to help him carry his luggage and supplies up to the cottage."

"It will soon be supper time," said Maude to the twins and Gilbert. "Maybe we can have the blow by blow conversation about both rides over supper tonight when we chat about what is the best thing that happened to you today."

"Great idea mom," said Ben. "I know I'm not going to have any trouble coming up with something to say today." Then showing a sign of how just mature he was becoming Ben walked over to Doc, stretched out his hand for a handshake. Doc reached forward and gripping his hand firmly Ben said, "Thanks again Doc. You've made our day."

CHAPTER - 16

Doc pulled a few items from behind the passenger seat and put them on the dock. Gilbert said, "I'll take the cooler if you want to take the duffle bag." Ben walked over and scooped up the duffle bag.

"That's a deal I'm not going to argue with you about. That cooler probably weighs a ton."

The two men and Ben brought the supplies up to the main cottage. Going in through the back door Gilbert put the cooler on the bench under the window in the kitchen and was surprised to see Ronnie in front of the stove stirring what smelled like a pretty delicious stew.

She turned when she heard someone come into the kitchen. "Oh, it's you Gilbert. I thought it was Doc." Gilbert immediately noticed that she was smiling and though he knew she must have been drinking earlier, there were no visible signs of it in her speech or demeanour.

"Doc is just putting the duffle bag in the bedroom," said Gilbert. "He'll be …"

"He'll be what," said Doc as he came around the corner from the living room and into the kitchen.

"Right here," Gilbert said finishing his sentence.

"Oh, hi Doc," said Ronnie resting her stirring spoon on the counter and walking over to give Doc a hug. "How were your flights? The twins seem to be pretty excited."

"The flights were great, weren't they Gilbert?"

"Amazing." There was an awkward pause then he added. "Guess I better get over to the stone cottage. I think the kids will bust at the seams if we don't get to compare notes about our airplane rides pretty soon."

As he made his way towards the kitchen door Gilbert heard Ronnie say to Doc. "I'm sorry I acted so bizarre when you showed up at the dock this afternoon. It was just such a total shock. It was so inappropriate for me to take off on you like that. I'm sorry."

Though it was not really in his nature to eavesdrop on anyone, Gilbert paused just outside the kitchen back door shaking his head in disbelief at the change in Ronnie. He was surprised by the transformation in behaviour. He heard her continue, "Really, I'm thrilled that you are thinking of buying that plane. I can't wait to go for a ride. Is tomorrow OK? Supper is just about ready and I made your favourite. It's Irish Stew. I just have to get the biscuits in the oven then we can sit down and you can tell me all about this plane."

As he walked towards the stone cottage Gilbert thought, *I don't know what Maude said to Ronnie while she was at the main cottage this afternoon but whatever it was it seems to have had some impact on her.*

*****

"Can I fix you a drink while you get the biscuits ready?" Doc asked Ronnie as he was unloading the items from the cooler into the fridge. He too was surprised by the change in her attitude but didn't want to do or say anything that might change it.

"No, I don't think so. I had a drink with Maude earlier this afternoon and I think that's enough gin for me for today. Maybe I'll have a glass of red wine with supper when it's ready."

"A glass of red wine with supper sounds like a great idea." Doc turned towards the door leading to the main part of the cottage but turned around and picked up the cooler. He put the empty cooler in the back porch then said, "I'll just go wash up and change into some shorts. It's still pretty warm out and these dress pants and long sleeved shirt I had on to do rounds this morning at the hospital are a bit too much for cottage life don't you think?"

"I think shorts and a T-shirt are just what the good doctor needs to get into cottage mode. And uh," she turned from the stove to face him, "lose the black socks and dress shoes too would ya?" Ronnie added jokingly.

Though he had shaved that morning, Doc rubbed the stubble that had already formed on his chin then shouted to Ronnie from the bedroom, "After supper perhaps we can go for a walk in the Narrows then sit and watch the sun set from the front porch. Seems like forever since we've done that just the two of us."

"Sounds divine." She smiled, then turned towards the stove to give the stew a final stir. She was glad she was pre-occupied with making supper and homemade biscuits because right now what she wanted more than anything else was a good stiff drink right out of the bottle of gin. On the outside she was all smiles and happy, but the inner Ronnie was in a state of turmoil like she had never ever been in before.

*****

It had been an unusually hot day for August. The clear blue cloudless skies had allowed the rays of the sun to heat the granite rocks around Cognashene to the point that even though it was nearly six pm, the rocks were still warm on bare feet. Maude and Gilbert, each carrying a towel for the twins, walked from the stone cottage to the shore line. Both were in shorts, both were bare feet and in a rare move that surprised even Maude, Gilbert had taken his shirt off.

"Nothing like a pre-supper swim for the kids to wear off a bit of that energy they have."

"They were so excited about their plane ride this afternoon I had to do something so I suggested they go for a swim before supper. They leaped at the chance and took off not even bothering to take a towel."

"You know what?" Gilbert said stopping on the path. "I think I'd like to go for a swim as well. It was pretty stuffy in the cockpit of the plane and I was awfully sweaty after an hour in there. You go on ahead, I'll be right back," he turned and headed off up the path towards the stone cottage once again.

When he opened the screen door he was struck by the heat that was trapped inside the cottage. He thought about the way the cottage had been built. The stones that were used on the cottage were a great idea to make it a solid and sturdy structure but when the sun beat down on the roof like it did today the heat became trapped inside and the rocks were almost as hot inside as out. Gilbert thought, *This is a great feature in the spring and fall but on a day like today...not so much. Maybe sometime I'll have to insulate the roof to block out some of the heat.* He pulled the small step ladder that was kept behind the chairs to the dining table and set it up under the window in the small unfinished loft. Stretching as far as he could reach he was barely able to open the window but with a steady upward shove he was able to open it about ten inches. *There*, he thought, *perhaps that will let some of the hot air trapped at the ceiling to escape.*

Quickly moving into the kitchen he retrieved his swimsuit from the box under the bed, slipped out of his shorts and pulled on the swimsuit. Still thinking about how hot it was in the stone cottage he thought, *Maybe another window in the kitchen would help create a breeze and cool things off a little. Oh well, maybe some other time.* Once outside he grabbed an extra towel off the clothesline from behind the cottage and made his way to the water.

The kids were waist deep in the water and tossing an old beat up rubber ball to each other. In the process they were accidentally (on purpose) splashing Maude as she sat at the water's edge. She didn't seem to mind. She was onto their tricks but appreciated the cooling water even though she was getting thoroughly soaked right through her clothes. The effects of the gin she had shared with Ronnie had worn off and it didn't take long for her to decide a full soaking was in order, so, clothes and all, she slid off the rocks and into the cool refreshing water. Somewhat preoccupied at that point with tossing the ball back and forth, Ben and Emma hadn't really noticed their mother sliding off the rocks until they saw her floating on her back about twenty feet from shore. With her arms tucked alongside her body she lay motionless except for flapping her hands back and forth at her side like the pectoral fins of a sunfish. Slowly she manoeuvred her way over towards them. Suddenly she started kicking her feet furiously to garner maximum splash and she too was soaking everyone around her.

The children laughed hysterically when they realized what Maude had done and as soon as they saw their dad walking towards the shore shouted, "Hey dad, look at mom, she's floating like a boat, clothes and all."

"Your mom is a good enough swimmer she could probably swim all the way to the end of the bay and back with all her clothes on and not even get short of breath."

"Come on in…the water's fine," Maude shouted to Gilbert not even turning her head to look up at him.

Though it had been a few weeks since Gilbert had gone for a swim he didn't waste any time getting wet. Moving to a large boulder that was sticking about three feet out of the water he climbed to the top of it. He crouched down with a slight flexion to his knees he straightened them suddenly keeping his knees together. As he stretched his hands above his head he pushed with his toes on the edge of the boulder and in one fluid motion completed what some might think of as an award winning perfect dive. He swam underwater for probably fifteen or twenty strokes, arms and legs moving in perfect rhythm and surfaced a good distance from shore. The water was deep, cool and felt amazing; he was relaxed in his element once again.

He loved to swim and often thought of going for a swim on the long hot days of summer but it seemed there was always work to be done, a tourist whose needs had to be met or chores that seemed to be piling up. He rolled over onto his back and stared up at the perfectly blue cloudless sky. Unlike Maude who could somehow mysteriously 'just float' on the water Gilbert had to keep moving to stay afloat. The minute he stopped he would sink feet first right under and down he would go till he hit bottom. Treading water was what kept him above the surface. Doing a modified lazy backstroke so he could continue to look up at the sky he lifted his arms to shoulder height and while moving them down to his side, did a frog kick with his legs. Soon he was near shore and taking part in the splashing, laughing, frolicking behaviours of his family. It seemed everyone had a lot of energy to use up.

Though it seemed like they had only been lolling around in the water for a few minutes it was actually closer to an hour before Maude decided to get out of the lake and towel off.

"I'm about as soaked as a person can get," she said rubbing the towel on her head to try and dry her hair a little. "I'm going to go up to the cottage and change into some dry clothes then start putting something together for supper."

"It's really hot in the cottage Maude," said Gilbert remembering what it had been like when he went in to change. "Don't bother lighting the stove to make a hot meal for supper. Maybe tonight we can just have something light like a sardine sandwich and some cheese."

"I'm all for that. The thought of cooking a meal on a hot wood stove right now just doesn't turn my crank at all," said Maude. "A nice light supper will be perfect in this heat."

After Maude had left for the cottage Gilbert took advantage of having a bit of one on one time with the twins and the three of them played in the water for another twenty minutes. When his arms were aching from repeatedly lifting and tossing the twins in the air, trying to glean maximum lift for cannonball dives, they started splashing, cavorting and tossing the ball to each other once again. When they grew tired of that the games moved on to diving into the deep water to retrieve an old silver spoon. The race was on to see who could find it first. Although both of the children were good swimmers like their father and mother, Ben could hold his breath the longest and seemed to glide through the water like a porpoise. As a result he was usually the one to find the spoon first.

Gilbert was really enjoying this time with the kids. It was a great way for him to feel reconnected with his children and he cherished this moment much like he did those times when they were younger and would snuggle up on his lap to watch the sunset. So often he was up at the crack of dawn and after a quick breakfast was gone for the day, his work as the area handy man seemingly never over. Not usually one to have lunch he often didn't get home until supper time and so he missed the children's day time activities. They always ate supper together as a family regardless of whether they were at the cottage or at home. Though it was just a little thing, Maude had insisted it be *their* little thing to keep each one of them in touch with each other. The 'best part of the day' routine at supper was yet another little thing but as the years went by, all four of them looked forward to that habit of sharing their day as it brought them all closer together as a family.

"Gilbert, Ben, Emma, it's time for supper. It's almost eight o'clock." shouted Maude from the front door of the stone cottage. Having spent so much time in the water, Maude had cooled off quite nicely and rather than getting fully dressed again and risk getting overheated in the kitchen she had just put on her nightgown. It was a lot cooler to wear just that. When the kids saw her they were a little surprised and Emma said, "Mom, are you going to bed? Did we tire you out that much?"

"No, I'm not going to bed right now but I just wanted to stay cool and this is the coolest thing I own. So, it's pyjama time for you guys as well if you want."

"That's a great idea," said Emma as she rushed into the kitchen to grab her box of clothes from under the bed and dig out her nightgown as well.

"I don't have any pj's to wear that are cool, they are all hot," said Ben. "Maybe I'll just leave my bathing suit on."

Maude turned to him, "You're right, all your pj's are made of flannel, you'll cook in those tonight. I don't think you'll be very comfortable sitting around in a wet bathing suit," said his mother. "How about if for tonight, since it's so hot, you just put on a light pair of boxers."

"If that's OK with you it will be just fine with me," said Ben as he too reached for his box of clothes under the bed.

Having towelled off outside the cottage on his way up from the lake, Gilbert went into the cottage to retrieve all the wet clothes from Maude and the twins. Scooping them up off the floor he turned to Maude and said, "Can you hand me those towels from the chair next to you and I'll go and hang all these wet things out on the line." Having heard the conversation between Maude and the twins about just wearing something cool rather than getting dressed again, once he was behind the cottage Gilbert shed his swimsuit and, pulling a dry towel off the clothesline wrapped it around his waist. *There*, he thought as he walked back to the cottage, *this will work just fine*. As a very modest person when he sat down at the table he made sure to keep the towel wrapped tightly around his waist. "OK everyone, let's eat. Ben, how about you start the conversation today and tell us about what was the best part of your day." It was no surprise to either Maude or Gilbert that it had to do with going for a plane ride.

*****

Ronnie and Doc ate their supper mostly in silence but for some reason it was a comfortable silence. For once there didn't seem to be any tension between the two of them. Once the meal was over, they made small talk about the weather, about his work, the patients that had been in the office and those he had seen at the hospital. As his office nurse, Ronnie was a good sounding board for Doc to discuss symptoms and diagnoses and treatment options. He appreciated her knowledge of medicine and her familiarity with their patients and the families in their practice. Many times her advice carried a lot of weight in helping comfort the frail elderly and the dying. It was one of the biggest reasons Doc missed having her in the office during the summer.

When dessert was over Doc said, "That was a delicious meal. You worked pretty hard to pull it together on a hot day like today."

"It's a good thing we have an electric stove up here now. I'd hate to have had to light the old wood stove and keep it going to simmer a stew."

Brushing a few scattered biscuit crumbs into his hand from the table and dropping them onto the plate Doc looked at Ronnie and said, "Well. You made supper, I'll clean up."

"You'll get no argument from me about that. I think I'll pour myself an iced sweet tea and go sit on the front porch. Maybe there will be a bit of a breeze there and you can tell me all about this airplane we have tied at the dock."

"I'll just put this stuff away and meet you there. Do you mind pouring an iced tea for me while you're at it?"

Ronnie walked over to the fridge. Pulling a full pitcher from the top shelf, she poured a couple of glasses of iced tea and added a spoon of sugar to each, then a few lemon wedges.

"Can you toss in a couple of ice cubes in mine please?" said Doc as he ran the water in the sink to let the dishes soak.

"Sure thing."

As she reached into the freezer to retrieve the ice cubes she immediately thought of Philippe. For a while during supper she had almost completely forgotten about him and about the mess that her life was in. She had to tell Doc, she had to do it tonight but the evening had been so perfect so far. Like old times. She wondered if she should interrupt this reverie by having such a difficult conversation at this hour in the evening. She thought, "Maybe I'll wait till morning, after we've had coffee and breakfast. And a plane ride." She turned toward Doc and smiled at his officious way of cleaning off the table and scrubbing the stew pot. It was like he was preparing for surgery.

She put the ice cube tray away and gathered the glasses. "OK, I've got the iced tea, I'll meet you out there," and with that she turned and walked from the kitchen. Once out of sight her smile faded into a frown and not for the first time that day her hands had an obvious tremor to them. Maybe it was because she needed another drink since she'd only had one during the day or, maybe it was because she was terrified of the conversation that was soon to take place. Regardless, she set the two glasses of iced tea down on the glass topped white wicker coffee table, pulled a few napkins from a holder on the end table and placed them under the glasses to absorb the condensation that was already starting to form. She brushed a few crumbs from her dress then settled herself on the settee waiting for Doc to make his way in from the back of the cottage. She could hear him whistling a mindless tune as he cleaned the kitchen. He seemed so happy today and to be very much at peace. She hadn't seen him like this in a very long time.

The Stone Cottage

She glanced around the front porch appreciating how nicely it was decorated in blue and white gingham, perfect colours for this waterside location. She was so glad she'd had Maude help her get it set up. She looked up above the front door at the wood carving Gilbert had done. Though it was now a few years old, it still looked as nice as the day he presented it to them. "MY SHANGRI-LA" it said. "Yes", she thought, "this definitely is."

Like a lightning bolt, a thousand thoughts flashed through her mind; the well appointed cottage, the boats, the rocky rugged expansive property, her good friends Maude, Gilbert and the twins, a beautiful home in town, a thriving medical practice that she had helped to build. She had it all yet somehow she had seen fit to risk it all by having an affair with Phil. How could she have done that? How could she? She was in a state of utter turmoil. What should she do? Maude, whose opinion she cherished, said that she should come clean with Doc and tell him everything and promise that she would end it with Philippe. She said she had to trust that Doc would understand and hope that in time he would forgive her. But…what if he didn't forgive her? What if he asked for a divorce? Then she'd have nothing.

She reached for her drink of iced tea hoping the distraction would help to settle her down. As she lifted the glass off the table she noticed her hand was still trembling and she put the glass back down on the table. She didn't want to spill any on her dress and she definitely didn't want Doc to see her like this. He knew she was a drinker. How could she hide it? He was the one who brought the booze up to the cottage week after week. If he saw her shaky hands he might diagnose that as the onset of delirium tremens. The DTs, oh my God, has my drinking gotten that far out of hand that I'm thinking about that? Maybe the shakes *were* a bit of that too. She had gotten into the habit of drinking to get drunk most days. The only time she didn't feel like she needed a drink was when she was with Philippe. He seemed to be able to take all her worries and throw them overboard. She was happy and carefree when she was with him. Could she ever be that way with Doc she wondered. Maybe she should keep her affair a secret. She would break it off with Phil and go back to town with Doc. It was near the end of the season after all.

The whistling in the kitchen stopped and she could hear Doc making his way through the living room towards the front porch. Then suddenly, "Ouch," followed by a short pause, then "son-of- a-bitch". She heard him stumble and glanced through the window in time to see him fall onto the couch. Immediately he grabbed his left foot and pulled it upwards for closer inspection.

"Are you all right?" she asked.

"Yeah," he sighed, "when I changed my clothes before supper I didn't bother to put on any sandals thinking everyone else walks around here bare feet why not me? Well, let me tell you, these city slicker toes were not meant for that. I just stubbed my toe on the coffee table."

Ronnie stifled a laugh. He wasn't the first one to stub a toe up here and he wouldn't be the last but, she had to admit, it was kind of funny when it happened to someone else. Doc hobbled into the porch and dropped down onto the settee beside her.

"Here, have a look, I think I cracked my toenail in half." He lifted his foot up and placed it squarely in Ronnie's lap. The nurse in her kicked in and she lifted his foot and turned it sideways to get a better look. "I really whacked it when I came around the couch."

"Well I don't see any blood but you did split the nail. I'll get the clippers and shorten that nail and you'll be as good as new. She gently put his foot back on the floor and started to get up off the settee. Doc reached up, grabbed her hand and pulled her back down next to him.

"This toe can wait. What can't wait is that I need to give you a kiss to thank you for that wonderful meal, for all the things you do, for always being here for me. I just want to let you know that I love you and I appreciate all that you do. You are an amazing person and I'm so lucky to have you." With that said, he leaned over towards her, kissed her quickly but gently on the lips and then pulled her even closer to himself and hugged her tightly.

His kiss and caress were so genuine, so sincere, so familiar. Ronnie responded to Doc in a way she hadn't in a very long time kissing him gently at first and then with a hunger for him that surprised even her. Though she appreciated what he had said to her, in the back of her mind she was thinking, *I'm not exactly the person he thinks I am. But, how can I tell him? Or should I?*

He wrapped his arms around her and held her tight, holding her, as if by sheer muscle strength he might keep her safe, warm and forever at his side. Gradually the trembling in her subsided completely. She sagged into him. He held her for a long while and then gently began to release her from his grip. With his right index finger on her chin he lifted her face towards him and drew her face up to his. He stared into her eyes.

Her eyes shone with desire revealing her need to be touched by him. To feel loved by *him*. To feel alive and to know she wasn't alone. She knew deep within herself that she needed to be forgiven for what she had done but was too afraid to risk this moment, risk the rekindling of the old embers of love for him that still resided within her.

He cupped both hands to her face and leaned into her. Only then did he kiss her with the passion she remembered from years gone by.

"We have built a beautiful life together Ronnie, I know I haven't been the easiest person to live with lately. I've been moody, cranky, even downright ornery at times but that has never been because of you. I hope you'll forgive me for that. It's just that when I get up here to this beautiful place and I see you I think I'm the luckiest guy in the world. We have so much and we have each other. Let's never let anything ever get in the way of that."

Ronnie's shoulders visibly slumped and she was glad that she was cuddled up next to Doc and facing the Narrows channel so that he couldn't see the look of inner turmoil on her face.

She was quiet for a moment then turning towards him said, "You're right. We have built a beautiful life for ourselves, we have everything we could ever want or need. Let's make a pack right here and now to never do anything to jeopardize that."

With his arms still holding her closely he pulled her tightly to himself in a bear-like hug. "It's a deal." He leaned forward, lifted his glass of iced tea and took a sip. "You haven't touched yours yet. Here I'll get it for you." Reaching forward again he handed her glass to her. She took it from him and was happy to see that her hands weren't shaky. Not wanting to push the limits though she took only a small sip and put the glass back down.

"How about if we go for a walk in the Narrows and over to the far point? There is a small island at the end of the point and I have an idea about that property I'd like to share with you."

"Do you mind if I go and get my sandals first?" he asked.

They both laughed and stood up remembering the incident with the coffee table. Doc disappeared into the living room on his way to the bedroom to collect his sandals. Ronnie flattened a few wrinkles from her sundress, adjusted the belt slightly and ran her fingers through her hair then sneaked a quick glance in the mirror at the doorway. She was quite pleased with her casual, suntanned, windblown look. *Life is wonderful here in Cognashene,* she thought as she opened the screen door and made her way down the steps of the front porch to the granite rock landing below. Immediately she could feel the warmth of the rocks on her bare feet. Doc appeared at the screen door opened it then sat on the top step as he adjusted the straps on his sandals.

"To bad you need sandals Doc, the rocks are nice and warm on my feet. It feels amazing."

"Be that as it may, I don't plan on risking my toes any further tonight." At the bottom of the steps he reached forward and took her hand in his and squeezed tightly. Together they headed off towards the dock and the path that led to the Narrows.

"Now what is this idea you have about the island at the end of the point?"

CHAPTER - 17

They walked along hand in hand like a couple of young lovers out for an evening stroll, sometimes talking about the scenery, the height of the water this year or watching the boats going by navigating the tricky shoals in the Narrows. At times they were silent, just the two of them simply enjoying each other's company and the peace and quietude that comes with a long- lasting comfortable relationship.

They found a rock formation on the side of a small granite rise that looked like it was a sofa carved out of stone and built just the right size for two. They sat down and when they straightened their legs, their feet where only a few inches from the water. A small fishing boat driven by one of the locals passed through the channel on his way to the outer shoals and prime fishing spots. A wave broke and the white of its crest slid smoothly across the rugged shore and licked at their feet. The dying wave hesitated for a moment and then fell back, the trough diminishing as it receded into the channel. It was a perfect place to sit, relax and see the Narrows from one end to the other. Another boat went by, though a lot faster this time, being driven by one of the local residents familiar with the channel. It was throwing quite a large wake behind the boat and the waves came to the shore more quickly.

"You better lift your feet up," said Ronnie. "Those waves are going to get your sandals wet."

Doc did so and just on time too. "Whoa", he said quickly jumping to his feet, "that was close. That wave came right up the shoreline and just about wet the spot I was sitting on. My shorts and ass would be wet too if I hadn't moved."

Ronnie, who had pulled the skirt of her dress up to well above her knees started laughing at Doc for the second time that evening. "I didn't think you could move that fast anymore!" she said.

"You must be wet too?"

"No, I'm OK. I hiked my skirt up just in time. The waves only came as high as my knees but I think the driver thought that I was flashing him or something. I could almost see his eyes bulging out of his head looking at me as he went by."

"You always have been a looker Ronnie," Doc said teasing her and messing her hair with his hand.

Doc sat back down on the rocks and made himself as comfortable as possible. "This is a great place to take a break and I bet the view of the sunset from here tonight is going to be spectacular. But," he paused as he readjusted his sitting position "without a cushion this rock is going to get hard pretty quickly."

"I often come out here by myself in the evening just to sit, relax, think and watch the sun set and… yes…I often bring a cushion with me. I find the backrest is just the right angle for me. I don't mind leaning back onto the backrest but you're right, the seat does get pretty hard."

Doc stood up again and made his way to the water's edge. "Look here," he said pointing to a small pile of rocks at the shore, "these rocks are perfect for skipping."

"That little stash of rocks is there for a reason."

"And what would that be?"

"Ben is always scanning the shoreline and sometimes even underwater for rocks that are flat on at least one side. See how they aren't too big, aren't too small. Just the right size to fit in between your thumb and forefinger. Perfect for skipping."

"Why would he leave them here?"

"He and his sister often come here and have rock skipping contests to see who can skip them the most times and also to see if they can skip them right across to the other side of the Narrows."

"It's a great way to amuse themselves I guess."

"It is. I think that Ben is starting to get a little bored with being up here every summer with very few friends to hang out with. He'll soon be a teenager and at his age, you can only fish, skip rocks, swim, dive and pick berries for so long before that starts to get old."

"Do you think he'll stay in town next summer with Gilbert's mom?"

"No, I don't think so, from what I understand, Gilbert is getting so busy with his handyman work up here that he's going to enlist Ben as his helper."

"What a great way for a young lad like him to spend the summer. I noticed when he was getting on the airplane that he's getting tall and strong so my guess is he'll be very useful to Gilbert as a handyman assistant. And who better to learn how to do things than from Gilbert?"

"Yes, that's right. And Emma; Maude tells me that she too is going to get commissioned as a worker as well, helping Maude." She paused. "She seems to quite enjoy helping her mom with the domestic chores." Ronnie flattened her skirt and held it tight to her legs when a sudden gust of wind blew through the channel and lifted the edge of it slightly. She then added, "You know Doc, I'm pretty well established up here now, I have everything I need. I have enough of the conveniences from home up here now. There isn't that much that I need Maude for any more. Don't get me wrong, I loved having her help in getting the cottage set up the way I wanted it but there really isn't that much more that needs to be done."

"So is Maude going to hire herself out to the locals like Gilbert does?"

"Yes. Maude wants to work for the tourists who are here for the summer but she just wants to work here within the bay. She wants to stay close to the stone cottage so she and Emma can go to her housekeeping jobs by canoe or with the rowboat. There are quite a few new cottages being built around here lately and I'm sure someone with Maude's talents will be in demand. Gilbert always takes their small boat for his jobs so he can take his tools with him and often goes pretty far. Some days he has work all the way down the Freddy Channel towards Musquosh and Bone Island. Seems the more he does for people the more there is to do."

"We were lucky we got them first. I hope we don't lose them. I count on Gilbert to keep things in tip-top shape around here 'cause I sure don't have the time or the inclination to do these things myself."

"I agree, we are lucky. Maude says that we will always be their first priority. And, that is what brings me to talk to you about the idea I mentioned when we were sitting on the front porch."

"OK. Go on."

"Well, the twins are getting big now and they are still sharing the bunk beds with their parents in that tiny kitchen in the stone cottage." She paused and swatted at a mosquito that was buzzing around her shoulders.

"So what's your idea?"

Ronnie stood up and walked about fifty feet further down the shoreline heading towards the lake beyond. "Come over here for a second Doc."

Grumbling slightly about having to get up again and walk on his sore foot he moved over to where Ronnie was standing and stood behind her. Placing his hands gently around her waist he pulled her close to himself and leaned his head down, resting his chin on her shoulder.

"Mmmm, this is nice," he said breathing in the fresh scent of her hair.

"Cut it out," she said laughing and twisting free of him, "I'm trying to be serious here for a minute."

"OK, what's this all about?"

Pointing with her finger she said "You see how the Narrows channel ends with two small islands just as you are reaching the opening to the lake."

"Yes. Those two little islands are so small they look more like shoals to me but go on."

Continuing to point she said, "Follow the shoreline. See how there is about a fifty or sixty foot gap between the last shoal and the next much bigger island. Right now, the water is high enough that the last bit of land is actually an island but I remember that when the water was low a couple of years ago, those shoals at the end of the channel were well out of water and were a part of the big island at the end."

"Yeah, the water between the last island and mainland looks like it is only about three feet deep right now. When I think about it, when we bought this property I do remember that island was more of a point of land sticking out into Cognashene Lake. It was a part of mainland, a part of our property. You could walk right to the end of the point and not get your feet wet."

"Exactly. Over the years that 'point of land' is sometimes the northernmost part of our property and at other times it is an island all onto itself. It looks like its about three quarters of an acre in size."

"And so, what is your bright idea my beloved?"

"I think that we should give Maude and Gilbert that island."

"Uh, what did you say?" he asked looking at her curiously.

"Oh, Doc" she said turning to face him, "they have done so much for us over the years. Nothing we ask of them is ever too much. We have so much land here, we are never going to miss that point, or island or whatever you want to call it.

We have become such good friends and I think it's time we do something really nice for them."

Doc rubbed his chin, "I think that is an amazing idea." He walked away from her and climbed the slight rise in the rocks so he was now standing on what would be the backrest of the rock sofa. This position afforded him a much better view of the shoreline of the Narrows and he could see how the channel emptied into the lake. From there he was also able to properly size up the island. He rubbed the stubble on his chin as if deep in thought then said, "It's a great idea Ronnie. Let's do it."

Ronnie joined him on the rocky outcropping. "Maybe Maude and Gilbert could build themselves a nice cottage on this island, one with a couple of bedrooms. Like I said before, the twins are getting so big now it would be really nice for them to have their own room and it would give Maude and Gilbert a bit more privacy as well. I'm sure it wouldn't have to be very big but it would be their own place to go to."

He dropped his hands into his pockets and reflexively searched the bottoms looking for some change to jingle around as he was thinking. Finding no change in his shorts he pulled his hands free and started rubbing his chin again. "Well, I think it's a great idea. A very nice gesture on our part to let them know how much we appreciate all they've done for us. We wouldn't be here today if it weren't for them."

"Do you think we will have a hard time severing that piece of property from our land?"

"I don't think so. We can work it out in such a way that if we refer to it as an island then the land *could* be considered to be already severed so it should be OK. I'll check it out with the lawyer we used to close the deal when we bought the property initially. It'll be interesting to see how it's demonstrated in the survey maps. If the water was high when the survey was done and it shows as an island then, voila, we're laughing. If the survey was done when the water was low and it shows on the maps as part of mainland then we'll have to submit a request for severance and put that forward to the township."

Ronnie turned to towards Doc. She walked quickly up to him and throwing her arms around his neck gave him a hug, quickly kissed his cheek and said, "I'm glad you like my idea. I've been thinking about this for quite a while now and I didn't know how you would feel about it. I know you really respect Maude and Gilbert and I just think that if we can move forward with this and get it sorted out, if anything ever happens and we have to sell our cottage we know that they'll be able to keep coming up here regardless if we are here or not."

Ronnie sat back down on the rocks and pulled her knees up to her chest. She seemed deep in thought but after a short while added. "I kind of think they consider this area more like home to them than their place in Penetanguishene. Gilbert, his brother and his father spent a ton of time on the water as they were growing up. They fished and camped in this area a lot. That's how he knows his way around so well. Then, with Maude's heritage, you know, being raised on the reserve up north and always being on the water it just seems so right, so natural for them. They probably couldn't afford to buy any property here but doing it this way, well, it's one way for them to own a little piece of the rock, a place they can call their own."

He sat down beside her, loosened his sandal and rubbed his sore toe. "I don't think we should say anything to them about it right now Ronnie. When I get back to town I'll chat with the lawyer and get him to search the land title and check the survey. That will be the first step. There might be some legal hoops we have to jump through to give land away. I'm not sure. This is way outside my area of expertise but we won't know unless we look into it."

Turning to face him Ronnie said, "Thanks Doc. This means a lot to me. I'm glad you are on board with it."

The sun was slowly setting in the west and the high feather-like cirrus clouds that had adorned the sky all day were now turning to a shade of pink that bordered on a soft crimson colour. As the sun slowly dropped closer to the horizon the soft pink hues turned into a stunning vibrant red that reflected on the calm, still water of the lake before them. The view from where they were sitting was spectacular.

Stretching out her legs and laying flat on her back with her eyes cast skywards Ronnie whispered, "The sky is almost magical the way it changes so much during the day and evening. That is one thing that I have noticed being up here all summer long. There seems to be so much more sky here than there is in town, the clouds are so much more dramatic and at night there are so many more stars than we ever see in town. When I'm at the cottage I find myself looking at the sky many times during the day, but when I'm at home I rarely ever look up."

Doc reclined on his back looked skyward as well for a moment then propped himself up on his elbows so he could see both the sky and the reflection of the sunset in the calm mirror-like water. "It does seem that we have more sky to gaze upon up here than we do in town. I think it's because in town there are so many trees and buildings and street lights there. All we have here is water, rocks and sky."

Ronnie added, "I have to admit, I don't know that I've ever even noticed a sunset at home. I guess we just get so caught up in the activities of daily living in town, there are so many distractions, so many people around, so much to do, we don't really take the time to look skyward and appreciate how beautiful the sunsets really are."

Doc swatted a mosquito that had decided to take a chunk out of his knee. "That little bugger isn't really that little you know. He's huge, I thought he was going to pick me up and drop me in the water."

"They do seem to be well fed up here don't they?" Ronnie added.

The two of them sat quietly for a while just appreciating the stillness and beauty of their surroundings. "Well, I hate to say this but, as lovely as this evening has been and as nice as it has been to just relax and chat, the sun has set and soon it'll be too dark to see the path to the cottage so I think we should make our way back." Ronnie stood quickly and brushed at a couple of mosquitoes that were buzzing her head. She stretched out a hand toward Doc to help him up and added, "Come on old man, let's get moving. These bugs are getting worse by the minute."

"Thank God Gilbert insisted on putting screens on our porch." And with that they headed off towards their cottage.

*****

The following morning as promised, Doc brought Ronnie for a ride in the airplane. A bit nervous about going at first she quickly settled into the front passenger seat, fastened her seat-belt and sat in awe of her husband's command of the aircraft's pre-flight check.

"You just seem to be so comfortable working all those dials, gauges, throttles. It's like you've been flying a plane for years."

"My instructor was really anal about his students learning their way around a cockpit. He drilled it into us session after session. I literally got so familiar with the instrument panel that I could reach for anything I needed to get my hands on with my eyes closed."

"That's comforting to know but for now, I think I'd prefer if you keep them open."

"OK," he said in a mischievous way. "All the better to see you with my dear."

"Ah, you know what I look like, so umm, just keep those peepers focused on the sky."

"You sound nervous. You aren't afraid are you?"

"No, I'm fine. It's just this is so new to me."

With Gilbert's help the airplane was cast off from the dock and with the engine revved Doc taxied out of the lagoon and into the bay. "Hang on," he said. "There's a bit of a chop out here. Nothing to worry about, in fact the breeze will give us a faster, smoother lift off but it will be a bit bumpy as we are accelerating." With that he pulled the throttle lever to half for a moment then to three quarters. As if they were being lifted upwards by a giant unseen hand the airplane ascended to five hundred feet within a matter of moments.

"Hey honey bun. How's that for a smooth take off?"

"Let the record show your honour, I am duly impressed," she smiled at her own joke.

"Wait till you see the scenery." Doc pulled back on the yoke and the plane lifted higher in the sky gaining more elevation. "I usually fly at around fifteen hundred feet. No need to go any higher than that around here." He adjusted the throttle lever slightly then turned to Ronnie and asked, "So, my dear, where would you like to go."

"Where ever the breezes take us I guess." She looked over at her husband and smiled. This was the happiest she had seen him in a couple of years. He was a hard working man, with a demanding medical practice. She often worried that he put in too many long hours and consecutive days without time off to relax but she could see by the look in his eyes and his posture that he was totally in his element. He seemed so relaxed and happy and at that moment she knew this was the perfect release for him from the pressures of life.

Ronnie relaxed in her seat and staring out the window began to fully appreciate just what it was they were doing. She leaned over in her seat slightly towards Doc and said over the drone of the engine, "How about if we head out over Giant's Tomb Island, then Beckwith and Hope Islands? I've seen them so many times when we are crossing the gap yet I've never been able to figure out just how big they are."

"I'm thrilled you are OK with this. I'll fly over towards The Tomb first, then I'll go over as far as Christian Island. You'll get a chance to see the beaches on The Tomb, and Beckwith that way." He pulled on the yoke and banked slightly to the left. The right wing rose skyward momentarily then levelled off.

"Look down below Ronnie. That's Cranberry Island right there. I didn't know there were so many small islands between Cranberry and Giant's Tomb."

Ronnie allowed herself to gaze downward. She knew there were lots of little islands down there. She and Philippe had spent more than their share of time on some of them. With a slight trepidation she leaned closer into the window and searched the water below until she found the island with the bluff that she and Philippe had gone to. Her heart began to pound in her chest with the thoughts of that amazing afternoon on the island. Her thoughts were racing as well. *That was the last time I saw him.* She closed her eyes and tried to picture the two of them on that island on that day but she couldn't conjure up a clear image. She resolved there and then on the spot. *And it will remain the last time I see him.*

"You seem pretty quiet, like you are deep in thought or something." Doc noted.

"No, I'm just trying to take it all in," she lied.

"Well just sit back and enjoy the ride. I have plenty of fuel so we can explore for a little while longer. Let me know when you are ready to head back to the cottage."

"Let's go for about another half hour then head back. You don't have to show me everything at once. We can save places like Musquosh, McCrae Lake and that area to the south of us for another ride."

"Sure."

Forty minutes later the plane had landed smoothly in the bay and taxied to the dock. Gilbert, Maude and the twins met them at the dock and as soon as the passenger door was open the twins started with a barrage of questions, "How did you like your ride, what did you see, where did you go, did you recognize everything?"

Calmly Ronnie stepped out of the plane and slid down onto the pontoon then jumped onto the dock with as much grace as she could muster. Oddly, though she wasn't nervous flying, her legs felt a bit wobbly which surprised her and she did seem to be a bit dizzy as well. She lost her balance when Doc stepped onto the floating dock and luckily for her Gilbert was standing right beside her and gripped her arm keeping her upright.

"Whoa," he said. "I'm glad I caught you, you almost fell."

"So am I." She took a couple of steps forward but still seemed to be off balance. Maude came up to her and grabbing a hold of her hand, led her off the dock onto shore. "Maybe once you're on solid ground you'll be better."

"I hope so. Maybe I just need to lay down for a little while."

"I'll go up with you," said Maude, "just in case you lose your balance again."

They followed the path from the dock towards the cottage. Gilbert, Doc and the twins were still on the dock talking about the airplane and its many features. When they were well out of range to be heard Ronnie leaned into Maude slightly and grabbed her hand.

"Maude, I have to talk to you about something very personal but you must swear that you'll tell no one, not even Gilbert."

"OK, what is it?"

"I think I know why I am dizzy. I was sick this morning when I got up. Doc was still sleeping and he didn't notice but this isn't the first time. I was sick a couple of mornings last week as well."

Maude, not knowing what to say said nothing. She had a pretty good idea about what was coming next but thought it best to let Ronnie tell her.

"Maude, I think I'm pregnant. I'm a month late for my period and that has never ever happened to me."

"Let's go inside so you can lay down and put your feet up." They made their way onto the front porch and Ronnie laid down on the settee and put her feet up on the cushioned arm rest.

"Maude what am I going to do? Doc and I haven't been intimate for months. He'll know right away that the baby isn't his. You don't have to be a doctor to figure that one out."

"Did you talk to him last night about Philippe?"

"No, I couldn't. He seemed so happy about the plane I didn't want to bring it up. We went for a long walk in the Narrows, sat and watched the sunset and then came home. We were both pretty tired so we went straight to bed. Then I thought I would tell him this morning and before I knew it we were on a sightseeing trip around the islands. I thought about telling him then but when I looked at him piloting that plane, he was so content, so thrilled to be taking me for a ride I just couldn't."

"Well I guess for now you can say the plane ride made you dizzy but that story is only going to get you so far. How long is Doc here for?"

"He is going back to town later today. I'm not sure but maybe I should go back with him."

"And do what? Sit in the big house by yourself. The new nurse that is working in the office in your place is still there. I seem to remember you saying she would be there until the end of September since you didn't know how long you wanted to stay up here this year."

"You're right. I guess I'll stay, at least I'll have you and your family for company. That will give me some time to get my head straight and figure a few things out. For the record, I don't plan to ever see Philippe again. I don't want him around anymore. I realized today that my life is with Doc and I'll do whatever I have to, to keep what I have."

"Ronnie, I'm going back down to the dock and I'll tell Doc that you are laying down. For now I'll just say that the plane ride gave you a bit of motion sickness."

"I've been in planes before and never had a problem but I guess we can say there is always a first time."

As Maude turned to leave Ronnie reached out and grabbed her hand. "Maude, you are the best friend a person could ever have. I just want you to know that I, we, really appreciate all that you do and all that you've ever done for us."

Maude smiled back at her friend. She knew she did a lot for them, that she often went above and beyond for them but it was nice to hear that her work, time and efforts were recognized. "Thank you," she said simply then turned and left the porch.

*****

After the oohing and awing over the plane was over and there wasn't much more to be said about it Gilbert rounded up the twins and the three of them started up the path towards the stone cottage.

"I think it's getting pretty close to lunch time. Who's hungry?" he asked knowing full well what the kids answer would be. "I know I could sure use a cup of coffee. I hope your mom has a bit of a fire going in the wood stove so I can make one."

"She probably does," said Emma. "She said she was making soup for lunch. It was so hot yesterday that she didn't make any bread for sandwiches but I think we still have a few biscuits left for dunking in the soup."

"You guys run along up ahead of me. Tell your mom I'll be right in. I just want to check to see how much firewood we have left. It's getting towards the end of summer now and soon we'll be needing to light a fire in the fireplace just to keep us warm in the evening."

The kids scampered ahead of Gilbert as he made his way around to the back of the cottage. Earlier in the summer there had been a pretty significant 'three day blow' and a couple of trees close to the inland lake behind the cottage had been uprooted. Gilbert walked over to them and kicked the root mass that was jutting up in the air. *Amazing how shallow the root base is for such big trees. Hard to believe they can even grow on this granite*, thought Gilbert. He was pleased to see that the roots, and branches for the two trees were already starting to dry out. It would take a year before the trunk was dry enough for burning but there was plenty of wood to get started with. Gilbert made his way into the stone cottage and immediately was aware of the fragrant smell of a good old fashioned chicken soup. Commenting on how good the cottage smelled Maude replied, "I used the bones from the chicken we had for supper the other night. It makes great stock and a good base for the vegetables and barley that I added to the soup."

Gilbert made his way over to the washbasin and scrubbed his hands. He turned to Maude and said, "How's Ronnie doing? She looked a little green when she got out of the plane."

"Oh, she'll be alright. It's nothing she can't get over."

By the tone in Maude's voice Gilbert could tell there was something more to the story but with the children right underfoot he didn't want to press the point. *I'll ask her about it later*, he thought.

*****

Doc showed up on the porch with his small weekender duffle bag packed. He dropped it by the porch door and walked over to where Ronnie was still reclined on the settee.

"I feel badly that I'm leaving you when you aren't feeling well," said Doc.

"Oh, I'm going to be alright. I'm sure it's nothing. It was just so hot yesterday maybe it's just that I got too much sun or something. I'll just lay here till this dizziness passes. I'm sure I'll be fine."

Always the physician, Doc felt her forehead to check for a temperature, got her to stick out her tongue to check for pallor and quickly took her pulse.

"You seem to be pretty good for the shape you're in," he joked. "It's a comfort for me to know that Maude and Gilbert are here close by. If you start feeling really lousy and it doesn't seem to be going away get Gilbert to take you to town. It would be nice if we had phone service up here so you could call me and let me know then I could meet you at the town dock but I guess we'll just have to rely on you getting better."

"Don't worry about me," Ronnie smiled weakly at him. "And don't forget to check with the lawyer about the land severance issue we talked about last evening. I still want to move forward with that."

"OK, I think I'll do that first thing when I get to town. I've missed two days of doing rounds at the hospital. I'm sure they are wondering if I'm coming in or not. That old head nurse Ruth doesn't like it when I'm hard to get a hold of." He shuffled his feet a bit and wiggled his sore toe in his shoe. "I guess I'll be going then." He turned towards the door and then quickly turned on his heel and in a move pretty much unheard of for him he blew her a kiss then headed for the door. He walked out the porch door and turned to hold it so that it closed softly on its frame rather than let it slam. He looked through the screen and said, "You're sure you're OK?"

"I'll be fine, just go," she said a little more harshly than she meant to.

"I'll be back this weekend. See you then."

Soon she could hear Doc, Ben and Gilbert chatting as they made their way down the dock. Within moments the plane engine started up and though it was loud Ronnie could tell that it was a finely tuned engine that ran smoothly without any sputtering. That was reassuring.

Ronnie propped herself up on her elbows so she could see out the screens and down to the dock. She watched as Gilbert and Ben managed to turn the plane to face out of the lagoon and after giving it the final shove from the dock they stood side by side watching as the plane taxied out into the bay. Ronnie thought, *Doc was right. Ben is getting tall.* Seeing him every day she didn't really notice but looking at them standing side by side on the dock it was pretty clear, Ben was turning into a young man."

Ronnie flopped back down on the settee and ran her fingers through her hair. All of a sudden she felt a tightness begin to develop in the back of her throat. Within seconds her breathing became a bit erratic. She put her hand to her throat to try to control her breathing and within seconds tears started to well up in her eyes. She was glad Doc had left; she didn't want him to see her like this. She was emotionally overwhelmed. Her breathing slowed down but each breath came in a sob. *Oh my God,* she thought, *what am I going to do? Just when I thought it couldn't get any worse, now I'm pregnant and not with my husband's child.* The more she thought about the mess her life was in, the harder she sobbed. The tears flowed freely down her cheeks. *What am I going to do, what am I going to do?* she kept repeating to herself as if by chance an inspiration would appear before her. Her repetitive thoughts of the situation she was in did little to comfort her. In fact, the turmoil she felt within herself seemed to magnify.

In the distance she could hear the swoosh, swoosh of the Swede saw as it ripped though the branches of the fallen trees. Gilbert and Ben were behind the stone cottage and had started to work on cutting up the fallen trees for firewood.

As she listened to the repetitive sounds of the saw it lulled her into a calmer frame of mind and she thought, *Life goes on. I guess mine will too but I don't think the path for me will be a smooth one for the first little while.* She rolled over to face the wall, curled her legs up into a foetal position and slowly drifted off to sleep, albeit a restless one.

CHAPTER - 18

Doc had arrived by plane on a pleasantly sunny, calm Friday afternoon around three. It was much sooner than anyone had anticipated.

"I wasn't expecting you to show up until after you did your Saturday morning rounds at the hospital," said Ronnie as she helped with securing the mooring lines from the pontoons to the floating dock.

"As it turns out, I only have two inpatients right now. The others have been discharged and I asked Jim Jacobson if he'll check in on them for me this weekend."

"Who is Jim Jacobson?" Ronnie asked a bit of a puzzled look on her face.

"Oh yeah. I forgot. You've been up here all summer. Jim is a new guy in town. He's young, just out of med school and is just in the process of setting up a practice. I think his office is going to be in that big brick house across the street from the old Canada House Hotel on Main Street. He's anxious for work and pretty keen."

"It'll be good for you to have another doctor in the town. That will give you a chance to offer him some work, maybe handle a few emergencies and cover for each other so you can actually get time off."

"That's exactly what I was thinking. So, right off the bat I've sent a bit of work his way. There is a new family in town and they came to the office looking to see if I'd be their doctor. I told them that my practice is full and I'm not accepting new patients so I sent them over to Jim's office. Figured they may as well start with the new guy."

Ronnie's mind was already racing ahead thinking, *Finally there might be a bit of a break with people coming to the door looking for the doctor.* That was the problem with having your medical practice right at the house. It was like always being on call, as long as you were home people came to the door, even if it was outside of office hours. With Ronnie being the office nurse, there were times when Doc wasn't around and she would fix some patients up, minor injuries needing a dressing or splint, that sort of thing. *Now Doc and I might actually get a bit more 'us' time rather than working all the time,* she thought.

Doc unloaded the plane and carried the boxes with groceries up to the cottage. On his second trip to the plane he noticed the twins swimming in the water near the channel. "Where are your mom and dad?" he shouted to them.

Emma answered, "My dad has gone into town to pick up some things and mom is up in the second lake cleaning that big white cottage. Those people have left now for the season and asked mom and dad to put their place in order for the winter."

"OK. I was just surprised when they didn't come down to the dock when I got here and I didn't see them at the stone cottage."

"I'm sure they'll both be back soon. They weren't expecting you until tomorrow. Is there something you need us to help you with?"

"No, I'm fine. But, yeah, you're right. I am here a day early aren't I?"

Doc pulled the cooler out of the back storage compartment of the plane and dropped it with a thud onto the dock. Stooping over to get a better grip on the handles he picked it up and started to walk towards the ramp.

"Here, let me carry that for you Doc," said Ben who had seemed to appear as if by magic on the dock.

"Where did you come from?" said Doc a little surprised at seeing the young lad standing there.

"I swam underwater from where we were at the channel all the way over to the dock."

"Wow!"

"I know, that's pretty far isn't it Doc? I've been practising."

With that Ben reached out his hands and tried to carry the cooler but it was just a bit too heavy for him. He too put it down on the dock. "What have you got in here?" he said turning to face Doc. "It must weigh as much as I do."

"It's some fresh steaks from the butcher and a whole bunch of fresh fruits and vegetables from the farmer's market. We are having a party tomorrow night and I wanted nothing but the best for my special guests."

Emma who had by now wandered over to the dock said, "Is it someone we know that's coming to your party tomorrow night? Do they have children we can hang out with?"

"Oh, I think you know these guests very well. They have children too, a boy and a girl the same age as you guys are."

Excited at the prospect of meeting some new people Emma asked again, "Who is it? Do we know them?"

"I'm not going to say. I want it to be a surprise." Turning to Ben he said, "How about if you take one handle of the cooler and I'll take the other. Between the two of us we should be able to make it up to the cottage." The cooler was a lot lighter to carry this way and Doc was amazed at how well Ben held up his end of the heavy metal box.

"Thanks for your help there young fella, I couldn't have made it up to the cottage with that heavy thing by myself."

"How did you manage to get it in the plane?" Ben asked.

"I have to be honest here. I brought the cooler and the vegetables to the butcher shop and left it there last evening. I asked the butcher to give me a call when he had finished cutting up the meat. He offered to wait until this morning to deliver it and he packed it for me with the meat and a bunch of ice to keep it all fresh. Then his delivery guy who is just a bit older than you are helped me to put it in the plane. I really don't think I'd have been able to lift it in there myself without taking something out of it first."

"I'm sure you and Mrs. Johnson and your guests are going to have a good supper tomorrow night," said Ben as he left the kitchen and made his way down the steps at the back of the cottage. Turning to look back briefly to make sure the screen door had closed tightly behind him he gave Doc a slight wave and said, "Let us know if we can help you with anything else."

Ronnie, who had returned to the kitchen, came up to Doc and together they started to unpack the boxes of items that he had put on the table.

"What was all that talk about having a party tomorrow night?" she asked. "First you show up a day early and now we are having a party." He looked at her a bit quizzically afraid he had offended. "Don't get me wrong Doc. I'm thrilled you are here early and I really don't mind having a party tomorrow night. It'll be a good way to wrap up the summer."

"Let's unpack the rest of this stuff. I'll load up the fridge, then get changed into some cottage clothes and then maybe we can sit on the front porch and chat about my visit with the lawyer this week. I think you'll see there is something to celebrate."

Laughing as she said it she added, "Don't forget to put your sandals on this time," she said joking with him. "I haven't moved the coffee table in the living room and in anticipation of you coming up this weekend the table has grown a couple of extra legs to tempt your delicate little tootsies."

*****

"The lawyer says he sees nothing wrong with us transferring the island at the end of the point to Gilbert and Maude. We talked about gifting it to them and about selling it to them and he said that because they aren't direct family the transaction would go a lot smoother if we sold them the property rather than gifting it to them."

"Oh Doc. I really don't think Gilbert and Maude can afford to buy it. I would prefer if we just gave it to them."

"I know, and the lawyer and I talked about exactly that and we came up with a plan that will work perfectly. We just have to…" he turned to look at the front porch screen door and saw Gilbert raising his arm to knock. "Hi there."

"Sorry to interrupt. I wasn't expecting you to be here so soon. Had I known I'd have been here to help you land at the dock." He looked back at the dock to see if the rowboat was tied there then added, "and I see that Maude isn't here yet either."

"That's all right Gil, Ronnie was here and we managed just fine. Ben was a big help with bringing stuff up to the cottage from the plane."

Ronnie added, "Thank goodness Ben was here. He helped Doc carry the cooler up to the cottage. With all there was in it I think someone would have ended up with a hernia carrying it by themselves."

"Gilbert, I have a question for you," Doc said.

"Sure what is it? You want another dock built for another airplane," he said winking at his friend.

"No. One is enough. I just wanted to know if you and Maude and the children can come over here for supper tomorrow night?"

The Stone Cottage

"I don't see why not. I'll check with Maude to make sure, but I do know our social calendar is pretty wide open these days so I'm certain we can make it."

"Perfect," said Doc. Turning to Ronnie he asked, "what's a good time?"

"How does five-thirty sound?"

"I think that will be perfect," said Doc turning from his wife to look at Gilbert. He was pleased to see him nodding in agreement as well.

*****

"Here's to the best friends a couple of city folk like us could have," said Doc as he lifted his glass of wine in the air. "When we moved to town we didn't know anyone. The two of you have been our saviours, helping us get set up at the house, renovating and helping us move in at the cottage and helping with just about everything we have ever needed. I'm sure we wouldn't be here if it wasn't for you guys, and for that, we are eternally grateful."

Maude and Gilbert raised their wine glasses. The children who were drinking lemonade raised their glasses as well. Responding to the toast Gilbert said "Thank you, we appreciate all the opportunities that you have given us as well." He looked around the dining room of the main cottage and then out the window towards the stone cottage. "There is no way that we would have ever been able to spend our summers here on Georgian Bay if it wasn't for your generosity. I feel like we've been on extended holidays for the last few years."

"Even though we have worked you guys to the bone?" asked Ronnie.

"It's been labours of love for us," said Maude joining in the conversation. "We truly love being here in Cognashene. The stone cottage feels like home to us. I know we have a house in town but being here is really wonderful. Like Gilbert said, we wouldn't have been able to be here on the bay if it weren't for the two of you."

The salad bowls were cleared from the table and steaks were served on a fancy platter Maude had never seen before. The vegetables were added to the table in large amber coloured glass dishes, home style for everyone to share from. Generous slices of Maude's home-made bread lathered with butter were enjoyed by all. The conversation around the table was light and airy and it would have been evident to anyone peering in the window that those sitting around the table were good friends enjoying each other's company.

When the main course of the meal was over, Ronnie and Doc cleared away the dishes from the table insisting their guests of honour just sit back and relax.

"Before we have dessert there is a bit of business that we need to look after," said Doc.

Sitting down and pulling his chair up closer to the table Doc began. "Ronnie and I have been talking and we have decided that just saying thank-you and paying you a wage is just not enough to show you how much we appreciate what you guys have done for us. You've been more than just employees to us. You have become truly valued friends and you can't put a price tag on that."

Gilbert and Maude looked at each other. The conversation seemed to be getting pretty serious.

Doc continued. "We have decided to give you something more than just a pay-cheque; we want to give you the island at the end of the point as a place that you can call your own. You are welcome to stay in the stone cottage for as long as you'd like but we know that those are very close quarters and I'm sure that at times it must seem like its getting smaller as your family grows."

Ronnie piped in. "We thought that in time you might want to build yourself a cottage of your own on the island property. Maybe something with a couple of bedrooms that would give everyone a bit more privacy. We know it isn't a big island but it would give you some room to spread out a bit."

Gilbert took a long slow sip of his wine obviously deep in thought. He cleared his throat a bit then said, "That's incredibly generous of the two of you but it is such a big gift. I don't know if we can accept it. Don't get me wrong, I love the idea of owning that small island at the end of the point and it would be wonderful to have our own place, but, for you to give it to us, well that's just a bit overwhelming to wrap my head around."

"I spoke to my lawyer in town this week and there is a bit of a catch to this plan," said Doc. "The municipality doesn't really like it when people *give* land to someone else, especially if they aren't a direct relative. I told the lawyer we don't really have any family that we could give anything to and the two of you are the closest we have to family, in fact we do consider you to be part of our family. I thought that might count for something."

Maude wiped a tear that was forming at the corner of her eye.

"What the lawyer suggested is that we '*sell*' the property to you." He looked at Ronnie and then back to Maude and Gilbert.

The Stone Cottage

"Oh," said Maude, "there's that bit of a catch you were talking about. As nice as this offer is, we really can't afford to buy another property. We still have a mortgage on our house in town."

"I think you'll like our asking price," said Doc.

"Now I'm really interested," said Gilbert who was feeling more comfortable with paying for the gift rather that accepting it.

"I have drawn up a letter of purchase for you to sign Gilbert," he smiled. "That way it can be registered as a legal transaction at the municipal level." Doc stood and pulled a sheet of paper out of the top drawer of the credenza that was often used as a side table in the dining room.

"This letter is brief and to the point." He looked up from the document in his hand and smiled at his friends. "According to the lawyer, having this bill of sale leaves nothing open to misinterpretation." Glancing back at the document he continued, "It says, and I quote:

> *"I Doctor Joseph Douglas Johnson, of the town of Penetanguishene hereby sell to Gilbert and Maude Valcour for the price of one dollar and for services rendered over the years, the island that is the north part of Lot 45 Concession 5 of the Township of Georgian Bay."*

As the possibility of actually owning property in Georgian Bay sunk in, Gilbert once again became pensive. Maude looked over at the Johnsons to see if there was something more she could read on their faces. It seemed too good to be true. What she saw was pure admiration and happiness in their eyes. Maude could tell the offer was genuine.

"Gilbert, you seem pretty quiet. Are you OK?" asked Doc. After a brief pause he added, "I hope we haven't offended you with our offer to sell the island to you for that price." He smiled kindly at both Maude and Gilbert then added. "The real key to all of this is not in the one dollar sale price but in the" he raised his hands in the air, curled his fingers to suggest an air quote then continued, "in the 'for services rendered' part of the offer."

Gilbert took a moment to compose his thoughts then began, "No Doc, I'm not offended. I'm just totally overwhelmed. I can't believe anyone could be so generous. It just seems to me that since we met the two of you only good things have happened to us. All of my life, my family has been very poor. My father, mother, brother and I, well, we always had to work very hard for every single thing that we have. Maude grew up on the reserve before coming to town. She and her family were certainly faced with many challenges and isolation that you and I can't even begin to imagine. Since Maude and I met, through hard work and determination we have made a life for ourselves and it seems like our life as a family has only gotten better since we met you. As a child growing up I spent a lot of time on the water with my father and brother. We fished in many of the back bays, camped in the Musquosh area and canoed around Cognashene more times than I can even count. I never in my wildest dreams ever thought for a moment that I could possibly own property here on the bay. I can't say it's a dream come true because it never occurred to me to dream that this could happen."

Gilbert looked over at Maude and saw tears streaming down both cheeks. He was moved that Maude too was seeing this in the same way that he was. "I know that I speak for Maude and our children when I say that we would like to take you up on your offer to *sell* us the island. We need you to know that your generosity will never be forgotten or taken for granted. We will continue to be the family you have never had and we will be there for you … always."

As though to seal the deal, Gilbert pushed his chair back walked over to Doc and shook his hand. "We really appreciate this." He then went over to Ronnie and with a wink of his eye bent down and gave her a quick kiss on her cheek. "Thank you so much."

Maude too stood up, made her way around to the other side of the table and first gave Doc a hug and then extended her arms towards Ronnie. The two women stood very close facing each other, awkwardly at first then wrapped their arms around each other and embraced for what seemed like an eternity to the children watching.

Ronnie spoke first. "Maude, in all my years, I have never known anyone like you. You have been my friend, my confidant, my rock and I will always remember all that you have done for me, and for Doc, over the years. We would not be here today if not for you and Gilbert."

Suddenly the tears began to flow. She tried to wipe them from her cheeks with the back of her hand but it wasn't enough. She ran from the room and into the bedroom.

"Mom, what's wrong with Mrs. Johnson?" Emma asked.

Knowing that there was more to the story than she could ever share with her daughter she turned to her and smiled, "I think those were tears of happiness. She is just so happy for us."

The silence in the room was uncomfortable for Gilbert. He looked at Doc who seemed a bit surprised by his wife's sudden disappearance. "Ben, Emma, why don't you guys go outside and find something to do. Doc and I have a bit of business we have to complete. We can call you in when it's time for dessert." Turning toward Doc he wiped his hands on his pant legs then rubbed them together. "How about if you show me where I have to sign on the offer to purchase letter?"

*****

"The thing we'll have to remember is that although the island looks big right now, there is a lot of flat land around it and when the water level goes up, even by six inches the island will get quite a bit smaller and quickly," Gilbert commented as he rubbed the stubble on his chin.

Maude and Gilbert had been standing on the shore at the northernmost part of the Narrows looking towards their new island. Maude wrapped her arms around Gilbert's waist and said, "Even though it's been a couple of weeks now, I still can't believe it. To think that next year we will be able to build a place of our own, the way we want it."

"We are going to have to pull in the reins on it though," Gilbert cautioned. "I have some ideas about how it can be built but we have to remember that all of the lumber and building supplies will have to be brought up here in our boat. We will have to go slowly. I'd like to be able to pay for the stuff as we go so that we don't owe any money on this. We still have the mortgage on the house in town and that will have to be our first priority."

Maude nodded her agreement. "Maybe what we could do would be to build a platform the size of the cottage floor first. We could put up a tent on it. I'm sure the twins would be happy to venture over here now and then during the summer months. Doc said we can still use the stone cottage for as long as we need it. We could use the stone cottage in the spring and fall and camp out here when it's nice out."

Gilbert turned to Maude, "I like your idea of building a platform first. There are plenty of rocks and boulders around that I can use to make a foundation under the platform. That will keep the wind from blowing under and reduce the chance of it lifting in a big storm. I bet the wind blowing down the length of the bay can get pretty nasty here."

"We are very exposed to the elements that's for sure," added Maude. "There's only one pine tree on the island and a few small cedars. That won't give us much protection from good old mother nature."

"I'm gonna take my shoes and socks off, roll up my pant legs and take a walk on the island. Care to join me?"

"You'll need to hike those pant legs up pretty high, the water looks to be about three feet deep between mainland and the island right now."

Gilbert looked around scanning the shoreline of the entire bay. "I like the fact there are no other cottages in the bay. That makes it good and private." Seeing no one but Maude he decided to just take his pants and underwear off and leave them on shore with his shoes and socks. His shirt tails barely covered his butt. Looking at Maude he shrugged his shoulders and said, "Nobody but you can see me. It's safer this way if I fall in."

"If you think I'm going to take my dress off to go over there you can think again."

"It never even occurred to me that you'd do that. You are the shyest, most modest person I have ever met in my life," he said teasing her.

"Oh shush," she said as she pulled the back hem of her dress up between her legs and tucked it in the front of the waistband of her house dress making it like a pair of shorts. She rolled the 'legs' as far up as she could.

"Not hard to tell that it's getting toward the end of the season, the water is colder than I thought it would be," Gilbert said as he ventured into the water.

"Yup," she said laughing and pointing at his snow-white privates, "looks like the water must be pretty cold."

"Oh, oh, the rocks are more slippery than I thought they'd be," added Maude as she waved her arms in the air trying to maintain her balance to keep from falling in the water.

"Here, take my hand, I see a couple of rocks that someone has placed here to make a kind of a bridge over the deepest part."

"What? You want to take my hand so that we both go down together?" Maude teased.

Gilbert groaned. "Augh, even my shirt is getting wet." As the water reached waist level he reached out to take Maude's hand.

Stepping carefully on the slippery rocks Gilbert added, "Looks like someone has gone before us. This rock bridge is stable even though it's a couple of feet under water." By now Maude too was in water that covered her waist.

"When the water goes down, maybe we can add a few more flatter rocks to extend the bridge to make walking on the stones a little easier."

"I'd say it would be a lot easier if we just leave a little old row boat pulled up on shore in this cove over here."

"You've got my vote on that."

The two roamed the island for the better part of an hour. It wasn't that the island was that big but they spent a lot of time debating things like the best place to put the dock, the location of the platform they were going to build and which direction they wanted the cottage to face.

"We have a few options here," Gilbert noted. "We can face the front of the cottage towards the Narrows because the view would be calm and serene for most of the time, or we could face the front of the cottage toward the far end of the lake to give us a full view of the lake. If we face it towards the west we'd see the sunset better."

"Or, we could face the front of the cottage towards the east and capture the sunrise," Maude added. "There's just so much to consider."

Hands on hips Gilbert said, "I think I'm going to have to mull this over in my head for a while before I settle on which view I think I prefer." He turned slowly assessing the view from every direction.

"I think I'd like to head back to the stone cottage and get changed out of this wet dress. I'm starting to get cold and I think the supper hour has come and gone. For a change I'll look forward to lighting a fire in the stove to cook supper. It'll warm me up."

Together they headed back across to the mainland hand in hand to give each other balance on the slippery rocks. "Well, I don't think I'll be going for a swim till next summer now," said Maude as she unwrapped the hem of her dress from her belt and squeezed the water from the material. "I was well over my waist when we were crossing back."

Once Gilbert pulled his pants and shoes back on he pulled his shirt off over his head without bothering to undo the buttons. Folding it over on itself a couple of times he wrung the water out then shook it back into shape. "Looks like I'll have to put this shirt on the clothes line when we get back," he said.

"Oh, poor you," Maude teased as she finished lacing up her shoes.

As they started to follow the shoreline of the Narrows back towards the stone cottage they noticed the sky was clouding over in the west and the wind was getting up causing Maude to shiver in her wet dress. "I'll be glad to get home and out of this wet dress. This wind is giving me a chill right to the bone."

Gilbert added, "It's not a good sign to see the wind getting up in the evening, usually it goes down with the sun."

"Where I come from when the wind gets up as the sun goes down it usually means there is going to be a three day blow," said Maude.

Gilbert said, "I hope that isn't the case now. It would be nice to finish off the summer with good weather."

CHAPTER - 19

The meal was delicious as always. For a meal prepared on a wood cook stove, that for most people seemed impossible to regulate the temperature of, it never failed to amaze Gilbert that Maude could produce such a fine meal. Maude had the innate ability to put together a scrumptious meal working with the few items she had left on the kitchen shelves. It was getting towards the end of the cottage season and Maude had insisted that Gilbert not bring any more food up to the stone cottage on his last trip to town.

Days earlier, Gilbert had asked her if she needed him to pick up any groceries when he was preparing to make a run down to town. There were a few building supplies he needed for a project he was working on in the Freddy Channel and he wanted to finish that job up before the end of summer.

"I still have plenty of canned vegetables and fruit preserves left from the summer. I'll use that up rather than have to bring it back down to town with us," she had told Gilbert.

"What about milk for the twins?" he asked.

"Let me check," she said. She made her way into the kitchen to check her pantry shelves. "I still have about eight cans of Carnation Condensed Milk. That will do."

"OK, that means my trip to town and back will be a lot quicker," said Gilbert somewhat relieved that he wouldn't have to make another stop in town at the grocery store.

"Well, I'll have to get creative with my cooking towards the end so we aren't eating the same thing every night but at least it will use up what we have and save us a bit of money."

"Anything you make will be fine and don't worry about us eating the same thing a couple of nights in a row." He smiled and shrugged his shoulders slightly, "It's what I do when I'm up here in the fall doing cottage winter close-ups."

Swirling around and around his plate with a crust of bread to soak up the last of the gravy from the stew Maude had made, Gilbert seemed thoughtful, like he had forgotten something he meant to say. Then it came to him, "Speaking of closing up the cottages for the winter have you heard from Isaac lately?"

"No I haven't. Last time I spoke to him was late in the spring before we came up for the summer. He said he planned to take a couple of weeks off from his job at the lumber mill so that he could come up here and help you out."

"I'm not surprised. He just loves being up here in the fall and it shouldn't be too hard for him to get time off at this time of year."

Maude got up from the table and closed the front windows and door. "Boy the wind sure is working itself up into something fierce. There are little white caps forming in the bay down by the dock."

"I hope it doesn't blow all night," added Ben. "After a big wind it seems there are always a bunch of fallen branches and pine cones and stuff like that in the pathways that will need to be cleaned up."

"And what else do you really have to do anyway?" asked Emma somewhat sarcastically.

"Hey, watch your tone young lady," Maude said. "Maybe it would be good for you to offer to help him with that chore instead of giving him a hard time about it."

The family finished the rest of the meal in relative silence. Satisfied there wasn't a speck of gravy left on his plate Gilbert pushed his chair back and stood up.

"I guess I'd better go down and check the boats before it gets dark," said Gilbert to no one in particular. Turning to Maude he added, "I'll be back up in a few minutes to help you with the dishes."

"Oh, that's all right. Take your time. I have Emma here to help me with that," said Maude winking at Gilbert knowing she had made her point to Emma.

*****

The wind continued to increase in strength as the sun set below the horizon. In the fading light of dusk the leaves fluttered and turned in the wind. On his way back from the dock Gilbert noted they looked shiny and a lighter colour as the wind blew them such that their undersides were in full view. He remembered his father saying that when the leaves turned over like that they were putting their face up looking for rain. He hoped that wasn't going to be the case tonight. He looked toward the main cottage and saw that Ronnie was in the front porch lifting the cushions off the wicker furniture and bringing them into the cottage so they wouldn't get wet should there be a driving rain. As he made his way back up the path towards the stone cottage he could hear the massive century old oak tree behind the main cottage groaning as its limbs strained against the wind.

I hope nothing happens to that tree, Gilbert thought to himself. *That would be a hell of a thing to have to cut up into pieces if it came down,* then he reassured himself thinking, *it's survived all these years, I'm sure it'll be fine tonight.*

As if to defy him a gust of wind blew with unusual force. It was enough to flutter Gilbert's pant legs and cause the branches of the old oak once again to groan and creek in protest. Rather than go in the front door of the stone cottage, Gilbert headed around to the back, took his shirt, Maude's dress and a few towels off the clothes line and went in through the kitchen door.

"Oh, thanks for doing that," Maude said, "I was just about to go out there and get them."

She took the clothes from him and started folding the towels.

"The wind is really whipping around out there."

"Were the boats OK dad?" Ben asked. "Mom said there were white caps in the bay at the end of the dock."

"Yup, they were fine. I added an extra spring line on our big boat at the main dock. I think I may have to add an extra anchor on the floating dock though before winter comes. It's swaying pretty good in the wind right now but the chains that hold it to shore are good and strong. It's not going anywhere tonight."

Gilbert sat back down on his usual chair at the table and added, "I noticed with this wind the water level is up about six inches already. If it stays up tomorrow I'll head over to our island to see just how the high water level affects where I'm planning on building our dock."

"Aren't you planning to make the anchor for the floating dock tomorrow?" asked Maude.

"Probably not. I need to pick up some cement on my next trip to town and I'll make another anchor like the other ones I…" He was interrupted by a sudden loud crashing noise the likes of which he'd never heard before. It sounded more like a canon fired at close range.

"Dad, come and see this," shouted Emma who was looking out the front window toward the main cottage.

The old oak tree behind the cottage had snapped in two halves about eight feet up the trunk. A part of it was still standing. The remaining branches swayed and dipped lower than they ever had in any wind before. It looked like just a matter of time before this part of the tree would crash to the ground as well. The half of the tree that had snapped off was laying across the power-line that fed electricity to the main cottage. The cottage itself was in total darkness, then suddenly the lights came on in the cottage, dimly at first then they surged brighter, then went out again.

Gilbert, Maude and the twins ran out of the stone cottage and made their way over. As they approached the main cottage the lights flickered once again. Gilbert raced to the back of the cottage, thankful that it wasn't totally dark yet. He reached for the main circuit breaker and shut off the power to the cottage completely.

Ronnie came running out of the cottage shouting to no one in particular, "what the hell is happening? I heard a crash and then the cottage went dark."

Seeing Maude and the children on the path she ran over to them and saw they were looking at the huge branch that was putting pressure on the power line. Gilbert came around from the back of the cottage and said, "Ronnie, I've turned the main power-line switch off completely. I don't think it's safe to leave it on with that branch leaning on the wire and causing those power surges like we saw. Don't anyone go near that power line until we can get someone from the hydro electric company to get up here tomorrow to disconnect it at the pole."

"Thank God you were here," Ronnie said. "I wouldn't have known what switch that was!"

They all stood there in the wind, silent for a few minutes staring at the old oak. What was left of the tree seemed to be struggling to stay upright in the wind. The part of the tree that had collapsed on the power line was not very stable but the branches that had reached the ground looked like they were strong enough to at least hold it up and prevent the wires from being pulled out of the fuse panel attached to the back of the cottage.

"Well Ben," Gilbert said rubbing his hand on the top of the boy's head. "looks like we have our work cut out for us tomorrow."

"Yeah, looks like we have a tree to cut down."

"Do you need me to help you with anything," Maude asked Ronnie as they made their way around to the front of the main cottage.

"I'll be fine Maude. I have a couple of kerosene lamps that are on the shelf in the butler's pantry. I'll just light them up until it's time for bed. This may be a good excuse to make it an early night."

With there being nothing else anyone could do at this hour Gilbert said, "Speaking of an early night, we may as well all head back and go to bed ourselves. We've got a busy couple of days ahead of us."

Emma led the way but half way down the path she turned for one last look at the old oak tree. In the fading light she could barely see it. "I liked that old oak. I'm gonna miss it."

Ben added to her comment, "you and I have spent a lot of time over the years climbing that tree and using the upper branches as our lookout. I'm gonna to miss it too."

*****

Ronnie made her way into the cottage by way of the front porch. She checked to make sure the screens were secure across the front of the porch and picked up the remaining cushions off the wicker chairs. She made her way into the living room and pulled the flashlight out of the cabinet by the fireplace. Using the flashlight she made her way from one bedroom to the next checking the latches on the windows in each room to make sure that a gust of wind wouldn't blow them open during the night. Satisfied they were locked and secure she decided she may as well go to bed. Not much else to do. She changed into her favourite flannel nightgown, crawled under the covers and tried to settle. Twenty minutes later she got up out of bed, she hadn't slept a wink, in fact she was as wide awake as she had been in the afternoon. She wasn't the least bit tired and thought she probably couldn't sleep because of the noise of the wind howling outside, or, maybe it was because of all the excitement of the last couple of hours. Either way she decided she'd just sit up and read for a little while. Maybe that would help her settle.

Using the flashlight to guide her in the darkened cottage, she made her way to the pantry and took out two kerosene lamps from the shelf. She pulled the glass chimney shade off the first lamp and lit it. She repositioned the chimney on the lamp and adjusted the height of the flame to give maximum brightness without smoking up the shade. Once satisfied the lamp was properly lit she carried it into the kitchen placing it on the table in front of the window. She liked that the light from the lamp reflected off the glass window panes and made it brighter. It was almost like having two lamps on. Next she lit the second lamp and placed it on the end table in the living room. Once she had readjusted the flame slightly she went to the bedroom to get the book she had been reading. Coming out of the bedroom she looked at the warm glow of the lamp and the yellow hues that it cast throughout the living room and thought how cozy this made things seem.

"Maybe next time Doc is here we should light the kerosene lamps. It would be more romantic that way," she muttered to herself as she settled on the couch with her book and pulled her legs up under herself.

She had only read a couple of pages when she heard yet another loud crash. This time it came from in the kitchen.

That was when her world started to fall apart around her.

She leapt from the couch and ran to the kitchen just on time to hear a "whumpf" kind of noise and the entire kitchen seemed to light up in front of her. Coming around the corner she saw the wind had blown open the kitchen window and knocked over the lamp she had put on the table. The kerosene had spilled to the floor and ignited the area rug beneath the table. Streams of spilled kerosene snaked across the floor spreading white-yellow flames as far as the kitchen cupboards on the far wall. The flames, fuelled by the wind coming through the open window, quickly began to lick the lower cupboard doors. She ran to the bathroom to get the bucket used for washing the floor and jammed it into the sink furiously turning both the hot and cold water taps to fill the bucket. Nothing. No water pressure then she remembered Gilbert had turned the power off. Because of this the water pump wasn't working either.

Yanking the bucket from the sink she ran to the front porch and screamed Gilbert's name for all she was worth. She tried to open the porch door but had to take time to unlock the latch she had used to secure it against the wind. As she charged down the front steps she saw Gilbert running from the stone cottage towards her. *Thank God he heard me*, she thought. She ran to the shore

The Stone Cottage

and filled her bucket with water. "The kitchen is on fire! The kitchen is on fire!" she screamed.

Within seconds Gilbert was at her side and threw open the door to the pump house pulling out the buckets he used to prime the water pump in the spring. Maude and the twins by this time were also out of the stone cottage and were running down the path. "Get buckets, get anything we can put water in," he shouted.

Ronnie ran to the cottage and tried to open the back kitchen door but was overwhelmed by the heat coming from the fire. She turned and ran to the front of the cottage spilling half of the water from the bucket she was carrying. She ran into the cottage but couldn't get more than halfway through the living room before she was again turned back by the heat and smoke.

A cottager from a neighbouring island was going down to his dock to check that his boat was securely tied to the dock. "In this wind you gotta check these things out before you call it a night," he said to his two buddies who had come up to spend a few days fishing. As they made their way to the dock he noticed smoke rising between the trees in the Narrows. "No one would be having a bonfire in this wind. We better get over there and check it out."

Gilbert, Maude, Ronnie and the twins were madly scrambling to fill buckets and basins and run up to the cottage.

"We can't get into the cottage, it's too dangerous," Gilbert instructed after he too had tried to throw some water at the fire. The only thing we can do now is douse the junipers and shrubs around the cottage to keep them from catching fire too. The last thing we need is to start a fire in the forest behind us."

As the neighbour and his buddies approached the dock Gilbert yelled. "Bert, let your friends out of the boat to give us a hand and go up into the second lake and get the fire pump and hose at the end of the McLean's dock."

Bert's friends were barely onto the dock when he reversed his engine and sped up to full throttle. With the approaching darkness and high water he had to be extra careful to navigate the shoals in the Narrows. Now was not the time to be hitting anything.

"We have to form a bucket brigade," instructed Gilbert. "No point in all of us running the whole distance, we'll just pass the buckets to each other. I know my way around the cottage in the dark so I'll go closest to the cottage and keep dousing the trees and shrubs."

Within minutes Bert was back at the dock with the portable fire pump. As he had been instructed at a training session - all the cottagers were taught how to use it when they had pooled their money together to buy the pump. He connected the shortest of the hoses to the pump and dropped it into the water. Next he connected the two hundred foot long fire hose and brought it up to Gilbert. He ran back down to the dock and luckily the gas powered motor kicked to life after the second tug on the pull-cord. After adjusting the choke and setting the throttle to maximum speed he went to the end of the pump that was in the water to make sure it was deep enough to prime the hose and not suck any air. Within a minute there was sufficient pressure to fill the hose and the water shot forcefully from the nozzle once the valve was opened.

Though it was extremely hot to be anywhere near the cottage Gilbert stayed as close as he could and continued to soak the lower outside walls of the cottage, the shrubs and anything that could possibly ignite. Occasionally one of the windows would shatter from the heat blowing glass outward. Being careful to avoid stepping on any shards Gilbert would spray water into the cottage through the blown out window in an effort to help soak the inside of the cottage. While he manned the hose the others continued to work the bucket brigade occasionally taking turns being closest to the cottage to afford them some relief from the burning inferno and the searing heat it generated.

By now the entire cottage was engulfed.

Within a half hour there were twenty people who had arrived to help. Philippe being one of the many.

Though Gilbert was concentrating on dousing the fire with the fire hose and making every effort to keep the fire at bay, through the corner of his eye he saw Philippe's boat come racing through the Narrows at full throttle. Philippe slowed the engine to idle just as he was approaching the dock and seeing no space left to park at he gunned the throttle and rammed his small work boat right up on a smooth rock at the shore. Barely taking time to turn the engine off he leapt from the boat and raced up to where Gilbert was standing.

"Ronnie!" he cried out. "Where's Ronnie. I have to find Ronnie," he shouted to Gilbert.

"She's a part of the bucket brigade. She's down by the dock," Gilbert responded.

Philippe's shoulders sagged with the relief he felt knowing Ronnie was safe.

"How can I help?"

"You've got a strong back and arms. This fire hose has a lot of force behind it and I've been hanging onto it for quite a while. Take over for me for a few minutes and I'll check in with the others to make sure they're alright."

Gilbert handed over the hose to Phil and then moved down the line of people who were busy handing buckets, basins and whatever would hold water up the brigade line. He quickly assessed that everyone was OK then checked in with Maude and the twins to make sure they were still safe. "Stay far away from the cottage," he commanded his children. "It's too dangerous for you to go anywhere near the fire." They nodded their agreement to their father. "Stay here by the shore. We need you here to help with scooping water from the lake and I can't be worrying about where you are right now."

"I saw the glow in the sky as I was getting ready for bed," offered one neighbour. "I could smell the smoke all the way from my place," explained another.

Gilbert thanked them for coming and made his way back up the line looking quickly at each person to make sure they had not hurt themselves. Though they all looked exhausted from the strain of their physical activity no one complained.

Ronnie however, was totally bereft. She continued to run back and forth down to the water and then up towards the cottage. She was in shock. Maude had tried to stop her but she wasn't listening. It was like she was possessed by some force within her to try to save her cottage on her own. On her way up towards the front porch steps she heard a crash and looked up on time to see the cherished "MY SHANGRI-LA" sign Gilbert had carved come down onto the porch floor in a blaze of flames. That stopped her dead in her tracks. She dropped to her knees.

"Ronnie. Get back. Get away from there. The whole porch is going to collapse," Gilbert yelled at her. She turned and started to run back to the shore but her foot caught in the hem of her nightgown and she tumbled forward landing splayed out on a large boulder that had often been considered the perfect spot to sit and admire the beauty of the Narrows. Maude rushed to her side.

"Ronnie, are you OK?"

It took her a moment to respond. Her breath came in panting gasps, "I think so, I just had the wind knocked out of me."

Maude helped her to her feet and supporting her under one arm took her to the bench at the stone cottage.

"I have to get back. I have to help," she insisted.

"Ronnie, you need to take a break. You're exhausted. Sit here for a minute and catch your breath. You're safe here. I'll come back for you in a few minutes." Maude rushed back to take a position next to her daughter in the brigade and when she looked up she saw Ronnie coming back down the path towards the shore.

"Mom, I think Ronnie must have cut herself on something when she fell," Emma said. "She has blood on her nightgown."

"I'll go check her out," said Maude.

Maude rushed to her side and took hold of her arm. "Ronnie, you can't help us right now."

"But I have to!"

"Ronnie, come with me, you're bleeding. We need to check it out."

"What? Where?" She turned her hands over to examine both sides, "I don't see any blood."

"It's on the front of your nightgown," said Maude.

The two women moved back towards the stone cottage, Ronnie moving slower than Maude expected she would. She paused mid-stride and gripped Maude's arm, "Oh Maude, I'm having such pain and cramping. She looked down at the blood on the front of her nightgown. "Oh no," she cried. She felt a trickle of blood running down her leg. The colour drained from her face. Her legs buckled and Maude had all she could do to hold her friend upright.

"Maude, I think I'm having a miscarriage. It must be from when I fell onto that boulder."

"Let's get you lying down."

She brought Ronnie into the stone cottage and closed the door behind her to keep the wind from blowing things around in the front room, and more importantly, to afford the women the much needed privacy.

"Maude, this cramping I'm having. It's so painful." Clutching her abdomen she bent over and groaned a low, guttural kind of groan.

Maude laid her friend on the bunk and propped some pillows under her legs. She lifted the nightgown and saw where the bleeding was coming from. "Ronnie, I'm not a doctor or a nurse but maybe if you just lay still you won't lose the baby."

"I can't lay still," cried Ronnie as she pulled her knees up towards her chest. "These cramps are too strong."

She relaxed her legs on the pillows but only for a moment. With a second guttural moan that seemed to emanate from deep within her she drew her legs up again and as the hem of her nightgown rose to her hips Maude saw that in that contraction Ronnie had expelled the products of conception. It was almost with relief that she took her friend's hand and said, "there, I think the worst of it is over. The baby is out and the bag of waters is out too."

"I'm still having contractions."

Maude tried to reassure her friend. "You will for a little while but those will subside soon." She pulled the nightgown up over Ronnie's hips and helped her get her legs back in place on the pillows. "Just stay right there. I'm going to get some towels and a sheet so I can make you more comfortable."

"Can you see the foetus Maude? Is it alive?"

Maude looked at the motionless aborted foetus that was lying on the bed between Ronnie's legs. It was small enough that it would have fit in a tiny tea cup. "It is very small. It isn't alive." With that comment Ronnie broke into a heart wrenching sob that caused her breath to come in gulps as she tried to get enough air into her lungs.

Maude took water from the reservoir attached to the wood stove. It was still warm from the meal that had been cooked that evening. Taking a bowl off the shelf she took some cloths, soaked them in the warm water and began to clean up her friend.

Ronnie's sobbing settled somewhat, her breathing was more even and in order to ease some of the tension Maude asked her, "how far along were you?"

"I think I was about two, maybe two and a half months at the most. I'm not surprised it didn't live."

"Did you ever tell Doc you were pregnant?"

"No, I never told anyone. Not Doc, not Philippe. The only ones who know are you and I."

Maude looked her friend in the eye and said quietly, "Gilbert knows, but he would never say anything, to anyone."

"No one will ever have to know," said Ronnie. She lay motionless on the bed as Maude cleaned her up the best she could by the dim light of the kerosene lamp that was on the kitchen table.

Once Maude was finished, she changed the sheet on the bed and helped Ronnie out of the bloodied nightgown. Maude pulled a clean one of her own out of a box from under the bed and helped her into it. "You just rest here. You've been through a lot tonight. I'm going to make some tea for you then I'm going back out to help with the fire."

Ronnie gripped Maude's hand and held it tightly as if not wanting her friend to leave. "Maude, thank you," she said, tears streaming down from both eyes.

*****

By the time Maude got back outside there was barely anything left of the main cottage. The roof of the main part as well as the roof of the kitchen had already collapsed. The fire brigade members had slowed down their efforts at trying to throw water on the cottage and were concentrating on soaking the shrubs around the foundation. She went over to stand next to Gilbert. He was watching Philippe who was still using the fire hose and instructing him where to aim the spray around the few still remaining upright walls.

"Philippe," he shouted, "direct the stream of water onto the floor of what remains of the living room. The embers are starting to glow pretty red again." Philippe complied.

He turned to Maude and said, "If I can use the word, 'luckily' the wind has gone down quite a bit in the last hour. That cuts down on the chance of the embers lifting and sparking a new fire."

Maude moved to stand a little closer to Gilbert facing him but with her back to Philippe. In hushed tones she recounted to him what had happened to Ronnie. "Oh, my God," he said. "Is she OK, is she going to be alright? I was just thinking that someone has to go to town to get Doc and bring him back up here because of the fire. That will be good if he can get here soon. He can check her out. Maybe I should be taking her to town with me when I go get the doctor."

"She doesn't want anyone to know what happened to her, especially not Doc. She never told him she was pregnant. I think this will be a secret she takes to her grave."

"But with what happened to her…doesn't someone have to check things out?"

"Women have been miscarrying at early stages in their pregnancy since the beginning of time. In our village, it happened a lot and there was never a doctor around. I think that as long as she rests for the next couple of days she'll be all right. Using your word, *luckily* this all happened really quickly and there wasn't a lot of bleeding. She wasn't very far along in her pregnancy. She'll get over it faster that way." Maude stepped away from him slightly as some smoke from the remaining embers drifted up to them, "but I agree, someone has to get to town and bring Doc up here."

"I'll go as soon as it gets light," he said.

"I see we still have about a dozen people here. I don't have anything to feed them at this time in the season but I can make coffee. She put her hand on his shoulder. "You must be exhausted. You haven't stopped since this all began." She scanned the group of people standing down by the dock and noticed the twins were there. Hardly anyone was talking.

"I'll get Emma to help me with the coffee and maybe you can keep Ben out of the stone cottage for a few hours until Ronnie has had some rest."

"What are you going to tell Emma?"

"She's the one who saw the blood on Ronnie's nightgown so I'll just tell her that when she fell on the rock she cut herself and she needs to rest because of the shock of her cottage burning down. I'm sure that will be enough of an explanation."

"What about the baby?"

She gazed at what remained of the cottage for a minute or two then said, "I've set it aside in a towel. Perhaps I can bury it for her in a secluded spot somewhere behind the stone cottage. I'll talk to Ronnie about that first though and leave that decision up to her. When she gets a bit of her strength back she may want to be with me for that."

Maude left Gilbert and headed back to check on Ronnie.

Eventually Philippe turned the nozzle off and put the hose down on the ground. He scanned the crowd of people who were standing at the shoreline. Some were already making their way to their boats and heading home after putting in a full night of firefighting under such extreme conditions. He made his way down to the dock where Gilbert was speaking to a few of the neighbours. He bent down at the fire pump and turned it off. Comically it coughed and sputtered as it shut down. It had been running steady for hours and the carburettor and frame around the pump were sizzling hot as well. "Better let this cool down a bit," he said to no one in particular. He turned to Gilbert and said, "I don't see Ronnie around anywhere. Have you seen her Gilbert?"

"She's up in the stone cottage. She was exhausted and totally in shock. Maude took her up there to be away from all of this."

"Thanks. I guess I'll just go up and see her to make sure she's OK."

"Phil, I don't think that's a good idea. I'm sure she isn't up to seeing anyone right now and besides, Maude told me she was sleeping on the lower bunk."

Feeling a little out of sorts about not being able to see Ronnie, Philippe wandered around by the shore chatting with those people who were still there. He knew everyone and within minutes had started up some lively conversations with them about the possible cause of the fire and chatting about what type of cottage the Johnsons would rebuild. Slowly he made his way over to his boat and eased it off the rocky shore. He gave a hefty final shove, leapt onto the deck then took out his paddle and slowly pushed himself away from the dock and the other boats. Before starting his engine he caught Gilbert's eye and shouted. "Tell Ronnie I'll come by tomorrow or the day after to make sure she's OK." He gunned the outboard engine and headed through the Narrows.

Gilbert thought, *It's not likely she'll still be here tomorrow but I'm sure it's best that he doesn't see her right now.*

CHAPTER - 20

The clouds had begun to dissipate and a few stars started to poke their way through. Soon the stars were beginning to blink out one by one with the pale light of the approaching dawn, on the eastern horizon the sky was brightening, announcing the arrival of a new day.

As Maude and Gilbert only had five coffee cups and one pot to make coffee in, it took quite a while before everyone who was there on the shore got a cup of coffee. Maude apologized for that but no one complained. They gratefully accepted the coffee as it came around to them and only one person asked about Ronnie. For that Maude was thankful.

The spare gas can for the portable water pump was completely drained and a couple of neighbours had returned home briefly during the fire to get more gas from their own supply. Once the sun had poked its way through the remaining clouds, the wind calmed to little more than a stiff breeze. Several neighbours offered to stand guard over the burnt pile of rubble in case the wind should pick up and stir the embers and Gilbert told them he was grateful for that.

Gilbert went to the stone cottage and changed his clothes. "I think these will have to be washed a couple of times to get the smell of smoke out of them," he said to Maude. He had changed clothes in the living room so as not to wake Ronnie who was finally resting on the lower bunk.

"I'm going to go into town and get Doc now. Is there anything you want me to bring back?"

"Nothing for me, but be sure to get Doc to bring back some clothes for Ronnie. She has nothing left here."

*****

Not sure exactly how he should break the news to Doc he met him at the office just as he was going out the door to do morning rounds at the hospital.

"Good morning Gilbert," he looked at his watch and added, "what brings you here so early in the morning?"

"Doc, I don't know how to tell you this but…" he was sure the look of shock and distress was written all over his face.

"Has something happened to Ronnie? Is everyone OK?"

"Ronnie is fine. She is mighty shook up but…"

"What is it Gil? Tell me!"

"Last night we had a horrific wind storm. A branch broke off the big old oak tree behind the cottage. In fact the tree actually snapped in two. It fell on the power line to the cottage and I had to shut the power off because it was still connected and surging electricity into the cottage."

"You didn't come all the way down here at this hour to tell me just that."

Gilbert continued. "Because there was no power to the cottage Ronnie lit a few kerosene lamps. The wind was so strong it blew open one of the windows and knocked over the lamp. I'm sorry Doc but there was a terrible fire and the cottage has burned down." He paused tears blurred in his eyes. It was difficult for him to continue because suddenly his mouth and throat had gone completely dry and a huge lump had formed in his throat. "I'm sorry Doc, we couldn't save it. There is nothing left." He paused for a moment to let Doc absorb what he had said.

"We need to get back there right away. There are some part walls that are still smouldering and a couple of neighbours are standing guard in case the wind gets up."

"We can leave right now," said Doc as he made his way out the door.

"Doc. You better gather some clothes for Ronnie to wear. She has nothing but her nightgown."

"Yes of course." He ran to the stairs and taking them two at a time rushed into the bedroom gathering a few clothes and stuffing them in a small travel bag.

When he came back downstairs he said, "we should take the plane we'll get there faster."

"I'm not sure that is a good idea. The wind has gone down now but I have a feeling it is just a reprieve Mother Nature has given us so we can catch our breath."

"Yes, yes. That's wise," said Doc rubbing his hands through his hair.

The Stone Cottage

"Is there someone you need to tell you are leaving?"

Doc turned on his heel. He quickly ran to his office and scribbled a note for Lydia his nurse asking her to get the new doctor to cover for him. They quickly got in Doc's car and went to Doc's boat at the town dock. "It's a faster boat than yours is. And, it's already gassed up and ready to go." Gilbert didn't question the decision as he agreed wholly with what Doc had said.

Gilbert drove the boat. He could see Doc was very shaken by the news and was deep in thought. It was a pretty sombre ride to Cognashene with neither man saying very much.

As a doctor, Doc had seen and comforted a number of people who had encountered traumatic experiences in their life. He himself had never before had a personal experience with loss except for the death of his parents. Yet this fire and destruction of his property was totally different. It shook him to the core.

*****

While Gilbert was gone to town to pick up Doc, Maude spoke to Ronnie about burying the foetus. Together they went out behind the stone cottage where there was a slight rise in the granite and a pretty overgrowth of sumac trees, the branches of which danced playfully in the breezes. In a crevice between the rocks there was a patch of earth which sustained the trees and was covered in a luxuriant deep green moss.

"I think this will be a perfect spot," said Maude.

"It is peaceful and quiet and will never be disturbed here," agreed Ronnie.

Silently they removed the deep verdant moss that filled the crevasse and removed some of the earth beneath. Maude carefully placed the tiny bundle between the rocks, covered it with the dark rich earth and solemnly placed the moss back over top. The women stood quietly side by side, each deep in thought. Ronnie gripped Maude's hand and held it tight for a moment. They didn't need to speak, they were on the same wavelength.

As they turned to leave they were afforded a perfect view. Not only of a small portion of the Narrows that could be seen between the trees behind the stone cottage, but also a view of the outer islands of Georgian Bay. The two women looked at each other, embraced in a long hug then wordlessly started back toward the stone cottage.

"Would you like to come in and lie down for a little while to rest?" Maude asked.

Ronnie said she needed a bit of time to herself and aimlessly wandered down the path behind the stone cottage. She made her way past the burial rock and followed the uneven path toward the inland lake, stepping over small branches, roots and moss as she went. Eventually she found the perfect place and sat on a small outcropping of rock. She gazed out at the beauty and serenity of the inland lake. The beds of water lilies near the shore gently swayed in the slight ripple on the water's surface and seemed to be waving to her and the sound of the frogs and cicadas seemed to be singing to her providing the perfect backdrop. The peace and solitude of this moment helped Ronnie to relax and she stayed for nearly an hour totally immersed in deep thoughts of what had happened to her in the last couple of weeks.

She had seen Philippe arrive to help extinguish the fire but surprisingly she felt no emotional tie to him then, or now. Especially now that she had aborted his child. It was like that loss had closed that chapter in her life. It seemed odd to her at first, but after a while she realized that it was because she was truly in love with Doc and knew only he would be able to provide her the strength she needed to get beyond this. Slowly she moved from beyond this reverie. She got up slowly. took a final look at the inland lake and made her way back to the stone cottage.

*****

As they approached the dock they were met by the horrific scene before them. Several neighbours had stayed as they promised but over the several hours Gilbert had been gone, some of the partial walls that had still been standing when Gilbert left for town had fallen over into the ashes. All that remained now was the charred remnants of the brick fireplace and a huge vacant space where the once beautiful, majestic, summer home had once stood.

Gilbert jumped from the boat as soon as the twins had secured the lines to the dock. He turned and offered his hand to Doc who he could tell was so visibly shaken by the sight before him that he was having a hard time standing up straight. Doc placed his hands on the hardtop roof of the boat to balance himself. He just stood there staring at the space where the cottage had been. Gilbert moved closer to the edge of the dock.

"Let me help you," Gilbert said as he placed one foot on the boat's gunwale and offered his hand once again.

Without any reluctance Doc raised his hand to his friend and accepted his support in getting onto the dock. "Oh my God, oh my God," he kept repeating.

"Where is Ronnie? You said she was OK. Where is she? I don't see her," he said as panic started to rise in his voice.

By this time, Maude, who had been watching for the boat to arrive, had made her way down to the dock. She answered Doc's question.

"She's up at the stone cottage. She's sleeping right now. She has had a really rough night and is totally worn out."

"Why don't we go up to the cottage and see what is left to see," Gilbert said gently guiding Doc by the elbow.

"I can't believe no one was hurt during the fire," Doc said.

As they made their way up to what remained of the cottage Gilbert said, "well I think we did have one neighbour twist his ankle slightly on the rocks as he was running to the shore to fill a bucket. Other than a few people who have sore backs from carrying water buckets for hours we are very lucky no one was seriously hurt."

Once on shore Doc stopped to look at some shrubs that had been trampled and others that were slightly burnt. Gilbert saw him looking at the bush and said, "A gust of wind came up and was stirring the embers around. This bush took a hit but, for the most part, other than those bushes closest to the cottage that were scorched by the heat we were able to keep the fire from spreading."

Doc started to move forward again towards the cottage. He stopped, hands in his pockets and didn't move. He wasn't jingling the change in his pockets. Gilbert looked at him and saw he was very pale. It was like the blood had stopped circulating in his body.

"I want to go closer but it's like my legs won't move," he said to Gilbert as he reached up and put a hand on Gilbert's shoulder for support.

Gilbert gripped Doc's elbow and began to steer Doc up the secondary path to the stone cottage. "Why don't you come up to the stone cottage and have some coffee? You've seen enough for now. Take a break, gather your thoughts."

Just as Doc, Gilbert and Maude were getting to the veranda of the stone cottage Ronnie came out the front door. Her hair was messed; she still had some blackened smudges under her eyes and around her forearms. She looked like a woman totally defeated.

"I'm so sorry Doc, I'm so sorry. I never should have lit the kerosene lamps." She buried her face in his chest and he put his arms around her. They both stood still locked in their embrace, saying nothing more, just cherishing the fact the two of them were together and safe. Maude and Gilbert went into the cottage and left them to be alone.

Doc turned to look at the remains of the cottage. When he was finally able to speak he hugged Ronnie tightly and said, "I don't blame you. You could never have known this would happen. It was an accident. What is most important right now is that you are OK." It was then that he noticed she was in Maude's nightgown.

"I brought some clothes for you from home."

"Oh, thank you."

"Don't thank me. Thank Maude and Gilbert for having the clarity of thought at a time like this to think of it."

The couple moved onto the veranda and sat on the bench. It was the bench where they had so often seen Gilbert relaxing in the evening. It afforded a great view of the Narrows but it also afforded them a view of where their cottage had been.

"What are we going to do Doc?" Ronnie asked gripping her husband's hand.

Maude came out of the cottage, "Do you want to have coffee here or would you rather come inside?"

"I think I'd rather go inside," said Ronnie. "I'm tired and I can't bear to look at what is left of the cottage for one more minute."

Ben came around to the front of the cottage. He had made himself scarce for a little while knowing the Johnson's would be needing some privacy.

"Ben," said Doc. "Would you be a good lad and get the travel bag I left in the boat. I'm sure Mrs. Johnson will feel a bit better once she is in her own clothes."

Happy to have something to do, Ben turned on his heel and ran down to the boat.

Once they were settled at the table Gilbert said, "I just don't know what to say Doc, Ronnie, other than I'm so, so sorry."

"You don't have to say anything. There is no one in the world I trust more than you guys. The cottage is destroyed but I know no one else would have worked

The Stone Cottage

harder to save it than the two of you. From the bottom of my heart," he paused and wiped a tear from his eye with the back of his hand. "Thank you. I don't have the cottage but I still have Ronnie and we still have you and your family."

"What will happen now?" asked Maude. "Will you rebuild?"

"It's too late in the season to do that," explained Gilbert, "but we can certainly make some plans over the winter and start in the spring. That would give us time to get some blueprints drawn up and the township approval and permits as well."

"I can't really think about this right now," admitted Doc shaking his head in a side to side motion and rubbing his hand across his forehead. "It's too soon."

"I totally understand Doc. Just let me know when you are ready to talk about it and we can take it from there," said Gilbert.

*****

The rest of the morning the two couples sat at the table at the stone cottage. At times there were prolonged silences each person deep in their own thoughts. At other times Ronnie, Gilbert and Maude filled Doc in on the details of the attempts made to squelch the fire. At noon, Maude got up and began to gather the coffee cups. She lit the old cook stove and busied herself with making a hearty soup. Once the reservoir water was warm enough, she took out a clean wash cloth, basin and towel and said to Ronnie, "I'll close the doors to give you some privacy. Why don't you go in the front room and get cleaned up a bit better. Get into your own clothes and by then the soup will be ready."

Once lunch was over Gilbert and Doc went over to survey what remained of the cottage. It was devastating to see what little there was left. They had a conversation about whether the fireplace and chimney should be knocked down or left standing to be used as the centrepiece of the cottage when it was rebuilt. They talked through the pro's and con's of each option. It was thought the fireplace might pose a hazard should it accidentally get knocked over when workers were nearby but it would be nice to leave it up as a feature of the new cottage. Gilbert wandered over a little closer to the fireplace and said to Doc, "I'm not sure if the fire has affected the integrity of the chimney structure or not." He moved to the other side of the foundation and scrutinized it more thoroughly. "Without the walls around it to provide some support I think it could tumble over unexpectedly during a heavy wind."

In the end Gilbert thought it would be best for it to be knocked over. Doc agreed and Gilbert added he'd make that his first priority once the embers had cooled enough to work in that area.

"Our friend Isaac will most likely be coming up in the next few weeks to help me with winterizing the neighbours cottages. I'll get him to help me with the chimney." They agreed it could wait at least that long and it was safer for Gilbert to have help with a job like that anyway.

When they returned to the stone cottage Ronnie was once again laying down on the bottom bunk. She sat up on the side of the bed when the two men entered. "Do you want to go over to see what it looks like?" Doc asked her.

"No, I don't want to remember it that way." She looked totally defeated. "I just want to go home."

"While I was making the soup I was thinking about something," Maude said.

"What is it Maude," Gil asked.

"Gil, you and Doc came up in Doc's boat. That means you and I don't have a boat to go back to town in." Turning to the Johnson's she said, "I have packed a few things and I wonder if the kids and I could hitch a ride to town with you? The twins start school next week so really we are only a few days early anyway."

"Of course, there is no problem with that, we could actually use the company and the distraction of having the twins in the boat with us," said Doc.

Maude added, "Well, I'm ready anytime you are so take your time and we can leave whenever you are ready. To Gilbert she said, "can you round up the twins and let them know the plan. They may have something special they want to take home with them that I didn't think of packing."

"That's a good idea and don't worry about me. I have the runabout to use up here and I have plenty to keep me busy for a good week without leaving the dock. Maude I think what you should do when you get home is try to track down Isaac. Let him know what's going on. When Isaac gets to the house just have him take *our* boat up here. Oh, can you be sure to send him up with the groceries he and I will need for a couple of weeks."

Satisfied with the plan they went out onto the veranda. Ronnie was careful to keep her back to the area where the main cottage had been. She really didn't want to see the ruins and remember it that way. Doc and Maude understood how she felt and tried to keep the conversation light and not related to anything

The Stone Cottage

about the cottage or the fire. Within minutes Gilbert had rounded up the kids and they were all headed down to the dock.

After a tearful thank you and long hugs on the dock they said their solemn goodbyes and Doc slowly backed the boat away from the dock. He wondered if and when he'd be back next.

*****

The boat ride home was a very quiet time. The twins understanding the seriousness of what had transpired in the last twenty four hours settled themselves onto the seats at the stern of the boat and said very little, even to each other. Once the boat reached the gap and the spray from the waves started to occasionally splash them, they just turned on the back seats facing away from the spray rather than crowd in on the bench seats under the protection of the roof.

Maude was quiet as well. Her mind was racing with a million thoughts.

When they arrived in Penetanguishene the conversation was again mostly about the business of tying up the boat, Doc retrieving the car from the parking lot and the process of finding room in the trunk for all the supplies and clothing Maude and the twins had packed for their return trip.

Doc drove to Maude's house first and helped the twins with unloading their supplies. Once that was done, Ronnie got out of the car and stood next to Maude. She said, "Well we're back and that chapter in Cognashene has closed. I just live down the street Maude so if there is ever anything I or Doc can do for you please don't hesitate to ask. We'll never be able to repay you for all you've done for us not just yesterday with the fire but for all those years leading up to it."

Taking it to heart Maude rested her open hand on her chest and smiled at her friend. "Maybe for now we can plan to have morning coffee on the front veranda a couple of times a week and chat about whatever comes up. And…" she smiled at her closest friend, "Knowing us, there will be plenty that comes up."

Doc came up to stand behind Ronnie and put his arms around her waist. "Well you better get in the car and I'll take you home. We have nothing to unpack but I think having a good stiff drink is in order."

"You go home and mix something for yourself Doc. I'll walk home, it's just a half block away and maybe I can work out a couple of kinks and sore muscles along the way."

When she got home she made her way up to the bathroom, filled the oversized tub with steaming water and had a long, hot bath. As she washed the smell of smoke from her hair some shampoo got in her eyes and they started to sting. Within moments she was full on crying. She remained sitting in the tub but turned on the shower and let the water run on her until it ran cold. The tears assuaged the guilt she was feeling about the fire, the affair she had with Phil and the remorse she felt about how it all ended. She vowed to herself she would never tell Doc about the affair, or the pregnancy. She knew she could count on Maude and Gilbert to do the same. She made a promise to herself that she would also never touch another drop of alcohol for as long as she lived. She was not a very religious person but something deep inside her felt she was somehow being punished for what she had done and what had happened. She was sure that never drinking again would be a penance that would last a life time and be a constant personal reminder of her transgressions and betrayal of her husband.

CHAPTER -21

The next day Maude was able to track down Isaac and made arrangements for him to stay with her on the night when he arrived back in Penetanguishene. She went to the grocery store first thing in the morning and with her shopping list in hand purchased all she would need to restock the house in town since it had been empty for the summer. She also picked up what Gilbert and Isaac would need for their remaining days in Cognashene. Next she stopped at the butcher shop and asked her uncle for four healthy sized steaks. She knew the men would be working very hard over the next couple of weeks and a couple of good steaks with fresh garden potatoes would be a meal they'd really appreciate.

Right on schedule Isaac arrived the next day. He was amazed at how much the twins had grown since he'd seen them last. Rubbing the top of Ben's head he said, "you'll soon be as big and strong as your dad."

Not to be outdone Ben replied, "I'm already as strong as him, I just have to get taller," and the two of them laughed at the joke Ben had made.

After supper, once the twins had settled for the night Maude and Isaac had time for a long chat. The conversation between them was easy and drew on the memories of their time growing up on the reserve and about all the things that had happened to the two of them since they had moved from Granite Bluff Inlet and gone their separate ways. As always with old friends there was no tension or posturing, it was just easy, relaxed and pleasant.

"When I got home this week there was a letter for me from my mother," Maude said.

"Oh, what did she have to say? Is she thinking of coming here for a visit?"

"No actually, she said that my dad is sick. Seems he has been for about six months now. He went to see the doctor in Parry Sound and the doctor says his heart is weak." Maude got teary-eyed and was quiet for a few moments. "She said she thinks it would be a good idea for me to go up to Granite Bluff and see them." She began to cry softly.

Isaac got up from his chair, took a tissue from the holder and gave it to Maude. She was the strongest woman that he had ever met. He had known her for her entire life and to see her this way was very sobering.

"This is the hard part of moving away from your parents," she said. "When you are young and adventurous you move away from home looking for something else to interest you. You never think of your parents aging. I always thought of my father as being so healthy and invincible. I never thought about him getting sick." She wiped the tears and looked vacantly out the window. "I don't regret having moved away but it is hard to think of my parents being there without me to support them as they get older." She took a sip of the strong tea she had made for herself after supper then said, "I was thinking Isaac, I know that you have to go up to Cognashene tomorrow for a couple of weeks but do you think that when you and Gilbert get back you could come up to Granite Bluff with me?"

"Of course I can."

"That way Gilbert can be at home with the kids when they get back from school and I can go see my mom and dad."

"At this time of year we'll have to take the bus up to Parry Sound but we can arrange to have somebody pick us up there. It will be a good chance for me to visit with my parents as well. It's been a while since I was home too."

*****

The next morning Isaac called a cab and he and Maude loaded the supplies she had set aside for Isaac to take to the stone cottage. It was a lovely calm morning and the ride up the lakes was totally uneventful. Though Isaac liked what he was doing working in the lumber yard up north, he thought about perhaps moving back to town permanently. He wanted to make this town his home. He didn't think either Maude or Gilbert would mind him crashing at their place until he found a job and a place of his own to live in.

By the time he reached the dock at the stone cottage he noticed that Gilbert had a small fire going down by the shore. Gilbert helped with tying the boat up and the two carried all the supplies up to the stone cottage. Once everything was unpacked Gilbert said, "Why don't we sit and have a coffee and get caught up on what has been going on. I know I'm ready for a break. We can take our cups down to the shore and that way I can keep a better eye on the small bonfire I have going."

"Yeah, sounds great," said Isaac. "I have to admit that I was a little surprised to see smoke coming from here when I came around Lee's Point over there."

"I'm just burning off what is left of the walls and flooring. I tried moving around inside the foundation and there were quite a few boards that were mostly burnt but had a lot of nails poking through. I thought it best if I pull those out and finish burning them."

"That wood is useless anyway at this point," added Isaac looking at the charred remains of the boards Gilbert had stacked by the bonfire ready for burning.

Isaac told Gilbert about the letter Maude had received from her mom and about the plans they had made to return to the Inlet.

"Well, perhaps we shouldn't doddle in the next few days with what we need to do here. The sooner we finish, the sooner we can get back to town and so you can get back up north."

The next two weeks went by in a blur. The men worked from sun up to sun down. In the last couple of months Gilbert had agreed to take on a few more cottages to close. At the time he had no way of knowing what the future would hold for them. Being a man of his word they met his commitment but it was hard work especially with the added work of cleaning up the ruins from the main cottage.

They had late suppers, played cards for a little while and slept soundly every night. Though the extra money was helpful this did add another couple of days to their work schedule.

The better part of the first week they were consumed by clearing the debris from the site of the fire. They dragged the burnt out remains of the kitchen stove and fridge from the carnage then lugged out the spring frames from the mattresses and the rod-iron bed frames. Once it was all pulled away from the rubble they made piles off to the side halfway to the shore. Loading it all on a barge in the spring for disposal in town would become a project for Gilbert when he returned next year.

Broken glass from windows and dishes made the clean up slow and tedious. Gilbert saw a glint of sunlight shine through the ashes amid the pile of rubble located close to where the butler's pantry had been located. He carefully with gloved hands wiped the ashes away and found it was a crystal decanter Ronnie had used to make dozens of pitchers of ice tea and Margaritas in. Over the years he had noticed she had carefully guarded this one keeping it on a high shelf so that it would not get accidentally knocked over. When asked if it had special meaning to her she said that this was all that was left of a crystal set her parents had received as a wedding gift so many years ago. It was obvious she cherished owning it. "I'm sure that over the years this decanter has been through many trying times and it has never once even ever had a scratch on it," she proudly proclaimed.

Gilbert continued to wipe it and carefully examined it in the process. Not only had it survived the fire, it had dropped down about fifteen feet onto the rocks below, its landing cushioned by a bed of embers and yet, there still wasn't a scratch on it. He carefully took it in both hands and brought it up to the stone cottage and placed it on the dining table thinking, "I'll wash it up in hot soapy water and take it to town. Ronnie will be so pleased to get this back."

Finally the next big task was to knock over the fireplace chimney. The bricks were completely blackened with smoke. Gilbert had noticed during the fire that even though there wasn't a fire burning in the fireplace at the time of the fire, the chimney had created enough of an updraft that smoke billowed from the top of it as if a roaring fire was burning inside. It was a messy, filthy job to do. Using a long rope Gilbert was able to lasso a line around the top of it about one third of the way down. Without any walls or roof to support it, there was already a significant lean to the structure so with he and Isaac standing well at a distance they heaved and pulled until they were able to topple it over.

"I'm not prepared to take the time this fall to start cleaning up those bricks. I'm sure they could be used once again if another fireplace gets built but for now, at least they don't pose a danger to anyone who may come poking around," said Gilbert. Isaac was in full agreement. Though he was not opposed to hard work, he agreed they didn't really have time to work on that right now.

"Maybe we can make that an early spring project," he said to Gilbert.

Gilbert raised an eyebrow, a quizzical look on his face. "Did you say we?"

"Yup, ever since I got back I've been thinking about moving back to town permanently. After seeing Maude and the twins and now spending time with you up here, I've come to the conclusion this is where I belong, not stuck up north at a lumber yard. If you'll have me as a boarder for a little while until I get a job and find a place of my own, I'd like to live with you guys. I have some money saved up 'cause there's nowhere to spend it up in Mactier, so I'd be happy to pay room and board."

"I'd like that and I'm sure the rest of the family will as well."

"Maybe we could even build a few canoes and rowboats over the winter."

"Sounds like a plan. It will be real nice to have you around and in our lives again," said Gilbert. To himself he thought, *Isaac is like a brother to Maude and is certainly a good friend to me.* He thought about losing his brother during the war and how difficult it had been for him to make friends after that. Isaac was a natural fit to the family and it warmed his heart to know he'd be around.

The rest of the week was spent completing the cottage close ups. Because the two men had a history of doing this for several years now, they had worked out the kinks in getting it done. They knew where to store the screens, where the storm doors and shutters were kept at each place and which cottage had an outhouse that needed to be cleaned and who had boats that needed to be stored either under the cottage or in the boat house. It was so much easier to do this year than the first year. Each man worked tirelessly sometimes not even saying much to each other as they completed the close up until they reached the dock and did a quick recap of what each had done to make sure they hadn't forgotten anything.

Soon the jobs were done and the last cottage to close up was the stone cottage. Shutters were nailed to the window frames, ashes were cleaned from the fireplace and the wood stove. The remaining groceries were boxed up and loaded in the boat. The crystal pitcher was carefully wrapped in Gilbert's duffle bag of clothes and placed under the deck of the boat so that it wouldn't get anything piled on it or accidentally stepped on. It would have been a shame to break it at this point after it had survived so much. Gilbert was excited to show it to Maude and when he did she said she had a plan. She took it upstairs and placed it on the top of her dresser.

"I'm not going to tell Ronnie about it," she looked sternly and jokingly said to Isaac and Gilbert, "and don't you guys tell her either. That is going to be her Christmas present from us this year."

"Maude you are such a romantic," said Isaac. Gilbert smiled in agreement.

EPILOGUE

It was a beautiful autumn day. The leaves were at full fall colour and the clouds had a wispiness about them. Gilbert, Maude and Isaac were sitting on the front veranda of the house in Penetanguishene having their morning coffee and admiring the view they had. From there they could see the full length of Penetanguishene harbour as it stretched out before them. It was perfectly calm and the leaves reflected in the water like a precise mirror image.

Gilbert spoke first, "I'm thinking I'll pull the boat out of the water next week. Would you be able to help me with that Isaac?"

"For sure. I need to go up to Mactier and get my stuff out of the boarding house I was staying at but that will only take me a day. What day are you thinking?"

"Thanksgiving weekend has come and gone. I don't start back at the hardware store until Friday of next week so you make your plans first and I'll work around that."

"Maude, can I interest you in one more boat ride up to the cottage? I just feel like one more trip up, just you and I. We can take lunch with us and be back before dark."

"I've been thinking the same thing and was going to bring it up when you weren't so busy. I'm so glad you asked. I haven't been up since the fire and even at that I left in quite a rush. It will be so nice to go up, take our time, check out our new island and maybe have a picnic on the shore near the Narrows. That will be a perfect way to close out the season as far as I'm concerned."

"I'm so glad you and Isaac were able to make the trip up to Granite Bluff to see your parents. I think the visit went a long way to reassure you that although your dad isn't feeling quite like the young man he used to, it sounds like he's still a going concern, just not quite like he used to be."

"You're right," Maude added. "I think mom was worried more than she needed to be. Dad isn't as strong as he was but mom says he still goes fishing almost every day and that's a good thing. I think that I'd like to go back up first thing in the spring though, and I'd like to visit a little more often from now on."

"You go as often as you'd like," said Gilbert "And, if I can swing it with my workload you'll have a hard time keeping me from going with you."

*****

It didn't take too long before they were ready to go. Isaac agreed to stay with the twins when they got home from school so Maude and Gilbert made their way to the dock. The ride up was one of the most beautiful they had ever had. The colours were scenic, at times breathtaking. The gap was calm, not even a ripple. No other boats were out this late in the season so there weren't even boat waves to contend with.

As they rounded Lee's point it was easy to see that Johnson's main cottage was no longer there. The majesty and allure of this former dwelling would be lost forever.

"Slow down a bit," Maude said to Gilbert. "Let's take our time from here. It pains me to see what has been lost. Out of respect we should go slowly."

Overcome by the loss of their grand cottage retreat the Johnsons admitted to Gilbert and Maude only days before they would not have the energy or the desire to rebuild. As their caretakers, they were never considered to be just "the hired help" but more like trusted life-long friends, so the Johnsons insisted Maude and Gilbert continue to use the stone cottage as their own for as many years as they wanted or until they had their own cottage built.

Maude and Gilbert slowly meandered through the Narrows and pulled their boat up on the south side of their island. The bay was totally quiet, the stillness interrupted only momentarily as a lonely loon called for its mate.

They unpacked their picnic lunch and sat on the rocks chatting about their wishes and desires for their new place. It was a glorious and peaceful day for the two of them and they cherished this time they had been able to etch from their busy lives to recharge their internal batteries.

As the sun started to edge toward the western sky a large flock of Canada geese in V formation flew overhead honking and chattering to each other.

The Stone Cottage

"I guess they are heading south. As nice as this is, we should take our cue from them," Gilbert said pointing to the geese, "and make our way back home before it gets dark."

Soon, everything was packed and they were heading back out of the Narrows. They slowed to an idle then Gilbert put the engine in neutral. They coasted up to the end of the floating dock.

As with all good things that must come to an end, so too did the point in time come for the caretakers to head home for the season. It was time to say goodbye to the stone cottage for another year. As their lap-strake inboard slowly pulled away from the dock they looked back one last time. Tears welled in their eyes as they thought of the many good times and deep friendships they had built over the years at the stone cottage and with the closely knit community of year round residents. These memories were not only of the full-time residents but of their summer-season neighbours as well who lived around the lake beyond the channel. Fondly they remembered the good times spent with the many guests that stayed, sometimes at length, at the owner's main cottage.

They thought too of all the good times they had shared on fishing expeditions with the guests. These fishing trips often culminated with shore lunches made from the day's catch. Picnics were held on the windswept outer islands reached only by cleverly dodging the many hidden shoals in the cedar strip canoes the owners so willingly allowed them to use.

Though there were many good times, their thoughts also raced back to the tragedies on the bay and the devastation those events inflicted on them as caretakers as much as it did on the owners. Their own personal stories of celebrations, good times, hardships and sorrow would never be forgotten. It left them with a certain sense of melancholy and hope that perhaps time would somehow heal the pain of those events. Perhaps time would not be that kind but, perhaps it would.

These were their stories of their life at the Stone Cottage. They looked forward to the new life they were about to build at their own cottage in Cognashene Lake.

ACKNOWLEDGEMENTS

This book is a work of fiction. Some of the stories however, are loosely based on the lives of my grandparents, Gilbert and Maude Vaillancourt, who lived in the Stone Cottage for a number of years acting as hunting and fishing guides and all around resource people to the residents and guests of the Cognashene area. Gilbert did work in the hardware store in Penetanguishene; he did repair radios and anything else that crossed his workbench. He was also a barber. The house on Water Street does exist and is the house my mother and her family lived in.

The other characters in the book are fictitious and any similarity to anyone is purely coincidental except for Wilfred and Winifred France. They did own and operate Franceville a resort like community on the Freddy Channel circa 1915 and on into the 1950s.

The location of Granite Bluff Inlet is a place purely from my imagination but is similar to a location on the eastern shore of Georgian Bay north of Parry Sound and south of Killarney.

Cognashene is a real place on the map in southern Georgian Bay ON. The Freddy Channel, Hangdog Channel, Giant's Tomb Island, Hope and Beckwith Islands, Go Home Bay, The Musquosh, Bone Island and McCrae Lake are actual locations in the greater Cognashene area.

Many thanks to the authors and contributors' (too many to name here) to the book *Wind, Water, Rock and Sky – The Story of Cognashene Georgian Bay*, for their detailed information about places such Franceville, Blarney Castle etc. The book is an incredible resource for anyone wishing to learn more about the area.

The Keewatin is an actual vessel that plied the waters of Georgian Bay for a number of years. It is currently moored in Port McNicoll ON, and is maintained as a historic site. Tours of the vessel are available daily.

Denis S. Lahaie

The McGibbon Lumber company actually existed on Water Street in Penetanguishene ON. The former office space has been renovated and is currently being used as a private residence.

It is true that there is very little of the Ojibway language and history that has been written. Much of it has been passed down verbally from generation to generation in the form of stories told by the elders. I believe from my research that the translations in this book are accurate however any errors are mine alone.

I would like to thank the Metis Nation of Ontario for their financial assistance with publishing this book.

*****

If you'd like to comment on this book please feel free to email me at lahaiedh@yahoo.ca or visit The Stone Cottage Georgian Bay on Facebook.

I am currently working on the sequel to this book. Watch for "**The Narrows Escape**" as I continue the story of Maude, Gilbert and their children as they make a new life for themselves in Cognashene.

Denis Lahaie

Printed in Canada